WAITING
FOR A

Love Song

JAIME CLEVENGER

Bella
BOOKS

2015

Bella Books, Inc.
P.O. Box 10543
Tallahassee, FL 32302

Printed in the United States of America on acid-free paper.

First Bella Books Edition 2015

Editor: Medora MacDougall
Cover Designer: Sandy Knowles

ISBN: 978-1-59493-453-7

Other Books by Jaime Clevenger

Bella Books
The Unknown Mile
Call Shotgun
Whiskey and Oak Leaves
Sign on the Line
Sweet, Sweet Wine

Spinsters Ink
All Bets Off

Acknowledgments

I am very thankful to have a wonderful editor and fabulous first-pass readers. Thank you to Corina, Kathy, Carla and Nancy for your time and unending patience. At times I thought of each of you while writing this story. Also, thank you to Karin Kallmaker for the pep talk—your words and wisdom meant a lot to me.

About the Author

Jaime Clevenger lives with her wife, two kids, two cats and a dog in Colorado. She spends her days working as a veterinarian and playing with her family. She loves to hear a good tale and is often running late because she's convinced someone to share their life story. Bonus points are given if they include a good romance—whether or not there's a happy ending.

May you hold love...

Alice was already dead when I met Michele. Not by hours or days, but by a few weeks at least. Of course, I didn't know about Alice's death that night. I pulled up a chair at an empty table in the Metro, a jazz lounge I'd passed maybe a hundred times but never entered, and was prepared to be unimpressed by the lineup of local bands. I was certain that the Metro wasn't on anyone's gateway to success list, but it was on my path from the grocery store to the apartment I had then. I'd glanced at the door enough times that when loneliness and boredom conspired to push me off the sofa and into the late spring evening, I'd walked directly there.

It was a Sunday night, and I quickly learned that jazz was saved for Monday through Saturday. The place was more crowded than I'd expected and mixed in age and gender. Everyone was better dressed than I was in a T-shirt and jeans. The bartender flirted openly. I ordered a Cherry Coke and got a cherry without asking. She wanted to know my name as if she expected that I'd be back.

"Jodi," I'd said, wondering if I should add my last name. It was a strange thing for a bartender to ask when all I'd ordered was a soda. Clearly I wasn't a regular.

"Tina," she replied, assuming I'd wanted to know.

Since she knew my name, I did want to know hers, at least for the sake of fairness. I didn't think that I'd end up using it again, but I did the following Sunday and then again on many more Sundays after that. I never thanked Tina and I guess I should have. Apparently Michele had seen us chatting and asked about me later that night. At that time, Tina knew that I liked Cherry Cokes and not much else. If she hadn't asked for my name that first Sunday, my story might have ended then and there.

The opening band played a mix of rock and reggae hits. They called themselves Snowball's Chance and I agreed completely. Michele's band came on second. I didn't catch the name of her band then, but I learned it later—Olive and Slim. Michele sung backup to a tall redhead named Sarah. Sarah's nickname was Slim. But there was no Olive in the band, past or present. For a long time, I thought it must be a cocktail drink.

Sarah had a breathy soprano voice that annoyed and captivated me in the same moment. She claimed the band's genre was folk, but their songs ranged from alternative pop to country, minus the twang. The thing was, they were good. Really good.

I liked Michele's alto right from the start, but it wasn't her voice I noticed first. When my eyes settled on her, she was tuning a guitar. She told me later that she'd lost her guitar tuner earlier that night. She'd tilt her head, ear inches from the strings, play a chord and then straighten up and tighten a peg. A moment later she'd repeat the process, strumming her fingertips across the long neck of the mahogany guitar, bending low, then sitting up again, eyes adrift as she concentrated on the notes. Her eyes were adrift, that is, until they settled on me. I didn't need to look at anyone else for the rest of the night.

KW didn't know about Alice then either, not yet. She read the *New York Times* on Sunday nights. The paper arrived five days late, but she always saved it for Sundays, since it was a Sunday paper. She told me later that she didn't need to test her brain on crossword riddles anymore. She was mostly interested in the music section, but she read the rest for good measure and after she'd finished reading, she'd spin her wheels on the Internet chasing down each new musician or recording that was mentioned. She found out about Alice via the same postman who brought the late paper. The letter may well have been on time, for all I know, but for KW it was late. Much too late. That the only letter KW ever got from Alice happened to be her obituary was an irony lost on no one, especially KW.

But on that night as I sat transfixed by a blonde with a pixie cut whose fingers seemed to drum on my body as they kept the beat on the belly of her guitar, I had no idea that the four of us were linked to a house on Granite Avenue. In fact, I would probably have laughed at the improbability of it all.

CHAPTER ONE

Two Years Later

Trimmed in dusty white, the pale yellow Craftsman house was nearly the same color as the dead grass of the front lawn. The roof was pockmarked with missing shingles, and the drainpipes were pulling away from the house on both sides. I parked my pickup across the street and pulled out my cell phone, searching for Carol's email about the listing. I found the price and dialed Carol to cancel the appointment. In the Old North End, even a dump was a big stretch for my price range. The call went to voice mail without ringing. Either Carol was showing another house, or she was screening the call. I hung up without leaving a message.

The sun was inching toward Pikes Peak. Dusk would settle in less than an hour. I climbed out and stretched. A cold wind gusted and I zipped my Carharrt jacket, turning the collar up to block the wind that whistled down my neck. I crossed the street and walked up the brick path toward the front porch. Under the overhang, I was shielded by two sides of the house and the wind had less bite. I tested the porch swing. The white paint had splintered off where legs had rubbed the planks and the chain whined, but the bolts were driven deep in the wood and the swing felt solid.

The longer I sat on the swing, the colder I got, but I stubbornly waited until Carol pulled up to the curb before hopping off. Carol kept her phone sandwiched between her shoulder and ear as she climbed out of her Lexus. The car was jet black and gleaming as usual. Carol was a regular at the car wash. My Ford had been black once, months ago, but winter storms had left their muddy mark. She waved, double clicked the lock button on her car, tested the door to make sure the lock button had in fact worked and then headed up the brick path. When she reached the front steps, she ended her phone call and dropped her phone into her purse. "Great location, right?"

"I think that might be all it has going for it."

Carol tested the porch handrail and smiled when it wobbled. "You know what they say about location."

"Be ready to dump a lot of money into a house if it's in the right location?"

Carol rolled her eyes. "I just got off the phone with Michele. She told me to tell you hello."

I had lots of practice by now at keeping up a front when Michele's name came up. The best way to keep anyone from noticing that her name threw me off balance was to smile and nod, then promptly change the subject. "I don't have the budget for this place, Carol. I don't think I should even waste your time going inside."

"I've wanted a peek in this place for a while. You're not wasting my time. And you know, you aren't going to see another property pop up in this neighborhood that is even close to your budget."

"Well, then, maybe the North End is out of my league."

I wanted to ask Carol why she'd been on the phone with Michele. They were friends, of course, but I knew Michele and Desi, her girlfriend of the moment, were considering buying a house together. They'd discussed the idea in detail at a recent dinner party, even asking my opinion about buying a fixer-upper versus a newer home.

The thought of them moving in together wasn't the worse thing I heard that evening, but it was close. That same night they'd gotten into an argument and Michele's parting words to me had been, "You'd be the perfect person to buy a house with. If Lynn lets you go, come find me."

This was, in fact, worse than hearing about her plans to buy a house with anyone else—worse because she could joke about it. She liked to try to get a rise out of Lynn, who had only shaken her head in response to the comment. No one in the room had taken it seriously, least of all me.

"Think of your profit margin. You can stick to making peanuts remodeling dumps in suburbia or sign on for a bigger loan and play the game with the big boys. Think big, Jodi. You're ready for this address."

"I think I'd need a business partner with some capital to qualify."

"Lynn would help, wouldn't she?"

"I wouldn't want to ask." There was no way in hell that I was going to ask Lynn for financial help. She might agree, but adding her name to the loan would mean I owed her—a debt I could never pay off. Carol was staring at me, so I added, "Lynn hates the idea of signing on to loans with anyone. She doesn't like shared risks." We'd carefully avoided sharing finances on her insistence. Besides that, we didn't need to add another potential issue to our already full list.

"I should know better than to stick my nose into someone else's relationship. Forget I mentioned Lynn. If you like the potential here, talk to the banks and see what you can take on. You might be surprised."

"Judging by the outside, I have a feeling the rest of it is going to need more than the usual facelift. I bet I'd get lots of surprises with this place."

"To tell you the truth, I thought you would take one look at it and cancel."

"I tried. You didn't answer."

Carol's sly smile confirmed that my call had been screened. Whatever Carol claimed as her reasons for thinking this was a good buy, it was, of course, in her best interest to show places at the high end of my budget.

Carol's cell rang, and she made an apologetic face as she reached into her purse for it. I glanced at the house across the street and then up and down the block. Every yard within sight was meticulous save this one with the For Sale sign. Without a doubt, this house was the one spot of blight in the neighborhood.

Carol was right. If I didn't lose my shirt, a remodel in the North End could radically change the look of my checking account. I stepped off the porch and walked the length of the dead lawn. The freeze-dried grass crunched underfoot, and the wind bit at my cheeks. March in Colorado Springs was fickle. A week ago, temperatures were in the seventies and I'd sweated in a T-shirt and jeans. Now I wanted my wool coat.

It was easy to find spots where the paint had curled away from the wood and less easy to find bits of siding that were in tolerable condition. The warped shutters and single-pane windows were simple, though not cheap, to replace. The roof was another expense. Some of the shingles were cracked and many were missing, but with a closer look the roof seemed in need of repair, not replacement. Still, the list of repairs was already extensive, and we hadn't crossed the threshold yet.

Carol finished her call and motioned me back to the porch. "You're sure this isn't a foreclosure?"

"I know the listing agent. It isn't a foreclosure. But it's been a rental for years. Lots of deferred maintenance, obviously."

"Think they'll come down much on the price?"

"You never know." Carol punched a code into the lock box and pulled out a key. "The renters moved out six months ago, but it first went on the market last May. Ten months is a long time to wait for a buyer. The owner's probably tired of paying the mortgage on an empty rental." Carol swung the door open and waved me inside. "They dropped the price ten grand last week. They're motivated."

The floorboards creaked. Beige carpet, worn threadbare in places, covered the entryway. I turned to look out the front window. Someone had taken down all of the drapes as well as the rods. White marks remained where the brackets had once attached to the gray walls. A woman jogged past the house. Carol's Lexus was parked halfway up the driveway, partly blocking the jogger's path. The jogger hesitated long enough to scowl, then veered into the street.

Carol closed the door and slid the deadbolt into place with one fluid move. She took off her coat and then took a deep breath. "Some places I walk into and immediately know they have a mold problem. No funny smells here. That's a good start."

She walked over to the curio cabinet to the left of the doorway and added her card to the handful of other cards scattered on the shelf, then picked up a fact sheet on the house. "Circa 1899. Well, you wanted a place with some character, right? And I know I said this before, but for the Old North End, this place is a steal. I sold a place on the two hundred block for just under a million, and that one needed work as well." She sighed. "The right buyer needs to come along and add a little sweat equity..."

"A little?"

The entryway opened up to a small living room with a brick fireplace on one end and a staircase on the other. A half bath had been added under the stairwell and a narrow hall led past this into the dining room. While Carol flipped through the business cards on the shelf, I wandered down the hall, stopping in the dining room. Sunlight poured into it through a bank of windows. Between the trees outside, there was a peak view of the mountains. Dark clouds had begun to gather in the north. A storm was predicted to blow in that evening, but whether it might bring snow or more icy wind was still in question. A narrow doorway opened to the kitchen. The kitchen was adorned with wallpaper featuring bluebirds hovering over bouquets of pale pink roses. Speckled white Formica countertops and white metal cabinets completed the scene.

Carol came into the kitchen smiling. She tapped the wall nearest the doorway. "You could take this wall out and open the kitchen up to the dining room. Did you see the view there? With this address, that's a million dollar view."

I went over to the sink and turned on the faucet. The pipes gurgled and spit for half a minute before the water flowed. I cupped my hands and tasted the water. City water. Lynn had gotten me used to filtered water. Above the kitchen sink, a small window looked out to the backyard, which was little more than a large rectangle of dead grass framed with a leaning wood fence. Past the fence, the neighbor's tidy yard sloped down to Monument Creek. Swollen with snowmelt, the creek seemed nearly a river as it coursed under a bridge and then disappeared from view. Tufts of evergreens dotted the far side of the creek. The mountains claimed the rest of the scene. Snow-capped Pikes Peak stood in center stage with layers of evergreen-splattered foothills framing the rest of the horizon.

"Now this view I could get used to."

Carol had come over to the sink and leaned to get the angle on the mountains. "Knock out these"—she tapped on the metal cabinets nearest the windows—"and put in a bigger window. You're still miles from the Peak, but it will feel like your backyard with that view."

We walked back to the living room and then up the staircase to the bedrooms. Two rooms shared one upstairs bathroom; the fixtures and tile suggested that it had been remodeled around the same time as the kitchen. From the master bedroom, a glass door led to a balcony overlooking the backyard. Several boards on the balcony were split, and the railing wouldn't meet code in any state. It had been reattached to its weak anchor on the house multiple times, judging by the jerry-rigged odd lot of screws and nails temporarily fixing it in place. Carol ventured out to join me on the balcony, stepping tentatively and then eyeing the railing skeptically.

"The layout's nice, isn't it?" She shivered. "I should have known not to pack up my winter parka until May." Without waiting for my opinion on the weather, she added, "And the rooms are larger than I'd expected. You're not going to find a better view for the price."

The sun was setting and the storm clouds darkened. "It needs a lot of work."

"And that's where you come in." Carol patted my shoulder. "You wanted a bigger project."

"Did I say that?" I grinned and Carol cocked her head. "I'm nervous about the loan amount."

"You've already been approved for three hundred. What's another hundred grand? Lynn won't kick you out if this place takes a little longer than the others."

"She might."

There was no reason to discuss my relationship with Carol, especially the money aspects of it. Lynn and Carol were friends. If she wanted, she could talk to Lynn about it. I turned to go inside before Carol had time to ask another question. Carol followed me, stopping to fuss with the lock. It had resisted movement when I'd first tried to unlock it, but with a little force, the bolt had screeched loose from the jamb. Relocking it seemed out of the question now. Carol glanced over at me and then shoved the bolt as far as it would go and left it at that. Halfway latched was probably sufficient. The door needed to be replaced with a glass slider. One more thing to add to the list.

I retraced my steps to the dining room and then to the kitchen. I'd never been much of a cook, but Lynn was, in fact, worse than me. I walked over to the narrow window above the sink and had a last look out the window. The view saved the place, but it still needed a lot of work before I would get any return on that. Carol was right—the kitchen needed a bigger window and the wall to the dining room needed to go. Knocking out walls was all pleasure. I'd found, with a little Metallica blasting, that swinging a sledgehammer into drywall was better than any gym workout and probably as good as a therapy session.

I peeked in the pantry and found a trap door. The door took a bit of work to budge and opened to a narrow staircase. I pulled the string on the fixture mounted on the wall. The bare bulb lit briefly before blowing, leaving me to depend on the dim light from two grimy windows for my inspection. It revealed a dusty, but dry basement with unfinished walls, a serviceable furnace, updated breaker box and a cement floor. Carol called for me, and I climbed back up the stairs. The trap door closed behind me with a thud.

"I pulled up another place that I thought you might want to look at as well. There's no view and it doesn't have the address, but it's a lot cheaper," Carol said, handing over a printout with a picture of a brick rancher.

The sterile look of the suburban rancher was enough to seal the deal. I handed the printout back to Carol. She was staring out the dining room windows and took a moment to reach for the paper. The sun dropped behind Pikes Peak and the mountains in the foreground grayed.

"I want to make an offer on this place."

"Without Lynn looking at it?"

"She's busy with her own work. This is my project." It was true that Lynn had helped choose the last house I'd remodeled, but I'd made up my mind that she didn't need to weigh in on the next. She'd gotten too involved with the last project, and the job had strained our relationship. "Anyway, I know what she'd say. That I'm taking too big of a risk."

CHAPTER TWO

The birthday party was nearing the two-hour mark. I poked my head inside the bounce house and hollered, "Time for cake." Nine seven-year-olds spilled out, each one either screaming or laughing. Roxanne came out last. She grinned up at me and then dashed off to join the others crowding around the picnic table. The air inside the bounce house was stale. I fished out a pair of sneakers and someone's watch, set these items among the pile of shoes by the back door and then went to join the party on the patio. The day was warm for April, but the wind was tugging at the treetops and snow was predicted for tomorrow.

Lynn had lit the candles, and Roxanne was seated at the head of the table, her knees tucked under her. She leaned over the cake, the song began and I pulled out my camera. No one would doubt that Roxanne was Lynn's biological kid. They shared the same amber eyes and auburn hair, though Lynn's was now highlighted to hide the wisps of gray slipping in at her temples, and they had the same smile with one dimple each. I glanced down at the image on the screen. The frozen faces were too quiet. Only a video would really capture the moment.

Lynn was on one side of Roxanne with a video camera in hand, and Sal, Lynn's ex and Roxanne's other mom, was on the other. Sal led the singing. Her voice overpowered all the kids as well as the other adults. She wailed on, oblivious.

As soon as the candles were blown out, Roxanne reached for them, dipping her finger into the cake as she did. The other kids leaned toward the cake, shrieking for a turn, but Sal whisked in and grabbed it before any other fingers could manage a swipe. She set the cake on the barbecue rack, and Lynn joined her, ready to weigh in on how the cake ought to be cut.

I found a spot against the fence and watched the scene. A hand brushed my arm, and I turned to see Michele smiling at me.

"Feeling outnumbered?"

"Maybe. Sometimes I think Roxanne has more than enough moms in her life."

Michele tilted her head toward the table of kids. "I was talking about the seven-year-olds. As Roxanne's aunt, however, I can officially say that she has exactly the right number of moms. And she adores you. Besides, you are nothing like the other two. She needs someone that isn't going to pressure her to get a degree at an Ivy League." Michele grabbed hold of my hand. "Come on, let's get cake."

Michele was not, in fact, Roxanne's aunt. She was Lynn's best friend. Lynn had given her the honorary title since there was no one else to claim it. Michele took the role seriously and spent a lot of time with Roxie. This meant she was at Lynn's house at least once or twice a week.

After nearly two years with Lynn, I still hadn't found a way to be comfortable around Michele. I kept expecting that I'd relax eventually and stop being attracted to her, but it never seemed to happen. She'd never mentioned having any feelings toward me and I wouldn't have dared voice mine aloud, but I knew we shared something. Calling it only "chemistry" seemed to diminish whatever it was that sparked when we caught each other staring or hazarded a hug. Naming it would only make the feelings harder to ignore. She usually dealt with it by teasing and even flirting if we ended up standing a little too close or there was an awkward silence between us. I played along, recognizing it as a necessary game. We both knew enough to avoid each other after any volley. Of late, however, I'd noticed that Michele had become less careful. She'd stare a moment too long or brush against me accidentally but not bother pulling away or teasing to lighten the mood.

I tried to focus on the party, eyeing the cake and not daring a second look at Michele. Sal had cut the cake in twelve slices. I did a quick double-count of the kids to confirm that we were going to be one piece short, then slipped inside the house at the last minute to avoid causing drama when Sal, or more likely Lynn, came to the same realization.

Sal had brought a bottle of wine along with the cake. She knew how to pick good wine and had a paycheck to support her talent, but I knew Lynn was irritated that she'd brought wine to a kid's birthday party. I uncorked the bottle and poured myself a glass. Michele came inside with a slice of Sal's chocolate cake balanced on a hot pink plate. She noticed my glass and nodded. We could be cool, even when tested, I thought. Anyway, this wasn't the first time we'd been alone.

"I saw you skip out of line."

I handed her a glass. "I may not have the Ivy League degree but I'm quick at math."

"You're quick at a lot of things. You don't give yourself enough credit." She sank down on the sofa, then took off her shoes and kicked her bare feet up on the coffee table. Her toenails were painted pink with white polka dots. She'd painted Roxanne's nails as well, white with pink polka dots. Roxanne had convinced me to hold the hairdryer over their nails so I'd had a long while to contemplate the artistry—and Michele's legs. She had nice feet, nice calves, nice knees…I wouldn't let myself look at her thighs. She had been wearing shorts at the time so I could have looked, but Roxanne's nonstop monologue about her party plans had provided useful distraction.

Michele took a sip of the wine. "We needed this about an hour ago. I've never understood how kids can make that much noise and still hear each other. After this, I'm going to watch a movie and call it a night."

"No plans with Desiree?"

"No." She sighed. "I broke up with her last week."

"Why? I thought maybe she had a chance of making the cut. She was good-looking and she had money."

"She has a lot of money...And money does buy a nice dinner. I might miss that." Michele shook her head. "And she's attractive. You two look a lot alike, you know? You're both tall, dark and *sporty*."

"Sporty?" Desi and I were close to the same height and we both had short brown hair, but that was where the similarities ended—at least in my mind. Desi did yoga and competed in triathlons. Maybe we both had muscles, but hers were perfectly sculpted and mine were only useful for making a living. "I don't think I'm exactly sporty. Desi's sporty. I'm...rugged?"

She shook her head. "I was going to say handsome."

I laughed.

"Don't laugh, it's true. You and Desi are both attractive in that handsome way. You have other similarities as well."

"Too bad my bank account doesn't look like hers."

"Too bad you're in a relationship with my best friend," Michele added.

"And too bad you don't do real relationships." I had to keep teasing her. I couldn't take any of this conversation at face value.

"Hey, that's going too far," Michele joked. She tried to kick me as I passed by her spot on the couch and then busted out laughing when I tripped over the end of the coffee table. I grinned and swatted her foot as she tried to kick me again.

And too bad I'll never qualify as dating material for you, I added silently. It didn't matter if we flirted or if she thought I was attractive. This was only more of our usual banter. I sat down on the coffee table, several feet away from Michele. She moved her feet over to make room, but I didn't move closer. I glanced out the glass doors to the patio. The kids had calmed down. For the first time that afternoon, everyone was sitting down. They were focused on Sal's cake. "Roxanne will sleep well tonight."

"If she's not winding down from a sugar high from this." Michele took a bite of the cake and murmured her approval.

"Damn, Sal makes a good cake. Sometimes I forget that there was something redeemable about her dating Lynn. She is a goddess in the kitchen."

"They weren't dating—they were married." Sal wasn't my favorite topic. It helped that Michele also found her overbearing and difficult to be in the same room with. "So, are you going to tell me what happened with Desi? Joking aside, you two seemed happy."

Michele shrugged.

"Lynn gave her two months. I thought she'd last longer. Guess I was wrong."

Michele cocked her head. "Are you two betting on my dates?"

"Not exactly. But you do have a pattern." I wasn't about to tell her what else Lynn had said about her serial dating pattern. Her theory was that Michele's standards were high, but she didn't like to turn anyone down—so she wasted time dating women she wasn't really interested in. I had a different theory. "You like the excitement of a new relationship, but then you get bored when you realize you have to put in time for daily maintenance."

"Is that so?"

I nodded.

"Is this what Lynn thinks or what you think?"

"Lynn thinks your standards are too high."

"Maybe you're both right. I do get bored." Michele held up a forkful of cake. "Try some."

Her eyes were locked on mine. I leaned over and took the bite.

The door swung open, and Lynn stopped on the threshold. She eyed me and then Michele. "Are you two escaping the seven-year-olds?"

"Not at all. Well, maybe a little. I came in for a glass of water, but Jodi offered wine," Michele said. Her voice was even and gave no hint that anything was out of the ordinary in our being alone together. There wasn't, was there?

Lynn's pinched expression made me want to stand up, but I kept my place on the edge of the coffee table. "There wasn't room on the picnic table," I offered.

"You're in here drinking wine?"

"Sal brought us a bottle." I wasn't a big drinker and her accusatory tone made me want to pull Sal down with me.

"I know who brought the bottle of wine," Lynn said. "And she's drinking lemonade."

"But we all know she would rather be drinking this." Michele took a sip and smiled. "Sal is damn good at picking her wines. This goes perfectly with her cake."

I stood up and went to get the bottle. Lynn had a glass of wine with dinner every night. She made her drinking seem cultured. "Can I pour you a glass?"

"No. I don't want to have wine on my breath when the other parents come to pick up their kids." Lynn took the bottle out of my hands and found the cork. She tried to jam it in, but it lodged halfway out at an angle. On her third try she gave up and set the bottle on the back counter, then grabbed a fork from the dishwasher. "I came to find you so that I could get a little help with the cleanup."

I took a sip and nodded. "Okay. I'll be right out."

Lynn's expression left little doubt in my mind that I was going to pay for the wine later. The door swung closed behind her. She passed the picnic table and went directly to Sal's spot by the barbecue.

"Think they're discussing the wine?" Michele pointed out the window at Sal and Lynn, their heads leaning together. "I think we're in trouble."

"You think?"

Michele smiled. She sipped her wine and then took another bite of the chocolate cake. "Seriously, have you ever had a cake this moist? It melts in your mouth."

Michele's eyes were closed as she let the bite dissolve in her mouth. I rinsed the wine out of my glass and took a sip of water, then found a pack of Lynn's gum and pulled out a piece.

Long before I came on the scene, Lynn had quit cigarettes and picked up a gum habit. She stashed Trident around the house like a smoker stockpiling cigarettes. The main cache, over a dozen packs, all the same mint flavor, was on the top shelf in the pantry. The mint ruined the lingering flavors of the Malbec. I handed Michele a piece and went outside.

The kids had finished their cake and returned to the bounce house. Sal was seated at the table, working her way through a slice of cake, and talking about the weather again. Lynn was halfheartedly listening. I knew this because she'd add "hmms" and "ohs" at appropriate times but didn't make eye contact with Sal. She did the same thing to me whenever I tried to tell her about something that had happened at work.

Weather was Sal's perpetual topic. She thought it would rain any minute despite the weather prediction that it would hold off for another few hours. Heavy clouds had rolled in from the north, obscuring the city view and the mountain peaks. Lynn had cleared the kids' plates and held out a plastic bag for me to hold.

I took the bag and said, "I don't think it will rain."

Sal cleared her throat and began to recite a litany of reasons that I was wrong. Something about an upper level disturbance and a warm front...Then something else about a drop in atmospheric pressure. When I shook my head at this, Lynn shot me a look that said more than words could have. She was still annoyed that I'd ducked inside and left her alone with the kids. But she had Sal for that, I argued silently.

Michele came out of the house, passed the table and went toward the bounce house. I couldn't help but follow her with my eyes. She climbed inside with the kids, and Roxanne's shrill voice distinctly announced the arrival of her favorite aunt. Sal wanted to know why I didn't think it was going to rain. In fact, I agreed with her. It looked like it was going to dump any minute.

* * *

Roxanne was finally asleep an hour past her usual time. There had been three separate requests for sips of water. I complied with each of these, but Lynn shook her head when Roxanne called for a snack. She was quieted, in the end, when I dug out the old giraffe from the closet and tucked it under the blankets. Roxanne closed her eyes and kissed the giraffe's head before whispering, "Good night, Giraffe."

I sank down on the couch opposite Lynn's reading chair. She had a pile of books on the coffee table and was wearing her reading glasses. I glanced at the television, knowing how it would irritate her if I turned on a show and annoyed at myself for wanting the simple relief of a sitcom.

I glanced again at Lynn. Her gaze was focused on the book. Now would be a good time to bring up the house on Granite Avenue. Miraculously, I'd been approved for the loan and my offered price, twenty grand below what they'd hoped to get, had been accepted. The closing date loomed in less than a week. All I had to do was keep my fingers crossed that the bank didn't find a reason to change their mind. If I thought that Lynn had any interest in hearing about it, I would have told her the details of the inspection and my plans for the remodel. I hadn't said anything partly because I didn't think she cared and partly because I could guess what her first words would be: "You're in over your head." I was worried she'd be right.

This would be my fourth remodel. The first two flips had gone well. I'd turned a good profit with less work than I'd expected, and the homes had been quick to sell. But I'd made a bad choice on the last location, and the place had been slow to move. In the end, I'd barely broken even. Fortunately, I'd stayed busy and afloat moneywise by working with Travis. He ran a general contracting business and always needed an extra hand on his projects. We'd agreed to a set hourly rate, and although I made less than when I worked on my own, I kept taking his calls because he taught me something on nearly every job. Travis had been a journeyman electrician in a union for several years before giving up the career to start his contracting business, but he also had a laundry list of other construction crew jobs that he'd filled over the years.

I figured I'd be able to work on Granite Avenue on the days when Travis didn't call and the weekends as well, but I needed to set aside at least a few evenings each week in case Travis kept me too busy. This was the part I needed to discuss with Lynn.

For the past year, I'd been Roxanne's ride to and from school most days. I was home with her every afternoon and had dinner ready by the time Lynn was home from work. Now I'd need those afternoon hours and a few evenings as well to work. We'd have to schedule more after-school activities for Roxanne and a ride home with one of her friends.

Lynn was upper management in a big accounting firm and often worked late. I'd never complained about taking care of Roxanne. There's something addictive about being needed, and it was in the hours after school that Roxanne had won me over. I'd never thought that I'd have a close a connection with a kid. Maybe the truth was that I'd never wanted any connection. Roxanne changed my mind.

"Carol dropped something off for you," Lynn said. She took off her glasses and rubbed the bridge of her nose. "She came by while you were out picking up the ice cream. I forgot to mention it earlier."

Apparently we were going to have the conversation about Granite Avenue after all. I wished I'd been the one to bring it up. "Thanks. It's probably an addendum to a house contract. A few things came up in the inspections." In fact, more things had come up in the inspection than I'd imagined. The seller had agreed to lower the price and I was satisfied with the new terms. Carol had promised to drop off a copy of the signed addendum yesterday. She was a day late.

"You've picked a new house? You kept this one a secret."

"I wasn't trying to keep it a secret. You've been busy with work and I didn't think you needed to be bothered with this." Lynn would see through my lie, but I doubted that she would argue with my point. She'd been too busy with work to make it home for dinner most nights in the past month.

"Carol says the place needs a lot of work. More than what you've done on the others?"

I nodded. Carol would have told her all about the place and then looked puzzled when she realized I hadn't mentioned anything about it. Lynn would have carefully remembered every bit of her conversation with Carol, then sorted through the details multiple times and saved it all as ammunition for a fight at the exact moment when we were both exhausted.

I knew she didn't really want to fight about the house. She was still upset about the wine and the one morsel of chocolate cake. Or, more specifically, Lynn wanted to tell me all the reasons why I shouldn't have taken that bite of cake. But I already knew all the reasons. That bite of Chocolate Diva Decadence, as Sal had called it, had melted in my mouth and then caught in my throat when I'd seen Lynn's face.

Lynn had once told me that Michele liked women who were my type—more butch, she'd said. She'd even asked if I found Michele attractive. I was adept by now at sidestepping questions about Michele, and she'd let me get away without answering. Later she'd joked that she thought Michele had a thing for me. Michele was friendly with everyone, I'd argued. And despite what Lynn thought, I had no illusions that Michele was interested in anything more than a game. I was fairly certain Michele enjoyed flirting with me only because there was no risk of anything more.

"If all goes according to plan, I close on Wednesday."

"It's a good address. But Granite Avenue appeals to a certain type of homeowner, you know. They are going to expect a high quality remodel. Are you sure you aren't in over your head?"

"It sounds like you think I am. I guess we'll see," I countered.

Lynn picked up her reading glasses and perched them on her nose. She opened the book with the leather marker and held it for a moment without looking down at the page. Then she set the book down and took off the glasses. "I should tell you something. I was going to wait to bring this up until I knew for sure but…" She rubbed her forehead and shifted back in the armchair. "Sal is in line for a promotion. It's a big move up in the company."

"And?"

"And it's unlikely she won't get it. The promotion comes with more than a pay raise. She'll need to relocate to corporate headquarters." Lynn fidgeted with her glasses and then set them on the coffee table and leveled her eyes on me. "She's waiting to hear if everything is approved, and if it is, she'll start this July."

Sal and Lynn worked at the same company. They were in different divisions, but their work frequently overlapped. I had never given it much thought since Lynn seemed so completely done with Sal. But something in her voice was different now. "Where is corporate headquarters?"

"San Jose."

"She'll be moving to San Jose?" It would be hard on Roxanne to have one of her moms move, but she saw Sal so infrequently as it was, I doubted that this would change things much. They could probably arrange for summer and holiday visits. "Roxanne will probably like taking vacations to California, I guess."

"Sal wants Roxanne and me to move with her." Lynn's face was as blank as if we were discussing what we'd have for dinner tomorrow night.

"And you're considering this?" I kept my voice as even as I could, but I could hear it shake. She had kicked me in the gut without any warning.

"I've already told her I would."

"Already?" I was reeling.

Lynn nodded.

I gripped the sofa cushion. Lynn and Roxanne couldn't move to California simply because Sal got a new job. Screw Sal, I thought. This is my family now. Sal had left them years ago. I wanted to remind Lynn that Sal had been the one to leave her, the one to insist on a divorce instead of a separation like Lynn had wanted…I wanted to remind her of the fact that Sal was overbearing, annoying and hardly seemed attached to Roxanne. Of course I couldn't say any of these things. Lynn would only argue in Sal's favor.

"Do you want to move?"

"I don't have many options because of the custody agreement," Lynn said. Her voice gave no hint that she was upset. She was simply practical, as always. "Sal and I have been talking over all of the possibilities. She wants us to try to do this move together, as a family. I haven't mentioned anything to Roxanne yet, of course. She'll finish out the school year here and then we'll move—probably mid-June."

I realized I was holding my breath and let it out slowly. Until the moment Lynn said the word "family," I had considered myself part of hers. My role wasn't clearly defined, obviously, but I knew I had a role to play. Apparently I was the only one who knew that.

"Are you saying that you're getting back together with Sal? Or is it only because of the joint custody thing?"

"I want to do what's best for Roxanne, of course. And, yes, there is the custody agreement to consider."

"But you want to get back together?"

Lynn shrugged. "I don't know…Sal suggested that we go talk with a counselor." She reached for my hand, and I pulled it away without thinking. Lynn sighed. "Maybe I should have waited to tell you. I wanted to know for sure before I mentioned anything. There's so many pieces to this equation. But I thought you should know in case this changes your position going forward with the new property."

"That's your reason for telling me?" My hands were shaking, and I clenched them into tight fists, fighting back the urge to raise my voice. "I'm not sure what I'm more pissed about—the fact that you've been considering getting back together with Sal without breaking up with me or that you and Roxy are moving to fucking San Jose in less than four months."

Only an accountant would approach this with such practicality. I wondered how I figured in Lynn's "equation." I didn't want to ask. I'd thought she hadn't wanted to talk during dinner because she was still upset about the chocolate cake and the wine or the fact that Michele and I had shared both. In fact, Michele had had nothing to do with her mood.

"Honey, what are you doing up?" Lynn's voice had changed, becoming more restrained, more patient even, than usual. Roxanne had suddenly appeared in the hallway. She had her monkey slippers on and was holding her favorite red cup. "You were supposed to be asleep an hour ago."

Roxanne didn't meet her mother's eyes. She only looked at me. "Jo, I'm thirsty again. And I can't find Giraffe."

I stood up and went over to her, taking the cup and the outstretched hand and hoping she wouldn't notice that mine was shaking. She'd never heard me swear or even raise my voice. I hoped that somehow she hadn't heard our conversation. We walked back to her room, and she paused at the door.

"Climb back in bed," I said, surprised at the steadiness of my voice. "I'll get your water."

I went to the bathroom sink for the water, then searched the hallway and Roxanne's room until I found Giraffe amidst the rumples in the comforter. I handed Roxanne the cup and sat down on the edge of the bed.

"Where's San Jose?" Roxanne asked.

"California." How long had she been standing in the hallway? I wished I'd noticed her earlier. Her wide eyes made it clear she'd overheard enough.

"Why were you and Mom talking about San Jose?"

"It's a long story, sweetie. You're up way past bedtime."

"We're going to move there?"

"Maybe." I smoothed the comforter and shifted on the bed. "You aren't supposed to eavesdrop, you know."

"Why do we have to move?"

"It's about Sal's new job." I pointed at her red cup. "Are you going to take a sip?"

Roxanne shook her head. "I'm not thirsty anymore. Why do we all have to move just because Sal got a new job? She can move by herself. I don't want to move."

"California is nice. You'll probably like it a lot once you get used to it."

"Do you like California?"

"Yeah, it's pretty." I reached for the cup and patted her pillow. "Lay down now. It's late. We'll talk in the morning."

Roxanne didn't budge. "Do you want to move to San Jose?"

I couldn't answer.

Roxanne continued, "Will we all live in the same house? With Sal?"

"I'm not sure, sweetie." Wishing that Lynn had already had this conversation with Roxanne was useless. Lynn wasn't good at fielding Roxy's questions. "We'll talk about it in the morning, okay?"

Roxanne folded her arms across her chest. "You don't want to move either. I can tell."

"You know I want to be wherever you are, right? But I think I might have to let you and your mom and Sal go on this big adventure to California without me."

"But who will take me to school? Mom doesn't even know how to pack my lunch. And she doesn't like cookies."

"She likes cookies. Everyone likes cookies."

"She doesn't buy them." Roxanne leaned across the bed and wrapped her arms around me. "I'm not moving. I'm staying here with you." Her small frame shook as she cried, her hands balled up in my shirt and her tears soaked my shoulder. "Tell Mom that, okay? Tell her tonight. Tell her that I don't want to move." She continued, but the rest of her words were muffled as I eased her back onto the pillow. Several minutes passed before she'd finally quieted enough to fall asleep. She didn't let go of my hand until she was soundly snoring.

I stood up and rubbed my eyes. The monkey night-light shone from the dresser, outlining birthday toys left like landmines between the bed and the door. I couldn't face Lynn and hoped that she'd already gone to bed. There was a mattress in the guest room that I'd never slept on. The couch was another option. Lynn's bed wasn't.

I looked back at Roxanne. Her small body was curled up in a fetal position with the giraffe nestled under her chin. Lynn had told me early on that she wouldn't introduce anyone to her daughter unless the relationship seemed serious. She'd waited a month to invite me over for an afternoon barbecue with Roxanne. I remembered that afternoon clearly. Roxanne had convinced me to play pirates and fairies in the backyard while Lynn read us stories from a thick book with Peter Pan's grinning face on the cover. When Roxanne's arms had wrapped around me for a goodbye hug that evening, I'd had a sinking feeling that my first real heartbreak was going to be because of a little girl. Part of me had expected things not to work out all along with Lynn. I knew this now because Lynn's words hadn't come as a total surprise. Of course we were going to break up. Of course. And yet, her disclosure had flattened me.

The problem was, I'd jumped in with both feet—maybe because of the fleeting feeling of it all. I had wanted the family, even if it wasn't mine. But now I had no rights to claim. I couldn't ask for visits or even an invitation to a holiday meal. I had lost a seat at the family table before I'd even earned it.

As I made my way to the guest room, I beat myself up with a repeating thread of "What was I thinking?" and "I should have known better." Who would get attached to a kid who already had two moms? I never even really liked kids, I reminded myself. I didn't like kids, I thought, but I had gotten attached to this one. And somehow I had to walk away from the past two years and not look back.

CHAPTER THREE

My cell phone rang at half past six. I finally located the phone in the back pocket of my jeans and for several seconds couldn't place where I was or why I was sleeping in my clothes. I answered the phone, and Travis cleared his throat. His phlegmy smoker's hack was unmistakable.

"I know it's Sunday, but I got a call from a homeowner who I need to keep happy…It's an easy job. You busy?"

"If I am, who else are you going to call?"

He paused. "I've got a list."

I knew he was lying. "When do you want me?"

He wanted me at the site in an hour. I agreed without bothering to ask more about the job. I guessed there'd be a ladder involved or that Travis had something too heavy to move alone. He'd fallen off a ladder when he was working as an electrician and had developed a nearly paralyzing fear of heights. He also had some issues with his back and hated heavy lifting. He promised to text the address as usual.

I'd fallen asleep on top of the comforter. The guest room mattress was hard as a board and the comforter was little cushion, but I hadn't wanted to find sheets to make the bed. I smoothed the wrinkled spots where my body had creased the material and then eyed my reflection in the mirror above the dresser. Wrinkles creased my normally smooth forehead, and yesterday's shirt was wrinkled as well. Dark circles under my eyes were telltale of the fact that I'd tossed and turned for most of the night. I needed a hot shower, but I wasn't going to risk it. Fortunately, my blue jeans were as good as clean.

I combed my fingers through the tangles in my hair. It had grown several inches on Roxanne's request. She wanted to see what its thick dark brown strands would look like braided. I'd given in, despite my usual preference to keep it buzzed above my collar. Now that it reached my shoulders I felt like I was staring at my high school self. I pulled it back in a low ponytail. I hadn't planned on getting a haircut this week, but today I needed it more than ever. I had developed a ritual of getting a haircut whenever I broke up with anyone. Lynn was the first person who had caught me by surprise. I brushed my teeth in the guest bathroom and slipped out the front door before anyone else stirred.

After a stop at Starbucks for a slice of pumpkin bread and two coffees, I pulled up directions to the address Travis had texted. His truck wasn't there when I arrived, so I listened to the radio and gulped down the bitter coffee. The caffeine fix would get me through the morning, and I could make it until noon before I needed a break for food. Travis pulled up ten minutes late and then took his time getting out of the truck. I rolled down the window and waited for him to make his way over. He looked expectantly at the coffee cup.

"How much do I owe you?"

"This one's on me." I handed him the coffee and the pumpkin bread. "What's the job?"

"I installed a ceiling fan for these folks last August. Now they want to take it out and put in a sunroof."

"And you don't like heights."

"It's not that." He grinned. "You know how I feel about spiders. Attics are full of them."

"Right. It's the spiders that you don't like."

"I could probably use your help for the next three or four days. This lady has a list of projects. Up for it?"

I finished the last of the coffee and hopped out of my truck. "You get me through Tuesday. I close on my new house on Wednesday."

* * *

If I'd really wanted to, I could have avoided going with Lynn to the Metro that evening. I'd spent dinner considering all of the excuses that Lynn would easily accept, but by the time I'd showered and changed clothes, the babysitter had arrived and Lynn was chatting with her. Roxanne was already watching a movie and making her way through a bag of popcorn. I grabbed my coat and Lynn's as well and waited by the back door.

The only good thing about going to the Metro tonight was that I wouldn't have to talk to anyone. I wasn't up for pretending everything was okay with Lynn and me, and I wasn't up for any questions Roxanne might think of about the San Jose move. I'd check in with her tomorrow when it would be just the two of us on the drive to school. Given how exhausted she'd been, there was a slim chance she'd forgotten the conversation about San Jose. I knew by their calm demeanor that neither Lynn nor Roxanne had brought up the subject while I was working. I almost wished that everyone could forget about it entirely.

Lynn took her coat from me without making eye contact. She opened the garage door and headed for her car with the keys in hand. We always drove Lynn's car whenever we went anywhere together. Lynn hated my truck's suspension. She drove a white Volvo with no scratches and a near pristine interior.

After she turned down the volume on the radio, she glanced at my seat belt to see that it was buckled and then backed out of the driveway. I hated the seat belt thing, even though I knew it was only a habitual response to years of buckling in Roxanne. I'd considered not buckling the seat belt tonight to see if she would reach across me to do it herself, then had relented. After all, although the habit annoyed me I'd never bothered to bring it up before this. Lynn was ten years older, and something about the way she almost expected to see my seat belt unbuckled always brought to my mind the age difference. Neither of us spoke during the twenty-minute drive downtown.

Olive and Slim was on the Metro schedule every other Sunday. The band also had a few other regular gigs, including two local pubs and a winery. But so far as I knew, they weren't known at all outside the city limits. Michele's singing role was always limited to the "ooh parts," as Roxanne called them, or the chorus. I wanted her to sing lead on a song, just once, but when I'd asked why she never did, her response had been, "I'm not the soprano."

The gig was a far cry from her usual job as a reference librarian at the college, and by the way she lit up as soon as she crossed the stage and the fact that her smile didn't leave her face for the rest of the evening, it was obvious that she loved it. I'd seen her quiet side, but when Michele took the stage, it was very hard to believe that her real job was spent in front of a computer screen or between stacks of books.

I thought of telling Lynn that I'd had a crush on Michele since the first night I'd seen her onstage. I wanted to say something to throw her off balance, but the more I thought about it, the more I doubted that she'd care. In fact, the reason I'd met Lynn was because I had made a point of going to the Metro whenever Olive and Slim played. I'd even gone to see the band play at the winery on the west side of town once. But mostly I stuck to the Metro shows because I could walk home. I also worried that I might be pegged as a groupie if I showed up at more of their gigs.

After several months of going solo to the Sunday night Metro shows, I'd spotted Carol. She was out of her usual realtor clothes and sitting at a table with another woman, someone who I'd immediately guessed was queer. Wondering if I had mistaken Carol as straight all along, I'd gone over to her table, mostly to find out if I'd been wrong. I wasn't. Carol was straight. But her friend wasn't. Carol had introduced me to Lynn and insisted I join them. Lynn let Carol lead most of the conversation, but she'd handed me her number at the end of the evening.

That same night, Michele had leaned over her microphone to blow a kiss at some woman seated at one of the front tables. I learned later that the woman in question was Michele's friend from work and the whole thing had been a joke between the two of them, but at the time Michele's air kiss to someone else and Lynn's phone number in my pocket had been what I'd needed to finally walk away from my daydream world. I realized that if after three months I still hadn't gotten up the nerve to talk to Michele, a date wasn't on the immediate horizon. Lynn was easy. She was a year out of a divorce and wanted company. When I turned my attention toward someone attainable, as opposed to the figure onstage, I realized I wanted someone real to fall asleep with. I was lonely.

Lynn's friendship with Michele made it difficult to completely let go of my fantasy however. We kept a regular routine of going to the band's Sunday night shows. Every time Michele came onstage a familiar feeling gripped my body. Although I tried to fight it, I couldn't look away when her hands strummed the guitar strings.

Tonight was different. I didn't feel anything when Michele and the band filed onstage. I could hardly look up from my glass of wine and didn't dare glance at Michele. The band began to play, and I nearly cupped my hands over my ears. The familiar songs I often hummed along with seemed...jarring.

Lynn finished her wine before I'd taken a sip. She didn't seem to notice or at least didn't say anything if she did. I'd had no stomach for dinner that night and thought the wine smelled like vinegar. We'd both ordered the same merlot. Hearing Lynn say, "I'll have the same," after I had ordered had pissed me off more than was reasonable. I didn't want anything in common with her tonight and wished I'd ordered a Cherry Coke. Sitting at the same table was hard enough—drinking from the same wine bottle was somehow worse.

The band took a five-minute break, and Lynn finally broke the silence with, "Maybe we should talk."

"I can't see how talking is going to help."

"You slept in the guest room last night. I know you're upset."

"You're moving to California to be with your ex. You gave me no clue that this was even in the cards. Yeah, I'm upset."

Lynn held up her hands. "Whoa, I'm not trying to start an argument."

I gripped the narrow stem of the wineglass and clenched my jaw. There was a lot I could say, but none of it was going to come out at a reasonable volume.

"I know there's a lot we need to talk about," Lynn said.

"Why? Why talk at all? You're always so damn practical about everything. What the hell is talking going to accomplish?"

Lynn shook her head. After a moment she said, "You have no idea..." Her gaze remained fixed on the stage as she continued, "I can't possibly make everyone happy. There are too many things that I have to balance here. And when it comes right down to it, this isn't about my choice. This is about doing what's right for my family."

"Right." I felt the sting once more of how completely wrong I'd been about my situation. I didn't want to hear Lynn say the word "family" ever again.

A waitress passed by our table, and Lynn asked for another glass of wine. I'd never seen her drink more than one glass. It was somehow comforting that she wanted a second one now. I wanted some sign that she was upset that we were breaking up. We had nearly reached the point of breaking up earlier in the year, but our fight then had fizzled more than exploded. Lynn had stated all of the reasons that things weren't working out, then validated her position with some quip from a relationship text that she liked to cite and shut down any discussion by preemptively saying she didn't want to argue. Her tears then had seemed mostly out of frustration or exhaustion. She had been going through a stressful time at work, and I didn't think the relationship had reached an end point. I'd considered sleeping at a motel that night. I knew we needed space. But then I had wondered how Roxanne would get to school.

"I'm not saying anything is definite. The move is a possibility. But if Sal has to move, Roxanne and I will too."

"A possibility? Last night it sounded like you had your moving date already set."

"She hasn't received the official offer. Nothing will happen until everything is approved. The CEO and CFO want to sign off on this one. That's how high up she's moving." The waitress returned with Lynn's drink. She took a sip and settled back in her chair. After a moment she said, "When Sal and I divorced, we agreed that we would always live within thirty miles of each other for Roxanne's sake. Sal has wanted to go to California for years and has been working her way up to this promotion. And, yes, I've known about the possibility of a move for a long time." She sighed. "I probably should have told you right from the start."

I wondered if Lynn added this last bit because of Roxanne. If I had known from the beginning that Lynn might take Roxanne away any day, would I have let myself get attached? But I'd never planned on getting attached to her kid. The whole thing had caught me off guard.

From what Lynn had said about her breakup with Sal, which was minimal even when I'd pressed for more details, the parting had been mutually agreed on and amicable partly because of Roxanne. Lynn had mentioned that they had both decided that the separation needed to be smooth for Roxanne's sake. I understood now how important that part was, and yet I was going to have no chance to maintain the same ties.

"I didn't want to come here tonight. The last place I wanted to be is some club where a bunch of people are trying to have a good time, you know?"

"So why did you come?"

"I thought maybe we might talk. I guess I was thinking about Roxanne."

"Well, I'm trying to talk." Lynn sighed. "We can still talk."

"We both know that there isn't any reason to talk anymore. If Sal moves, you and Roxanne move. End of story." I flicked my finger against the wineglass. The sound was barely audible. I had the urge to flick it hard enough to crack the glass, but I doubted one finger would be enough. "I considered moving out last night. But then I decided I couldn't do that to Roxanne. Maybe I'll be ready to say goodbye to her in June. Maybe."

Lynn glanced again at the stage. The band members had taken their places again, and Sarah was thanking the audience for letting them play a second set. "I want you to know that I'm sorry. I really am."

The music filled the space, but I had nothing else to say to Lynn anyway. I'd spent most of the day taking stock of the past two years. Working with Travis afforded plenty of time for introspection. He kept headphones on when he worked and rarely spoke until we took breaks. I knew that I hadn't been in love with Lynn. She'd been convenient right from the start. We liked the same music and the same restaurants, checked the same boxes at the voting booth, kept the same sleeping schedule and enjoyed spending an evening home with Roxanne as much as going out on the town. But after the first six months or so, Lynn seemed less and less interested in spending time together and made excuses whenever I suggested we have a weekend away or even a date night. Then sex became an issue or rather a nonissue. We hadn't done anything in bed other than sleep together for longer than I wanted to admit. I'd lost track, in fact, of the last time that she had even let me give her a massage. More often than not, she'd tense her shoulders at my touch and say she only wanted to go to sleep. We rarely hugged anymore, and our daily kiss before leaving for work felt like little more than an empty promise.

When Olive and Slim finished their second set, Lynn reached for her coat. I hadn't tried the wine and couldn't recall any of the songs that had been played. I pulled on my coat and followed Lynn to the door. Michele was tucking her guitar into the case and raised a hand to wave when she spotted us at the door. She often sat with us after the band finished playing and was probably wondering why we were leaving early. The three of us had spent countless Sunday nights together listening to the other bands play while Michele still glowed from her turn onstage. Tonight, however, I didn't want to see anyone glow. I couldn't even look up to meet Michele's eyes.

CHAPTER FOUR

The green suede couch was easy enough to get out of the truck by tipping it on its end, but I broke a sweat maneuvering it across the lawn, up the three steps to the porch and through the narrow front door. I positioned it in the middle of the family room, set up the cushions and then sat down. Carol had sold me the couch for twenty bucks because her cat had clawed up the backside. She claimed she wanted to replace all of her living room furniture anyway. The cat's temper tantrum on the back of the couch was enough of an excuse. I think she would have paid me just to haul it away. Given how much trouble it had been to move, I wasn't sure how good a deal I'd gotten, but its plump cushions were comfortable, and it had a long enough stretch to serve as a bed in a pinch. At present, it was also the only piece of furniture in the place and thereby enjoyed an elevated status despite the scars on its backside.

A knock rattled the front door and I nearly jumped. I'd gotten used to the quiet of a house without a first grader bouncing off the walls. I took my time getting up, ready to explain to a solicitor that they'd wasted a knock on my door. Michele stood on the porch with a bottle of wine in one hand and a bakery box in the other. We hadn't spoken since Roxanne's birthday party. I also hadn't given anyone the address of my new place. Not even Lynn knew more than the street name.

After a long moment, Michele smiled and said, "So, are you going to invite me in?"

"I'm sorry. It's been a hell of a day." I paused and stepped back from the door, waving Michele inside. "Come in. It's good to see you. Unexpected but good, especially since you brought wine."

Michele walked into the living room and pointed at the couch. "Isn't that Carol's old couch?" She set the wine and the bakery box on the floor and then sank down on the couch, brushing her hand along the armrest. "She has good taste in furniture."

"So does her cat. You should see the work he did on the back." Carol and Michele were friends, through Lynn, and it wasn't hard to put two and two together. Carol had given Michele the new address. I wondered what else Carol had already told Michele. "What's in the box?"

"Cupcakes. I thought maybe you could use a little celebration."

"Celebration?" I glanced around the mostly empty room. I couldn't admit aloud how little I had to celebrate. "I guess so, maybe. But the way my week has gone, I don't know if I'm up for celebrating."

"Housewarming then?"

"This place is only a job, you know. I'll do the remodel and then unload it as quick as possible. This house is going to have to wait for someone else to warm it."

"Rough week, huh?" Michele smiled again, but her expression was more sympathetic than anything else. "Carol told me about Sal's promotion."

Of course Carol would have told Michele about the promotion—and everything that went with it. Carol was the biggest gossip in the group. She wouldn't have been able to resist talking about a breakup.

"I was surprised I hadn't heard anything from Lynn," Michele continued, "but she hasn't confided in me in a while. Still, I expected to hear it first from her."

Expected? I clenched my jaw when I felt tears press at the corner of my eyes. Why had she expected Lynn would tell her? Had she known about the possibility of Sal's promotion and the necessity of a move at some undetermined time? Was I the only one who hadn't?

Michele continued, "You probably don't have a corkscrew here, do you? I should have thought about that."

"There's one in my toolbox. I'll go grab it." I headed out to the truck, content with an excuse to be out of Michele's gaze long enough to wipe the tears from my eyes and regain some composure. I unlocked the toolbox and stared at the neatly arranged tools. I had a bottle opener with a corkscrew in a pullout tray with other infrequently used items. Everything had a place in the toolbox and I was meticulous about keeping it organized. Travis gave me a hard time about it; his own box was a mess. I grabbed the corkscrew and slammed the lid. The latch wouldn't hook otherwise. I locked the toolbox and turned back to the house. If circumstances were different, I could have been thrilled that Michele had come just to see me. I knew she'd come because she felt sorry for me, though, and pity was the last thing I wanted tonight.

By the time I came back inside, Michele had left her spot on the sofa. I heard the floorboards creak in the dining room and guessed she was checking out the rest of the place. I opened the bottle of wine and then the bakery box. The closing had run late, and I'd gone straight over to Carol's place to pick up the sofa after so there'd been no time for dinner. My stomach growled. Two chocolate cupcakes stared up at me with silly yellow icing grins and polka dot eyes.

"I like it. You have a lot of work to do, but the layout is great and you have one heck of a view. The sun's setting over the mountains now. You can see it perfectly from the balcony off the master."

"Someone is going to love having a drink in the evening with that view," I agreed.

Michele reached for the wine bottle. "I want to be that someone. Come on." She headed down the hall toward the stairs without looking to see if I was following her.

The cupcakes stared up at me, willing me to be happy. I closed the lid and carried the bakery box upstairs. Michele was already out on the balcony. She was sitting cross-legged and drinking straight from the bottle. She turned her head and smiled when she spotted me.

"Well, you certainly found a damn good view. Gonna sit with me?"

I hesitated. I had no inclination to argue with her, and yet I didn't want anyone to pull me out of my funk. Her skin had turned golden in the setting sun's long rays and her pixie haircut shone the same shade as warm honey. It would be easier to be friends if Michele were less attractive.

I stepped out onto the balcony and opened the box again. *Damn happy faces*, I thought grimly. I picked out a cupcake and handed the box to Michele, then sat down, being careful to leave a good distance between Michele's legs and mine. The first bite of the cupcake was decadent. I ate the entire thing in five bites, all without pausing for wine. I wiped my lips with the back of my hand and realized Michele was watching me.

"Missed a spot," she said, reaching across the cupcake box to swipe a bit of chocolate from my cheek.

I grinned and she laughed out loud. I'd always loved the sound of her laugh. Back when I was compulsively attending the Sunday night Metro concerts and before I met Lynn, there was one night when I'd nearly asked Michele out. After a break between their sets, one of the other band members had told a joke to the audience and Michele had laughed into her microphone. The sound had warmed up the room and left nearly everyone smiling. I'd decided then to ask her out—her laugh had somehow broken the spell that had me believing she was unattainable. But when she stepped off stage, she walked right into the arms of a woman with an expensive-looking black leather jacket.

Michele was staring at me.

"What?" I had to look away from her blue eyes. I looked instead at the mountains. The sun had already slipped behind the peak and the clouds were beginning to change from hazy orange to pinks and purples.

"You inhaled that cupcake. I should have brought you dinner too." Michele passed the bottle of wine and then leaned back against the glass door. "I could get used to this view."

I felt Michele's gaze on me and turned to see the upturned corner of her lips. She was still staring at me when I looked away again. The sunset wasn't enough of a distraction, but I resisted glancing back at Michele and instead took a sip from the bottle. The wine was a perfect contrast to the icing. I took another sip and then offered the bottle back to Michele. She shook her head and I took another long sip. I was drinking too fast. "So, you were expecting Lynn to break up with me?"

"No," Michele said, pausing to lick the icing off the edge of her cupcake. "But I was expecting Sal's promotion. Lynn told me that there was a good chance Sal could get moved to the California office if she continued her corporate ladder climb. And Sal likes to brag about her accomplishments."

"You could have mentioned it to me."

"I'm Lynn's friend, Jodi. I had no place telling her girlfriend anything that would hurt her relationship. And as much as—"

"Why are you here then?" I asked, cutting Michele's sentence short. "I don't need Lynn's friends at the moment. I need my own."

I stood up and grabbed the railing, leaning my weight on the wrought iron and staring at the dirt yard below. I knew I should apologize, but the words were stuck in my throat. Of course Michele would take Lynn's side. They'd been friends long before I came on the scene. In the past two years, I'd managed to lose all of the casual friends I'd had before I met Lynn. I didn't have the time to keep up my own friendships. Lynn had plenty of friends for the both of us.

"Carol acted like she wasn't surprised about the promotion or the move either. Everyone else somehow knew this could happen, and no one bothered to tell me. Or Roxanne."

"Lynn was worried about Sal moving to California way back when they were going through their separation. We talked about it, so yeah, I've known for a long time." Michele paused. After a deep sigh she continued, "I know this is hard, but it isn't really about you. It's something that has been in the cards and maybe you should have known, but..."

"But what? Get over it? Is that what you are saying? Fuck you. The only one on my side right now is a seven-year-old kid. Roxanne doesn't want to move."

"Of course she doesn't want to move. She's seven. And yes, she's going to miss you. I flatter myself that she'll miss her auntie too." Michele wrapped up the rest of her cupcake and tossed it into the box. She closed the lid and pushed the box aside. "Lynn and Sal settled all of this three years ago when they decided on the terms for joint custody. Because of Roxanne, obviously, they wanted to make certain that if something like this happened, it wouldn't mean a custody fight."

"I know."

"Are you frustrated because you have no control over what happens or because you've just realized that you've never been part of the long-term plan?"

"Frustrated? Whose side are you on?"

"I'm not taking sides, Jodi."

"Then did you come over to make me feel worse?"

She shook her head. "Look, I'm sorry."

"Whatever." I gripped the railing, fighting a sudden urge to pull it loose from the bolts and throw it as far as I could manage. "You know, I want to be mad. I want to yell. But who's listening? Who the hell cares if I yell? I know Lynn doesn't care. And it doesn't matter anyway. Like you said, I'm not in the long-term plan and never was. I hate the fact that I'm going to lose Roxanne. I hate it. And I hate that I've gotten so attached. And, yeah, I hate that I'm not part of anyone's long-term plan."

"You're wrong. About a lot of things."

Michele stood up and put her hand on my back. I pushed away from the railing and turned to go inside. As much as I could use a friend, I didn't want Michele to play that role.

I went down to the living room and stared at the couch. I'd planned on going home or rather back to Lynn's house, but I'd downed the wine with only a cupcake in my belly. The couch didn't look like a promising night's sleep, but I was too buzzed to drive and I didn't want to risk seeing Lynn in my current mood. Because of the closing, Lynn had taken off work early today to pick up Roxanne. The two of them were probably battling over bedtime at the moment. I went out to the truck and found a blanket I kept rolled up in the cab. I could drive to Lynn's in the morning and make it in time to get Roxanne's breakfast together and get her ready for school. Roxanne might not even know that I'd slept somewhere else.

Michele was sitting on the couch when I came back in with the blanket. "You're sleeping here?"

"I was thinking of finishing off the rest of that bottle of wine. And I don't want to go back to Lynn's house tonight. I've been sleeping in the guest bedroom, and the bed is terrible. This couch can't be much worse."

Michele's phone beeped with a text and she glanced at the screen. "Desi wants to see me tonight."

"Oh." Did I care if she was with Desi tonight? Of course I did. But I couldn't expect her to want to stay and keep me company considering the mood I was in.

"'Oh'? That's it?" Michele sighed.

I had nothing else to say. Or too much. I wouldn't blame her for going to see Desi tonight. And I could easily imagine Desi and Michele getting back together. Desi was easy to like. Several weeks before they'd broken up, Lynn had invited Desi and Michele over for a dinner party. The four of us had played board games after dinner. Lynn and I had joked and laughed more that evening than I remembered doing in a long time. Desi was mostly to blame for keeping us all in a good mood. But it was still hard not being jealous of her.

Finally Michele said, "She's been texting me nearly every day since we broke up. I keep texting her back, though I've told myself that I should let her go. I think I'm bored. Or lonely." Michele glanced over at me. She set the phone on the armrest. "Admittedly, lonely. Anyway, I'm thinking of saying yes."

"Desi will be better company tonight than I will."

"Maybe. But I'd still rather spend the evening with you… If you want me here."

I met Michele's gaze. Of course I wanted her to stay. I wanted it so much that I couldn't manage to tell her so out loud. I could hear my pulse thumping in my ears when I shook my head.

"If that's what you want…Okay."

Michele got up from the couch. She headed to the door, pausing in front of me as if considering a hug. When I didn't move toward her, she seemed to change her mind.

"You know my number. I'd like it if you called me sometime."

I nodded.

"I don't want to lose you as well as Lynn and Roxanne." She waited for me to assuage her concern, but when I didn't speak up, she said, "Don't worry, I won't show up uninvited again."

* * *

Carol's couch was, in fact, less comfortable than the guest bed. Between that and the wine, I needed more than a hot shower to get my body moving the next morning. I stopped for coffee, buying one for Lynn out of habit, and made it home before either Roxanne or Lynn were awake. Roxanne always smiled when I woke her up. I crowed like a rooster, and she tossed her pillow at me, grinning. After I'd helped her pick out her outfit for the day, I went to the kitchen to pack her lunch and get breakfast ready. Lynn appeared in the kitchen, dressed in her good business suit and sporting a pair of heels, something she rarely wore unless she had an important client or a meeting with one of her bosses.

"You look good," I admitted. I handed her the coffee and wasn't surprised when Lynn smiled as smoothly as always. If she could show a little more emotion about our breakup it would help make things easier, I decided. I wanted to know that she was sad, or mad, or felt something beyond indifference. She acted as if it was perfectly natural that I had picked up coffee and would be getting her daughter ready for school as usual. It was almost as if our conversation on Saturday hadn't actually occurred. Or that Lynn didn't care how the news would affect me and took for granted that I'd be willing, maybe even happy, to stay and help out until the move to California.

She grabbed her car keys and briefcase and, balancing the coffee cup in the same hand, reached for the garage door. "I'll be home late. I have a dinner meeting with Duggard. Someone's coming in from the San Jose office."

"Okay, no problem. By the way, I'll be moving my things out this weekend."

Lynn had one foot on the first step down to the garage. She stared at me as if suddenly jarred into the reality that we were in fact breaking up. I hadn't considered moving out early until the moment she'd taken the coffee cup without so much as a thank you. I had had it in my head to stay as long as I could to make things easy on Roxanne but watching Lynn casually sip the coffee, I realized that it would be too painful to try and stay longer. If I got my things out this weekend, I could set up at Granite Ave and start working on the remodel sooner than I'd planned. Waiting until June wouldn't make losing Roxanne any less painful. I could still pick her up from school if Lynn allowed it, and she would. She would need the help, as much as she'd hate to ask for it.

Roxanne walked into the kitchen. "Oatmeal? I don't like oatmeal."

I held out a glass of milk. Roxy took the glass and went to sit at the table. She sipped the milk but pushed the bowl of oatmeal to the center of the table. I cleared my throat and Roxanne looked up at me. She pulled the bowl back but didn't reach for her spoon.

"We're out of your cereal, and I didn't have time to make anything else. But how about we make this oatmeal a little more interesting? How about a marshmallow mud fight?" I sprinkled a handful of miniature marshmallows on top of the oatmeal.

Roxanne looked up with a wide grin on her face. "Mud fight?" She drove her spoon hard into the closest marshmallow, dunking it under the oatmeal. She took a bite and added, "This is so good. Can we always have marshmallow mud fights when you make oatmeal?"

I glanced over at Lynn, still standing in the doorway. "You got it."

Lynn was staring at Roxanne's back. She set down her briefcase and walked over to the table. "I'll be home late, sweetie. You'll probably be in bed."

Roxy nodded without looking up. She dunked another marshmallow and laughed. "This is the best breakfast. Ever."

Lynn kissed her head. "I love you. Have a good day at school."

Roxanne took another bite. "I got two marshmallows," she said, her mouth still full as she looked over her shoulder and grinned. "Bye, Mom."

Lynn headed to the door a second time. She picked up her briefcase and left without another glance back.

CHAPTER FIVE

The bank of west-facing windows in the dining room that I'd fallen in love with in late winter were less appealing when the summer sun baked on the glass. An air conditioner had been on the list of items to add to the house early on, but there had been so many other things that became more important as the remodel progressed that I'd yet to get around to that purchase. The new double-pane windows were ordered, and they would help some, but I figured that since I'd already made it to late August, the air conditioner could wait.

Fortunately, I was rarely home during the heat of the day. Travis had kept me on the clock nearly full time since April and I'd welcomed the distraction. If nothing else, Travis kept things interesting. Lately days with him were long, usually ending at six or seven in the evening, and that meant there was little time left to think about Lynn, Roxanne or Michele. The current project, a bathroom remodel, was in limbo for the next few days while we waited for a picky owner to decide on tile and the city to give us a permit. We finished what we could do and agreed not to take on a new project in the meantime. We both needed a break.

I propped open the front door when I came inside and then stood for a moment listening to the eerie quietness of the place. I switched on the ceiling fan I'd installed in the hall, turned on the radio and walked from room to room opening every window. The newscaster's voice competed with the whirring fan and filled the emptiness of the house. But the house was too still. I'd thought of buying a television, but then it would be one more thing to move when I sold the place. The radio was enough company most nights, and when the news became too depressing, I switched to a music station to fill the space.

The master bedroom didn't feel like my room even though the closet was crowded with my stuff. Aside from my clothes, which only partly filled one side of the closet, the rest of the space was taken up by boxes. I had moved into Lynn's house with the same boxes and never gotten around to unpacking most of them.

I stripped out of my work clothes and changed into a tank top and shorts. The bed was from Lynn's house, and since it'd been the guest bed, I somehow felt like a guest sleeping in it. Lynn hadn't wanted to move it to California since it was an awful mattress anyway, and the new house in San Jose was only a two-bedroom. I tried not to think about the fact that this of course meant Lynn and Sal would be sleeping in the same room, though Roxanne had brought it up in one of our phone conversations. I'd asked Roxanne how she liked the new house, and her response had been that it was too small. She thought that if they had a bigger house with another bedroom, there would be a place for me to sleep and she'd petitioned her mom on my account for this. I wondered silently how Lynn had possibly responded to Roxanne's request for me to have a bedroom in their new house. Lynn had agreed that Roxanne could call me when she wanted to, and at first the calls were almost nightly. Now, though, weeks passed before I saw Lynn's cell number pop up on my screen and I had to fight back tears when Roxanne shouted hello.

I went to the kitchen and opened up the refrigerator. I hadn't gone grocery shopping in a while and the shelves were empty enough for me to think I ought to clean them. After a long minute of deliberation and a longer minute of self-pity, I decided on a bowl of cereal. The doorbell startled me. I heard Carol's voice hollering over the fan and the radio and went to open the screen door. "Carol, come on in."

Carol smiled. "Am I interrupting anything?"

I smiled. "I wish you were."

"My daughter has volleyball practice tonight, and I kept meaning to stop by sometime and see how you were getting on with this place…I thought tonight was as good as any. She's playing varsity and the practices are over two hours long. I can't sit on the bleachers that long." She held up two bags from the burger drive-through. "And don't tell me you aren't hungry. I never get fast food, but I love these burgers and I'm not eating alone."

"Don't worry. I'm starving."

"Stopped eating since you moved into your bachelor pad? Or did you start lifting weights to trim down?" Carol squeezed her own arm to mimic a biceps curl and then laughed. "I need to work out. Maybe I'll join your gym."

"I don't go to a gym. When would I have time? Talk to Travis. He either has me scaling ladders or doing all of his heavy lifting. Anything over thirty pounds and he hands it off to me. He's freaked out that he'll throw out his back." I took the offered bag and glanced at the sofa. There was no table or chairs, which hadn't been a problem since it gave me no excuse not to eat on the sofa. "It's a nice night. Do you want to sit out on the porch? Then I can show you around, though I haven't gotten nearly as much done as I'd hoped."

Carol pointed to the floors. "So there was hardwood under the carpet after all. It looks great."

"That was one of my first projects. The weekend I moved out of Lynn's place I came here and started yanking out carpet."

"Wood throughout?"

"And in near perfect condition, after I refinished it." I held open the screen and waited for Carol. I sat down on the first step and pointed Carol to the porch swing. "That was my second project. I'm out here almost every night on that swing and I got tired of splinters pretty quick." I'd sanded down the wood, repainted it and replaced the chains. With little competition, the swing was the nicest piece of furniture in the place.

"And you've got green grass to mow."

I unwrapped the burger and took a bite. "New sprinkler system too, so I've got the water bill to pay. I put the sod in early for the neighbors."

"Have you met any neighbors?"

I shook my head. "I've waved to a few."

"How's everything else?" Carol asked, wiping ketchup from her lips.

"About the house?" By her tone, I figured she wasn't talking about the house. I was stalling.

Carol shook her head.

"To tell you the truth, this is pretty much my life. I work with Travis six days a week…" I paused to take another bite of the burger. "Then I come here and work until I'm too tired to stand up straight in the shower. I collapse in bed or your old sofa, and the radio wakes me up before the sun."

"No company?"

Did I have to answer all of the questions from my nosy realtor? Carol was a friend as well as my realtor, but she was more Lynn's friend than mine. Of course, I'd said that about all of the friends we'd had in common. It was an easy excuse to keep me from calling them now. I pointed to a blue jay that had perched on the crab apple I'd planted. "I have nice neighbors."

Carol continued, "Have you talked with Lynn since she moved?"

"I get calls from Roxanne every once in a while, but I haven't wanted to talk to Lynn and she hasn't tried to call me."

She nodded. "I had lunch with Michele today. She mentioned how much she missed Roxanne. I told her she ought to think about when she's going to have her own baby. She laughed it off, but she'd be a great mom. She'll need to hurry up or find someone younger to have a baby for her, though. She's pushing forty-one."

"I think she likes the single life."

I wasn't entirely sure Michele preferred single life, but in the two years I'd known her, she didn't seem to have any desire to settle down with someone nor did she ever mention wanting kids.

"I guess it isn't for us to decide who has kids and who doesn't, is it?" Carol laughed. "Michele also said she misses you. She's finally thinking of leaving her condo—apparently her landlord keeps threatening to up the rent and she's already paying too much. I took her around to see a few listings, but I think she should consider waiting until this place comes on the market."

"I doubt she'd want to wait as long as it's going to take me, especially if she's checking out listings now. Travis has kept me too busy to get much done around here." As much as I needed the paycheck and the distraction, working for Travis meant that I only had a few hours to do my own projects each night before exhaustion won. "Anyway, she's seen the place already."

"Well, not since you've done all of this," Carol said. "And Desi would need to see it too, of course."

"Desi? Why would she need to see it?"

"Desi is the one with the down payment. They'd have to go in on a place together. By the way, did you know Desi is vegan now? They came over for a barbecue a few weeks ago. I invited them over after we'd been out looking at properties. Tom made his usual ribs and I made potato salad. And then Michele mentioned Desi had stopped eating meat. I think she had to get by on bread and watermelon."

From what Michele had said when she'd brought over the cupcakes, I'd guessed that she'd be getting back together with Desi. The confirmation of this, however, hit unexpectedly hard. If they were looking at places with Carol, things must have become a lot more serious. I changed the subject. "How is Tom?"

"He's fine. Busy. But we both are busy. He's got a boat race coming up."

Tom had a strange obsession with model boats, and one of the rooms of their house was filled with miniature sailboats and navy ships. Some of the boats were radio-controlled; he took these up to the reservoir to race. When Carol had first told me about Tom, she'd mentioned the boats and I'd thought it was a strange hobby for a grown man, but somehow it fit his quiet nature. I imagined him standing at the edge of the water with a remote control in hand, eyes intent on a toy boat. "Do you go with him to the boat races?"

Carol shook her head. "He likes his alone time."

"I can understand that." Maybe I'd take up radio-controlled boating. Once the remodel was finished, I'd need a hobby if I didn't have a girlfriend.

"But you know, you can have too much alone time. I asked Michele if you'd been to the Metro lately and she said she hadn't seen you."

I hadn't called Michele back after the night she'd stopped by with cupcakes, and I wasn't going to show up at the Metro without talking to her first. I couldn't go back to being a stranger in the crowd.

It wasn't that I hadn't thought of her however. I'd spent entirely too much time thinking of her. Every Sunday night I thought of going to the Metro. Someone would recognize me, though, even if I managed to avoid Michele. I longed to go and sit in the back and listen to her sing harmony. The fact that Desiree was still in the picture meant that Lynn's analysis of Michele's relationship history was now completely defunct. Unfortunately, proving Lynn wrong was the only good thing about Michele dating Desiree.

"So Desiree and Michele are seriously thinking of getting a place together?"

"Between you and me, I don't think it's a good idea. You know how often Michele changes her mind. How long is it going to be before Michele is tired of living with Desi? And then what? Anyway, I hope I'm wrong." Carol crumpled up the wrapper from her burger and tossed it into the bag. "So, show me around."

I led Carol around the outside of the house without much interest. I wanted to call Michele and was distracted with the thought of what I would say if I actually did. Fortunately, Carol had no problem keeping up both ends of a conversation, and I had to do little more than point out the repairs. The gutters and roof had been one of the first projects, in anticipation of the rainy season. The exterior was still the color of dead grass with paint peeling off the siding in too many spots.

"When are you going to paint? I'd be happy to throw in a vote for colors," Carol said. "Although any color you pick is going to be an improvement."

"I have a friend who does stucco. And he owes me a favor so I'm getting a good deal. But I wanted to wait on the stucco until I get the new windows."

We headed back inside the house and Carol went right to the kitchen. "You took out the wall," she said, standing between the kitchen and the dining room where the wall had been. "This is much nicer. And you've put in tile. Did you lay this yourself?"

I nodded.

"Instead of, what was it, flowery linoleum?"

"The matching wallpaper is gone as well. And my bay window is coming next week. I'm taking out those cabinets." I pointed to the metal cabinets on either side of the narrow window over the sink. "With the bay window, the view will be about four times the size."

"I have a contact for granite countertops if you want me to give you a name."

"Is he cheap?"

"Not really. But I'll put in a call for you and see if I can get his price down. I've given him a lot of business over the years, and he's about due to cut me a deal. When are you getting the cabinets?"

"I have new ones picked out, but I'm waiting for another paycheck before I order. If I had money to burn, this place would be finished by Christmas. As it is, I think I'll be paying the mortgage for another year."

Carol peered out the window over the sink. "I'd trade houses for a year just to enjoy this view."

"Better yet, you guys could buy this place. Why have the view for only a year?"

"Tom would never leave unless we were moving to the coast. He keeps talking about retiring to someplace with a view, but he wants to see water. You know how he likes his boats. In his dreams, I tell him. Besides, we have two more kids to get through college." Carol sighed. "Are you going to do the windows yourself?"

"No. Brandon over at Ames Windows owes me a few favors. He's slow, but I like his work." I tapped on the cabinets. "Of all the projects around this place, this is the one I've been looking forward to—ripping these things out and punching the hole for that bay window. Brandon gave me a good price on a big one. I can't wait to see the mountains right here."

"You might like it enough to stay."

"In my dreams, maybe."

After Carol left, I went up to shower. She had to get back to her daughter at volleyball practice and then there was a full house waiting for her. The only thing waiting for me was an uncomfortable mattress with stiff sheets.

I stretched out across the bed, and my cricket made his first tentative call. I didn't try to hunt him down tonight. I knew he was somewhere in the room though I had yet to find his hiding spot. The past few nights I had tried unsuccessfully to convince him to leave by keeping the back door open. I'd even called for him, fully aware of the futility of this as well. It seemed he had taken up residence. Ah, well. He was some company.

It was past my usual bedtime, but I wasn't sleepy. I went out onto the balcony and stared at the mountains. Bathed in the weak light of a crescent moon, they were hunched and dark blue, cold in their distance and less company than my cricket. I decided against going to bed. Once Carol had mentioned Michele, I'd been unable to think of anything other than calling her. I had her phone number dialed into my cell, but I couldn't bring myself to make the call. Loneliness was too easy to recognize on the phone.

I considered texting her. At least then my voice couldn't betray me. I wanted to see her on Sunday. I'd checked the schedule and knew the band was playing this week. The thought of actually going to the Metro made me obsess about what I would say when or if Michele noticed me. That Desiree was still on the scene wasn't surprising, though I guessed Lynn would say that it was. Michele didn't like to be alone. The cavalier attitude she'd had before toward her relationship with Desi easily convinced me that now she was only passing time with her.

I pulled on a T-shirt and shorts and went to get my toolbox. The kitchen lights switched on with a blinding rush. I laid out the tools I'd need and then hopped up on the counter.

The narrow cabinet to the right of the sink came off quickly enough. Behind it was a sheet of yellow plaid wallpaper that didn't match the blue birds and roses on the wallpaper I'd torn down already. I wasn't certain that the birds were an improvement over the yellow plaid. I carried the cabinet out through the back door and down the half flight of steps, tossing it on top of my growing junk heap.

The cabinet on the left side proved to be more of a project. Someone had overtightened and stripped nearly every one of the screws that attached it to the wall. Worse yet, a breadbox had been added underneath it and it was attached to the cabinet as well as the wall with a mixture of screws and nails. On closer inspection, I realized the edges of the breadbox had even been caulked. I nearly laughed at the ridiculous attempt someone had made to ensure that the breadbox didn't budge.

After ten minutes of fighting with the screwdriver, I was no longer in a laughing mood. I managed to pry out only half of the screws. I went to get a crowbar. It didn't matter if I punched a hole in the drywall getting the thing out since the whole section of wall would be cut out when the window arrived.

Once I'd finally wrestled the second cabinet and the breadbox off the wall, I set them both in the middle of the kitchen and poured myself a glass of water. I wiped at my sweaty forehead and stared at the strange set of rectangles that the missing cabinets had created. It took me a moment to see the hole that the breadbox had covered. Newspaper had been stuffed in the wall and it was nearly as yellow as the wallpaper surrounding it. It wasn't uncommon for newspaper to be used as insulation and I'd run across old news in more than one teardown project. I'd also run across my fair share of rodent nests. I poked at the papers, wondering if a mouse or some other critter had made its nest in the wall.

The longer I stared at the hole, the more certain I became that it hadn't been made by an animal. Whoever had hung the breadbox had done so to cover this hole—or more likely they'd pulled down the breadbox, made the hole and then jerry-rigged the breadbox back in place to cover their handiwork. The hole was several inches smaller than the breadbox and cut symmetrically. I pulled out fistfuls of the newspaper and didn't spot any mouse droppings. I tried to decipher the date. The month and the year were fairly clear, but the day had been creased into oblivion. September something 1954.

Once I had the newspaper out, I spotted a light brown wooden object. I pushed at it, still worrying about mice. It was a wooden jewelry box jammed tightly in the cubbyhole that I guessed had been made especially for it. When I pulled the box out, I spotted a matchbook behind it. The hole was otherwise empty.

I flipped the matchbook open. All twenty matches stared at me in perfect condition. The matchbook was from a place called Uptown. The address listed on its back was in the less desirable part of the Springs—undesirable, that is, unless one desired meth. I hadn't been south of the expressway in a long while, but I didn't recall ever seeing a place called Uptown. There was a good chance it no longer existed. In the fifties, East River Street wouldn't have had meth dealers. It might have been an entirely different sort of place.

I stared at the jewelry box. It was an old wooden box—likely an heirloom as old as the house or maybe even older. It was well-made with dovetailed corners and hand-carved details. A pattern of leaves and vines decorated the sides and a flowery design covered the lid. I traced the swirling vines and each leaf, considering what might be inside. Tiny brass hinges and a locked latch kept me from finding out. I shook it and listened for any rattling. The box wasn't heavy and the contents made only a rustling sound. I reached into the wall again and searched for a key. Nothing. I could easily jam a screwdriver in and crack the box open, but something made me hesitate.

After tapping the screwdriver against the lid, considering, I set the box aside and set about flattening all the sheets of newspaper. I read the headlines, hoping something might provide an explanation for the box. Nothing stood out. I realized that the newspaper and the matches might have nothing to do with the box.

I picked up the box again and fidgeted with my screwdriver in the lock mechanism. It held solid. I didn't want to ruin the box by cracking it open if there was a chance that I'd come across a key hidden somewhere. But now it was too late to search the house for a key. I stared at the box a moment longer, suddenly feeling that I had ghosts for company in the old house, and then left it on the counter with the newspapers and the matches. A secret that had been safely contained since the fifties could wait for daybreak. Regardless of what it contained, the mystery of the box was a welcome distraction. My mind needed a break from Michele.

CHAPTER SIX

It was never the light that woke me at daybreak. Nor was it the garbage trucks, which screeched by twice weekly. I didn't have the money to waste on garbage service and trucked mine to the dump every few weeks. And it wasn't the barking terrier that lived in the house next door either, though he barked at the same time each morning to be let out to pee by the old man who hobbled with a cane and hacked up half his lungs as he waited for the terrier to do his business. It was the blue jays.

I knew it was no use to try to fall back asleep. The blue jays were insistent that a half hour before sunrise was when the neighborhood needed a wake-up call. I pushed the pillow against my ears and squeezed my eyes shut. There was no reason to wake up early. Travis wasn't going to be waiting for me, and I didn't have to get anyone ready for school or brew the coffee. I'd yelled at the birds countless times, to no avail. When their squawking became too loud to ignore, I closed the balcony door.

Even if the birds hadn't woke me, I wanted to get an early start on the kitchen before the sun had a chance to cook the place.

I headed downstairs to get the coffee brewing and remembered the jewelry box only when I saw the mess that filled the kitchen. My coffeemaker was next to the refrigerator and the path to both was blocked by the old cabinet. I stared at the cabinet and the breadbox for a moment and then at the hole in the wall. The contents of the hole were still strewn on the counter. I contemplated where to begin the cleanup and quickly decided I needed coffee first. It was only five blocks to the coffee shop. The coffee was quite a bit better than what I could brew and the baristas knew me by name.

Granite Avenue lived up to its fame on summer mornings. By the time I was dressed and out of the house, the jays were as quiet as the worms they'd been after. Big elms let the sun slip through their leaves irreverently and every lawn was as green as the next. The old bungalows and Craftsman homes, all better than a hundred years old, gleamed behind diligently swept sidewalks. Dog walkers and joggers passed, waving as they did, as if each one knew all of the neighbors. I recognized a few of their faces or their dogs, but I hadn't bothered to introduce myself to anyone. It seemed pointless to make friends since I was only in the neighborhood for a quick flip. *Quick flip*, I reminded myself, thinking again of the jewelry box. I didn't need the box distracting me from the planned project for the day. Now that I had the old cabinets out, I needed to make the initial cuts for the bay window.

The coffee shop was at the start of the trendy part of downtown. Bicycles lined the bike rack, and the patio tables set out on the sidewalk were all filled with eager recipients of a morning caffeine rush. Molly was working the register and waved when I came in. The couple in line in front of me kept their arms entwined and their bodies sandwiched together while they ordered, each taking painstakingly long to decide on their beverage. Molly's smile never wavered as they changed both drink orders from hot to iced after she'd swiped their credit card.

"How's life?" Molly asked.

"It's Saturday."

"Tell me about it." She sighed. "You haven't been in for a while."

"Missed me?"

"Maybe."

Maybe was exactly what I wanted to hear. I'd been wondering if Molly was queer for months. If I were smooth, I'd figure out a way to hand her my phone number. But I wasn't smooth, so I only stood there grinning. She didn't ask if I wanted my usual order. She took the cash that I handed over and handed back the change.

When I slipped a tip into her jar, Molly leaned around the register and said, "Check out the hottie at the back corner table. I'll bring your coffee over there if you want to snag the table next to hers."

"Thanks, but…"

"Your loss," Molly interrupted. She went to fill my travel mug. When she returned, she said, "I left you room for milk, but you have to go over to that back counter and get it yourself this time. I'm too busy."

I always took my coffee black and she knew it. I took the mug. "I think I overtipped today."

"You didn't tip enough for what I'm trying to hand you," Molly shot back. "Add some milk and sugar and tell me if I'm wrong. Unless, of course, you're scared."

I laughed. The challenge was obvious. I'd never discussed anything beyond work and the weather with any of the baristas, but I'd guessed Molly was gay, or maybe bi, the first time I'd met her. At least now I knew for sure. Too bad she wasn't interested in me. "I'll even say hello."

Molly winked. "So brave."

Some days I did add milk when I made my own coffee, but I always thought coffee with a packet of sugar added tasted like dessert. Since there was room, I poured milk into the mug and because it was Saturday added sugar. Days off were for decadence. I reached for a stir stick and snuck a glance at the table in the back corner. The woman had her back to me, but I immediately recognized the black ball cap with blond strands peeking out from the edges.

Molly came over to the counter with a jug of milk and a carton of half-and-half. She refilled the carafes and whispered, "You actually have to walk over to the table and say hello to win this bet."

"I don't remember making a bet."

"Whatever." Molly shook her head and spun to leave.

I caught her before she went behind the register. "I know her. She isn't single."

"She looks single to me. Anyway, don't tell me that you can't say hello because she's dating someone else. I'm dating someone and you flirt with me all the time."

"Wait a minute, I don't flirt. You flirt with me." I felt my cheeks burn. "I'm only being friendly in return."

Molly stepped closer and whispered, "You're blushing. And I know you aren't only being friendly but whatever. It's possible that there have been some days I even wished I were single, because maybe I've even thought of asking you out on a date. But, as luck would have it, I'm already happily in love. She, on the other hand," Molly pointed to Michele's back, "isn't happy. If you do know her, make her day and say hello."

I gripped the travel mug and glanced at the door. I didn't need Michele today. I needed to turn and walk right out the door. Instead, I walked over to her table.

"Hi."

She looked up from her book and stared at me as if she were trying to remember something. She set the book down but didn't say anything, still looking up at me.

"Should I leave you alone?" I asked. As soon as I'd reached Michele's table, I knew it had been a mistake to give in to Molly's pressuring. I felt the usual ache of desire take hold, but there was something more mixed in now. Regret? What did I regret? That I hadn't said hello that first night at the Metro—or that I'd let her leave to go back to Desi when I was still in the middle of breaking up with Lynn? I waited for Michele to say something, and after a long minute of her silence, I added, "Feels like it's been a long time."

Michele nodded but remained silent.

"I didn't mean to interrupt your reading. I only wanted to say hello. I'll catch you later." I turned to leave. Michele reached out and caught my arm.

"Wait. Don't walk away." Michele's voice was hoarse. She'd either had a long night of singing or she'd been crying. On closer look, I saw that her eyes were ringed in red and I guessed the latter. "Sit down. Please," she added.

I pulled a chair over to her table and waited for Michele to say something more. Her gaze was fixed out the window. "What's wrong?"

"My cat died."

"I'm sorry." I remembered her gray tabby. He was a grumpy old cat that tried to bite me when I first pet him. I never tried a second time.

"And then I got a call from my lawyer."

"You have a lawyer? Are you being sued?"

"No, no…The lawyer is helping me with a paperwork issue. Or trying—and failing. Anyway, it's a long story. I don't want to get into it. And I don't know why I'm so upset about Beastie. He was a complete pain in the ass."

"That's been my experience with cats. And lawyers."

Michele smiled. "I'm not going to laugh at that. But I've missed all of your terrible jokes."

"I really am sorry about your cat. What happened?"

"He was old. The vet said kidney disease. He used to bite everyone—except me. He ripped up my furniture, way worse than Carol's cat, and he started peeing on Desi's clothes…But for some damn reason, I loved that little bastard. Most days we barely tolerated each other. Still, he was with me for sixteen years."

I reached across the table and set my hand on hers.

"Ridiculous, right?" She sniffed. "He used to torture my old dog, Boss. I think Boss died just to get away from Beastie." She laughed, but the sound choked in her throat.

"I cried my eyes out when my cat died. That was high school, but I get it."

"I'm not in high school and it's already been a week. I'm not even sure if I'm still crying about the cat." She smiled weakly.

"This stuff takes time. Give yourself a break."

"Is that my pep talk?" Michele asked sarcastically. "I've missed you. You know, you're an asshole for not calling me. What if I'd needed you? What if I broke a window or the garbage disposal stopped working?"

"You would have called me. Or your landlord."

"No, I told you to call me when you were ready. And don't get me started about my landlord. Anyway, I didn't want to push you, especially after you practically kicked me out the last time." She sighed. "As soon as I heard about Lynn's move, I had this nagging feeling that I was going to lose both of you. I didn't realize how boring my life was until you both were gone."

"Have you been in touch with Lynn and Roxy at all?"

Michele nodded. "I'm planning on flying out to spend Thanksgiving with them. Roxanne is so excited about it I feel like November must be right around the corner."

"I want to come," I almost said. I swallowed my words before they even had a chance to elicit a nod of pity from Michele. My throat was tight. I knew Michele was watching my reaction closely. "That's great. You're going to have to give Roxy a big hug from me."

"I bet you've missed her. Been in withdrawal?"

"Almost enough to want my own kid. Almost. And how's Desi?" I didn't want to ask, but it was the only thing I could think of to change the subject.

"Oh, she's fine. We're roomies now. She moved in a little over a month ago. She's the reason I'm sitting in this café, in fact."

"Why's that?"

"She told me the Humane Society was having a pet fair. She thinks I should go pick out a kitten." Michele shook her head. She held up the book. "I took myself to a coffee shop instead, thinking I'd spend the morning reading. I've been staring at the first page, but I haven't read a word. And then you waltz in." She smiled. "Of all days, why did you show up today?"

"What do you mean?"

"I've been thinking about you, that's all... I was sitting here wishing I could drive over to your new place and invite myself over. And then suddenly you were standing in front of me. I miss talking to you." She let go of my hand and tapped the book. "This is one of Desi's books. She writes her name on the inside cover." Michele pointed to the inscription. "In case I was thinking of nabbing this one, she'll track me down."

"Can't trust a librarian to return a good book, I guess."

"She's even more anal than I am. I don't think my place has ever been so organized." She paused. "But I don't know how we're going to do once we're past the honeymoon period. We haven't lived together long enough, but I'm already worried that she doesn't seem to have any faults. I've had roommates before that seemed great for the first few months, and then all of these weird issues start to come to the surface."

She opened the book and stared again at the inside cover, then closed the book and shook her head. "Anyway, so far, so good. We've even planned out a garden for the house we might buy together." She glanced out the window. "How would you feel about a walk? I've been sitting here too long."

We stood at the same time and without thinking, I reached for Michele and pulled her into a hug. I hadn't hugged anyone since the day the moving truck came to pick up Roxanne and Lynn's things. I'd given both of them big hugs and it had been hard to let go.

Hugs were something I'd never really thought much about. Lynn was a big hugger and so was Michele. Maybe they'd gotten me into the habit. As soon as Michele was close to me, I realized how much I needed the contact. I wasn't sure if it was the feel of being held or the feel of holding someone else, but I could hardly let go. Michele didn't try to pull away. She leaned into me and her face pressed against my neck.

I finally had to step away. Hugging her had always made me want more. I wanted to kiss the cheek that was inches below my lips and, even more so, to find her lips for a real kiss. Instead, I reached for Desi's book and picked up my travel mug. "Let's get some air."

Michele followed my lead through the maze of tables in the overfilled coffee shop. Molly grinned and held up her thumb as we passed the register. I wasn't sure if Michele noticed and decided against bringing up Molly's challenge.

When we stepped outside, Michele let out a deep breath. She glanced up and down the sidewalk. "Sometimes I get sick of this sunshine. Rain would be nice today, wouldn't it?"

"Not for a walk."

"I think you're wrong. A walk in the rain can be lovely." Michele tilted her head to the few puffy white clouds on the horizon. "Why don't we go to your house? You can show me what you've done with the place."

"It isn't exactly ready for company."

Michele tilted her head and squinted up at me. "I'm not going to whip out white gloves and swipe for dust, you know."

"Yeah, it's just…" I stalled. I couldn't exactly admit that the problem wasn't *any* company but her company in particular.

"It's just what? Come on," Michele said, turning to head toward Granite Avenue. She walked several steps and then looked back. "I want to see what you've been up to, and you had better have been busy because I haven't heard any other excuse for why you never called me."

Michele was now several yards ahead. I knew well enough that once she had decided on something, it was useless to try and convince her to change her mind. "Okay, fine. Hold up," I called.

"No." Michele smiled over her shoulder. "Catch up with me."

Once I'd caught up, we walked side by side and close enough to touch. I resisted the urge to reach for her hand. We reached my house and Michele paused at the front yard.

"This one, right?"

I nodded. "It still looks pretty bad from the front. As Carol would say—no curb appeal. I'm getting new windows on Monday, and then I'm having the stucco done when I get the money for that. It should look a lot better in a month." I walked up the stairs to the front door and then hesitated before placing the key in the lock. "It's such a nice day. Maybe we should keep walking."

Michele took the keys out of my hands. She brushed against my chest as she maneuvered in front of me to unlock the door, then left the keys in the lock as she walked inside. Pointing to the sofa, she said, "Don't tell me that is still your only piece of furniture."

I closed the front door and stood in the entryway, staring at Michele's back. She was wearing a tank top that showed off her shoulders and black jeans that hugged her butt. I followed her into the living room. "Of course not. I have a bed too. I don't recommend sleeping in it, though. It's almost as uncomfortable as the sofa."

"If I ever get the chance to test it out, I'll keep your advice in mind." She winked. "No sleeping."

"I missed your teasing."

"Who said I was teasing?" Michele countered. She'd turned away from me, and I couldn't see her expression. "The floor looks great. Is this the original wood?"

I tossed the keys on the mantel and shoved my hands in the pockets of my jeans. Michele had wandered down the hall, not waiting for an answer about the floor. The staircase creaked as she headed up to the bedrooms. I followed, several steps behind. Michele poked her head into the bathroom and said, "Well, you've done a few things, all right. This bathroom looks great. I like the tile you picked. But the wallpaper?"

"You don't like roses?" I grinned.

"I would have ripped that down first thing. Why put in a new shower stall and tile when you still have to stare at that?"

"It's on my list."

Michele continued on to the bedrooms, glancing in at the smaller room and then pausing at the entrance to the master bedroom.

"I didn't need to do much to the bedrooms. Just the usual—new baseboards, closet doors, a fresh coat of paint and light switches. Uncovering the original wood floor made a big difference in here as well." I could hear the nervous edge in my voice, and I wondered if Michele noticed. I followed her into the master and then wished I hadn't. Michele had stopped in front of the bed and seemed to be staring at the single pillow. I didn't need more than one. She turned around and we were inches apart. Every nerve that had signaled to reach out and grab Michele on the walk here fired once more. I glanced away from her and only then noticed the unmade bed, the open closet door and the overflowing laundry basket. "It would look better if it wasn't a mess."

"Relax. I already gave you a bad time about the wallpaper. I know when to shut up." Michele smiled. "You've been busy."

I didn't breathe until Michele walked past me. The floorboards creaked when she headed back down the stairs. I pulled the sheets up on the bed and closed the closet door, shoving dirty socks and yesterday's T-shirt into the laundry basket along with a pair of shorts I'd hung on the closet door handle.

Michele reached the kitchen before I thought to stop her. I heard her say, "Holy cow." And then a moment later, she hollered, "What the hell is this hole for? Jodi, did you cut the wall or was this here before?"

Michele was already reaching her hand into the hole when I walked into the kitchen. "It's some sort of secret hiding place, isn't it?" She glanced down at the newspaper and matchbook and then eyed the jewelry box. "Was all of this inside there?" She didn't wait for me to answer, picking up the top page of the newspaper and scanning it. "September 1954. Old newsprint feels so much thicker than what they send out nowadays."

"I didn't notice." I walked past her and picked up the breadbox that had concealed the cubbyhole. "I'll be right back." I tossed the breadbox down on the junk pile in the backyard and came back for the cabinet. The cabinet wasn't heavy, but it was unwieldy and an awkward squeeze through the doorway. I heaved it on top of the trash heap and it collided against the other metal cabinet with an awful racket. It was useless to wish that I hadn't left the papers or the box out in plain sight. Michele knew as much as I did, but I wasn't ready to share the discovery with her—or with anyone. Last night, it had felt as if I'd had some sort of connection to the person who had nailed a breadbox over a secret. But now that strange connection that I'd felt was gone. I wanted more time alone with it. I wanted to open the jewelry box alone.

When I came back to the kitchen, Michele set down the newspaper and looked up at me. "This article is about the McCarthy witch hunt. They have names listed for the local suspects. Front page. Unbelievable. I knew they went looking everywhere but imagine reading names of your neighbors? Somehow this makes it all the more real. This one article probably destroyed these people's lives."

"Witch hunt?"

"You know, commies, McCarthy's Red Scare and all of that. Don't tell me you don't remember that from your high school history class."

"Red Scare? Right. No, I remember it. Vaguely." I paused. Michele was reading the article, head bent and eyes squinting at the faded print. "It's possible that I wasn't paying all that close attention to my history teacher in high school."

"Too distracted by your high school social life to pay attention to history?"

"I wouldn't say I had a social life in high school. But there was this one girl...I paid a lot more attention to her than anything my history teacher said."

"Now that I believe." She smiled. "But think back to your history class for a minute...This is someone's big secret. Right in front of us." She paused. "This jewelry box was in the hole too, right? What's inside?" She brushed a finger across the lid, waiting. When I didn't answer, she said, "You haven't tried to open it yet, have you? Have you looked for the key?"

"I only found this stuff last night."

Michele picked up the box and turned it upside down, exactly as I'd done. She shook it and held it against her ear like a seashell. "Let's break it open. Got a screwdriver handy? I used to sneak into my sister's jewelry box all the time to borrow earrings. These locks are easy to crack."

"I want to look for the key first. If this is someone's big secret, I don't want to destroy their box just because I'm curious."

"Why not? Are you going to track them down and give the box back to them?"

"Well, no. I don't know. Maybe." I hadn't thought past not wanting to break the box. Michele's suggestion that I might consider returning the box to its owner sounded crazy, but I didn't want to rule it out.

She set the box down and folded her arms across her chest. "I never took you for the sentimental type."

"Maybe you don't know me as well as you think."

"Maybe not." Michele walked over to where I stood. She reached for my hand. "But did I tell you how much I missed you? I can't even remember why I was so upset earlier."

"Your cat died." I didn't want Michele to let go. The feel of her hand in mine was dizzying.

"Thanks for the reminder. I didn't actually forget about Beastie. A lot of things hit at once." She paused. "I've missed you. And Lynn. And Roxy too, of course. I feel like I lost all of my best friends the day you guys split. Sal was camped over at Lynn's almost as soon as you moved out and you know how well Sal and I got along. I stopped going over unless Lynn asked. And you—you fell into a rabbit hole." She started to let go and then leaned in and kissed my cheek. "Come on, Alice, let's find your magic key."

I was frozen in place. It could very well have been Wonderland that I'd slipped into that morning. Or yesterday when I'd discovered the cubbyhole. Everything could have been in Technicolor since that moment.

I watched Michele open every cupboard. "I've already looked there."

"So I'm looking again," Michele said. She got down on her knees and felt under the sink. Michele had never kissed me before. I tried not to let my mind leap to any conclusions.

Michele glanced over at me. "Do you mind that I'm looking? I think I might be channeling Nancy Drew. It's been a long time since I've felt this excited about anything." She pulled open the drawer where I kept my few pieces of camping silverware and slipped her hand inside, feeling around the drawer. "How often do you get this in life, you know? We have this mystery right in front of us!" She closed the silverware drawer and pulled open the next one in line. It was mostly empty save for an odd assortment of napkins, packets of mustard, taco sauce and other single-serving condiments. "Come on, Jodi. If you aren't going to let me crack open the box, at least help me find the key."

"If I had something to hide, I'd pick the basement. Unfinished basements are creepy enough to keep everyone out except the mice and spiders."

"Then lead the way," Michele said, closing the last drawer.

"There's a trap door over here." I went to the pantry and pulled on the chain light. The trap door took a good tug before it opened with a whine. I started down the narrow staircase, glancing over my shoulder to see if Michele was following. "Are you coming?"

She leaned her head through the opening. The light in the basement was weak, and I doubted we'd be able to find anything without a flashlight. I made room for her, standing in the open space below the stairwell. Michele still hesitated at the top of the stairs.

"You're not coming, are you?"

"I'm not a big fan of small spaces," Michele admitted. "Can you look around and I'll hold open the door?"

"Prop the door open with something and see if you can grab my flashlight. I can barely see anything down here. The flashlight's under my bed."

"Should I be worried about what else I may find under your bed? No dirty magazines, right?"

"If you don't come back with the flashlight, I'll assume you found my collection."

Michele had already shoved a box of macaroni and cheese in the corner of the door and disappeared from view. We used to trade sexual innuendos back and forth all the time. Now her joke was strangely steadying. We had made good friends. There was no guarantee we'd ever make good girlfriends.

I took a deep breath and exhaled. The air smelt of dirt and concrete dust. I leaned against the railing, not wanting to venture further without better light. I had a hard time ignoring the way Michele smiled at me. But maybe I could ignore how much I liked her… Maybe there was a chance we could be friends again.

"Found it!" Michele shone the light down the stairwell, directly at my face, inadvertently blinding me. "Nice vibrator collection, by the way."

"I don't keep vibrators under the bed." I reached for the flashlight with my eyes closed until Michele redirected the light. Once I had it in my hands, I quickly directed it back at her, returning the favor, and was rewarded by a screech. I turned the flashlight into the basement depths and said, "They're in a drawer in the bathroom. I wash them after I use them."

"You have always been good at making me slightly more uncomfortable than I tried to make you."

"You're welcome," I replied. "By the way, I haven't looked through the pantry yet. If you want, there's a stepstool in the corner so you can get to the high shelves."

"I'll start right on that, boss. Once I can see again."

"Can't take what you give, huh?"

"I can take it. But I can hand out a lot more, so you might want to watch it. Now focus, Watson. We need to find the key." Michele had disappeared from the door.

"No way," I shouted. "I found the secret cubbyhole. I get to be Sherlock."

"Too late. I'm Sherlock. Not only do I have a pipe, I know how to smoke. And I've got a tweed hat that I will so pull out if you fight me for this." Michele's face popped back into view. "Besides, I'm a research librarian. Do you know how exciting my daily life is? Let me have this one."

"You have a pipe?"

"Look for the damn key."

"Why the hell do you have a pipe?"

"It might have belonged to one of my exes. But I don't want to get into that because I know you are going to ask too many questions, and then you'll be distracted. We have a key to find."

I combed the walls and the crevices between the stairs with my hands, running them through cobwebs and over layers of dust so thick it made me think of powdered milk, then angled the light further into the recesses. I hadn't been in the basement since I first toured the place. It had more potential than I remembered. The ceiling height didn't drop off suddenly like in many old basements. It was at least eight feet high all the way across, and with the two windows already in place, it wouldn't be hard to turn the space into an in-law unit. There was at least eight hundred square feet of useable space and it was partially above ground. I'd have to cut in a new entrance... I stopped short. It was useless to dream of a finished basement when I didn't even have the budget to do everything I wanted to do upstairs.

After a twenty-minute search, I decided that if the key was in the basement, someone had done a damn good job of hiding it. I was edgy in the dank space and wanted air. When I returned to the kitchen, Michele had the sheets of newspaper laid out across the length of the counter and was snapping pictures of them with her phone. I filled a glass of water and handed it to Michele, then grabbed another for myself.

Michele glanced up from the newspaper. "No key?"

"Nope."

"I didn't have any luck in the pantry either, but there's a jar of cinnamon that's so old it smells like wood chips. It's the only thing on the top shelf aside from mouse droppings. I wonder why someone would leave one jar of cinnamon."

"Maybe it's for good luck."

"It's cinnamon, not a penny. Where's your screwdriver?"

"I'm not breaking the lock."

Michele sighed. "I was thinking that maybe someone on this list," she pointed to the McCarthy article, "might have been living here. I'm going to look up the names and see if I can link anyone to the address."

"Why not check the county records? They keep a registry for everyone who has a house deed."

Michele arched an eyebrow. "Not bad, Watson. In fact, I was planning on starting with the county recorder. But the person who hid the box might have been a renter and not listed on the deed. So, don't worry, I won't stop there." Her phone rang and she glanced at the screen, then hit the button to silence the call and slid the phone into her pocket. "Desi probably thinks I'm going to come home with an entire litter of kittens at this rate. I hate to say it, but I need to get going." She restacked the newspaper sheets and then picked up the box. "You sure? One quick turn and I can crack it open."

"I'm not done looking for the key."

"You're more patient than me." As she set the box down, she noticed the matchbook. She flipped it over, reading both sides and then opened it and ran her finger across the match tips. "Was this in the cubbyhole as well?"

"Yeah. I was thinking of taking a drive down to that address to see what's become of the place."

Michele set the matchbook on top of the box. "Maybe the newspaper isn't connected to the box at all."

"That was my first thought. People used to stuff newspaper in walls for insulation all the time. But the more I consider all of this, I think everything that was put in the hole has a reason for being there. I have a feeling it's all linked."

"Maybe." Michele looked at the hole thoughtfully. She took a sip of water and then glanced at her watch. "Shit. I don't want to go to look for a kitten. Why don't we go for a drive and check out this address together?"

"I don't have time for a drive today," I said. I could make the time, I knew, but I wasn't ready. Michele had always been too easy to fall for and I could feel my body lunging for the edge. "I've got a lot of work to do around here. I shouldn't waste any more daylight." Fortunately this was the truth. I hated to lie to her.

Michele stared at me as if she was formulating an argument. Finally she said, "I should get home anyway. But I want you to promise to tell me when, or if, you find the key. I want to be there when you open the box." Michele seemed reluctant to leave. She opened one of the drawers directly under the hiding spot. She'd already checked the drawer, but she felt the underside of it once more, shaking her head as she did. She closed the drawer and sighed. "Anyway, I'm glad you found me in the café. This morning was nice."

"It was." I could have added more, but I didn't want to risk ruining what we'd had that morning. It felt like old times, only better. The problem was, Michele seemed happy enough with Desi. It wasn't my place to admit to feelings that may or may not matter while Michele was with someone else.

"And I think I'm finally done moping." She headed out of the kitchen and then paused in the dining room. "Hey, I know you haven't been going to the Metro lately...I can understand avoiding the place since you and Lynn met there, but I miss seeing you in the audience. The band is playing tomorrow night. I'm singing lead on one of the songs. I'd love to see you there. I could use a friend in the audience tomorrow. Moral support, you know."

Avoiding the Metro had nothing to do with Lynn, but I couldn't admit to the real reason. It was Michele I hadn't been able to face. Still, I couldn't resist an invitation, even though I knew I should give some excuse. What was a little more torture?

"I'll be there."

CHAPTER SEVEN

Nearly all of the tables in front of the stage were filled, and most of the seats at the bar were taken as well. There was a table near the side door with a limited view of the stage but good cover. I headed for this but paused when I spotted Desi getting a drink at the bar. As hard as it would be to watch Desi and Michele together, I knew it was harder staying away from Michele entirely. Getting better acquainted with Desi might help suppress the feelings I had for Michele. I'd hardly gotten anything done since Michele's visit yesterday and hadn't been able to sleep well. If I was going to have any chance at a friendship with her, I couldn't be jealous of her girlfriend.

Desi sat down alone at a table on the opposite side of the club, and I reluctantly headed toward her. She waved as I approached and gestured to the empty seat.

"Jodi! Good to see you," she said, getting up to give me a hug. She sat down again and pointed to the seat next to hers. "Keep me company? I hate sitting alone."

I'd gotten used to sitting alone but didn't admit this aloud. The chair was a little too close to hers, but I sat down anyway. "How are you?"

"Good." She sighed and took a sip of her cocktail. "It's been a long weekend. You know how it goes. By the time Sunday night comes round, the last thing I want to do is go out to a club. But Michele was so excited about the new song they're doing tonight. I couldn't stay home."

The band members filed onstage, and my eyes latched onto Michele. The applause provided enough distraction for me to be able to shift the chair a bit further from Desi's. When the clapping died down, Desi began describing her weekend in detail, beginning with how she'd tried to get Michele to adopt a new cat and a quip about Beastie's passing. Facing her more than the stage, I avoided sneaking side glances at Michele and tried to keep up my end of the conversation, which mostly only required a nod or head shake at the appropriate time. After everyone had tuned their guitars and settled into place, though, I gave up any pretense of listening to Desi and focused on the stage. The first chords slipped into the air and Michele's alto voice filled the room in a long "ooh." Sarah began the melody and Michele's voice was relegated to the background.

It was easy to slip into a trance as I homed in on Michele's voice. Her voice was as familiar as a lover's kiss. I felt closer to her when she sang than at any other moment. When the song finished and a new one began, I excused myself to get a drink at the bar. I wanted to be able to watch Michele without feeling guilty. With Desi next to me, that was impossible.

Tina smiled when I came up to the bar. She filled a glass with Cherry Coke and stabbed a cherry on an umbrella toothpick. She pushed the drink toward me. "Long time no see, Jo. What do you have to say for yourself?"

I shrugged. "Not a whole hell of a lot."

"Avoiding me?"

"No. I've been busy."

"I watched you walk in alone. You haven't been that busy." She grinned. "Isn't that woman you were sitting with Michele's gal?"

"Don't worry, we're all friends." That wasn't exactly true, but it was close enough. Tina could be a gossip, and I didn't need her telling Michele anything. I knew I should go back to Desi's table, but I was more comfortable sitting by myself at the bar.

I watched as Tina filled other orders at the bar and then concentrated on the stage. As she strummed her guitar through the verses of the next song in the set, Michele stared out at the audience. She didn't seem to be paying attention to anyone in particular; her thoughts were either tuned to the music or very far from the Metro Lounge. I'd always longed to ask her what she was thinking when she played. The question was too personal, I thought, for anywhere but in bed. Chances were slim that I'd ever get the chance to ask if I waited for that however.

"You know, it's been proven that you are more likely to get asked out if people think you aren't available," Tina said, mopping up a puddle of spilled beer with a dishtowel. "Why don't you go sit back at that table?"

"I don't believe anyone's ever proven that. Anyway, I'm not here hoping someone asks me out."

Tina shook her head. "Travis was in a few weeks back. He said you've been working for him lately. Are you still doing your own stuff as well?"

"Some. Travis keeps me busy."

"Well, say hi to him when you see him and remind the guy that he owes me ballgame tickets. He'll know what I'm talking about." She tossed the wet towel over her shoulder and made her way over to a couple waiting at the other end of the counter.

I glanced over at Desi. The trouble was, I really liked Desi. She'd never rubbed me the wrong way. And I didn't question why Michele would want to be with her. In fact, there was no good reason that I could think of for Michele to want to break up with her. I took another sip of the soda and headed back to Desi's table.

Desi smiled when I sat down. "I was getting lonely."

"Tina's chatty."

"Tina?"

"The bartender." I didn't mention the fact that Tina seemed to know her even if Desi didn't know her.

When the next song began, I immediately recognized the chords. Lynn used to invite Michele over for dinner nearly every weekend and she had sung the tune often as she helped in the kitchen. I remembered standing next to her, distracted by our closeness in those cramped quarters, and hearing Michele softly singing about a lovesick cowboy and his heartbreak. I didn't remember many of the words, but I could picture Michele's face perfectly as she belted out the chorus as well as the sad last line.

Instead of Michele taking the lead in the singing as had been planned, Sarah began the song. Michele only came in with the chorus. Desi and I exchanged a wordless glance. It was a country ballad, and Sarah's voice wasn't as well suited to it. Sarah was a good singer, but it was immediately clear that Michele's version, even sung in Lynn's kitchen over a pot of stew, was far better.

Where Michele had taken long pauses between the verses, Sarah sped through the breaks. She also didn't have the twang or the emotion I'd remembered in Michele's voice. Without these things, the song lost its passion. Suddenly it was only a story about a lonesome cowboy.

The cowboy had set out to strike his fortune but soon fell in love with a farm girl. Sarah smiled as if oblivious to the words when she sang about how the cowboy had promised to return to the farm girl after his summer's work but he'd gambled away his hard-earned money and refused to return penniless. How could she smile? I wondered. Summers passed and still the cowboy refused to return until he'd earned enough money to satisfy his pride. Too late he'd learn that the farm girl had married another. The crush of emotion that was palpable when Michele had sung the final verse was entirely absent in Sarah's version.

I shook my head, and Desi said, "Tell me about it. She's got this song all wrong. Why the hell didn't she let Michele sing this one?"

"I guess the plan changed."

"Well, that's crap. Michele totally owns that song. Sarah can sing everything else. She can't sing country. I don't know why she's even trying."

When the cowboy's ballad ended, the band switched back to their usual folk-rock beat and did a cover of a love song that was one of their usual closers. Sarah announced a ten-minute break and I glanced at the door. It would be hard to leave without Michele noticing, but I didn't want to sit at the same table with her and Desi. Michele set her guitar in the stand and stared straight at our table as she made her way off stage. I knew I was stuck.

"Hey, you made it out of your hermitage," Michele said, slapping my shoulder. She slid into the seat on the other side of Desi and continued, "So, do we have to tie you down to get you to stay through the next set? Or will you stick around for old times' sake?"

Desi interrupted. "Why the hell didn't Sarah let you sing your song? She can't do country."

Michele shrugged. "It's a long story. What are you drinking?"

Desi pushed her drink over to Michele. "I'm too upset to enjoy it. You should have been the one to sing that song. You've got the country voice. Why aren't you upset? I am."

"I told you—it's a long story. I think she did a great job with it—it was different, but that's the folk process."

"Well, screw the folk process. You were supposed to sing lead. She can't step back from the limelight for one fricking song?"

"We aren't a country band, Desi. Yeah, she gave the song a different feel, but that's how these things work."

"You said the rest of the band wanted to do a country piece—that's why you guys picked that song and why you were going to sing lead."

"Sarah changed her mind," Michele said flatly.

I eyed Desi. "I think she's saying 'drop it.' But, for the record, I completely agree with you."

By the time I made it home, the sugar high I'd felt from two sodas was long gone. My stomach growled, and I went to the kitchen for a glass of milk and a slice of leftover pizza. I sat on the counter opposite the new hole I'd cut for the bay window and stared at the sheet of plastic that I'd stapled in place over the space. Every time the breeze caught it, the plastic billowed inward, crackling as it did.

I'd looked a little more for the key for the mystery box, but had no luck finding it and had moved it, along with the matchbook and the newsprint, upstairs to the bedroom closet. Michele hadn't asked about the key or anything else from the cubbyhole while I was at the Metro. I was glad; I wanted to keep the secret between us. Michele's silence on the subject in front of Desi confirmed that she wasn't interested in sharing it either.

I finished the pizza and downed the last of the milk. It was past midnight, and I hadn't stayed up past eleven for months. I'd planned to leave once Olive and Slim had finished their second set, knowing Brandon and his window crew would arrive at daybreak. But with a little arm twisting, Michele had convinced me to stay. After their argument about the cowboy ballad, Desi and Michele hadn't talked much. Desi had seemed distracted for the rest of the evening, in fact, yawning frequently.

The bands that followed were better than expected, and in the end, we had all decided it was worth staying until the last song. The evening passed with little of the awkwardness I'd expected. It helped that Desi and Michele were not the type of couple that wrapped their arms around each other, sat close enough to whisper into each other's ear or even kissed in public. With little effort, I could easily imagine that Michele wasn't that into Desi. I'd seen her be plenty affectionate with other women she'd dated and guessed that it was Desi who wasn't interested in a public display.

Unfortunately, the fact remained that they were living together. Worse yet, Desi had mentioned that they'd gone to a few open houses that morning. No matter what Michele's dating history showed, Desi didn't seem to be going anywhere anytime soon.

I rinsed out the milk glass and headed upstairs. As uncomfortable as it was, the bed was a welcome sight.

CHAPTER EIGHT

Michele sent me at least one text every day after our night at the Metro. I referred to it in my head as "our night" even though we'd had no time alone together during it. Hearing her sing again after so many months had solidified everything in my mind. I had hopelessly fallen for her.

Because of this, I didn't reply to any of her texts. Most of them were short—updates on her search for information about the home's prior occupants or details about local happenings in 1954. She sent me a link to an article on McCarthy and a podcast on the US Communist movement. I scanned the article and even listened to the podcast. Travis had raised his eyebrows when I showed up for work with earphones, but then he wanted to listen to the podcast after I'd finished.

None of her texts were personal though she had invited me to come see Olive and Slim at the West Side Winery on Thursday night. Sarah worked there, but she had Thursdays off and the winery often scheduled the band as live entertainment that night. I wasn't up for going out or maybe I wasn't up for seeing Michele yet. I hadn't quite figured out how to act around her. While she obsessed about our shared mystery and seemingly wanted to discuss nothing else, I couldn't stop thinking of all the other things I wanted to talk about instead.

Friday's text was different. She hadn't sent me anything until after five and then only one word: "Home?"

Travis had wanted to work late, and I didn't return her text until I was leaving the site. I didn't stop to pick up dinner, hoping I could squeeze in a shower before she showed up. I slammed the truck door and then caught sight of the house. The new windows were overshadowed by scaffolding that wrapped around the house and by a coat of gray cement that had replaced the siding for the time being. My friend in the stucco business had called the night before to say he'd had a project fall through and didn't want his crew standing around for a day. He gave me a cut on the already low rate and I'd managed to come up with half down. Applying the stucco was a process that took weeks longer than it seemed to be worth, but I didn't need Carol to tell me how it would raise the value of the house enough to be worth the money and hassle.

I had barely unlocked the front door when I heard Michele's car pull up to the curb. It's easy to recognize a Prius: the engine sound cuts out before the wheels hit the curb. It was easy to tell it was Michele's too, given the bumper stickers. She had an assortment of HRC and rainbow stickers along with my favorite—an outline of lips over the words "Reading is Sexy" all clustered on the car's back bumper.

Michele hopped out and waved. She was wearing black heels, a short black skirt and a dark red blouse. Clearly she'd come from work, but she looked so good that I wished I could convince her to go out to dinner. The idea of going on a first date with someone I'd eaten dinner with too many times to count was ridiculous. And yet it wasn't.

I waited until she reached the front porch. "So—are you here because you wanted to see me or because you want to crack open that box?"

"Guess."

"You are really getting into this, aren't you?"

Michele grinned. "I've been slightly obsessed."

"I know the feeling," I said, regretting the words as soon as they slipped off my tongue.

"Really?" Michele tilted her head. "You haven't responded to any of my texts until tonight. I was starting to think that you weren't interested."

Of course I was interested. I was also distracted. I held the door open. "Coming in?"

"That depends. Can I see the box?"

"Yeah, it's up in my closet. I'll bring it down. And feel free to have another look for the key. I've had no luck."

Michele walked in and pointed at the new windows. "I didn't even notice them from the outside. They look great. How did the kitchen window turn out?"

"Go take a look. Mind if I hop in the shower?"

"No. But if you leave me alone for too long, I'll be scouring the whole house in search of that damn key."

"Good luck." I headed upstairs. This time I was careful to clean up the bedroom after I stripped. I headed to the bathroom and hopped into the shower, taking only a quick rinse to get the day's stench off my skin.

I stared at my reflection in the mirror as I toweled off afterward. I had no business grinning like a love-sick schoolgirl every time Michele stopped by. Behind me, the wallpapered roses glowed in the fluorescent glare. Michele was right, of course. The wallpaper should have been the first thing to go, but I'd gotten a deal on the tile and once that was in place, the roses didn't bother me as much. I still had every intention of peeling off the paper and texturing the walls, but the project kept slipping to the bottom of the list.

The edge of the wallpaper near the border of the mirror was already curling up and I tested the corner with a light tug. The paper peeled away from the wall as if it had been waiting for an excuse. Normally it took a bit more work to get wallpaper to loosen, but I guessed the glue was weakened by years of moisture. I worked off one entire strip and then crumpled it into a ball and tossed it in the trash can. Not surprisingly, there was another layer of wallpaper under the roses. I hesitated when I recognized this one. It was the same yellow plaid print that had been behind the cabinets in the kitchen. That layer hugged the wall tightly, however, and I realized that, unlike the sheet with the roses, it was going to take the right tool and lots of elbow grease to get this one off. That wasn't going to happen now, however, not with Michele waiting for me downstairs.

I changed into a T-shirt and jeans and grabbed the jewelry box from the top shelf of the closet. Michele was in the kitchen, leaning against the counter and staring out the bay window.

"This is worth however much money you spent."

I walked over to where Michele stood and set the box on the counter. "Yeah. Not bad, for the price."

Michele spotted the jewelry box and smiled. She stepped closer to me and to the box and said, "You smell better. I wasn't going to say anything before, but…"

"But I stunk? Travis had me crawling in an attic for half the day." It was hard to resist the urge to wrap my arms around her.

"How do I get you to relax? I don't remember you being this serious." Michele laughed. She tapped her finger lightly on my chest. "I was teasing. I didn't think you smelled bad before. Just like you'd been working. And you've smelled worse."

"Thank you, I think."

Michele was close enough that we easily could have kissed. As soon as the thought crossed my mind, I took a step back. "Do you want a drink?"

"No. I want a damn key. Not knowing what's inside this box is driving me crazy. Let's admit we aren't going to find the key. The key moved out along with whoever left the box fifty years ago."

"You don't know that for sure." I considered telling Michele about the layers of wallpaper in the bathroom upstairs. Something about the yellow wallpaper—the same that had hung in the kitchen behind the cabinets and the breadbox—made me think that the key might be hidden there. Maybe between the layers of paper…I didn't have any reason to think this other than the feeling I'd had while I'd peeled the paper, and while I usually trusted a hunch, there was a good chance I was wrong.

The fact that I might be wrong wasn't what was stopping me from sharing my hunch though. I wasn't ready to be stripping wallpaper in a small space with Michele that close. "Give me another week. If I still can't find the key, I'll let you crack the lock."

"I'm not sure I can wait another week." Michele sighed. "You know what I keep thinking? What if this secret is something awful?"

"Like what?"

Michele shook her head. "I don't know. Someone went to a lot of trouble to hide it."

"Yes, but they clearly wanted to keep whatever it was. If it was something awful, they would have tossed the box or whatever is inside it. I'm sure plenty of things go missing in the river." I poured a glass of wine and held up the bottle. "You sure you don't want a drink?"

"I can't stay. I'm going with Desi to see a movie tonight."

"Yeah, of course." I set the bottle down, forcing a smile.

"Do you want to join us?"

I shook my head. I wanted her all to myself tonight, but I had no right to think along those lines.

"You sure I can't change your mind about opening this?"

I shook my head again. In fact, it wasn't true. She could do a few things that would make me instantly change my mind.

"You got my text with the name of the guy who owned this place, right?"

"I got the name. Randall Johnson."

"Just when I think you aren't paying attention, Burkitt." She smiled. "Good memory."

My last name is Burkitt. It'd been a while since she'd called me that however. She would whip it out when Lynn and I played card games with her, and I'd often wondered if she was trying to throw off my attention by saying it. Now it seemed as close to a term of endearment as I'd heard from her.

"I'm always paying attention. But I couldn't text you back."

She met my eyes briefly and then continued. "Anyway, this Johnson owned the place from 1952 to 1962. It wasn't hard to find information on him. Turns out he was a professor at Sutherland. He taught economics there until 1962 and then took a job in Atlanta. I didn't follow his story any further. I know he had a wife and two kids, who were both born here. As far as I can tell, nothing in that newspaper can be linked to anyone in the family." Michele glanced at her watch. "I guess I should go. Desi likes to get good seats."

"Did you only come tonight because of the box?"

"I was hoping you'd found the key. Or were ready to give up and let me crack it open."

"I'm stubborn."

"Yeah, that I knew. But the sentimental thing was a surprise."

If I mentioned my hunch about the wallpaper upstairs, I knew she'd cancel her movie plans. I thought of Desi and sipped my wine. Michele sighed. She turned the box over a few times and then shook it lightly.

"It's light. And I think, by the sound of it, that there's only paper inside. Damn it, this is driving me nuts…Please, can we break it open?"

I nearly went for a screwdriver. The chance to crack open the box would be enough for Michele to call Desi and cancel their movie plans even if the wallpaper wasn't. And she'd said please. But as much as I wanted her to stay, I only nodded. "Paper's my guess too. Or maybe there's paper wrapped around something else light—like a ring."

Michele handed the box back to me. "Your place is on my way home from work, you know. The college is only a half mile from here."

"It's good seeing you. Whatever your reason is."

"Whatever my reason? You think I came here for something besides this jewelry box?"

I didn't answer.

Michele hesitated a moment longer, staring at me as if she were about to say something and then deciding otherwise. "You've got a week. I'll be here next Friday with my own screwdriver."

It wasn't exactly a date, but it was close enough. I walked Michele out to her car and waited for her to drive away. Then I went over to the truck and searched through my toolbox for a putty knife. My hair was still wet and a breeze sent a chill down my spine. It was the first cool evening and felt like a promise that summer was on its way out.

I headed back inside and upstairs to the bathroom. With the lights switched on, the yellow plaid was even harder to appreciate. The roses had definitely improved the place. I stared at the section of wallpaper that I'd stripped, then at the stubborn yellow plaid. It was definitely the same paper from the kitchen. Maybe there was a good deal on yellow plaid wallpaper. I slipped the putty knife under the edge of the paper and set to work.

Within a short time, I found a rust spot in what might have been a shape of a key, but no key. I set the putty knife on the counter and rubbed my head. My stomach reminded me that I'd skipped dinner. The thought of heating up a frozen dinner was unappetizing, but my stomach insisted on a meal.

Standing in the kitchen, waiting for the microwave to heat some enchiladas, I had a strange feeling that someone was standing behind me. I glanced over my shoulder but, of course, nothing was there. If I believed in ghosts, which I didn't, I'd swear that something wanted me to go back to the bathroom and finish stripping the paper.

By the time I'd eaten half of the enchilada dinner, my non-existent ghost was getting antsy. The more I thought about it, the more convinced I was that the key was hidden in the bathroom. Taking the second enchilada with me, I went back to the bathroom, took a seat on the counter with my feet propped on the toilet seat and ate the rest of the meal while staring at the strips of yellow plaid paper. Aside from the wallpaper, the only other thing I had left to remove were the gold-trimmed mirrored faceplates over the light switch and the electrical outlets.

I scanned the sheets of wallpaper searching for a hidden key. I kept seeing shadows that made me convinced something might be underneath the paper, but every place I felt was smooth. I eyed the rusty spot I'd found earlier, traced its outline with a light touch and the drywall crumbled in my fingers.

I picked up the putty knife and started to work on the next sheet of wallpaper. It was slow going. In many places when the glue peeled away it took drywall with it. Deciding finally on repairing the drywall rather than trying to save it, I began ripping the sheets with less care. As strip after strip peeled away, I scanned the back sides for any clues before crumpling each one carefully and tossing the wallpaper balls in the shower stall.

I came to the last sheet of wallpaper. It was the spot closest to the door and I'd left it for last because the outlet faceplates would have to be taken off before I could get the paper all the way off. I ran my hand up and down the wallpaper. No trace of a key. Still, there was no sense in leaving the project unfinished. I unscrewed the faceplates and set the ornate mirrors on the counter. On my next trip to Home Depot, I'd replace these faceplates with the usual boring almond plastic covers—something that had entirely much less character.

I stripped the last sheet of wallpaper off and stared at the wall. No key. I picked up the old faceplates, ready to toss them along with the balled-up paper. I'd seen faceplates like them before in homes decorated in the early sixties and guessed that they had been added then. They didn't fit the remodeled bathroom, but I liked them and decided they could stay until I'd picked up new ones. When I went to replace the cover over the electrical outlet, I spotted a bronze key. It was sitting in plain view at the bottom of the outlet box. Somehow I'd overlooked it.

It was such a little thing to find—no treasure that anyone would give any money for—but my heart thumped in my chest and I could hardly stop grinning. I knew the ghost who'd been with me for the past hour was smiling as well. I picked up the key, still hardly believing I'd found it at all, and turned it back and forth. No inscription. It was lightweight and small, and I imagined it hanging from a cord around someone's neck—more a piece of jewelry than a key at all. What secret was I about to unlock? I thought of racing to unlock the box but hesitated...I sat down on the toilet, squeezing the key inside my fist.

I wanted to text Michele. I would only need two words: "Found it." I didn't reach for my phone. Instead I slipped the key into my pocket and stared at the outlet covers. Who had bought those ornate things? Was it the same person who had hung the awful wallpaper? And what treasure had they left behind for me to find?

I couldn't open the box without Michele, I decided. But I also couldn't ask her to come back tonight. Each time we were together I felt my resolve weaken. Tonight she'd left me feeling more weak than ever. If she came back now, there was no way I could resist telling her what I'd longed to say for years. The possibility that those words would push her out of my life was enough to keep the key a secret, at least for the night.

CHAPTER NINE

The stucco crew arrived early Monday morning. I was out watering my new crab apple and recognized the sound of their truck before I spotted it. The brakes screeched when the driver hit the curb. Stucco Jon, as he had been introduced to me when we met years ago, had come the first day, but he had sent only his crew thereafter and I couldn't remember anyone else's name. The guys were friendly enough, but they weren't interested in chatting. The men would mill about until Stucco Jon showed with his truck and their supplies. By the end of the day, the house would be dark beige with lighter beige accents around the windows and the trim. Beige wasn't what I'd pick if I actually planned on living in the place, but it was the best choice for resale. I'd painted the front door a deep burgundy and hoped the colors would work well together. If it didn't the front door was easy enough to repaint.

I finished the watering and headed inside to fill a lunch cooler with two sandwiches, several pieces of fruit, a bag of cookies and a canister of Pringles. Since I'd been working nearly full time with Travis, we had set up a lunch schedule to save money and time. Mondays and Wednesdays were my designated days to bring lunch. Travis was in charge of Tuesdays and Thursdays. We splurged on Fridays and ate at one of the food trucks. Travis knew where all of them parked around the city, and he kept a mental list of the ones we'd tried and liked. I filled the water canteen and headed out to the truck with the cooler. Travis had texted saying that he had scheduled us for repairs on a deck that morning. It was light work, he promised, at least compared to what we'd had for the past few weeks. We should finish early.

It was time, I decided. I would drop by Michele's work after we finished.

The key, the box, the newspaper and the matchbook were tucked between the sweaters and winter gear on the top shelf of the closet. I had resisted the urge to unlock the box the night I'd found it, though I did slide the key into the lock and turn it to be certain of the fit. For the rest of the weekend, I had tried to forget that it was in the closet at all. I put the box, with the key still in the lock, in an old backpack and headed back out to the truck.

Stucco Jon arrived, pulling a flatbed trailer layered with the bags of stucco. He waved as I headed for my truck.

"You don't want to change your mind on the color, do you? Last chance."

"I always pick beige on my realtor's advice. It's not like I'm going to be living here for long."

"Why not? Can't beat the neighborhood."

"That's what I'm counting on when this thing goes on the market."

He came over to my truck and waited as I climbed inside. "What color would you pick if you weren't selling?"

"Blue."

"I've always liked light blue," he agreed. "With navy accents and a crisp white trim. But neither of us is probably ever gonna live anywhere long enough for it to matter which color we pick. You know we aren't going to be picking our favorite colors in a neighborhood like this." He raised his hand as I turned the key in the truck's ignition, then turned to oversee the crew that had gathered round to pull bags off the trailer. Stucco Jon flipped houses as well and had traded work with me more than once. I was paying for the supplies and his crew's hourly wage. The deal was impossible to beat.

I watched the men for a moment, briefly reconsidering the beige. It was too late to change my mind, despite what he'd said. Besides, Carol would give me an earful if I went with any color besides a shade of brown. She'd likely raise her eyebrows on the burgundy door as it was.

Travis had scheduled a four o'clock appointment with his chiropractor and left me to finish a closet door repair. We'd finished the deck by noon, but the homeowner had given Travis a list of other projects. I cleaned up our worksite and met the owner of the house as she was pulling up in the driveway.

The owner, or the owner's wife, for all I knew, was distractingly pretty in that meticulously groomed sort of way. She pronounced her name—Alana—with a faint Spanish accent. I loved the accent. Not a strand of hair was out of place and she was returning from the gym, or so she said, with perfect make-up. She smelled like she'd bathed in a Hawaiian vacation—coconut oil mixed with piña colada. It might have been her lotion or her shampoo. Whatever it was, I couldn't decide if I wanted to roll around naked with her in a sandy island cove or step away quickly so I could get a breath of fresh air. The longer I stood with her, hardly listening as she talked, the more certain I was that I'd take the beach scene.

Alana winked when she said that she could make good use of my muscles if I wanted to stick around for a few other projects she had in mind. I admitted that I had to leave to meet someone, and her lower lip jutted out in a pout that I could have kissed. Her coconut lotion was going to my head. When she asked if I'd mind if she tested out the closet door to make sure it was to her satisfaction, I willingly followed her to the bedroom. The door had been hung poorly and wouldn't close before. She also wanted the paint touched up—because apparently it was important to not have any minute scratch marks on a closet door. Since she wanted to pay top dollar for it, I didn't mind the work.

Alana closely inspected the spots I'd painted, and then swung the door shut. It closed snugly, but there was a faint squeak. I offered to grab the WD-40 before she could complain. She watched while I sprayed and then swung the door back and forth. Her satisfied nod was well worth my extra hassle. Distractingly pretty, and if she'd asked, I would have helped her test out the bed for squeaks as well. After she'd written a check to Travis for our day's work, she asked for my number so she could call me directly if she had any little issues that came up. By the time I got into my truck, I had almost forgotten about the jewelry box and Michele. Almost.

It was close to five. I thought of calling Michele to catch her before she'd left work but decided just to drive there. Anyone could walk into the university library without an ID card. I'd taken Roxanne there more than once.

Michele's light blue Prius was easy to spot in the nearly empty parking lot. I pulled into a space near her car and grabbed the backpack, glancing at the rearview mirror as I did. I considered driving home and texting Michele from there. My hair was a mess, and I had a smudge of white paint on my cheek. Apparently Alana hadn't minded. I rubbed at my cheek until the paint was gone, but a red spot took its place. The hair was another story. I needed a shower. I combed my fingers through my hair, short enough now to not need a brush, and eyed my reflection a moment longer. Fine lines creased the corners of my eyes, accentuated by the mirror's small rectangular shape. I'd never thought much about getting older, but I realized I was beginning to look every bit of thirty-five. At the moment, I didn't feel nearly as mature as my face looked. I decided that my appearance wouldn't matter given what I had to show Michele. I shouldered the backpack and climbed out of the truck.

Michele had an office at the back of the library. The office was lined with windows that looked in at the library, but the blinds were drawn. There was a desk in front of the office door with a button buzzer to call the librarians out of their offices during posted "Research Desk" hours. According to the clock above the desk, I'd missed those by fifteen minutes, but I pressed the buzzer anyway.

The office door opened a few minutes later and a young man poked his head out of the doorway and peered at me. "The research desk is closed until tomorrow."

"Yeah, I know. I have a meeting with Michele Galveston. She asked me to ring for her here."

The young man squinted at me as if he were trying to place me in his mind. Sutherland was a private university and enrolled only a few thousand students. I knew from Michele that everyone knew each other or thought they did.

"One moment," he said, closing the door and disappearing from view.

A long minute passed before the door reopened. Michele cocked her head to one side. "In case you didn't notice the sign, I'm afraid you're here after hours. The Research Desk is closed until tomorrow." She came up to the desk and crossed her arms. "And I'm fairly certain we didn't have a meeting planned. There's nothing on my scheduler and it's never wrong."

"I have a surprise." I held up the backpack. My heart raced just seeing her. I blamed Alana, at least partly. She'd gotten me thinking about squeaky mattresses and all the things I'd like to do with a beautiful woman.

"Please tell me that's what I hope it is." Michele bounced up and down grinning. "You found it?"

"Maybe."

"Damn it, Jodi, get in here. Don't make me wait a minute longer."

I followed Michele through the office door and past several desks. The young man who had greeted me earlier was slipping his laptop into a carrying case. Other than Michele, he was the last one in the office. He glanced up at Michele as we passed his desk. "Okay if I head out?" he asked.

She nodded. "See you tomorrow."

He headed for the door with the computer bag slung over his shoulder. Michele's desk was the last one in the row. The window behind it offered a view of the grassy quad, now deserted save for the trees that lined the space. I guessed that when the fall semester began, the area was rarely empty.

Michele sat down on the corner edge of her desk and crossed her arms. "So, tell me where you found the key. And when."

"Why when?"

"Did you have it when I came on Friday?"

"No." I hadn't anticipated that question. "But I found it that night. I almost texted you."

"Damn it, Jodi."

"I'm here now."

"And I'm mad that you made me wait all weekend. You know I would have been there in a second."

"You were at a movie with Desi."

Michele waved her hand as if this were beside the point. "Okay, where was it?"

"You know that awful rose wallpaper in the upstairs bathroom?" I waited for Michele to nod and then continued, "There was a second layer—yellow plaid—under the roses. After you left I decided to peel off that wallpaper. Something about that paper got me to thinking that maybe the key was hidden between the sheets of wallpaper. It wasn't. But when I went to take off the faceplate on the outlets to get the wallpaper all the way off…"

"They hid the key in the outlet?"

"There's a metal box around the outlets and the key was left there. It's a perfect hiding spot, really, since whoever left it behind would have easy access with only two screws to remove…"

"You should have called," Michele interrupted.

I shook my head. "Desi and you were…"

She interrupted again, "I'll get over the fact that you made me wait as soon as you tell me what you found inside the box."

I opened the backpack and took out the jewelry box, checking that the key was still in place. I held the box out to Michele. "I don't know what's inside. I've been waiting for you to open it."

"You waited for me? All weekend?" Michele's smile lit up her face. She reached past the box and grabbed my shoulders.

Her kiss was much too quick. She had the box in her hands and was setting it on the desk while I was still registering what had happened. The sensation of Michele's lips pressed against mine lingered.

I focused on the key, watching it turn in Michele's hand and unwilling to risk a glance at Michele's face as she lifted the lid. She pulled out a stack of yellowed envelopes and flipped through them. She held up the first one in the stack. "Ready to find out our mystery?"

I nodded. Someone had used a letter opener to carefully open the side of the envelope. Michele slipped out a single handwritten sheet of paper and then read the cursive handwriting swirling across the page. If I'd concentrated, I probably could have made out a few of the words, but I was still unsteady from the kiss.

"It's a love letter," Michele said. She held one finger up to her lips as if she were quieting the silent room. She did the same thing whenever she was concentrating on a play in a card game. She turned the page over and then handed the letter to me and reached for the next envelope.

The first letter was addressed to Alice and signed by KW. The sheet of paper was frayed on one side and as yellowed as the envelope it had slipped out of. After a brief glance, I agreed with Michele. KW was in love with Alice.

I hadn't finished the letter by the time Michele handed me the next one. It was Alice's reply. The words were smudged with what were likely long-ago dried tears. Most of Alice's letter was an apology. It wasn't clear what had happened between them, but Alice seemed to blame herself. One line in particular caught me: "What would I give to hold you for one night?" I couldn't move past it. Michele had gone on to the next letter and then the next while I considered this single sentence. I scanned to the bottom of the page and read the last few lines: "Of course we are in love. How else could we cause each other this agony?"

I glanced over at Michele. The expression on her face made it clear that she was miles, or years, away. I flipped through the stack of envelopes. Half of the envelopes were blank and the other half were addressed to Alice Johnson at 514 Granite Avenue. The puzzle piece clicked into place.

"Alice Johnson never sent her replies to KW's love letters. Turns out Alice was a terrible pen pal," I added, trying to break the somber mood I'd felt after realizing the box's secret.

"Randall Johnson owned the house. Alice was his wife. I remember reading her name in one of the documents I tracked down last week." Michele glanced up from the letter she'd been reading. "How many letters do you think there are?"

I quickly counted the envelopes addressed to Alice Johnson. "There's close to thirty letters addressed to Alice."

"And she answered each one. Why didn't she mail the letters to KW?"

"Probably because of a certain Randall Johnson," I answered. When I saw Michele's eyes roll, I added, "Do you have a better guess?"

"Can you imagine how KW must have felt writing all of this and never receiving a response?" Michele carefully folded the letter in her hand and replaced it in the envelope. She folded her hands and stared out the window. "It must have been agony to never know if Alice felt the same."

"Maybe Alice eventually told him."

"Him? No way." Michele reached for one of the letters and held it up for me to see. "KW is a woman. Look at this handwriting."

"You can't always guess someone's gender by their handwriting. I write like a guy."

Michele laughed. "And? Are you trying to prove my point?"

"Well, I'm saying that I think KW could have been a man with good penmanship."

Michele shook her head. "I'll bet you on this one." She tapped her finger on the stack of envelopes. "I'm going to figure out who KW is and I'll bet you dinner that this was a love affair between two women."

I knew better than to bet against Michele. I'd never won against her. In this case, winning wasn't the point. I wasn't about to turn down a dinner date. "Okay, deal."

Michele glanced at her watch. "Oh, shit. I'm supposed to meet Carol and Desi at six." She glanced at the box. "Think they would mind if I canceled? I'm not going to be able to think about houses anyway." She picked up the letter on top of the stack. It was in a blank envelope, one of Alice's responses that KW never had a chance to read. "I want to sit here and read every one of these letters. Want to order pizza?"

"You know, you can keep the box here, if you like. I don't need to read each letter and I can tell there's no way you'll sleep if you don't."

"Don't you want to know their story?"

I shrugged. Before we'd opened the box, I had wanted to know everything about the person who'd made the hidden cubbyhole. Now that it was obvious that the story wouldn't have a happy ending, I wasn't eager to learn the details.

"I think this is all I need to know. I think the mystery is solved. I'm not sure I want to know any more. KW loved Alice, but for all she knew Alice didn't care. Alice locked up the secret and moved away with her husband. End of story."

Michele stared at me for a long moment. "Really? You're going to leave it at that?"

"I'll still buy dinner if KW turns out to be a woman."

Michele replaced the letters in the box and turned the key in the lock. She slipped the key into the top desk drawer and then made room for the box in the bottom drawer. She hesitated as she closed the drawer. "I don't want to go look at houses tonight. Let's order a pizza and sit right here and pore over these letters."

I shook my head.

Michele sighed and reached for her purse. "Okay, but what if this story has a happy ending?"

"How'd you know that was what was bugging me?"

"You've never been hard to read." Michele smiled. "Alice locked up the secret, but these two were in love. Maybe Randall Johnson sold the place because his wife left him."

"She wouldn't have left the love letters behind."

Michele tapped the box. "This isn't the end of our little mystery. We're only getting started."

CHAPTER TEN

"Knock, knock."

I could see Carol through the screen door and waved her inside the house. The day had been unseasonably hot and by the time I'd gotten home, the place was an oven. I'd opened all the windows and the front door to cool things off, but the kitchen, with its big bay window and no blinds, was still much too warm. I was listening to the news, stretched across the sofa under the fan with my legs propped up on the armrest. I got up to turn off the radio and then realized Carol hadn't come alone. Desi and Michele were testing out the porch swing.

Carol set her purse down on the sofa and glanced around. "You've been busy in here as well. By all accounts, 514 Granite Ave is no longer the eyesore of the neighborhood. I bet the neighbors are happy. I don't know about your color choice for the front door, however."

"I guessed you wouldn't like it. But the stucco is beige just for you."

"Burgundy is too dark. I'd settle for a flashier red."

"I'll consider it." I motioned toward Desi and Michele on the swing. "Showing your clients houses in the neighborhood?"

"Only one house," Carol said. "I don't know what you are hoping to get money-wise once you've finished, but I'm guessing this should still be in their budget."

"What's their budget?" I'd heard Michele complain about bills and couldn't believe that this house, even unfinished, would be something she could afford. Maybe she was enjoying Desi's money after all and they weren't planning on splitting things.

Carol tilted her head toward the screen door. "Let's just say that Desi has got the down payment and then some, even if you list this at the high end of the market. Michele mentioned your place when we were looking at some other properties. I think Michele has been comparing all of the other houses we've looked at to this one, and they are all falling short of the mark. I thought Desi should have a look too so she can be comparing the other houses as well. I figured you wouldn't mind us popping in last minute. If they were regular clients, I would have called to warn you."

"'Warn' her, huh? Jodi probably would have appreciated some advance notice," Michele said, pushing open the screen door. "Then again she might have told you she was too busy. Good thing we aren't 'regular clients.'"

I met her gaze but said nothing.

Michele looked away quickly. A week had passed since I'd dropped in at her work and we hadn't spoken since. I'd come up with excuses when she texted to ask about getting together, claiming work was too busy. She had read through all the letters apparently and wanted me to read them as well.

She had texted me over the weekend too, saying she had more information on Alice and asking if I was interested. I hadn't responded to that text nor to the one inviting me to drive over so we could check out the club from the matchbook.

I wondered if it was actually Carol's idea to drop in tonight or if Michele was using the house as an excuse. Then again she could have easily dropped in alone if she'd wanted to talk to me.

Desi came in behind Michele. She glanced around the living room and her gaze settled on the couch. "Somehow I'm not surprised that you're into the minimalist approach to home decorating, Jodi. But I could give you a good deal on a coffee table if you're interested."

"There's less to dust this way," I replied, forcing a smile. I tried to focus on Desi. Michele's presence was hard to ignore. I couldn't help but watch as she headed down the hall and climbed the stairs up to the bedrooms.

"I tried to convince her to take some of the other furniture we were selling along with the couch, but she insisted she didn't need it. So much for staging a place." Carol sighed. "Desi, you have to see the view from the dining room."

Desi followed Carol into the dining room. I headed up the staircase, pausing when I saw where Michele had stopped. She was standing in front of the bathroom.

"I love the new bay window in here!" Carol hollered. In a lower voice directed at Desi, she continued, "There used to be a narrow window here above the sink, but this really opens up the space. Look at that view. This is what is going to sell this place right here. Doesn't even matter what countertops or cabinets are put in now…"

I heard the back door open and guessed Carol and Desi were headed out to the backyard. I'd spent a day cleaning up the yard and then made a trip to the dump that weekend so the space was much more presentable than it had been.

Michele glanced down the staircase, and her gaze met mine. She had tears in her eyes. I climbed the stairs two at a time. Michele met me at the top of the stairs. Her arms wrapped around me. Our embrace was brief, and by the time she'd pulled away, she'd rubbed off any evidence of the tears. Her face was still close, however, and it was impossibly hard to keep from kissing her. My hands shook and I braced myself on the railing. I swore that Michele wanted the kiss as much as I did, but neither of us moved to close the space between our lips.

"The wallpaper's gone."

"But I kept the faceplates. I'll replace them too, eventually."

Michele glanced at the light switch and then the outlet. "Wow, those are tacky. I can't believe no one wanted to replace them sooner."

"I don't know. They've kind of grown on me."

Michele laughed and then wiped her eyes again. "To think of how many times Alice must have touched them, knowing what she had hidden…" She leaned against the doorway. "It looks good in here. No one would know."

"No one knew Alice's secret for years… But now we know."

"We only know part of it." Michele sighed. "I can't figure out who KW is and it's driving me crazy. I've scoured that newspaper, every article, and there is no one with the initials KW in it. I tried to find out more about Alice, but every lead seems to be a dead end. For all I can tell, Alice seemed to be a happily married mother of two who did very little that made it into any archive. But we know there was more to her story."

"I keep thinking about how hard it must have been for Alice to have left that key behind, knowing those letters were never going to be delivered and that her secret was going to be lost. But in a way, Alice finally shared her secret." I paused. "Maybe this is where it ends."

"It can't be. For KW's sake, I'm not going to give up," Michele said.

"What if she isn't supposed to know? Alice went out of her way to hide all of this. Maybe it isn't our business finding KW at all. Maybe there's more to this that we don't know."

"How would you feel if you were KW? Is it our business deciding what she should or shouldn't know?"

I shrugged.

"If she is out there, wouldn't you want to give her the closure those letters might bring? I know you didn't read many of them," she paused, "but I seriously was ready to fall for KW after I'd finished reading everything. There was no doubt how much she loved Alice. And Alice wanted her so desperately. She said she was 'caught'…" Michele shook her head. "One thing in particular that KW wrote keeps haunting me. She said she'd found an inscription in a book that she wanted to share with Alice so she copied it down for her. It said, 'May you know lust, may you accept loss, may you hold love.' KW wrote that the inscription was signed Fearless."

"No one's fearless," I countered.

"That was what Alice wrote back to KW, almost verbatim," Michele said. She touched the wall above the light switch. "I can almost see Alice in here, worrying about where she could hide the key, thinking about KW's words. She was filled with fear… KW knew that. That was her point. She was asking Alice to be fearless with her. And Alice couldn't. It's heartbreaking. KW didn't sign her last letter to Alice. She ended it with 'May you hold love.'"

"We don't know what happened after those letters. Maybe they ended up together. Like you said, maybe there is a happy ending. Maybe they are in some old folks home now."

Michele shook her head again. "I found Alice's obituary in an Atlanta newspaper. She passed away over two years ago, 'survived in death by her husband of sixty years—Randall Johnson.' There was no mention of anyone named KW."

I reached for Michele's hand. "I'm sorry about this week. I've been—"

"'Busy.' I know. You haven't been busy—you've been avoiding me. But whatever." Michele pulled her hand away. "I'll admit that I've been a bit obsessed. I don't blame you for tiring of it."

"That's not it at all."

Michele nodded. "There's more to the story, right?"

I opened my mouth and then shut it again. When I tried an explanation, Michele waved her hand to stop me.

Her voice was soft when she said, "Don't worry about it."

"Jodi, this place is great. I'm not surprised Michele keeps bringing it up." Desi's voice came from the bottom of the stairs.

I glanced down at her, stepping away from Michele in what I hoped seemed like a natural move. "It's getting there. You guys are here a few months early. It isn't exactly in show condition yet."

"Don't worry about it." Desi waved her hand. The gesture was identical to the one Michele had made earlier. So were their words. Even their tones matched. My heart sank. "From what Michele tells me and by what I'm seeing so far, you have done a lot of nice work in here. Aside from the kitchen, it doesn't look like you need to do much more." Desi started up the stairs and then hesitated. "Is it okay if I come up and check out the bedrooms?"

"Yeah, of course."

Michele had already turned to head into the master bedroom. I watched her open the new sliding glass door and walk out onto the balcony. I wanted desperately to follow her. Instead, I waited for Desi to reach the top of the staircase.

"Two bedrooms up here?"

"Yeah, though one of the rooms is pretty small. There's one full bathroom up here and a half bath under the staircase." I was ready to downplay the house in any way I could, I discovered. I didn't want to imagine Desi and Michele living in this house. I'd never felt possessive of it until the thought of them sleeping together in the master bedroom entered my mind.

"Well, the bathroom up here looks great. I like the texturing on the walls. You've added some nice touches." Desi wandered out of the bathroom and into the master bedroom.

Michele was still out on the balcony. Desi walked out to join her. They stood next to each other but not touching. Desi pointed to the mountains and said something to Michele. Were they really in love? Did it matter? I turned and headed downstairs. The house didn't feel like a home, but it was mine, for the moment. Still, it was only another project; I'd have to hand the keys over to someone else eventually. Some stranger would buy it and Alice's secret would be lost with the wallpaper. So, why shouldn't Michele and Desi buy the place? Still, it was the only space I had to claim at the moment and I couldn't bear to imagine them together in it.

Carol was on the couch, flipping through printouts of other homes. She glanced up at me. "I forgot how comfortable this old couch was. Our new one looks better, but you can't sink into it like this one."

"I think I'll keep it when I move."

"I'm glad to hear you're thinking ahead. Desi likes this place and I already know Michele does. We might have to talk about numbers. Shall I call an appraiser?"

"I'm not ready to have it appraised."

"What if they want to buy it as-is? They could hire you to finish up the projects that aren't complete and have some say in the details. You still have work to do in the kitchen, but we could get an appraisal now. You can still make money selling this in the present condition."

"I'm not selling until I've finished the job. I don't want to be coming in and working on it while someone's living here."

"But you do that all the time with Travis."

"This is different. I know these people."

"Why does that matter?" Carol cocked her head to the side. She stared at me for a minute before clearing her throat and standing up. She gathered her papers and her purse and then smiled. "I think something just clicked. Sometimes I'm a little slow with these things."

"What are you talking about?"

Desi and Michele came down the stairs, and Carol's attention immediately shifted to them. "So, what do you guys think?"

"It's exactly what we've been talking about wanting," Desi answered immediately. "And none of the other places we've seen can compete with this view." Desi glanced over at Michele and waited for her nod of agreement. "I guess it depends on what Jodi is going to want for the price."

"We were just talking about that. She wants to finish the kitchen before the appraisal. You two wouldn't want to be living here through a kitchen remodel anyway. But there isn't much else left to be done, right Jodi?"

Everyone's gaze leveled on me. I glanced at Michele and then regretted it as I felt a warmth creep up my neck, a certain sign that I was blushing. "I do have a few other things I'd like to do." I turned to Carol and continued, "But I guess if I already had a buyer, I could concentrate on the kitchen and then get it appraised."

"Okay. Well, why don't you give me a call tomorrow and we can get a timeline for this. Obviously Michele and Desi need to know if this is in their price range before we go further." Carol glanced at her watch. "Gals, if we want to get to that house on Holbrook, we should get going."

I followed them out as far as the front porch. I leaned against the railing, wondering if Michele would glance back and feeling foolish for even wanting this little thing. Carol and Desi climbed into the car, but Michele hesitated opening her door. She looked up and down the street, then briefly at the house before reaching for the door handle. I nearly called her name, but it stuck in my throat.

As the car pulled away, I headed back inside the house. The screen door slammed behind me and tears threatened. I found my phone and texted Michele, "Come back, please." I hit send before I could delete the message, unlike the dozen other texts I'd nearly sent earlier that week.

Michele's response was immediate. "Why?"

I stared at the question mark but couldn't answer honestly. Instead, I texted, "I want to hear the whole story."

"I don't know the whole story yet. Only pieces. Monday?"

Monday was much too long to wait. I tossed the phone on the couch and headed to the kitchen. The fan and the cool breeze coming down from the mountains had chilled the room. I switched off the fan but left the windows open. The mountains were close enough for an afternoon's hike, but it had been years since I'd hiked. Lynn hadn't ever wanted to, and Roxanne was more interested in a day at the park. I tried to push away the thought of Roxanne. Breaking up with Lynn had made me certain of a few things. I needed someone who would be upfront with their baggage and I needed someone who was kid-free. I didn't want to get attached to another kid that wasn't my own. In fact, I was fairly certain that I'd turn down a date with anyone who had kids solely for that reason.

I finally went upstairs to shower. It was early, but I was done with the day. A long shower seemed like the best way to end a crappy night. The water pelted my neck and shoulders until my skin was flushed and my fingers were pruned. I dried off and then stared at my naked reflection. My hair was dark brown, but it looked black when I got it wet. I pulled a comb through it until I'd smoothed the shaggy mop, then reached for the light switch. My hand paused as I caught sight of the doorway that

Michele had leaned against earlier. I touched the spot and then pulled my hand away. "Give it up," I said. My voice sounded like a strangely distant sigh. "She belongs to someone else."

Even as the words left my lips, the thought of Michele reaching for me replaced my own reprimand. The look in her eyes after we'd hugged had been enough confirmation. She might be with Desi, but she didn't belong to her. I had imagined Michele touching my body so many times before that the fantasy sprang quickly to mind. I opened the drawer where I kept my vibrators, knowing I was already wet. It wouldn't take long to finish the job. I stared at my collection. My hand went to my favorite toy first, but I didn't pull it out of the drawer. Suddenly I didn't want a toy at all. I wanted to touch Michele's body and I wanted her hands on mine. With effort, I finally reached over and hit the light switch. The doorbell rang and I startled at the sound of it.

I slipped into the same pair of jeans and T-shirt that I'd been wearing earlier and nearly ran down the stairs. I didn't want to hope it was Michele and yet as soon as the possibility occurred to me, I couldn't imagine it being anyone else.

Michele pressed the bell again as I opened the door. She stared at me, waiting for the doorbell to fall silent. I stepped back expecting her to come in, but she didn't move from the doorstep.

"Should I not have kissed you?" she asked.

"What are you talking about?" I stalled, knowing full well what kiss she was referencing.

"When you came to my office with the key. Did I cross a line?"

I searched Michele's face, wondering how I could possibly answer the question honestly. Finally I reached for her. She stepped through the doorway and into my arms. Our lips met. The kiss wasn't quick. Neither of us pulled away and only when I worried about the open door did I think of anything other than her lips pressed against mine. I knew she didn't want to stop either. If Michele had already crossed a line, I was ready to follow.

I closed the door, and the sound was enough to break the moment. Michele looked at the floor. I reached for her hand, and she looked first at my hand and then up to my face.

"I'm not sure this is a good idea," she said.

I let go of her, feeling every ounce of conviction slip away, but in the next moment, she reached for me and pulled me into another kiss. I felt the room spinning when we separated. I needed to ask if she had an open relationship with Desi. Maybe she wasn't crossing any line. Maybe she had already talked to Desi about coming here tonight. But if her answer was no, I didn't want to hear it. She kissed me again, opening her lips as she did. I couldn't resist.

When she pulled us toward the sofa, I considered saying something, asking if we should stop. She was an adult and could make her own mistakes, my mind countered as she slipped out of her shirt, revealing a black bra that cupped her breasts. I brushed a hand over the silk, and she closed her eyes, moving into the touch. I took off my shirt too and Michele pulled me down on top of her, stretching across the length of the sofa. I kissed her lips and then moved down to her neck and chest, hardly able to believe that what I was doing was real. Blood pulsed in my ears, my body trying to drown out the louder voice from my brain. "What are you doing?" it repeated over and over again. I didn't want to stop. I wanted Michele so much that desire had taken over.

I undid her bra and kissed her breasts, shaking off the thought that I could stop there. She unbuttoned my jeans and pushed them down on my hips, her hand moving between my legs. She wasn't slowing down, and I realized that she wanted to touch me as much as I wanted to touch her. I shifted off of her and undid her pants, then slipped out of my jeans as she kicked off hers. I paused a moment, wondering if she would have second thoughts in the morning, but she reached for me, pulling me back on top of her naked body.

I couldn't keep track of her hands or her lips as they traveled over my skin, wakening every nerve with the rush of her own desire. I moved between her legs, realizing how wet she was when I felt the slickness on my thighs as she pushed into me. We moved together, riding a wave that didn't seem to have an end.

If I could have held on to that moment, I would have, but I felt her hands press against my shoulders and knew what she was asking for. I shifted lower, wanting to taste her as much as she wanted to feel me there. Her hands slipped behind my neck and she pulled my face toward her center. I slipped my tongue over her clit and heard her moan. Then I knew I had no intention of slowing down.

She cried out when she came—nothing like the tender sounds I'd long imagined but more an animal sound of desire—a desire that had finally been satisfied. Her legs squeezed together and she turned to her side. We lay together for a moment, but before I had time to wish that we might stay in that position for at least the rest of the night, she reached for me, her voice a soft murmur as she repeated my name. We kissed again and again. Her hand moved between my legs, fingers encircling and then strumming my clit all while she kept my lips busy with her own. I came in a hard rush and was shaking when I finally pulled away.

Several minutes passed. I knew Michele was watching me, but neither of us dared to speak. We sat on opposite ends of the sofa, our legs crisscrossing each other in the middle. I couldn't meet her gaze. Finally I pulled my legs free from hers and stood up.

Michele shivered and turned on her side, pulling her knees up to her chest. I found her shirt and handed it to her. I didn't have a throw blanket or anything else to offer. Michele took the shirt and slipped it on, then looked up at me. She reached for my hand, pulling me close.

"You okay?" she asked softly.

"I don't know. I'm not sure that should have happened."

"What do you mean? I think it was pretty clear we both wanted the same thing," she said, her voice full of doubt.

"Yeah, we want the same thing. We have for a long time. But that doesn't mean one of us isn't going to regret it tomorrow."

"Are you?"

I shook my head. She reached for my hand, and I let her hold it. I knew I ought to ask about Desi. But the lump in my throat stopped all the words. If Michele wasn't going to bring it up, did I have to? Was there some rule about this? The fact that Michele was here when Desi was at home, likely waiting for her, was too much. I couldn't understand why Michele hadn't stopped us. And I was mad at myself for wanting to shift the blame to her. Michele could see my desire and I could see hers still; she wanted more. There was no use denying it. But what game was she playing?

Michele let go of my hand and rolled to her other side. She was silent for a long moment and then quietly asked, "Should I go home?"

"I don't want you to go." She'd turned me on like no one before. I wanted her hands on my body again. Once wasn't enough. I nearly reached for her. I knew she'd let me kiss her again, let my hands touch her breasts... "But maybe you should. I wish..."

What did I wish exactly? I answered the question a moment later. I wished Desi wasn't in the picture. I wished that two years ago when I'd first seen Michele onstage, first fallen for her, that I'd had the guts then to catch her after the show and say something.

"You know, it doesn't matter what I wish right now. I wish you could stay, but I think we both know this shouldn't have happened. Staying the night would only make things worse."

The full weight of my words sank in as I waited for Michele to respond. I held my breath, wanting her to argue, wanting her to say that she was free to sleep with anyone she wanted to and that Desi already knew. Michele was silent. What was left to say? Desi was home waiting for Michele, wasn't she? I wondered what excuse Michele had used to get out of the house, and the thought of her lying to come over made me feel even worse. I'd never cheated in any of my relationships, but I'd never longed for anyone the way I longed for Michele. And I was sick with the thought that if Michele reached for me again, I wouldn't try to fight it. I was gambling here with everything I had left. If Michele called my bluff, I'd fold.

Michele didn't look at me when she stood up finally. She sorted through our clothes, tossed together on the floor, and slipped on her underwear and pants. She didn't bother putting her bra back on and her blouse gaped open when she reached for the bra, balled up by the leg of the sofa. She was dressed too quickly. I watched her head to the door, wishing I could think of something to say besides "Don't leave" and saying nothing even when she glanced back at me.

CHAPTER ELEVEN

Michele's perfume was still on the cushions. She always wore the same subtle scent, and it had left the sofa smelling vaguely of lavender. It wasn't so much sexy as it was familiar, and I couldn't bring myself to leave the sofa after she'd gone home. When I woke up stiff, I regretted the decision. Sleeping anywhere but a bed usually turned out to be a mistake. I found my phone and checked for a text or an email from Michele. For the first time in several days, she hadn't sent one. I went to dress and stopped short in the hallway outside the bathroom. I touched the doorway she'd leaned against again and shook my head.

It was as much Michele's decision as it was my encouraging, I reminded myself. Regardless, I felt like crap. Part of me did anyway. The other part of me was hungry for the feel of her body again. But Michele had never mentioned having an open relationship with anyone, and I couldn't imagine her to be comfortable with cheating.

Maybe I didn't know her as well as I'd thought, I decided. Her routine had always been to break up with someone before she got to the point of cheating—she'd even told me as much. Either she'd broken her routine or she had some agreement with Desi. I hoped for the latter but suspected that she would have told me if it were the case.

Worrying about what should or shouldn't have happened wouldn't change a thing. I decided on a shower to clear my head. Every time I used the bathroom now my gaze went right to the outlet where I'd found the key. One question went round in my head—and I doubted that the answer was in the jewelry box. What had prompted Alice to leave the key in the house? I'd come to two possible conclusions. Either she'd wanted someone to eventually find her secret or she'd left too quickly to take the key. Since she'd read all the letters, Michele might have a better idea about Alice's motives, but after months living in Alice's old house, I thought I had enough in common with her to guess that it was the former. I would have wanted someone to know.

Last night's secret plagued my thoughts. If I'd had a best friend, I would have called her so I could get it off my chest. Now the guessing game was over—Michele wanted what I had wanted all along. At least she wanted the sex. Whether she wanted a relationship or not was unanswered—and couldn't be answered so long as she was with Desi.

This thought had passed through my mind as I'd fought sleep, still scarcely believing that what had happened wasn't a dream. Michele had come back to the house for only one reason, and in one moment everything was perfect and better than I could have imagined and in the next I was sending her home. If it had been a dream, it was a terrible one.

Travis had wanted the day off, but I dressed in my cargo work pants anyway. I had an appointment to pick out granite for the kitchen counters. One of Carol's friends was giving me a good deal, but I had to meet him at the warehouse and arrange for my own delivery. As much as I wanted to chew over what had happened last night, I knew it was probably better that I had plans to keep me from my thoughts. Otherwise I'd likely spend the morning rehashing the ways our evening could have ended on a better note—or not ended at all.

My thoughts drifted back to Alice and KW. Had they slept together? The answer was probably in the letters. I considered asking Michele if she'd figured out whether it had been only a mutual attraction or a proper affair. I went downstairs, found my phone and texted the question to Michele, using only initials and deleting the word "affair." Had there been an affair? Had Alice gone to her grave with the secret? Or was the answer in her letters?

Then I sent another text, this time asking Michele if I could get the box back, saying I wanted to read the letters after all. I stared at the screen, waiting for an answer. After several minutes, when none came, I tossed the phone on the sofa and went to make coffee.

Knowing that Alice had stayed with her husband until her death made me wonder more about KW. Who was KW, and what had happened to her—or him—after Alice? I realized I hadn't asked these questions earlier because I'd been too focused on my own questions about Michele. With those now answered, however, I was still drinking my morning coffee alone.

I stared out the bay window. The early sunlight changed the mountain rocks from gray to purple. When the remodel was finished and I'd found a buyer, I was going to miss drinking coffee with the mountain view more than anything else, even if I was drinking alone.

I headed out to the truck and stopped before I'd made it to the front steps. Alice's jewelry box was on the porch swing. The key was in the lock. I turned it and stared at the letters inside. I put the box inside the house and locked the door, trying to decide if I needed to read the letters after all.

* * *

Carol's granite friend was in a good mood. He agreed to deliver and install the pieces I needed for half his usual rate, so long as I agreed to have Travis use him on future jobs. His granite was high quality, and I didn't hesitate with the handshake.

My next errand was picking up the cabinets. They were on the other side of town, and I had to swing by Travis's place first to borrow a trailer. Travis was sitting on his front porch tossing a ball to his Labrador when I pulled up. He scooted the jet-black dog into the backyard and helped me hitch up the trailer, then jumped into the passenger seat of my truck.

"What are you doing?"

"Helping you."

"Why?"

He slapped the driver's seat and a cloud of dust mushroomed up. "Get in and say thanks," he said.

I climbed in the truck and looked at him out of the corner of my eye. "Thanks. You in trouble with Traci?"

"No." He squinted at his house as I checked the mirrors and turned onto the main road. "It's possible I used you as an excuse. Traci wanted me to go up to Denver to have lunch with her folks."

"And you wanted to move cabinets instead?"

"I'm only along for the ride." He grinned. "But I'll help if you buy lunch. And this way I finally get a tour of your house."

He'd asked for an invitation several times, but I'd wanted to at least have the kitchen finished before showing it off. But an offer to help with the cabinets was too good to refuse.

"What's for lunch?"

"I don't know. Sandwiches?"

"We had sandwiches yesterday," he argued. "I feel like that Mexican place over on Williams and South Teller. I haven't had a decent steak burrito in months."

"There's more to life than planning your next meal."

"Yeah, but I try not to think too much about all the other crap. Have you tried their green chile sauce?"

"No." I concentrated on the road, annoyed that Travis was messing with the radio stations I'd programmed. He found his favorite station and turned up the volume, slapping his thighs to the beat. He only knew the words to the chorus and tried to get me to sing along with him. I reminded myself that I could use his help and chimed in. "Mexican sounds good. I'd buy you anything for helping me with this load. How's your back?"

"Good. Rock solid. You know me, I'm as fit as I was when I was thirty and thirty pounds lighter. But I like to hide it."

"Right."

With help from the guys in the warehouse, the cabinets were loaded on the trailer in no time. I didn't argue when Travis promised burritos for everyone in the place, four guys in total, on the condition that his friend in the showroom help unload the cabinets. I knew him well enough to realize he was lying about his back. He was wearing his brace and was too eager to have someone else help with the lifting. With two of us lifting and Travis using the dolly, the oak cabinets soon filled my living room.

* * *

Travis drove with his friend back to the warehouse, and I went to pick up the order from Cantina. The Mexican restaurant was south of downtown and I'd rarely had a reason to drive that direction. As I crossed East River Street, something triggered in my memory. A red light popped at the next intersection and I hit the brakes. Cantina was only one block away. I glanced back at East River, trying to recall why the street name sounded so familiar. As soon as the light changed, I remembered the matchbook in Alice's cubbyhole. The matchbook had come from the club Uptown on East River.

After dropping off the burritos and taking Travis home, I decided to drive back to East River Street. Uptown was a dodgy place, at least from the outside. The building had no windows on the street level. The front of the club had been painted over many times, but never completely, and the result looked like a patchwork quilt of gray and beige swatches. Graffiti artists had also clearly picked the club as a favorite spot to tag. If not for its sign, replete with a neon pink arrow that buzzed and sputtered off and on as if in some code, I would have guessed that the club had shut down long ago. There was plenty of street parking and only a few cars in the lot behind the place. I parked on the street and checked that my tools were locked.

The front door was solid black and unlocked. Inside, the stench of smoke and stale beer was overwhelming, at least at first. I let my eyes adjust to the dimly lit space and the stench lessened quickly. A bartender motioned me forward. Apparently I looked as if I needed encouragement.

Two gray-haired men were seated at one end of the bar. They were focused on the television screen hung in the far corner and did little more than glance up as I entered, unfazed by me joining their group. Aside from tracking down the matchbook's address, I hadn't given much thought to what I was looking for or what I expected to find. When I sat down at the bar, and the bartender stared her question at me, I realized a drink was the furthest thing from my mind. "Cherry Coke?" I asked hopefully.

She chuckled. "In this joint? Try again."

"Whatever you have on tap is fine."

She nodded and filled a glass with a frothy amber ale, then took my money and set my change on the counter. I tried to sneak glances at the rest of Uptown's interior and was unimpressed by what I saw. There were a handful of tables around a good-sized dance floor, but a pool table claimed the center of the space. Beyond this was a stage, far bigger than the one at the Metro but with little more than a microphone stand and an amp in one corner.

The place had a desolate feel to it, but I reminded myself that it was four o'clock on a Saturday and let my attention wander to the ball game. The beer was better than I'd expected. I watched the screen for a full inning, sipping the beer slowly. It had been months since I'd watched TV. I'd grown so accustomed to radio that I found the television strangely annoying with its flashes of brighter than life images.

The bartender eyed me and I wondered what she was thinking. Clearly the other two were her regulars. "You're early for my evening crowd."

"You get an evening crowd?"

She grinned. "You'd be surprised. This place is never exactly hopping, but some nights I break a sweat. I make most of my tips on Fridays. That's our karaoke night."

"The beer is better than I was expecting."

"I hear that a lot. Mitch—the owner—stocks his favorite brews." She smiled. "I'm Val."

I shook her hand. "Jodi."

"Since I know you didn't come for the beer, what else were you looking for when you wandered into this dive?"

"'Dive'? She said it—not me." One of the old men staring at the game had spoken up, but neither turned their attention from the screen so I wasn't sure which one had spoken.

Val ignored the comment and looked expectantly at me.

"It's a long story." I hadn't planned on answering questions or on sharing any part of Alice and KW's story. I wasn't even certain that the matchbook belonged in their story. Besides this, I doubted that Val, who looked to be in her late forties, would know enough about Uptown's past to make any part of the secret worth telling.

"I've got time," Val said. "These guys won't move until the game finishes. And then they will probably only gripe when they can't figure out how to get the remote to change the channel. There's another game starting at five." Val paused. "So far, you are the most interesting customer of the day. No one's ever asked for a Cherry Coke before." She ended her sentence with a wink.

Val was clearly working the friendly bartender angle to get a better tip when I ordered another drink. She had wavy brown hair that fell below her shoulders and a curvy figure. Her blouse was low cut, showing off enough cleavage to make me realize, a moment too late, that I was staring.

"You were saying?" Val asked, grinning when I quickly met her gaze.

Of course she'd noticed me staring at her breasts; there was nothing I could do about that now. My guess was Val was used to getting looks, but I felt sheepish about it nonetheless. I tried not to slip up with straight women. "I was following an address on an old matchbook. I think this might be a wild goose chase, but the matchbook came from here. I'm not sure what I'm looking for, but I was in the area…"

"Must have been a really old matchbook. I haven't ever heard of us having anything like that." She glanced over at the two men and said, "Ever seen a matchbook from this place?"

One didn't seem to hear the question. The other shook his head.

"Well, you're welcome to take a walk around. There's not a whole lot to see, but we've got some old pictures in the back hall. This place has more stories than those pictures will tell though, that's for sure." Val paused and then said, "And I'd be happy to try and answer any questions you have about the place. For better or worse, I've worked here long enough to know a thing or two about Uptown's past."

I decided I didn't have anything to lose by asking Val a few more questions. "Do you know what this place was like back in the fifties?"

"My guess is these guys were still lining up at noon to get in and watch the ball game, but it was on a black and white screen."

The old man who had shook his head earlier now raised his middle finger. He didn't look away from the screen.

Val continued, "The fifties, huh? Is that when you think that matchbook was printed?"

"That's my guess."

"Well, all I know for sure is that we don't have matchbooks anymore. I've never even seen one, in fact, and I've been working here nearly fifteen years. As for what this place was like in the fifties, I've heard that it was a hell of a lot different than what you see in front of you now. I wish I knew more what you were after…"

I quickly decided on a lie. "My grandmother passed away, and when I was going through some of her things, I found the matchbook. I'm guessing she would have come here before she was married. I couldn't help but wonder what this place was like back when she was going out for a night on the town." I paused. Val certainly seemed interested in the story. I'd never been good at storytelling or lies. Still, I needed to keep this one going. I wanted to know if the matchbook was a big enough part of the story to lie about it. I wasn't about to let anyone else in on the secret I'd found. "Who knows why Grandma held on to the matchbook...I've been wondering about it because she wasn't the type to have keepsakes. I thought maybe there was a story behind it."

"Uptown used to be full of people with good stories or secrets, I guess...I can tell you this—those two were kids when this place had its heyday." Val motioned to the pair focused on the game. I guessed they were both in their seventies. She continued, "Uptown was a disco hotspot for a long while, though it was well known that in the seventies people came here more to find drugs than good music. Before the disco, you came here to get hash and your groove on...And before that it was a swing club. Long before swing was popular, this place was a speakeasy. Going way back, I've been told, men came here for the women more than the drinks, if you know what I mean. Uptown has probably seen it all."

One of the men held up his empty glass and Val went to fill it. Over her shoulder, Val continued, "There's a floor above us that was used for the dancing, but now the owner has it split into apartments that he rents out. There's a third-floor apartment as well. That's been rented out to traveling musicians mostly. Supposedly the third floor was once split into smaller rooms and used for women to take their men way back when...The back hall used to be the main entrance to the basement when this place was a speakeasy. Now the basement's for storage and the back hall's our museum. They used to take pictures of all of the bands that came through when this place had a better reputation."

One of the old men laughed, and I realized he was listening to our conversation and no longer really watching the ball game. "A better reputation? What are you saying about it now?"

Val grinned back at him. "Billy, you know I'm not saying anything you don't already know."

Billy reached over and swatted at the head of the other man, still focused on the game. "She's saying we're bringing down the place." Billy's associate waved him off without looking away from the screen, and Billy continued, "I'll add my two cents to

Val's story. This place has never been somewhere you'd want to be recognized. My old man used to be a regular here when I was a kid." He smiled. "He came here for the men, not the women, and for the booze. Long before Uptown was a disco club, it catered to the kind of folks that couldn't buy drinks anywhere else. The place was raided more than once…'Course, I only found out about that after my old man died. Never knew he went with men. Funny what you find out when people die."

Billy paused and leveled his gaze at me. "You might find out something you never wanted to know about Grandma if you go barking up this tree. Chances are, Grandma had some skeletons if she was holding on to a piece of this place."

I was surprised that neither Billy's friend nor Val seemed surprised at Billy's admission about his father. Likely they'd all heard the story before. "I need to use the restroom. Then maybe I'll check out the pictures you mentioned."

"The bathrooms are at the end of the hall. You won't miss the museum." Val pointed again to the back hall. "There's a few boxes with more signed pictures in the storage room. I'll go grab that too. Billy, we might find your old man in there."

Billy laughed. "No one would have taken a picture of his ugly mug. I'll bet you my next beer on that."

"Family resemblance must run strong then. I'll agree with you and not take that bet."

I left them arguing about past bets and the free beers that had or hadn't been exchanged afterward. I headed for the women's restroom, which was surprisingly clean. It clearly hadn't been remodeled since the disco era: it still had a mirror ball swinging from the ceiling and a silver-speckled mirror. Val's comment about the drugs made me guess the walls would still test positive for cocaine residue.

The back hall leading to the restroom was indeed filled with photographs. The frames went end to end in four solid rows. The photos were black and white, mostly, and all hand signed and stamped in the corner, "Uptown." I read each name, squinting in the dim light to make out some of the scribbled signatures. I stopped when I spotted E. Katy Warren. The woman in the picture had a wry grin and was holding her index finger up to her lips as if she had shared some secret with the photographer. None of the photos was dated, at least not anywhere visible, and since they were almost entirely headshots in black and white, it was difficult to guess the decade. The hairstyles were the only clue. E. Katy Warren had a tie around her neck, but it was loosened, and the first button on the men's dress shirt she wore was unbuttoned. Everything about her look, though, confirmed my suspicion that this was Alice's KW.

Val came over to where I stood. She glanced at the photograph I was staring at and then took the frame off the wall. She handed it to me. "Looks like you found what you were looking for. This is Grandma then, huh? She was handsome, wasn't she? And maybe a little cocky?" Val smiled.

I understood what she was hinting at well enough. KW was certainly more handsome than beautiful. And her expression certainly was cocky. I wanted to admit that KW wasn't my grandmother. She belonged to Alice, not me. Still, I had to keep up the cover story with Val.

Val glanced at me and then at KW's photograph again. "I can see the resemblance," she said. "And I'd bet you your drink that before Grandma met Grandpa, she wasn't only coming here to sing." Val waited for me to argue otherwise. "Is that why you came here? Did you suspect she went for women? I like the tie. Classy."

"She never mentioned anything. I didn't know she came here at all. It was only the matchbook that made me wonder…"

"Well, you're welcome to take that picture," Val said. "The owner already rifled through these and sold the ones he could… He's told me to box up the rest, but I can't bring myself to take them all down. I've boxed up half of them, but something about seeing all of those faces piled up in a storage box, well, I had to stop. Anyway, I'll fill her space with one of the others from storage. There's plenty ready to take her place."

"Thank you."

"Don't mention it. These faces are strangers to the rest of us."

I took the picture out of the frame and handed the empty frame to Val. She rehung it on the wall. The blank space inside the frame made me regret taking the photograph, but Val headed directly to the door labeled Storage, and I guessed she was sincere about having more faces to fill this frame.

I stared at the woman's face, wondering if this was in fact Alice's KW. Katy Warren would have been attractive in any decade. Her notable features were her dark almond eyes, with long lashes and finely arched eyebrows. She had a strong jawline that made her look more sexy than beautiful. I turned the photograph over. Someone had put the date on the back: June 3, 1953.

Val came out with another photograph in hand. "I've been meaning to put this one up." She held it up to show me. The woman in the picture had one foot up on a stool and was looking at the photographer over her shoulder, pulling up her skirt as she did. Val grinned. "Want to guess the year?" Val didn't wait for her answer. "1936. Can you believe it? Gals were racy back in the day."

We walked back to the bar together. An ad was playing on the television and Billy had gotten up to fill his own beer. He held up a finger to Val. "I've already marked my tab so don't start complaining."

I finished the last of my beer and pushed a tip across the bar toward Val. She waved it off, but I said, "I'm not sure what I was expecting, but it wasn't her picture hanging on the wall. This made my day. Thank you."

"You're not going to tell us her story?" Billy asked, motioning to the photograph.

I hesitated, eyeing KW. "You know, I'm not sure I knew her as well as I thought I did. I never guessed she had her picture up on a wall in a nightclub. I think she kept a lot of secrets."

"I'm going to my grave with all of my secrets." Billy slammed his glass on the counter to make his point. "And if someone comes poking around for me after I'm gone," he jabbed his finger at his friend, "you'd better tell them I was one smart, handsome son of a bitch and leave it at that."

"No one's gonna come looking," his friend countered. "You ain't got your damn picture on the wall."

Billy scoffed and started to argue, but his friend pointed at the television. The game was in the ninth inning and the player at the plate cracked the ball far into the outfield, recapturing Billy's attention. I waved to Val as I let myself out. The sunlight was blinding and my eyes took a moment to adjust. A man leaned against a street sign at the end of the block, but the sidewalk was otherwise deserted. He seemed to be playing with his phone, but I saw him glance in my direction and guessed that I was trespassing in his territory. I headed for the truck, not wanting to wait around to see if the guy was in fact a dealer who wouldn't be happy with an audience for his next transaction.

I reached for my phone, thinking of texting the news to Michele but changed my mind when I realized Michele still hadn't texted back after my three earlier messages. It wasn't like her to not return a text. If she was upset about what had happened, maybe she needed space. I wanted to see her in person before I texted anything more.

CHAPTER TWELVE

I'd stashed the jewelry box on the top shelf of the closet. I went to get it as soon as I got back from Uptown. I set KW's picture on my bed and unlocked the box, eyeing KW and wondering how she'd feel knowing I was going to read her letters in earnest this time. At Michele's office, I'd only scanned the words. Now I wanted the story or at least as much of it as KW was willing to share.

I picked out an envelope in the middle of the stack. I've never been one to start a book at the beginning. Whenever I read a book or even a magazine article, I flip to the middle, sometimes even the end, and read a few lines to decide if I am interested. I didn't mind a spoiler…I liked knowing what I was in for.

The letter I'd picked was addressed to Alice and KW's penmanship was painstakingly perfect. I glanced over at the picture of her. "This is awkward with you staring at me." I flipped her photo upside down and leaned back on the pillows.

Alice,

I've gone back to count the ripped pages from my journal and know that this is my eleventh note. Between your ripped pages are the new songs I've scribbled. I'm writing like a fiend since they've thrown me out of Sutherland and since, well, since everything. I thought I'd stop writing to you after the last letter, to save my pride if nothing else, but a week has passed and time has done little to erase you from my thoughts. If anything you are all the more present. Still, I expect no reply and so to save my ink, my precious notebook pages, or something that I once gave more worth, I have decided to stop writing to you when I reach the thirtieth rip. That's all you'll have to suffer from me. The thought has passed my mind that perhaps you don't even open the envelopes I send—perhaps this note will become tinder for your evening fire. Then I think I should write volumes to warm your hands more—fingers that were cool on my skin in summer must now be cold as ice.

The floorboards shake tonight and this old building groans in protest as the dancers pound the floor below. Merlin's playing with a full band and I don't expect any rest until well after two. You may be happy to hear that I turned down a free drink this evening. I knew the buyer well, from before we met, and drinks from her are never without a catch. But it isn't only that. I've been off liquor since the last bottle we shared.

I've just come back in from a smoke on the balcony. The snow's started again. No, I haven't given up cigarettes. I know you'd be after me about that if you could. The cigarettes keep my fingers busy, though I'd rather they were busy with something else. Tonight's my first night off the piano in two weeks. I think I played your favorite "Bugle Boy" piece in my dreams last night. I've had a new song in my head for the past week, but the words are all wrong. I've ended it with the girl gone and the man heartbroken, and no one buys sad songs nowadays.

My father wrote to me this past week. My mother is ill, has been for months and no one told me, but he says she's taken a turn for the worse and so my bags are packed. I'll hitch a ride as far north as I can make it in the morning. Merlin's playing Denver tomorrow night so I'll get at least that far with those boys and then buy a bus ride to Cheyenne if I have no luck past Denver.

Do you remember the first night we danced together? Merlin's band was playing then. I can't tell you if they've kept the same songs or added new ones—because that night I wasn't listening to the music at all.

I'm going for another smoke and I might have that drink with Charlotte, after all. Will you blame me for it? If I do go, it won't mean anything, you know. Nothing does anymore. I wonder how you're still so under my skin after two months without a glimpse. That isn't entirely true. I saw you last week at the intersection of Union and Montgomery. You had your arms full with groceries, and I wanted to run over and help you into your Buick. Of course I only stood there. The Buick is Randall's car, after all, and I know you wouldn't want to be seen with me. I should despise Randall but I don't. I only envy him. And now for that smoke.

- KW

I folded the letter and replaced it in the envelope, then flipped KW's photo face up. "I hope you had that drink," I said, staring at KW's face. I picked up another letter and eyed Alice's handwriting. By the date, I knew this was Alice's response but I didn't want to read it. I only wanted to know what KW knew. I refolded her note next to KW's eleventh envelope and then reached for another envelope. It was the fifth one in the stack and by the tattered look of it, this one had been reread more than all the others. The folded crease was nearing a breaking point so I handled it gingerly.

Alice,

What is it about music that makes us forget all of our troubles and remember all of our pain? My fingers ache from playing nonstop for five hours last night. I thought of you hosting the Economics Department dinner and played all the harder. The image of you serving those scrounges coffee and slices of your pie bring only dark thoughts to mind. Randall has no business asking you to keep up this hoax…but I digress. I promised, at least to myself, that I would leave him out of this. Please disregard that mention. It has never been about Randall, has it? I remind myself that my lot in life is not so bad. Unlike some, I have no one who expects me to keep up a lie.

The sun is warming my room and it's well after one, but I've nowhere to be today. I thought about going for a walk and yet I keep to my room. Breakfast was a stale biscuit from last night's unfinished dinner. Williams bought me dinner. He feels sorry for me, I know. It was his work that landed us in this mess, not mine, but it isn't for his sake that I took the fall. Are you still angry about all of that?

I must tell you something. How to tell you this has nagged at me for the last few days so much that I haven't slept. I've thought of all the ways that I might reach you, but I'm at a loss. Your friend Agnes won't hear from me and neither will Kay. I bumped into Lola at the cinema and she wouldn't pass on a message to you either. She was there with her lover, some bloke who called me a name I'd not care to repeat, and though it is no business of mine whom she takes to the cinema, I think it's only her folly that she's taking the high ground on giving you a message considering her husband is someone I know well. Perhaps she knows I won't sink to her depths.

The sad bit of it all is that I've never trusted the mail. I can't think of another option, though, and so I'll take this risk along with all the others.

My aunt Reba passed two years ago this March. She lived in Chicago and was married to a banker named Clive Hendrickson. I'm giving you the names because I won't think the less of you if you research my claims. Uncle Clive passed years ago and he left Aunt Reba all of his fortune. She managed their estate and the small fortune he left fared better with Reba than with Clive making the decisions. They had no heirs and when Aunt Reba passed, her estate was given to my father, with funds to be passed to my sister and me on his death.

My father phoned this past Monday to tell me all of this. He wants to pay for a lawyer to represent me against Sutherland. I don't want that. But if I'm not getting any doctorate, he wants me to move back home. I think he misses my help. He's said that the money is mine if I ask for it, no matter what I decide to do with it.

I'm telling you this because I don't want you to think I'm penniless. I'm not. This thing with Williams, and the article that's caused all the trouble, will pass. I know it will. And if you change your mind, you know I will change mine. I'm quite certain that I will love you forever regardless.

- KW

With care, I replaced this letter in the envelope and closed my eyes. Maybe I didn't want to read anything else. I glanced again at KW's photograph. How could she still smile? But, I reminded myself, the picture was taken before the letters were written. I found the first letter that KW had written and flipped it over in my hands.

Alice,

Sorry. That was all I wanted to say but you wouldn't answer my call. Well, the truth is, there is much, much, more to say but sorry was all I wanted to say over the phone. I have this awful feeling that the phones are tapped and that my mail is being read. Have I gone mad?

I've been released, as you may already know, pending further investigation of Williams. I was held for twenty-four hours at the courthouse but the attorney never showed and the bailiff uncuffed me after the first hour. The bailiff wasn't bad company, though I was at my worst. He told me a joke about a fish and a shark, but I didn't laugh at the punch line and that made him too sullen to talk which I didn't mind. I've wanted silence more now than ever. The judge told me to point my finger at Williams when the time came, though not in so many words. You know I won't point my finger at anyone. There is no saving you and me, so what is the point? If they need to take someone down, I'll go without bringing anyone else with me. I know they aren't after little fish. I was only charged because they're hoping I'll squeal. I won't. And although I am scarcely a minnow to McCarthy, one sweep of their net and my world has been destroyed.

I love you. I know I shouldn't write this. I know the risk those words bring to us both, but I must tell you. I love you. I don't need to hear the words from you. I left you in a terrible way. I wish I could take back the words I said that night. Do you know I only said those things because I felt myself falling down a dark hole? It broke me to see you cry. I don't expect you to feel the same any longer, not after all that has been done and undone, but I wanted you to know the truth. Nothing will change how I feel.

There's a song that I've started for you. Maybe one day you will turn on the radio and hear it. But how will you know I've written it for you? I'll think of some secret phrase and then even if I have to sell it to a broker for pennies to pay for my meals, you will know it was written only for you. There's no use starving if only for the possibility that someday you would be mine.

   - KW

CHAPTER THIRTEEN

By the third week, rather than weave between the cabinets that filled the hall between the front door and the dining room, I lined them up against the wall by the fireplace. Aside from the old cabinets, or Alice's cabinets, as I thought of them now, I hadn't begun pulling out any of the others yet and the unfinished kitchen nagged at me every time I walked in the front door.

Travis had agreed to a basement remodel that should have been estimated to take six weeks, but the homeowner offered a bonus if he could finish the work in four. I doubted we would complete it on schedule, despite working twelve-hour days, but the pay kept me from complaining. The work kept me from thinking of Michele—at least from sunup to sundown. It was the nights that killed me. I'd eat alone wishing I could simply ask her out to dinner like any normal person would do. I couldn't sit on the couch without thinking of what we'd done, what she'd let me do to her and how her body had felt under mine. I couldn't lie in bed without wanting to touch the places she'd touched, then I'd regret it afterward. The satisfaction was too brief and it only made the longing all the more acute.

I called her twice after the unanswered texts, but when she didn't return the messages, I finally took the hint that she wasn't interested in talking. After what had happened, I didn't blame her. If I mentioned that I'd found KW's picture, I knew she'd call back, but I didn't want her to call because of that. Still, the temptation was hard to resist. I'd even thought of dropping the photograph off at the library so I could have an excuse to see her.

Without the frame, KW's photograph seemed to be missing something so I stopped by the drugstore after work and picked up a plain black frame like the ones in the back hall of Uptown. Partly because I didn't want to tap a nail into any of the walls and partly because I couldn't see having it out on display anywhere else, I set KW up in the bathroom. Alice had claimed the space as hers when she left the key there and I decided that she would have wanted the photograph in a place where she could look at her with some privacy.

The phone rang and I jumped at the sound. I'd been thinking of calling Michele and my first thought was the silly hope that Michele was the one calling. Lynn's number flashed on the screen, and I hesitated answering the line. I had no excuse not to answer, however, having spent the past twenty minutes poking at my microwaved dinner and watching dark gray clouds collect over the mountains.

"Jodi!" Roxanne's voice exclaimed. "I got to buy a bag of marshmallows at the store and I'm going to put them in my oatmeal!"

"Wow. Lucky kid." I tried to steady my voice, fighting back a sudden rush of tears. It had been weeks since she'd called and I only realized how much I'd missed her when I heard her voice. I exhaled slowly and continued, "So, what'd you do to get that special treat?"

"I didn't do anything! I start school tomorrow, silly. Did you forget tomorrow was Monday?"

"You know I always forget the days of the week. That's why I have you—to remind me." I'd taught Roxanne a song about the days of the week and she used to sing it over and over on our drive to school every Monday. I pushed this thought from my mind and asked, "Are you excited about the new school?"

"I guess. I don't know. The playground's small. We went and visited it last week. And Mom said I could get a special cereal at the store so I asked for oatmeal with marshmallows!"

"Are you going to dunk the marshmallows or eat them right off the top?"

"I'm going to dunk each one! But Mom says I can only have five."

"Five is a lot."

"Five isn't very many at all. Ten or twenty is a lot. Thirty is a lot."

"Thirty marshmallows? That sounds kinda disgusting."

She laughed. "You're wrong. It'd be the best thing ever… Mom says I have to go. I promised I'd be fast. I only wanted to tell you about the marshmallows."

"I'm happy for you, Roxy," I said. "Dunk one tomorrow just for me, okay?"

"Okay, bye."

The line fell silent and I stared at the phone, willing it to ring again. Finally I stood up and carried my dish to the kitchen. In a few months, I doubted Roxanne would call at all. School would occupy her time and then the holidays would come. And before long, her old school, old friends and old house, would all be a distant memory. I was jealous that Michele had been invited to spend Thanksgiving with them, though I would never admit it aloud.

The phone rang again and I answered it quickly, hoping to hear Roxanne's voice again. Carol answered instead. She didn't waste time with niceties like hello.

"I want to go to the Metro tonight, but I don't want to go alone. So you're coming with me. I'll be over to pick you up at eight."

"What if I have other plans?"

"What other plans? Don't pretend you have something else to do because I know better. You don't even have a TV."

I sighed. "Why tonight?"

"I need to get out of the house. Teenagers and grumpy husbands…Is that a yes, then?"

"Did I have a choice?"

"Good. It's settled."

Carol rarely said goodbye when she ended a call. I rinsed the dishes in the sink and considered calling Carol back to tell her I wasn't up for the Metro. The problem was, I did, in fact, want to go. Olive and Slim was scheduled to play, and I'd been thinking of going all weekend. It would be hard to avoid Michele however. If Michele needed space or time or both, I didn't want her to think I was chasing after her. Running into Desi again wasn't high on my list of things I wanted to do either. I'd weighed the pros and cons of going alone so many times that I'd finally given up and decided to stay home. Now Carol could be my excuse and a buffer, if needed.

I was waiting on the front porch swing, showered and changed into a dress shirt and my best jeans when Carol texted to say she was running late. Ten minutes later she texted to say that she wasn't going to force me into going out after all. Her daughter was having some kind of teen meltdown and her husband's moodiness had become contagious. I stared at the long text and then typed a quick reply: "Next time."

I hopped off the swing and went inside, more depressed about Carol's canceling than I knew I should be. I glanced at the radio and then at my sofa. The last thing I wanted to do was stay home. I was overdressed and needed to see Michele. Somehow I had to avoid her seeing me.

The Metro was less crowded than usual and empty seats dotted even the front tables. Chances were slim that Michele wouldn't spot me, even if I picked one of the tables in the back. Fortunately, Desi wasn't there. I picked the table Lynn and I used to sit at on the far side of the bar and waited for a waitress. The opening band wasn't one that I recognized. Unfortunately, the audience didn't seem that engaged in the music, and an audible murmur of conversations and clinking glasses fought the lead singer's attempt at a mellow acoustic piece. After the band finished their second acoustic piece, I decided that I didn't blame the crowd. With little effort, Travis could have outdone the lead singer. Olive and Slim was in a different league entirely and it occurred to me that they had outgrown the Metro. They weren't scheduled to perform until nine thirty and the bartenders were going to be busy in the meantime, despite the small crowd.

"Are you saving this seat?"

I looked up at Michele, instantly recognizing her voice.

She sat down without waiting for me to answer and handed her cell phone to me. "I was going to send you this tonight, but I couldn't do it."

I read the lines on the screen: "I want company tonight. Meet me at the Metro?" As much as I would have loved to read that text on my phone, I realized that it wasn't exactly what I wanted her to say. Would anyone's company do? "Why didn't you send it?"

"Because I've been trying to ignore you for the past three weeks. You didn't notice?"

"Yeah, I noticed."

"So why would I break down tonight?" Michele took the phone back and deleted the unsent message. "The truth is, I agree with you. I didn't that night, but I do now."

"About?" I knew what Michele meant too well to admit it aloud.

"We shouldn't have gone there. But it happened…I spent a lot of time thinking. Finally I decided that I like you as a friend and I think you are right that we shouldn't mess that up."

"Wait, you're saying this has nothing to do with Desi?"

"Desi?" Michele furrowed her brow. "No."

"But you wanted company tonight because Desi's not here, right?"

The waitress finally appeared, interrupting Michele as she started to answer. I ordered a glass of wine and Michele asked for a Coke. As soon as the waitress turned away, Michele said, "You know that Desi and I are only roommates, right? Housemates, I guess, is more accurate. She has a new girlfriend.

Well, newish, anyway. They've been together for two or three months I think—I haven't kept track. She's with her tonight." Michele paused. "You didn't think that I was still with her, did you?"

I opened my mouth to answer and then clamped it tight. Hadn't Carol said that Michele and Desi were together? I was nearly certain that was what she'd said, but I couldn't remember the conversation clearly. Maybe I'd heard the names and put them together. And although I remembered Michele calling Desi her roommate, at the time I'd assumed this was Michele's way of downplaying the relationship.

"Do you honestly think I would have slept with you if I was still with Desi?" Michele shook her head. After a long pause she said, "Jodi, now isn't the time to be the strong, silent type."

Being the strong, silent type was never my goal, especially now. But the words stuck in my throat when she looked at me.

The waitress reappeared with our drinks and Michele glanced at her watch. "I've gotta get backstage in ten minutes…" She took a sip of her drink and glanced at the empty stage. "You know, I wouldn't have done that to Desi. Or you. I have relationship issues, I'll give you that, but I'm not going to cheat on someone."

I wanted to say something, knew Michele was waiting for me to do so, but too many things came to mind and I didn't know where to start. If she wasn't with Desi, then why hadn't she told me that night? Why hadn't she argued that there was no reason she couldn't spend the night?

"I wish I could ask for a do-over. I want to redo that night. I didn't know…"

"I don't want a redo of that night." She paused. "We need to go back to when we were only friends and forget about everything that's happened since."

"I can't forget about it." The band had returned for their second set and I glanced at the stage to avoid Michele's gaze. I wanted to take Michele home. I wanted to show her Katy Warren. If she wanted to be friends, then I wanted to spend the night talking—with no distractions. I wanted to start at the beginning. Was there any way we could start over from the beginning? "I don't think I can go back to how things were." I already knew that I wanted more.

"Why not?"

"Because of everything."

Michele shook her head. "Lynn used to say that women needed friends more than girlfriends but with lesbians the lines got messy. I argued with her about it, but I think she had a point. Relationships are fun and I like the diversion of looking for love as much as anyone else. But this thing with Alice and all of the secrets that she kept from the world...I keep wondering if she ended up happy. What if Alice and KW hadn't tried to have an affair? What if they had been satisfied only being friends? Maybe they would have stayed friends forever...And then I think about what I need to be happy. I don't think I need a serious girlfriend, but I know I need a friend. I want to have someone I can tell anything to, you know? No secrets. And I want someone who is as happy to see me as I am to see them but doesn't expect me to be anything more than who I am. I want someone who won't judge."

"Yeah—you want a best friend. But a girlfriend is supposed to be your best friend—with benefits."

"And probably sometimes that actually is the case," Michele agreed. "You're right, I guess, in an ideal world. But I've never found it to be true."

"Can we go back for a moment?" My head was spinning. "Are you still buying a house with Desi?"

"Maybe. It's Desi's idea." Michele continued, "I'm along for the ride. It's funny that we didn't click as girlfriends considering how well we get along as roommates...I'm fine with renting, but she's convinced now's the time to buy and my place is tight for all of our stuff. I like having someone else around, but we don't have much elbow room in the condo. I think we'd be happier in a house. Besides, I hate my landlord."

"You said you were going to try and get back together with her. What happened to that?"

"Last spring? I tried. She turned me down." Michele added, "Thank God. I can't believe you thought I was still with Desi."

"She turned you down?" I couldn't believe anyone would walk away from Michele.

"You don't need to rub it in. Anyway, I don't think I really wanted to be with her. And I'm pretty sure she knew it. I was lonely."

"So you've been single this whole time?"

"I've been on a few dates, but there's no one serious." Michele sighed. "That sounds like the story of my life these past few years, doesn't it?" Her laugh sounded forced. "Which is why I'm convinced I only need a best friend. Last I checked, you were at the top of my list for the spot."

"I don't know if I can be a best friend. I'm not sure I can be your friend at all." I swallowed hard after the words slipped out.

"I was worried you'd say that." Michele sighed. She glanced at her watch, then took another sip of her Coke and stood up. "Are you going to be here when my band finishes? We only have a half-hour slot tonight."

"Yeah. I'll be here." I didn't think I could will my body to move at all. I watched Michele until she disappeared through the side door. The door led outside and there was a second entrance backstage to the side of the Dumpsters behind the bar. Michele had taken Lynn and me backstage once. I imagined the room we'd gone to, filled with couches, and crowded with instruments on stands or hung on the wall. I imagined Michele joining her bandmates, pictured her opening her guitar case and picking up her guitar to tune it…

I had to close my eyes to stop these thoughts. I wanted to chase after Michele, wrap my arms around her and hold her in place long enough to admit to everything—to over two years of pretending to care about Lynn when all I wanted was her, to the past several months of painful longing, to the past weeks with every night a memory of the night we had together and to the past half hour that had torn everything loose from the careful straps I'd used to keep my emotions all in place.

I hadn't touched the wine and took a sip now. The taste of it brought my attention back to the moment. The sounds of the lounge pierced my thoughts in a deafening rush. The band onstage ended their song and I clapped automatically, glancing about the room. We were strangers, but we clapped in unison so efficiently, so well trained were we to conformity. The crowd faded in and out of focus. I eyed one person at a time, lost that person to the crowd and then picked another. When the clapping ended, I sipped my wine again, concentrating on the red swirl in my glass.

One question lingered. If I had let Michele stay that night, what would have happened the next day? Had Michele only wanted that one night? It was altogether possible that even if I hadn't sent her home, she would have admitted the next morning that she only wanted me as a friend, maybe a friend with benefits, but with none of the ties of a girlfriend.

I suddenly didn't want to stay. I didn't want Michele to sit next to me after her band finished and chat about anything other than all the reasons why we should be together. I even didn't want to watch Michele onstage. I was done pretending that one day she'd gaze out at the crowd until she found me, then sing—as if she didn't care if anyone else heard—a song that was meant only for me. It seemed like such a ridiculous fantasy now, something that would never come true.

I picked up my phone and typed, "Not feeling well. Going home early." But I didn't send the message. I stared at the words and then, in fact, began to feel nauseous. I set the phone facedown on the table and sipped my wine, giving up my fantasies one at a time.

The opening band finally cleared the stage. Olive and Slim would be on in minutes. I couldn't bring myself to send the text or to stand up and walk out the door. The waitress came round again, but I waved her past, knowing the last thing I needed was to get drunk. I needed to slow down. I glanced at the strangers near my table, wishing someone was sitting in the seat next to mine. The loneliness that had been jabbing at me for months was suddenly impossible to ignore.

Sarah came onstage, raised her hand in greeting, then took her place at the microphone. That was unusual. She was often the last one to come onstage. She seemed more focused tonight than usual. I'd met her at a party that Michele had thrown over a year ago. She'd been more than friendly but also very drunk, and I'd avoided her for most of the evening. When I asked Michele about her afterward, joking about her drunken friendliness, it came out that Sarah's drinking was a regular source of contention for the band. They'd lost a bass player over the issue. He'd since been replaced.

Michele and the rest of the quartet took their places and their first number was soon filling the space. It was a mellow folksong that showcased Sarah's voice. Michele's hands moved smoothly over the strings of her guitar, and I forgot that I'd promised myself not to stare. They were so mesmerizing that the thirty-minute set was up before I had a chance to think about making a break for the door. I couldn't leave then either. Before Michele placed her guitar gingerly in its case and made her way backstage, she looked right at me, as if making certain that I hadn't left and wouldn't.

She reappeared at the side entrance several minutes later and headed straight for my table only to be stopped midway when someone waved to catch her attention. I couldn't hear their conversation but saw Michele smiling and guessed at the compliments. They had played their usual songs, nothing new, but they sounded better than usual and the small crowd had clapped enthusiastically.

Michele reached my table and a smile lit up her face, erasing any desire I had to have a serious conversation. "That was fun. What's next?"

"You guys were great tonight. The band was really on."

"We sounded awesome, didn't we? Not bad for a lounge act." Michele grinned. After a moment, she added, "Sarah's been sober for a month."

"So this is her sober?"

"Yeah. This is her actually remembering the words." Michele reached for my wineglass and took a sip. "I think that's the reason we've been hitting it lately. We've all made a deal. No drinking at practice time or when we have a gig. She's tried sobriety before and failed—you know she works at the Winery, right? She's a chef…but the wine is free. I think this time is different though. Anyway, my fingers are crossed."

"I was wondering why you ordered a soda earlier."

Michele still hadn't sat down. She glanced at the door. "I want to get out of here. How would you feel about leaving early?"

"It isn't early anymore."

Michele finished the last sip of my wine and reached for my hand. "Good. Let's go."

We went out through the side entrance. Michele slipped into the back room to grab her guitar, and I waited by the Dumpsters for her. The wind had picked up and cool air bit at my neck. I turned up the collar on my jacket only to feel Michele's hand push it down again. I glanced over my shoulder at her.

"Trying to look cool?" she asked.

"I don't need to try," I said, grinning. She kissed my cheek, and her warm lips sent a shiver through my body.

"You're right about that." She swung her guitar and walked past me toward the main road. "Where are you taking me?"

I considered the options. Her kiss had me going in circles, wondering what she wanted from me. More than anything else, I wanted to take her home. If we were only going to be friends, I wanted to spend the rest of the evening talking, just the two of us, without distractions.

"I want to show you something." I reached for her free hand and she clasped mine tightly.

"I like the sound of that."

The warmth of her hand made me shelve the hesitations I'd had earlier. I led the way to where I'd parked and then opened the door for her. I was only being practical; she had her guitar case in one hand and I wasn't ready to let go of her other one. I prepared to offer that as an excuse if she teased me for it, but she didn't tease and no one else was watching.

Michele picked out the radio station while I drove, not bothering to ask where we were going. When I turned down Granite Avenue, I felt her watching me.

"You're taking me to your place?"

"Don't worry. You are going to like my surprise."

"Surprise, huh?"

I parked in front of the house and then hesitated. I considered asking Michele to wait in the car while I grabbed KW's picture. Sitting in the car with Michele only inches away from me, I decided that none of the reasons I'd thought of earlier for having a genuine relationship seemed all that important now. I was nearly certain that Michele would agree that we could have a good time tonight as friends with benefits and no one would be hurt by it. *No one*, I thought, *except maybe me*.

"Is it something out here?"

"No. I was just thinking."

"Should I worry?" Michele asked. She was staring up at the house, her expression hidden.

"You're going to like this. I promise." I waited for Michele to look my way. Instead, she reached for the door handle and hopped out.

She was waiting at the front door by the time I started up the path. I unlocked it and switched on the lights, then regretted it; the glare was much too bright for the mood. Michele set her guitar case in the front room and looked at me expectantly.

"It's up in the bathroom," I said. "I'm going to get a glass of water. Can I get you something?"

"Water's fine," Michele answered, clearly distracted. "Nice cabinets," she said, sliding her hand along the edge of the nearest one as she passed the fireplace and headed toward the stairs.

"They'll look even better when I finally get them installed in the kitchen." I went to get the water. The evening had not gone at all as I'd expected. I filled two water glasses and went upstairs.

The frame I'd picked up at the drugstore was sitting on the counter in the bathroom, but the photograph was missing from it. I found Michele in the bedroom. She was stretched across the bed, angling the picture to catch the weak light coming in through the sliding glass door.

"You could turn on the light, you know," I suggested.

"Where'd you find her?"

"Uptown—which isn't uptown anymore, and I'm not sure it ever was. But the place is definitely an interesting step back in time. Remember that matchbook?"

Michele murmured, "Unbelievable."

I took a sip of water and then offered the other glass to Michele. I set both glasses on the floor beside the bed when Michele shook her head. I didn't miss having a nightstand or a chair until moments like this. I sat down on the corner of the bed, feeling strangely awkward in my own room. I waited for Michele to say something, but she settled the picture on her chest, KW's face staring at the ceiling, and covered her eyes with her hands. "You okay?" I asked quietly.

"Yeah. Tell me how you found her."

"Travis wanted me to pick up burritos from this restaurant way at the south end of town. I'm never down in that part of the city so when I recognized the street name from the matchbook, I decided to take a detour. Turns out Uptown is still there, but it's more of a neighborhood dive bar now. I found KW up on the wall. She was in their back hall by the restrooms along with probably a hundred, maybe more, headshots of other almost-famous people. Apparently the bar's owner sold all of the photos of the truly famous ones."

Michele picked up the photograph and stared at KW's face again. "So, you spotted this name and checked the date on the back and knew it was Alice's KW?"

"I knew it was her before I saw the date. I mean, I was pretty sure. She was the only one who looked like a dyke."

Michele touched the signature. "I remember this name from the list. 'E' stands for Edith. Edith Warren."

"What list?"

"That newspaper article about suspected communists. She was on the list. There weren't many last names beginning with W so I checked all of them. I didn't find anyone with even a middle initial of K. I guess McCarthy and his boys didn't know her nickname. And, by the way, you owe me dinner."

I smiled. "I was waiting for you to say that."

"You've had this picture for a while, haven't you?"

"Long enough to pick up a frame and get used to seeing her smile when I brush my teeth. You didn't respond to any of my texts." Hearing the defensive tone in my voice, I added, "Anyway I knew you were mad…and now I know you had a reason to be. I did try to tell you about this as soon as I found it."

"I wasn't mad," Michele argued. "It's possible I was upset… And maybe hurt. But I wasn't going to tell you that part."

"I'm sorry." And I was, about so many things. "At least now you know why I sent you home."

"You should have said something then. I can't believe you thought I would have come over in the first place if I was still with Desi."

"I wanted you to come regardless," I admitted. I sat down on the edge of the bed but didn't look at Michele. There were too many reasons for why we shouldn't be this close to each other— on a bed, no less. But all I could think of was shifting closer yet. "Yes, I thought you were with Desi, but you guys didn't seem that into each other and when you looked at me that way…I had to ask you to come back to see if you would even respond."

"I'm not sure that makes it better." Michele shook her head. "You know, I don't think I want to talk about this tonight."

"What do you want to talk about then?"

Michele sighed. "Do you want to know why I was really pissed? I finally got to see you naked. And then you sent me home early."

"You're upset because of that? You could have tried harder to stay." I laughed. "You wanted to see me naked, huh? For how long?"

"I'll probably regret telling you." Michele stared at me for a long moment. "Lynn had a barbecue a few months after you two started dating." She paused. "You were joking with Roxanne and pretending to squirt her with ketchup and then she got the bottle and really squirted ketchup all over the place. Your shirt was covered. We were all laughing so much Lynn spit her food out. You went inside to change your shirt. Lynn had Roxanne hosing the ketchup off everything, so I cleared the dishes. I saw you when I was carrying everything in. You were standing at the kitchen sink rinsing the ketchup off your shirt. You hadn't put a new one on yet and I stared at your back for longer than I should have. I started to worry suddenly that you were going to turn around and call me out for staring at you, so I set the dishes on the counter and practically ran out.

"When you came back outside, I was waiting for you to tease me about it. I even had a quip all ready about how you looked ready to pose in some calendar, showing off your shoulders and back. But you never said anything. You never heard the door, I guess."

"A calendar?"

Michele grinned. "All I'm saying is that you look great with your shirt off."

"I heard you come in," I admitted. "I remember that day pretty well. I was too embarrassed to turn around."

"You shouldn't have been. Anyway, I'm not the type to chase after someone who's in a relationship."

"Wait. Are you suggesting that I am?"

"You did ask me to come over the other night," Michele countered. "What were your intentions?"

"As it turns out, you weren't with Desi anyway."

"You told me that you didn't know that at the time, remember?"

"Can we change the subject?"

"I shouldn't have brought that up anyway," Michele said. "Though it was fun reminiscing about that barbecue." She handed me the picture of KW. There wasn't anyplace to put the picture so I held it, eyeing again the face that I was certain I would recognize if we ever crossed paths even if the years had changed her.

"Who was Edith Warren?"

"I don't remember anything that stood out about her. I'll have to search the name again tomorrow. I was only trying to link the 'W' names to the right initials."

"I want to find her." I stood up and set the photograph on the shelf in the closet. I closed the door and stared at Michele. I knew I ought to ask if she wanted a ride home.

"Let's hope she's still alive." Michele paused. Finally she said, "You know what I said earlier when we were at the lounge—about us staying friends? Are you okay with that?"

We had flirted more than we probably should have while I was dating Lynn, but it was Michele's personality to be friendly. I'd figured that the attraction was mostly on my part, just like qualms about the situation probably weighed more heavily on my conscience than it did on hers. Since she'd admitted that she'd been attracted to me all along, even when Lynn and I were together, it didn't make sense to me that we wouldn't date now.

"I don't understand you sometimes," I said. "Like now, for instance, I think I know what you want but…"

Michele didn't try to help me finish the thought. She only stared up at me waiting.

"I think you're into me and then you say 'let's be friends.' And the way you're looking at me now…You want more."

"Maybe I do want more. I've been into you, Jodi, for over two years now. We both know there's chemistry or whatever you want to call it." She continued, "But I don't think it would work. I don't want to try and then lose you as a friend."

The only person who would understand our dilemma, I thought, was Lynn. I wondered what she would say, not that I'd ever ask. As rational as she was, I still doubted Lynn would ever discuss the pros and cons of a relationship that involved one of her best friends getting together with her ex.

"Okay…So you go through girlfriends in two months. I'm not scared. In two months we can go back to being friends," I countered.

"I can't go into a relationship with you on that premise."

Of course it wasn't what I wanted either. I didn't want Michele for only two months. I wasn't in the mood to casually date her—or anyone else for that matter. After breaking up with Lynn I'd realized that I wasn't interested in wasting my time on relationships that were only convenient or women who were only easy to be with because we both knew it wasn't long-term…

I wanted long-term. I wanted someone who was willing to work through hard stuff and wanted to plan for something

beyond dinner. And I wanted someone who'd count on me—
someone who'd say I was part of their family. But I wouldn't
admit this to Michele. The truth was, with her, I'd settle for a
two-month fling. Starting tonight.

"Then we won't call it a relationship."

"With that look, you could convince me of almost anything,"
Michele said.

I wondered what look she meant. The longer we talked with
her lying in my bed looking up at me, the more turned on I
was getting. Maybe she could tell. All the reasons of why we
shouldn't date didn't matter one bit.

"Can I convince you to spend the night?"

"You have no idea how much I want to say yes. But…"

I shifted closer to her. I wanted to touch her so badly that
I could hardly hold myself back. "Maybe we don't need to say
anything at all. Maybe we both need to relax and see what
happens next."

"I think we both know what would happen next." Michele
paused. "And maybe that's okay tonight." She reached up and
touched my lips with her fingertip. "Maybe," she repeated. "But
tomorrow…"

I was ready to beg for one kiss. One kiss and then… "So let's
not think about tomorrow."

Michele shook her head. "Tomorrow comes even if you
don't think about it. We both know it's safer if we stay friends."

"Safer for who?" I wanted Michele tonight. Tonight I could
pretend that a friendship with occasional sex was a compromise
I could live with. I would deal with tomorrow later.

Michele sighed and shifted away from me and I knew her
answer. Not tonight. Maybe not ever. I wanted to argue that
it was only sex. But I knew better. For me, it wouldn't be only
sex. And instead of doing what we both wanted, she was telling
me no because she didn't want me to get hurt. I couldn't think
of anything worse. Was it that obvious—how easily she could
crush me?

I needed air. The new sliding glass door didn't squeak. I
stepped out onto the balcony and closed the door. The railing

was cold, as was the breeze coming off the mountains. I took a deep breath and let the cool air fill my chest. Stars dotted the moonless night sky and the mountains were only distant shadows. If the balcony had had stairs down to the backyard, I would have taken them. I wanted to walk and think. As it was, the balcony provided little escape. I felt caught. I couldn't turn down Michele's offer for friendship. Part of me wanted to, though, if only to see if Michele would actually walk away. A few minutes passed and I heard the door open, then felt Michele's arms wrap around my waist.

"I need a ride back to the Metro. I left my car there."

I didn't turn around. "So hugs are okay?"

"Friends hug," she said in response. Her chest was pressed against my back, and I could feel her breath on my neck. Her arms held me tight, as if she was worried that letting go would mean she'd lose me.

"I don't think friends hold like this."

She let go of me and I wished I could take the words back.

CHAPTER FOURTEEN

The blue jays were calling when I woke. Most days I was sure they were fighting over their worms when they called loud enough to wake me, but this morning they only seemed to be making the noise because it was sunrise and they seemed to think this was enough reason to be happy.

That anyone was happy at six a.m. pissed me off. I rubbed my eyes, searching for my phone. I hadn't left it on the top slat of the headboard where I normally kept it and I couldn't remember now if I'd brought it upstairs at all. The light coming through the windows made me guess it was near dawn. I finally found my phone in the pocket of my jeans. I'd missed a text message from Travis. He'd sprained his back playing a pickup basketball game with his friends and was going to call and cancel our day's job. I sat down on the edge of the bed. We hadn't had an unexpected day off in months.

I got dressed with one thought in mind. I needed coffee. Good coffee. The walk to the coffee shop was long enough that I had time to consider all of the things I could have done and said differently with Michele last night. But it might not have changed anything.

Molly's taciturn look changed instantly when she saw me step up to her counter. "Hey, stranger," she said. "Beaming" seemed like a ridiculous way to describe the expression of anyone who wasn't a kid at Christmas, but that was the way she looked. I couldn't help but smile back at her.

"Hey yourself."

"Missed me?"

I nodded. I didn't know I'd missed Molly until she was standing in front of me beaming. But suddenly it was true. Too bad she wasn't single.

"You want your usual?"

"I think I want something different today."

"You came to the right spot. I got a new roast in yesterday and I've been making killer mochas with it," Molly suggested. "These beans have a nutty flavor and with the chocolate added in, well, you won't be disappointed."

That was exactly what I needed—no disappointment. "Perfect."

"Have a seat and I'll bring it over."

I paid for the mocha and found my way over to one of the empty tables by the windows. It was a slow day, apparently, or still too early for the morning crowd. Only two other customers were in the place, both quietly immersed in ignoring the rest of the world. Another customer came in the door as I was searching for the free copies of *The Independent*. I found the magazine and settled in to my seat, scanning the calendar listings for local events. I needed to meet someone new, that's all there was to it. I needed to stop thinking about Michele. A new wine bar had opened up and they were offering half-priced wine tasting. It seemed promising but I didn't think I was desperate enough to try going alone.

The magazine didn't distract me for long and I was soon watching Molly. She helped the customer who had come in after me to a glass of orange juice and then sliced a quiche for their to-go order. When the customer headed out the door, she glanced my way and held up a mug.

She came over to my spot and set the steaming mug on the table. "So what are we doing Saturday night?"

"Um…"

She pointed to the magazine page. I'd left it open to the calendar of events. "I'm off at three."

I glanced at the magazine, not really looking at the words. Molly was asking me out? "Wine tasting?"

She found the listing I'd mentioned and gave one satisfied nod. "That place is a few blocks from my house, but I haven't been there yet. My favorite wine bar is a few blocks in the other direction."

She reached for a pen in the pocket of her apron and wrote a street address on the napkin she'd set under my mug. The bell clanged at the front door and a customer walked in. He glanced around until he spotted Molly.

"I'll see you Saturday at seven then?"

"Yeah, definitely." I grinned. It was too easy. "Wait, I thought you were dating someone."

She'd started back toward the counter but paused at my question. "Love of my life? Yeah. I was. Not anymore. Turns out she wasn't single."

I watched Molly serve the man at the counter, hoping that she'd come back to my table. But when she'd finished with that customer a crowd of people came in and the line only seemed to grow longer as I sipped the mocha. It was hardly coffee. But it was damn good. I'd finished my drink by the time there was a break in the line.

Molly walked back to my table and picked up the empty mug. "What'd you think?"

"Delicious."

"Best mocha you've ever had?"

"Best I've ever had."

"One more question. You are single too, right? 'Cause as much as I want to go out with you, I don't want to get mixed up with anyone who's already in a relationship."

"I'm single," I answered. It was true, of course. But it wasn't the only question she could have asked and I felt a twinge of guilt. Did she care if I was single but wanted to be in a relationship with someone else?

"Good. See you Saturday."

The walk home gave me plenty of time to think about my plans for the day—and my date on Saturday. I couldn't remember the last time I'd been on a first date with someone I hardly knew. Yes, I had known Molly for almost a year, but I hardly knew anything about her. My thoughts spun back to Michele. Molly was a perfect reason to clear things up with Michele, get things on a friendship-only basis. I needed to move on.

I dialed Michele as soon as I got home.

"Travis sprained his back."

"You sound pretty happy about that."

"I am. It means I have the day off. Want to call in sick? I want to go for a hike in the mountains." Because friends did things like that. And I figured a hike would be a good excuse to talk without the closeness of a bed clouding my thoughts.

"That sounds lovely, but I'm not going to call in sick. A hike does sound nice but...I never call in sick unless I really am. I think it's bad luck. Anyway, I want to use my desk job for something important this morning. I'm going to track down our KW." She paused. "Were you only calling to ask me if I wanted to go for a hike? Or are you trying to let me know that you aren't mad about last night?"

"I'm not mad." Sad was a better description, but it fell short of the mark. Fortunately Molly had pushed me out of my funk. "I'm calling to let you know I thought about what you said."

"And?"

"I'm fine only being friends." The alternative of losing her entirely was far worse. I wanted to tell her I had a date for Saturday to prove that I could let go.

"I'm glad one of us is."

"What's that mean?"

"It's gonna be hard, Jodi, that's all. I like you."

This was not what I needed to hear. No way was I going to argue with her. I didn't have a chance anyway. She had to end the call abruptly when someone interrupted asking for her help on something. When the line went silent, I stared at the phone considering all the things that I hadn't said.

* * *

Two of the new cabinets were in place by the time I was ready for lunch. I made a sandwich and took it out to the backyard, choosing my favorite seat on the bottom step of the stairs. The old metal cabinets were piled in a heap that claimed center stage only because there was little else but scrub grass for competition. The sandwich was gone before I was ready to go back to work, and I leaned back against the stairs and closed my eyes.

As I worked, I'd been distracted by thoughts of what had nearly happened with Michele. Not with thoughts about Molly. I knew that was a problem, but I told myself it was only because I hardly knew Molly. After several hours of thinking about what Michele had said last night and then what she'd said over the phone, I realized I wasn't angry or even annoyed. I was resigned. And yes, sad—which was much more pathetic to have to admit. It didn't matter if Michele said she liked me. She didn't want a relationship with me.

I shifted my position on the stairs. Warmed by the sun's rays on my black T-shirt, my skin was in perfect juxtaposition to the crisp autumn air. I thought of bringing a blanket outside to lay out in the scrub grass but made no move to get it. The ring of my cell was only enough motivation to remove the screwdriver wedged under the back door. The door slammed shut, muffling the phone. It was on the kitchen windowsill and I had no interest in leaving my spot to answer the call that I guessed was from Travis.

Travis had already called twice that morning. He was laid out in the middle of his family room watching television, propped up with pillows and too much pain medication. He'd called the guy about the basement job and explained that he'd thrown out his back and would need at least two days to recover. Travis knew the delay was going to piss off the guy, but he was grouchy as well because now there was no way we'd finish the job in time to get the bonus. Travis had tried to convince me to go over to the jobsite for a half day to at least placate the homeowner. Our next project in the basement required both of us. I had argued that it was pointless for me to go alone, but he wouldn't let up. I'd finally agreed to drop by the site to get him off the phone. Tomorrow I'd go.

Today the only person I wanted to see or talk to was Michele. I'd rinsed Michele's water glass in the sink and the smudge left on it by her lips made me want to kiss her. When I noticed Michele's guitar case in the living room, I barely stopped myself from sending her a text joking that she must have left it at the house on purpose so she'd have an excuse to come back.

I wanted to ask her about the letters too. I hadn't read all of them. After the twelfth one, I'd suddenly gotten too depressed about the whole thing. I'd folded them all up and locked the box. I knew Michele had read all of them, probably more than once, and I wondered what she'd learned about Alice and KW's relationship. I wasn't interested in clues about KW now. After I'd found her in Uptown I felt like I knew her well. But I wanted to know what had happened between her and Alice. I was ready to know their story, even if we already knew that it didn't end with them together.

Something held me back from simply opening the box and reading everything. I think it was mostly because I'd wanted a happy ending for them. I was too depressed to read anything more, knowing that they hadn't ended up together.

Storm clouds had collected over the mountains and were now slowly creeping eastward. When the sun slipped behind these clouds, I stood finally and stretched. I'd learned to ignore the clouds. Sometimes they brought sheets of rain or even pelting hail in July, but more often than not, it was a thunder and lightning show with a light sprinkle that the wind quickly pushed out to the range.

I headed back to the kitchen, pausing as I passed the windowsill to check for a message from Travis. The missed call was from Michele, but she hadn't left a message. I started to text her, but the doorbell interrupted.

"I found her." Michele pushed her sunglasses up on her head. She held a notebook and her purse was swung over her shoulder. "I've got the address. Want to go for a drive?"

"An address for KW?"

She nodded, a wide grin stretching across her face.

"Wait, aren't you supposed to be at work?"

"I took the afternoon off," she said, stepping past me to come inside before continuing, "and tomorrow as well. Guess who is listed in the phone book?"

"Edith Warren?"

"No." Michele smiled. "As it turns out, there is no listing for Edith Warren anywhere. Edith disappeared shortly after a certain newspaper article was printed in 1954."

"But KW didn't?"

"Katy Warren lives on a ranch in Wyoming. It's a five-hour drive, if we're lucky with Denver traffic. She's expecting us for coffee tomorrow morning."

I glanced at my watch. "We could make it for a late dinner."

"You owe me dinner. I decided I didn't want to share my date." Michele set her notebook on the sofa. "Fall semester starts next week and then I won't have any time to do something like this. As it is, I have plenty of vacation days saved. I haven't taken a half-day off in I don't know how long. One of the other librarians actually thanked me. She regularly needs time off for her kids and says I make her look bad. It's also possible that I've been totally useless at work today."

"Researching KW all morning?" My mind spun with the thought that Michele's dinner plan meant we'd have to find a hotel for the night.

"It only took me twenty minutes to find KW. Then I wrote you an email that I didn't send…" Michele walked over to where I stood. She dusted the wood flecks off my shirt. "I didn't get anything done this morning. It's possible I was distracted thinking about last night. You're really okay with everything?"

I thought of too many things I could say in response. When she stood close enough to kiss me, I wanted to say yes to anything she asked. "Yeah, sure." It wasn't exactly the truth, but it was easier than the truth.

"Good." She continued to stare at me as if she wasn't certain I was being honest but then said, "So, drive to Wyoming with me?"

"Definitely. I wouldn't miss meeting KW. Let me send Travis a message about tomorrow." I went to the kitchen and quickly texted Travis that I wasn't going to be able to go to the jobsite after all. I didn't wait for his response, knowing he would try to convince me that the job was too important to skip. The job wasn't even close to being as important as a road trip, especially with Michele. "Can I shower first?"

"Please," Michele said. "And I'll drive. I think we should give her everything you found, but I want another look at some of those letters first. And I want your opinion on a few things."

I grabbed the jewelry box, the newspaper and the matchbook from my closet and then picked up the picture from the bathroom. The bathroom seemed empty without KW's face. I emptied a small cardboard box from my closet and set the items inside, knowing I was going to miss KW's picture and feeling ridiculous for it.

I showered quickly and changed into clean jeans and a button-down shirt, then nearly changed out of the shirt, thinking I was probably overdressed. As much as I wanted it to be, tonight wasn't a real dinner date. I was taking the woman I'd had a crush on for over two years out for dinner only because I'd lost a bet. One look in the mirror and I decided to keep the shirt on. Even if it wasn't a real date, it didn't hurt to make Michele think twice about wanting to only be friends. I packed an overnight bag with a T-shirt and a flannel one for tomorrow's breakfast meeting.

Michele was sitting on the sofa. She glanced up at me as I came down the stairs. "I remember that shirt. You don't wear it often."

"I don't go out to dinner often."

"Lynn had a dinner party celebrating something, I can't remember what, but she had sent you out for something last minute and then you came back when everyone else had already arrived. I caught you in the hallway to let you know that everyone had shown up early. You were wearing a Pink Floyd T-shirt and I sent you upstairs to change. You gave me this funny look, and I realized that you weren't planning on changing. Everyone else was dressed up so I went with you and pulled out that shirt," Michele said, pointing at it, "and you changed in front of me without so much as glancing at my face."

"So, how many times did you see me with no shirt on while I was with Lynn?"

"Only twice. I'm not going to lie, though. I wanted to unbutton that shirt for the rest of that evening. God, that night was uncomfortable. And you don't remember it at all, do you?"

"I remember it. Lynn was pissed because I'd forgotten cilantro when I'd done the shopping that morning, so she sent me back out for that. Then I grabbed parsley instead. She barely spoke to me the rest of the night. I think you must have caught me in the hallway right after Lynn had gone off about the parsley." I laughed, recalling how I'd tried to avoid Lynn's eyes the entire evening but kept making mistakes like forgetting the names of Lynn's work friends while Lynn was glaring at me. "I honestly didn't remember that you were even in the room when I changed."

"You were distracted," Michele said, straightening the edge of my collar. She glanced at the jewelry box on top of the other items for KW and sighed. "Did you read all the letters?"

I shook my head. "I didn't even make it halfway. I was too damn sad."

"There are a few later ones I think you should read on the drive. I'd like to know what you think about a couple of things Alice wrote." Michele reached for the jewelry box and quickly popped it open. She fished out the letters she wanted and set them on top.

"It's too bad I didn't find all of this sooner."

"Before Alice died?"

I nodded. "How is KW going to feel? I keep wondering if she had any idea that the woman she loved so much actually loved her back. And now she's going to find out when it's all too late."

"Is it too late? To find out that it wasn't an unrequited love? Besides, we wouldn't be bringing KW the letters if Alice were still alive. We would have had to ask Alice first. And there's a good chance she would have told us to burn everything."

At first I'd tried to remain impartial about KW and Alice's relationship. There was no way I could judge Alice's decision to not reply to KW, but since I'd found KW's photograph, I'd picked sides. I couldn't help but align with KW. Even though I was living in Alice's home, using her bathroom, doing dishes in the same place where she had once stood scrubbing, I couldn't see Alice's perspective. How could she write all of the letters but not send them? But Michele was right. If Alice were still living, we couldn't possibly tell KW about the letters without Alice's permission and I doubted she would have given it.

Michele continued, "When I called KW, I told her that we had found some letters that she should have received a long time ago. Her response was, 'Oh, the mailman's always late around here, I don't mind. Better late than never.' I nearly started to cry when she said that. I was going to explain who the letters were from, so she had some time to get used to the idea, but I didn't get a chance. She got off the line after telling me to come by for coffee tomorrow, saying something about a dog that was after her chickens. There was a lot of barking." Michele picked up her keys. "Ready?"

We passed the city limits before Michele motioned to the pile of letters in my lap. "Read. There's a lot there, and I want to make sure we have time to talk about things before we meet KW."

"I have five hours, right? I think there'll be time." I didn't want to talk about KW as much as I wanted to talk about last night.

Michele shook her head. "Read."

"Is that your librarian tone?"

Instead of a sharp counter, Michele tilted her head and said, "Now, there's the Jodi I remember. It's been a long time since I've heard your sarcasm."

"Maybe I needed to let go. The more I think about it, the more I'm convinced we can just be friends. I'm going to try anyway."

"Good." Michele reached across my leg and picked up the top letter. She kept her eyes on the road as she held it out to me. "The question is, was Alice the one who couldn't just be friends or was it KW?"

"Don't you feel a little weird reading these letters now that we found KW? When they were both only strangers' names, I didn't feel like I was snooping, but now that we are going to meet KW, I feel like maybe we shouldn't have read the letters at all."

"If we hadn't read the letters in the first place, we wouldn't have searched for her. We're leaving the letters with KW. You're not going to get another chance. Don't you want to know?"

"I'm not sure what I want to know. I guess I want to know if KW ended up happy, but I already know that I'm not going to find that out in these letters." I glanced at the first line of the letter Michele had picked out, then refolded the letter and slipped it inside its envelope. "At first, I only wanted to know what was inside the jewelry box. After I found KW's picture, I wanted to know their whole story. But after I started reading, I realized I wasn't going to find a love story."

"There's a love story there. Not all love stories end happy, you know."

"I think they're called tragedies then," I countered.

"You only go for the stories with happy endings?"

"Maybe. I don't know...Even this morning I thought about reading the letters—all of them—to know exactly what had happened between them."

"So, here's your chance. The view out your window is going to be the same for the next hour."

"I don't think I can read these letters now," I replied.

"Why not?"

"Because we know there is no happy ending and because these people are real now. We are on our way to meet KW. It isn't our little Nancy Drew mystery anymore. These were real lives." Michele shook her head as I continued, "I guess I imagine someone reading a letter that I'd written...A love letter is private."

"Who knew Jodi Burkitt was a hopeless romantic?" Michele said, glancing at me for only a second and then refocusing on the road. "Fine. Don't read them."

Michele had picked out a radio station that crackled with static not long after we crossed the county line. I found a new station and then settled back into my seat. The letters weighed on my lap, tempting me, and I finally gathered them up to refill the jewelry box. I reached into the back seat and found the jewelry box, then carefully filed each letter based on the date of the postmark on KW's letters and Alice's handwritten date on the unmailed reply. Michele shook her head as I closed the lid on the box and turned the key.

"Can we talk about something else?" I asked, annoyed at the tentative sound of my voice.

Michele shrugged. "I want to talk about KW and Alice, but you don't know enough of their story."

"Tell me what you know."

"Uh-uh. You already made me feel guilty for rereading those letters. Maybe you're right. Maybe it was too personal. Anyway, it's too late for me. If you want to be virtuous, go right ahead."

"Virtuous, huh? You say it like it's a flaw. I'm guessing that's not one of your requirements in a girlfriend." The change in Michele was immediate, a barely perceptible tensing of her shoulders and then a forced smile. It was too late to second-guess my words. I added, "I mean a friend."

"Whatever," Michele returned.

"Anyway, I'm not reading the letters. We're about to meet KW. It's too late." I sighed and shifted in the chair. "Want to switch off driving every couple hours?"

Michele nodded. Several minutes passed before she asked, "Okay, what else did you want to talk about?"

"What didn't happen last night."

"I don't think we should," Michele countered. "We aren't going to agree on that either."

"How do you know we aren't going to agree? Maybe I was going to say I really liked hanging out with you."

"Maybe. Or maybe you were going to say that you don't understand why we aren't going to try to be friends with benefits." Michele sighed. "I'm not dense, Jodi."

"But you are difficult," I countered. "Which I like, don't get me wrong."

"'Difficult'?" She arched her eyebrows. "You told me you were fine with everything."

"I am. But I want to know why we are making this choice. The real answer—not some excuse about not wanting one of us to end up hurt. Tell me why you want to settle for being friends and then I'll drop this. I promise. I won't ask you again."

"I don't want to talk about it."

"At all? Or not now?"

Michele shrugged.

I had a stack of arguments ready for this moment, but Michele's somber expression made me decide to drop the topic.

I stared out the window. Cattle grazed in the fields, but they were little more than dots on a blurred landscape. I could only focus on one dot when they were still too far away to confirm them as anything more than cow-shaped blobs. But by the time the car was close enough to the herd to differentiate a cow from a sheep, the single dot that I'd strained to focus on was lost to the herd. I practiced focusing on one cow at a time until a headache started pulsing at my temple.

I closed my eyes and leaned back in the seat. The reality was, I had spent way too long considering all the possible reasons Michele might have for not wanting a relationship with me. The one thing that I came back to over and over was simply that Michele didn't think I was girlfriend material. I'd known most of Michele's past girlfriends, at least those from the past two years, and the one thing that they had in common was some sort of professional job and a degree to back it up.

I glanced over at Michele. "I wish you had some habit that I couldn't stand. Maybe you could be a compulsive gambler or chew tobacco when no one's around. Do you leave your toothpaste cap off?"

"Are you kidding?" Michele laughed. "I am way too OCD to leave the toothpaste uncapped. I think you already know most of my weird habits."

"I only know about the commitment phobia."

Michele shook her head but didn't argue.

"How well can you ever know someone anyway? Sometimes I think I know you and then…I have all of these questions. I don't know anything about your past—before you moved to Colorado. Why'd you move here anyway? For the job?"

Michele nodded.

"And you were in Tucson before that?"

Michele's jaw clenched at the mention of Tucson, but her tone was smooth when she answered, "Yeah, I was born there and didn't leave until I moved here. I always thought I'd go away for college but…I decided to stay. Then I was stuck in Tucson for a long, long time."

"Why?"

"A lot of reasons…Money is probably the easiest answer. I worked my way through college, taking some semesters off along the way, and then took some more time off before I started my master's program because I was so broke. I always had this dream that I'd move to LA or New York. I wanted new scenery and something bigger than Tucson. I'm not sure this town's any bigger, but the scenery is better." Michele smiled. "I started waiting tables when I was seventeen. After too many years serving buffalo wings and watered-down Coke, I realized I needed to go back to school if I wanted to do anything more than dream about leaving.

"It took me a while to figure out what I wanted to do. I didn't graduate until I was twenty-nine and then I still wasn't sure what I wanted to do. I'd always loved libraries…but I never thought I could be one of those shushing librarians who comes unglued when someone smacks their gum. But I liked how everything in a library had a place, though, the way everything was so orderly and quiet. And I liked how the old books smelled. Books had answers that the real world didn't have.

"When I finally looked into it, I realized Tucson wasn't a bad place to be. The same university where I went to college had a master's program for research librarians and I qualified for a grant. But I knew I had to get out of town as soon as I finished. A position at Sutherland opened up and here I am."

"Do you miss Tucson?"

"Sometimes. Then I remember how hot it gets. And how miserable I was."

"Okay, how about your family? I know your mom still lives in Tucson, and you don't like to visit her except on Christmas. Why?"

"It's too damn hot in Tucson the rest of the year. My turn to ask you a question now?"

"Wait, that's all I get? You lived there for, what, thirty-five years and you won't go back now because it's hot?"

"Thirty-eight. I'm forty-one now. Thank you for trying to make me younger, but I'm happier at forty-one than I've ever been."

What made her happier now? The job and the band were the easy answers. I knew better than to think it had anything to do with me. "Thirty-eight years in Tucson couldn't have been all bad."

"It wasn't all bad." Michele kept her eyes leveled on the road. "The thing is, even if you don't know everything about who I was in Tucson, you know who I am now better than anyone else."

"That's not saying much." I sighed. The truth was I knew Michele well enough to realize that she was keeping something from me.

"Remember that night at the lounge when the place was packed and I had the flu? I barely stumbled off the stage in time to vomit. You found me retching behind the Dumpster and held on to me while I tried to yank out my stomach lining."

"That doesn't mean I know you better than anyone else. It means I've seen you vomit."

"You knew where to find me. And how many times have you covered me with a quilt when I fell asleep on Lynn's favorite couch after we all watched a movie together? You know what I look like when I'm sleeping on a sofa—propped up with pillows, mouth half open, maybe drooling and probably snoring. Attractive, right?" Michele laughed. "I loved the fact that you bought me a toothbrush so I could have one at your guys' place for all of the unintentional sleepovers."

"It was a multipack. I needed a new toothbrush anyway."

Michele shook her head. "And you know how I am when I first start dating someone—head in the clouds—and how much of an asshole I am when I'm ready to break up with them. Remember how I made a total fool of myself when I first met Desi?"

"Namaste," I said, bowing my head slightly and not bothering to hide the grin. "Yeah, I remember."

"We don't have to rehash that one. I'm only mentioning it now because it proves my point. You know me better than you think."

Desi and Michele's meeting was tied up in a strange mix of emotions in my memory. Lynn had tried for months to convince Michele to join her in a yoga class. She had finally succeeded after Michele had gone through a particularly rough breakup. At the yoga class, Lynn had introduced Michele to Desi, a yoga friend who was a compulsive yoga fiend. Desi apparently planned her schedule so she could make it to a class seven days a week and often wore her yoga pants to her desk job in case she could stretch during breaks. Lynn hadn't seen any of these points as deterrents and was convinced that Desi was perfect for Michele. She cajoled Michele and Desi into agreeing to a bike ride foursome. On the morning of the bike ride, I had tried to back out, but Lynn was stubborn. I wanted no part in Lynn's matchmaking where Michele was concerned. Lynn convinced me that a foursome was needed and when Michele showed up dressed in red lycra biking shorts with a matching slim-fitting bike shirt that showed off her arms, I guiltily realized that I was probably going to enjoy the ride.

As we were waiting for Desi to show up at the bike trailhead, Michele had made a big deal about how she wasn't interested in getting involved with anyone so soon after her last breakup. Then, right as Desi wheeled up behind her, Michele had added that she couldn't deal with anyone who groaned loudly throughout the yoga class and whispered "namaste" with her eyes closed and head uplifted like some sort of enlightened being. Both Lynn and I had tried to motion her to stop when she began to mimic Desi's "namaste." Michele didn't get the hint. She turned her head and spotted Desi several seconds too late. Despite this, Desi had done a good job flirting with Michele throughout their bike ride. Desi had later made a joke about enlightened yogis and Michele had blushed a lovely crimson that nearly matched her bike shirt. Within a few weeks they were together.

Michele continued, "You already know how bad my hair looks first thing in the morning. And how many times have you seen me cry? Wait, don't answer that." She waved her finger at me. "Seriously, don't answer. I don't need the reminder of how pathetic I can be. I think I've showed up on your doorstep after every one of my major breakups."

"Every two or three months."

Michele punched my arm playfully. "And you already know I don't like commitment. See? You know me well."

"You're right, I guess. If I only wanted to be your friend, all of that would be enough." I waited for a response but Michele only stared at the road, her lips tight. "So the truth is everything would be a lot easier if I didn't like you quite so much."

Michele glanced at me but quickly turned back to the road.

I sighed. "And at the moment, I'm trying not to think of all the possible reasons you wouldn't want me to be your girlfriend."

"Don't go there, Jodi. Please." Michele set her hand on my thigh. We drove for several minutes with neither of us saying anything. I wanted to reach for Michele's hand but was afraid that any movement would make her pull away.

Several minutes later Michele said, "For the record, being *just* friends with you has never been easy. If I wasn't attracted to you, a lot of things would be easier. And after seeing you naked and having my hands on you, I wasn't sure I could go back to pretending I wasn't attracted to you…I'm still working it out in my head. I don't want to think about what happens when you find your next girlfriend. It's going to suck when I know someone else has their hands on your body."

The feel of Michele's hand on my leg was enough to make me want more. I tried to block the steady string of arguments that came to mind for why we should try dating. "It can't be only the heat that keeps you away."

"From Tucson?" Michele asked. "No, but it's a good excuse. I could come up with a list of other reasons if you needed them. Have you been to Tucson?"

"I've only been as far south as Sedona. Went hiking there with a girl—long, long ago. It's a beautiful place."

Michele perked up at this. "You know, I've never heard you talk of anyone else. I've often wondered about who you dated before Lynn, but I couldn't ever ask. Was she a long-term girlfriend?"

"Eleven months. Lynn was the only one who I've ever dated longer than her though. My track record isn't as bad as yours, but I don't have any long-term relationship history."

"Did you love her—the Sedona girl?"

The question surprised me. I nodded but felt my own hesitation. "That was ten years ago…I don't now if it really was love. I was twenty-five and we had good sex. At the time, I don't think I needed anything more."

Michele shook her head. "I didn't need to know that."

I grinned. "And the trip to Sedona was nice. Beth liked it so much she left Colorado a month after we got back. I wasn't heartbroken. Our relationship had pretty much run its course." I didn't remember much about the trip. It was winter, and Beth had wanted to go to Arizona to escape the snow. We had planned to drive all the way to Phoenix but ended up staying in Sedona. It was beautiful and snowy, which I'd thought Beth would hate, but she seemed to love the snow so long as she wasn't driving to work in it. We'd spent a lot of time hiking and the rest of the time in a hot tub.

I didn't want to talk about Beth only because there wasn't a whole lot more to say. We were together for a while, and then we weren't. It was one of those relationships that was never bad but was never all that good. When Beth decided to move to Sedona, I promised to visit but I never did. She only asked once and then we went our separate ways. I realized that my relationship with Beth wasn't that atypical. The first few weeks were always a buzz of excitement. Initial feelings wore off quickly and I'd be left wondering why I'd been interested in the first place. Michele was the only one who had broken that pattern.

"So what's another reason you don't like Tucson?"

Michele took her hand off my leg and gripped the steering wheel. "Well, my older sister lives there. And no matter how hard I try to avoid it, every time I go to visit my mom, somehow my sister always drops by to tell me how my lifestyle, as she calls it, has ruined my life."

"Did I know you had a sister?"

"I think I've mentioned it. Although there have been times when I pretended she didn't exist," Michele said with a wry smile. "She's four years older than me and was engaged to some born-again Christian before I was out of middle school. My sister found religion around the same time I started dating girls. We never saw eye to eye after that."

"I've never wanted to visit Tucson anyway."

"Good. It's settled. No road trips to Tucson."

"Mom and sister are it then? No other family?"

Michele hesitated. Finally she said, "My dad moved to Florida with his new wife when I was two. They never had kids. We exchange birthday cards, but he's practically a stranger to me. He's never really been a parent. I have so few memories of him that I have to look at photos to recall his face. I've told my mom that when she met him, all she'd found was a cheap sperm donor. She didn't see the humor in that." Michele turned down the radio volume when a commercial interrupted the music. "I think I'm done talking about family. Ask me something easy."

Michele's tight grip on the steering wheel and focused gaze

on the highway made me decide not to push the subject. "Okay, favorite color?"

"Purple."

"Favorite animal?" When she paused to think, I continued, "Too hard? I'll give you an easier one." I considered all the things I'd long wondered. "Want to have a family someday?"

"Off limits."

"Wait, that's off limits? I can't ask you about animals?"

She tilted her head. "Family," she corrected. "We already said we were done with questions about family, right?"

"Well, yeah, but this is different. This is about making a family—not about the one you were born into."

Michele didn't answer.

I sighed. "And the favorite animal question is off limits too?"

"Aren't you glad we're only trying to be friends? Imagine if you were wanting to be my girlfriend!" Michele forced a laugh, but the sound of it was flat. "Sorry. Bad joke."

"Whatever." I was feeling testy now. "Okay, fine. Favorite thing to do in bed?"

"As if I'd answer that!" Michele laughed again. "Maybe I'll give you a list of things not to ask. But knowing you, eventually you would get me to talk anyway."

"Weren't you the one who said you wanted to be friends so we could be honest with each other?" I added, "But I won't ask about family or about your favorite animal. If anyone asks, though, I'm saying it's a penguin."

"How'd you guess?" Michele smiled again. "I'm a total pain in the ass, aren't I?"

"Not completely." I tried to think of another easy question. "How'd you fall in with the band?"

"Sarah's friends with Carol. You didn't know that?" Michele reached for the radio volume when a new song began. "I feel like Carol introduced me to everyone in this damn town. Who knew my straight realtor was going to help fill my social calendar? Sarah asked me to fill in one night when her last backup singer had left town unexpectedly. The girl never came back, and so I took her place. I'd never played in a real band that did gigs and actually made money. It was a huge rush the first time we were up on stage. Sarah's such an awesome singer that she makes the rest of us look good even when we screw up."

"I never even notice Sarah."

Michele smiled but quickly glanced out the window. A moment later she continued, "Being onstage, especially when we're on like we were last night, makes me think anything is possible. It was a dream of mine for so long and here I am— actually doing it. I don't have any illusions that we're going to be famous or anything. I don't need that. I do love performing though. And I've made so many friends through the band. That might be the best part."

"Yeah, friends are good." I sighed.

Michele was silent for a long minute and then finally said, "Okay, I think it's my turn to ask you a question."

"Blue. And I'm not afraid to tell you that I like gorillas."

"I already know what your favorite color is."

"How'd you know?" I asked, feigning surprise.

"ESP." Michele tapped her finger against her temple. "Seriously, you only wear blue and black."

"My favorite color could have been black. And I wear gray too."

"No one's favorite color is gray. I knew that you liked gorillas too, so I'm not giving you any credit for that one either."

I leaned across the car console and kissed Michele's cheek. It was an awkward kiss, but I was rewarded with Michele's smile. "You know what I love? And, yes, I'm changing the subject. I love that we are on our way to meet KW."

"I'm giddy." Michele bounced in her seat. "I don't think I've ever truthfully been giddy before."

"I like you giddy. You were kind of giddy last night too, though."

"No, last night I was horny. But that's why nothing happened. I want you as my friend, Jodi. Not someone I fuck around with and then have to stop talking to when things get weird."

"*Horny.*" I wished she had used almost any other word. I stared out the window, trying to push away the gloom that had caught me off guard. I hated the idea of loving someone who couldn't or wouldn't return the emotion. I pushed away these thoughts and said, "Do you think KW kept track of Alice?"

"I doubt it. What are the chances that she's kept tabs on an old flame from that long ago? Especially one who broke her heart."

"Maybe Alice was the one with the broken heart. She's the one who saved everything."

Michele pointed to the jewelry box. "If you'd read the letters, you'd find out that by the end they both had broken hearts."

"How old do you think KW is now?" I imagined the rush of emotions that KW would feel when she saw the stack of letters. If she had broken her heart sixty years ago, would Alice trigger all of that again? "Maybe she's too old to want us to be bringing all of this stuff up."

"From what I've dug up on her, which wasn't much, she was at the start of a PhD program in English when the McCarthy article came out, so likely in her early twenties. She never completed the PhD."

"That would make her in her eighties now."

Michele nodded. "But if you are asking if I think we are going to be giving some old lady a heart attack, my answer is no. My impression of KW was that she was a pretty tough cookie back then," Michele pointed again to the jewelry box, "and if she's been on a cattle ranch since, I doubt a box of letters is going to do much more than make her reach for a Kleenex. I remember my grandma saying 'the only thing I have left is memories.' In the end, I think she cherished the bad memories almost as much as the good ones. They're all part of your life." She paused and then said, "You got us off topic. I still get to ask you a question."

I wanted to ask Michele to stop the car. I wanted to give her a hug but didn't have a good reason for wanting this and doubted she would stop without a reason. I didn't have to pee and couldn't think of any other excuses to pull over. Beside that, we'd just passed an exit and the sign had warned there were no services for the next twenty miles. The highway cut a straight line through the open range with little more than shin-high grasses covering hills that rolled, one after the other, onto the next. Occasional rock outcroppings called attention to the lack of trees and marked the passing of miles more believably than the green plastic mile markers, identical in every respect save the number.

"Did you love Lynn?" Michele finally asked.

"That's your question?" I asked, stalling. I didn't want to talk about Lynn at all, but the question was also problematic. If I admitted the truth, it would only bring up the issue that we were avoiding. I'd fallen for Michele first, and Lynn never had a chance. "Why didn't I get the family question?"

"I met your mom and dad. Remember the pie? Anyway, they told me plenty."

"Yeah, I remember the pie. You ate it even though you hate bananas."

"True friend, right?"

My parents had called one evening out of the blue. They were driving through Colorado en route to New Mexico for a Fourth of July weekend with friends and had parked their RV out front of Lynn's house and were calling curbside to ask if it was okay that they drop in for a visit. It had been well over a year since I'd seen them, but my mom regularly posted online about their RV travels and I felt like I'd kept up with their route. We emailed regularly and my dad called on Sunday nights. Neither had mentioned that they were headed my way, but that wasn't unusual for them. In fact, they had made a habit of not telling me any plans when I was growing up so they wouldn't disappoint me if they changed their mind. I'd grown up expecting impromptu drives to the ocean as much as a movie night. It also wasn't unusual for them to drop in on my life unexpectedly however. I wasn't exactly surprised by their call, but they hadn't been to Colorado in years and hadn't met Lynn.

Lynn was mad that they hadn't called earlier. She said she needed advance notice for visits from in-laws. As soon as I hung up the phone, Lynn began listing her reasons for why she found the impromptu visit appalling. Her list was cut short when my mom knocked once and then let herself in the front door. Michele was over at the house for our weekly movie night and Mom instantly mistook her for Lynn. Michele didn't have a chance to correct her before Mom threw her arms around her and said, "Oh, Lynn, I'm so happy to finally meet you." She handed Michele a banana cream pie and then enthusiastically hugged her a second time. At one point or another, I guess, I had mentioned banana cream was Lynn's favorite. More surprising than their visit was that Mom had somehow remembered Lynn's favorite pie.

Michele went right along with the whole thing and Lynn, who was too pissed to correct the mistaken identity, scooted Roxanne off to bed. She disappeared to her room for the rest of the evening and was still upset the following morning. Only months later did Mom ask about the third woman in the house, the one who wasn't very sociable. I decided to let my parents believe Michele was Lynn and never did set the record straight.

"You know, Mom called a few months ago. She asked about Lynn and I mentioned that I broke up with her. She was crushed, really, and even told me that she thought I was making a mistake. She liked you a lot."

Michele laughed. "And her banana cream pie almost made me like bananas. I wish my parents were like yours. They are both so sweet, if not a bit clueless. And I did notice that you avoided my question."

"I don't want to answer that question. You got to take a pass on my first question."

"I guess I can't make you," Michele said. "But that means I can ask about something else."

"And I think I used up my one pass so you might as well make this one good." I thought of the one question I wanted Michele to ask me and it had nothing to do with Lynn. Maybe Michele wouldn't ask the question because she already knew the answer.

"Where are you taking me for dinner?"

"That's your new question?" I asked.

Michele shook her head. "No, I'm trying to think of something good to ask you, but while I figure out what that is,

I want to know what we're eating. I skipped lunch. We'll pass through Cheyenne around dinner time, if you want to stop there."

I pulled out my phone and started searching restaurants in Cheyenne. "I keep wondering things about Alice and KW. Like, did they ever go out to dinner together? Back then, could two women go out to dinner together and not draw attention to themselves?"

"You should have read all the letters, Jodi."

"I couldn't."

Michele glanced over at me. "Well, they never went anywhere together—aside from Uptown. From what I could tell, that was the only place where they thought it was safe to be seen together. Even Uptown was a big risk for Alice. But a lot of Alice's letters mentioned the places she wanted to go with KW." Michele reached for a CD case in the center console. She switched off the radio, which had started to crackle again, and inserted a CD. "Bob Dylan?"

"Sure."

Bob Dylan's harmonica hummed through the speakers. Michele turned the volume down so the words were hard to hear, but I knew the song well enough. My parents loved Dylan and I'd grown up listening to little else. I could sing along to every song, though I rarely sang unless I was alone and there was no chance I'd sing with Michele in the car.

Michele continued, "There was this one section in one of Alice's letters about how she'd gone to a grocery store and spent over an hour walking up and down the aisles, imagining what they might cook together. And she wrote a sweet passage about standing too long in front of the rows of canned soups and beginning to cry because she knew KW ate canned soup for dinner nearly every night, all alone. She went on about how, if she only could, she would have invited KW over for dinner that evening and then never let her go home to her canned soup again."

Michele sighed. "Of course, what makes it that much worse is that KW didn't know any of that. She didn't see Alice crying in the grocery store over her or know that she was daydreaming about the dinners they could have together." Michele motioned to the jewelry box at my feet. "And that one was your freebie. I'm not answering any more questions that you could figure out if you just read the rest of the letters."

Options in Cheyenne were limited, at least online, but I found a restaurant with good reviews and scanned the menu. "Do you care what type of food we eat?"

"I'd like a milkshake. Pick something low-key." Michele glanced at my phone and then turned her gaze back to the road. "Nothing fancy tonight. The milkshake isn't a must, but you get extra points if you can find a place that serves one. I'm pulling off at the next exit. It's your turn to drive."

We arrived in Cheyenne after five. I let my phone's GPS direct us to the restaurant. Michele had unlocked the jewelry box as soon as we'd changed seats and had spent the past hour leafing through the letters. I'd tried to convince her to share something more from the letters that I couldn't in good conscience read myself. Not surprisingly, Michele had refused, quietly leafing through the pages and ignoring my sporadic questions. She broke away from the letters every so often only to glance out the window at the passing landscape.

It wasn't hard to find parking at the restaurant. I got out to stretch while Michele replaced the letters and tucked the jewelry box under her seat. We headed into the diner, which according to the online reviews, had better food than atmosphere, and followed the instructions of the sign inside the door: "Take a Menu and Find a Seat. WE do the rest."

It was Monday and early for a dinner crowd but half of the tables were already filled. Michele picked out a booth with a street view, while I used the restroom, then she took her turn in the bathroom after the waitress came by with two tall glasses of water.

I stared at the menu, too hungry to be picky, and glanced around the place. The kitchen was separated from the dining tables by a half counter and there was a clear view of an overweight cook working the grill. He boasted a crisp white cap and a full gray beard. A teenage boy, wearing a similar white cap, was chopping vegetables on the counter opposite the grill. Two waitresses bused between the kitchen and the tables, and despite their workload, they didn't seem rushed. Several of the diners were alone at their tables, and only a handful of couples were present. One family with two young kids was paying their tab.

"So I'm having a hard time settling on one question to ask you," Michele said. "Can I have two?"

I smiled as Michele sat down, wishing I didn't have to hide my excitement at going out to dinner with her. This couldn't be a date, but it felt like the best date I'd ever had. "You can ask whatever you want. But I think I want to answer your earlier question first."

"About Lynn? I shouldn't have asked that. Don't tell me." Michele picked up her menu. "What are you having?"

"The burgers smell too good to pass up."

Michele agreed. "And split a shake?"

"If it's chocolate."

"Sold." She set her menu on top of mine and folded her hands. "I thought of a couple things I don't know about you. Why did you move to Colorado?"

I leaned back against the cushion. "My parents have always loved to travel. When I was in high school we took a road trip to see the Rockies and I fell in love. I figured college would be a good excuse to come back here. But as it turned out, I liked the mountains a lot more than school. I never finished my degree. I started in Boulder...was there for a year, then took a year off to travel. It was only supposed to be for a semester, but I didn't know what I wanted to do when I went back to college so I wasn't in any hurry...then I ran out of my student loans, so I decided to start back up at a junior college in Denver."

"Reality check?"

"I wish," I paused. "Reality didn't hit for another few years. My parents wanted me to skip college and get a job. Thinking back, I would have saved a lot of money if I'd taken their advice. But I met some cute girls at that junior college so it wasn't all bad..."

Michele winked. "I bet you were a player."

"No, that's never been my style."

Michele sighed. "Okay, heartbreaker?"

I laughed. "Maybe…I can think of a few. Anyway, I finished two years at the junior college and then got a full-time job to pay down the loans. I always thought I'd go back to finish my bachelor's but I never did. One job led to another…Probably I should have stayed in Oregon and gone to school at the community college near my folks' place, then transferred to Boulder, but I wanted an adventure. As it turned out, I wanted an adventure more than I wanted a college degree."

"So is that a regret?"

I shook my head. The answer wasn't entirely truthful, but I could hardly explain it to myself and didn't want to tackle this with Michele. Maybe I wished I'd finished college but that wasn't because I wanted to be able to say I had the degree. I didn't think I'd likely use what I could have learned in college in my current job either. My regret was that I had missed out on the chance to have a few more years in college. I felt like I'd missed out by not going back.

I'd had no idea what I wanted to do after college, though, and the loan debts I'd already amassed weighed heavily on every decision. A cousin in Denver had set me up with a summer job on a construction crew. It was supposed to be a temporary thing after finishing my junior college stint and before transferring back up to Boulder. Initially, they'd hired me on as a gopher and then cleanup, but I was soon doing more than running errands and sweeping. The company that had hired me for the summer kept me working full time for three years. I'd finally left for a better position on another construction crew. Soon the idea of going back to college was a distant memory.

But I didn't want to explain all of that to Michele now because I knew what she would say or guessed it anyway. She'd say it wasn't too late to go back and I knew that it was.

"I wish I had traveled in my twenties," Michele said. "Or my thirties. I've decided that I've been saving up all the destinations I've always wanted to go to for my forties."

"I like road trips," I volunteered.

"Good. I'll want company. And I'm terrible with maps."

Maps I could handle. Spending long periods of time in close quarters with Michele might be more difficult. But I'd be willing to try it…"What's the second question?"

"Why didn't you ask me out two years ago?"

I laughed. "I wasn't expecting that."

The waitress came up to our table and smiled, "Ready to order, folks?"

We ordered burgers, salads and one chocolate shake. The waitress didn't write anything down, but she went directly from our table to the kitchen counter to holler the order to the cook.

"I guess I never asked because I didn't think you would say yes. Was I wrong? Would you have said yes back then?" I waited for Michele to answer. After a moment, I picked up my glass of water and clinked it against Michele's. "Okay, never mind. I get another question now, right?"

"Not yet. I'm not quite done with this one." Michele reached for her purse and pulled out an overstuffed blue canvas wallet with frayed seams and Velcro tabs that couldn't possibly hold the thick flaps together now, if they ever once had. Michele pulled out her license, credit cards and then several business cards. She sorted through the cards until she found what she was looking for and then held the card out. "Remember this?"

"Sure, it's my old business card. How'd you get it?" I took the card from Michele and flipped it over. The backside was blank. "I don't remember ever giving it to you." I hadn't used business cards in well over a year. Once I'd hooked up with Travis, I hadn't taken many of my own jobs. I didn't have the time for more work and fortunately, he paid well enough. He also took care of all of the business aspects that I used to hate.

"I didn't get it from you." Michele took a sip of water. "You know Tina, the bartender at the lounge?"

"You got it from Tina? That must have been a long time ago." I couldn't recall when I'd given Tina the card, but I vaguely remembered her asking for a quote on a job.

"Probably two and a half years ago, give or take. It was before you started dating Lynn. You'd been in a few times and then this one night…you came in looking so good I couldn't take my eyes off you. I watched you chatting with Tina at the bar for a while after our set and I almost went over to talk to you. I was with a friend that night though, and I kept thinking, 'what happens if she just stares at me after I say hello?' Anyway, when you got up to leave I pulled Tina aside. She'd already told me your name. I wanted to know if you were single. She pulled out this card and told me to call and ask you myself." Michele took the card back and slipped it inside her wallet, along with all the others. She closed the wallet and tossed it in her purse. "Surprised?"

"Why didn't you call?"

Michele's eyes locked on mine. She seemed as if she were about to say something, but finally she shrugged and leaned back in her seat. "I don't know. I guess I've gotten braver since that night."

"So, you're saying that your braver self would ask me out now?"

"If I see a cute stranger staring at me, I might walk over and introduce myself now, yes."

"And then they get two months with you and as soon as things started to get serious, you'd break up with them, right?" I smiled. "Well, maybe I'm glad you never called then. I get more than two months as a friend. Maybe you're right after all."

Michele didn't smile. She shifted in her seat and a look of relief crossed her face when the waitress appeared with our plates.

"Enjoy. I'll bring your shake out in a few minutes," the waitress said.

I lay awake, listening to Michele's breathing. What was bothering me wasn't that I couldn't remember the name of the town where we had finally stopped or the name of the motel, though the picture of a bison on the sign was clear in my mind, but that I couldn't stop wondering about what it might be that Michele didn't want to talk about. The questions hadn't sprung to mind until after Michele had fallen asleep. Now I couldn't sleep and the red beady lights on the bedside alarm clock seemed to taunt me. I turned away from the clock, trying to ignore it, but then I was face-to-face with Michele, so I'd turned back again. It was well after midnight. I'd read somewhere that dogs could hear the ticking sound of a digital clock as the seconds clicked. Some nights I thought I could go crazy straining to hear the time pass.

Michele rolled over and draped an arm over my side. We had only gone two hours outside of Cheyenne before deciding to get a room. I hadn't wanted to let Michele go to sleep, but I also didn't want to talk anymore. I only wanted to hold her close. Her breath was warm against my neck, and I could feel her breasts brushing against my shoulder blades with each breath. She was wearing a thin T-shirt and a pair of light blue pajama pants that hung on her hips with only a drawstring tie. If I could keep her from changing out of her pajamas, I would. In real clothes, she was as unattainable as ever, but in pajamas and in this bed she was somehow mine. I knew she wanted to head out first thing to meet KW, and there was no way I was going to convince her to spend the morning in bed.

CHAPTER FIFTEEN

Michele volunteered to drive the short distance that remained to KW's ranch. The county road was paved and smooth enough that when I closed my eyes I was soon startled awake by Michele's hand.

"We're here."

I rubbed my face and sat up. We were parked next to an apple tree, heavily loaded with small green apples. Sunlight filtered through the leaves and glared against the car's windshield. It was nine, on the dot, and I was already sweaty. I unbuttoned my flannel, balled it up and tossed it into the back seat. My undershirt was wrinkled but clean enough and still smelled like laundry detergent.

Michele glanced over at me. "Were you just smelling your shirt?"

I nodded.

"You know, I'd tell you if you were stinky."

"Yes, you have before. But I already know how good I smell. Clean and fresh."

"Good. Do you mind carrying the box?" Michele motioned to the cardboard box in the back seat. "My stomach's been off since that motel coffee."

Beyond the apple tree was a corral where two horses stood, nosing the sand, a long white barn and past this, a barbed-wire fence that seemed to stretch the length of the horizon. As soon as we got out of the car a dog barked, and then several more distinct yips were added to the first call. The sound was distant and the dogs were nowhere to be seen. We ducked under the apple tree's low-hanging branches and passed a blue shed in need of a fresh coat of paint. The ranch house was a darker shade of the same blue. Michele grabbed the brass knocker and the sound, low and dull, echoed in my ears. We waited only a moment before the door swung open.

A man in his late fifties or sixties stared at us. He had blue overalls that hung loose on his thin frame and ruddy, pockmarked cheeks. "Can I help you?"

Before Michele could answer, a raspy voice behind the man called out, "Jarvis, they've come all the way from Colorado Springs to have coffee with me. Let them in, will you?"

"Colorado Springs?" Jarvis mumbled.

When Michele nodded, Jarvis stepped aside, holding the door open until we had passed, then slipped outside as if that had been his plan all along and our knock had only been a brief interruption. We stood in the entryway eyeing each other. Michele shrugged and I motioned in the direction of the voice we'd heard. She shook her head as if she didn't want to leave the small brown-tiled space filled with philodendrons on pedestals. Each plant was positioned to catch a slice of sun streaming in through the narrow windows on either side of the door. I wondered if this was KW's handiwork.

KW appeared a moment later. I was wrong, I thought instantly. I wouldn't have recognized her at all if we'd crossed paths. The face in the fifties' photograph bore little resemblance to the person who stood in front of us now. I squinted, trying to find something familiar. Wrinkles crisscrossed her skin, attesting to a long life in the Wyoming sunshine, and the years had given her deep frown lines. There was no hint of the knowing smirk that I'd fallen for when I'd first seen her photograph at Uptown. She was nearly my height but stooped some. A faded green John Deere ball cap was pulled over her silvery white ponytail and she wore the same blue overalls that Jarvis had worn.

I wasn't sure what I'd expected, seeing as how over sixty years had passed since the photograph, and I tried to push away the suspicion that heartbreak had changed her instead of time. Only her eyes, steel gray and searching, were unchanged. I focused on her eyes and wondered what reflected when she turned her gaze on me.

"You've just missed milking. The girls will all be out enjoying the pasture now. There's fresh milk if you're interested." She cleared her throat and added, "If you've never tried milk the day it squirts out of a cow's teat, you're in for a treat."

I tried not to squirm at the image. "This is a dairy farm then?"

"No, we're all about beef. But we've always kept a handful of cows for our own milk. Some of it goes as partial payment to the boys working the steers and Jarvis sells some to the neighbors. We even have a couple of family friends down in Cheyenne that get weekly orders, but we make our money on the beef. Well, come on in." KW turned and motioned for us to follow. She led us through a hallway, lined with more philodendron-laden stools and through the family room to a spacious kitchen. I glanced at the walls, half expecting yellow plaid wallpaper or maybe roses, but the walls were painted a sedate light blue. The cabinets were whitewashed wood and the floor was a well-worn speckled gray linoleum.

KW pointed to the kitchen table. "Have a seat. And you go ahead and put the box down wherever you like. Since I got off the phone with one of you, I've done nothing but think." She took out three coffee cups and filled the first, then hesitated and looked over at us. "I forgot introductions, didn't I? You know I'm Katy. And one of you is Michele?"

Michele spoke up. "Yes, I'm Michele. I'm the one who called you, and thank you for letting us drop in on you like this." She sounded nervous. She pointed to me and continued, "And this is my friend, Jodi. She's the one who found the letters."

"Sugar is on the table. I'll leave room for milk."

Katy set the three coffee cups on the table, managing all three better than I would have done. She didn't move like a woman in her eighties, I decided. She went to the fridge and pulled out a thermos, then set this on the table saying, "Today's milk." I'd half expected a metal pail. She placed a bread basket next to the milk and added, "And biscuits, of course."

The biscuits were golden brown and as big as the palm of my hand. The butter dish and a jar of jam were already on the table. My stomach churned, but I wasn't certain I was ready to eat. Michele took a biscuit but only set it on her plate and eyed me.

KW sat down finally. She drank her coffee with enough milk to turn the color light beige. I reminded myself that I needed to call her Katy, as she'd introduced herself, though in my mind she'd remain Alice's KW. She glanced at the box and then at Michele. "That's not all mail."

Katy's statement was more of a question and Michele shook her head in reply. "I'm not sure where to start." Michele glanced at me. "Maybe you should explain how you found the letters?"

The coffee smelled strong. I decided to brave the unpasteurized milk and poured a bit into my cup. I hadn't eaten or drunk anything at the motel and took a sip to chase the fog from my mind. Michele stared at me, as did Katy, and I felt a lump form in my throat. Of course, I could have spent last night's sleepless hours planning out this conversation but instead I'd thought of all the things I should say to Michele. I leveled my gaze on Katy, hoping it wasn't a mistake that we were in her life at all.

"About six months ago, I bought a house to remodel," I started. Michele cleared her throat, as if from relief that I was going to speak after all, and then suddenly I wasn't sure I knew what to say next. Where exactly, and when, had the story begun? "I remodel houses and then sell them, hopefully for a profit of course, which sometimes happens and sometimes doesn't...

"It's not that unusual to find things left behind, especially if you're buying a foreclosure to flip, but this time, well, this was different. I came across something…" I paused. Probably I should have just handed her the box and not said anything, I realized. Katy was still staring at me, and I had a sinking feeling that I was about to ruin her day.

I took a deep breath and continued, "Anyway, this time what I found was something that I wanted to give back to the rightful owner. It took us a while to track you down, but as we were driving up here, I started to doubt if we should be coming here at all. I don't know if you're going to want what I found."

I stood up and went over to where I'd set the cardboard box. I opened the box and took out the jewelry box. The key was at the bottom of the box and I reached for it, remembering the feel of the metal in my hands when I'd first slipped it out of the outlet box. I held it for a moment, wondering how Alice would have felt if she knew Katy was about to receive all of her letters. As much as I'd tried to ignore it, I'd had an eerie feeling that Alice had been in the bathroom with me the night I'd found the key. Certainly now she would have stopped my hand, I thought. Or would she after all these years? If she were alive, would she care?

I set the jewelry box in front of Katy but held onto the key. "I found this jewelry box in the kitchen. It was hidden in a cubby someone had cut into the wall. They'd hung a breadbox over the hole to conceal it. But the key," I said, setting the key on top of the jewelry box, "Alice hid that in her bathroom. I think she wanted to make sure she kept the key close to her."

"Alice?" Katy's hand came up to cover her mouth. She stared at the jewelry box as if she recognized it.

I sat down, more uncertain than ever that we should be in Katy Warren's house. Michele seemed about to say something, but she glanced over at me, biting her lip. It was quiet enough to notice the metallic tick-tock of a clock and I quickly traced the sound to an old grandfather clock on the wall opposite the table. After a long minute, Katy stood up and went to the kitchen window. The window had a white lace header with a sheer below this that did little more than blur the view outside.

The edges of the window framed a scene almost too idyllic to be real: the blue barn with a green tractor parked in front, a picnic bench shaded by another apple tree, and a stretch of closely mowed green grass.

Katy's hands shook. She gripped the edge of the sink and gazed out the window. "And you found my letters in the box then? The letters I wrote to Alice?"

"And all of the letters that she wrote back to you." I waited for my words to sink in, watching Katy closely. "I found a few other things as well. She'd saved a newspaper article and a matchbook from Uptown." I went back to the cardboard box and pulled out the picture frame, turning it around so Katy could see the photograph. "We couldn't figure out who KW was until I found you on the wall at Uptown."

"Hard to imagine why someone hung on to that picture." Katy shook her head. "Uptown was one hell of a place, back in the day. Back in my day, that is." She took a deep breath and exhaled slowly. Again, the only sound in the room was the grandfather clock's rhythmic ticking.

Finally she let go of the sink and stepped back. She looked right at me, but her gaze seemed bleary. Her thoughts were likely far from the kitchen and far from her present company. Her hands were shaking considerably more, and she clasped them together as if this might steady them. Michele shifted in her chair, and the noise seemed to focus Katy's attention.

"I'm sorry," Katy said. "You'll have to excuse me for a moment." She passed by the table but didn't look at the jewelry box or at her photograph.

After Katy had left the kitchen, Michele glanced at me. She pointed toward the front door with a questioning look on her face. I shook my head. A door creaked, and I guessed that Katy had gone to a bedroom. Several minutes passed, and Michele finally stood and walked around the kitchen. She went over to the sink where Katy had stood and pulled the sheers back to look out the window.

I took another sip of the coffee and then added more milk and a spoonful of sugar. My stomach growled. I stood up and went over to Michele. She reached for my hand.

"Maybe you were right," she whispered. "Maybe we shouldn't have come here."

I pulled her into an embrace. Michele dropped her head against my shoulder. "It's too late now. This is out of our hands."

"I should have told her over the phone," she said. "Why did we think this was a good idea?"

She pushed away from me and went over to the wall with the telephone. The phone had a long cord, coiled round itself too many times to bother untangling, and was mounted on a small shelf along with a pad of notepaper and a desk organizer. Michele found a pen and jotted a note. She ripped off the sheet and went over to the table. Katy's photograph and the jewelry box disappeared once more, inside the cardboard box. Michele closed the lid and left her note on top. She turned back to me. "I think we should go. I wrote down your number."

"Why mine?"

"Because this," Michele waved to the box, "is suddenly too much for me." She smiled, but the look on her face was pained. "And you didn't read their last few letters. Let's go."

"Don't leave," Katy said, her voice coming from the family room. "Please… Give me a moment."

There was no way I was leaving. Not now. I ignored Michele's gestures toward the door and went to find Katy. She was sitting in a faded brown recliner and staring out the window.

"Jarvis is my nephew. His son, Cody, has been staying with us for a few months now. Jarvis is trying to teach him something about horses." She pointed to the window. I could make out the profile of the man who had answered the door earlier. He was leaning against the arena gate and a horse loped in circles around a younger man standing in the center of the arena.

"Cody graduated college last year, but he has no intentions of working a real job anytime soon. I don't give Jarvis any advice on that boy. None of my business." She paused. "Cody wants to train that one. Romeo. I named him the day he shot out of his mother. That mare gave us nothing but trouble until she had Romeo. Now," she pointed to a horse tied up alongside the arena, "Miss July is sweet as can be. She needed a baby, I guess. Jarvis runs the place now, though he lets me pretend to have some say in things so I picked the sire for Miss July. He's a cutting horse from a big barn outside of Cheyenne—he's named Montague but they call him Tag. It's better than mispronouncing his real name, I guess."

"The three of you live here?" I asked.

"Cody's only visiting. He doesn't like waking up at five to start milking the cows. I know he won't stay long. Jarvis has two other boys besides Cody and they've all spent a few months working here over the years. By the time winter comes, a desk job starts to look pretty good compared to ranch work. I think that's what Jarvis is hoping, anyway.

"Once Jarvis goes, those boys will likely sell the place. There's no one else to inherit it and none of them want the burden. I can't blame them. You have to love a place like this to break your back over it. Jarvis and I thought, a while back, of turning this all into a dude ranch. We'd let a management company take over and their hired cowboys would put on a good show with the steers. But when it came right down to it, neither of us could let the place go."

"So where are all the cows?"

"We only keep our milk cows close to home. This time of day they are in the pasture behind the barn." She pointed to the barn. "Otherwise, the steers are all in the south pasture at the moment. You'll hardly see them until the boys do their roundup. We've got eight hundred acres to run and the herd has their favorite hangouts. Fortunately for us, those spots aren't close. Otherwise you'd be holding your nose."

"How long have you been here?" I had so many questions I wanted to blurt out, but I didn't want to rush Katy. Michele was watching and listening, but for some reason, she kept her distance, leaning against the counter that separated the kitchen from the family room.

"I was born here. The day I left for college, I swore I'd never be back. Dad nodded and said, 'Good luck.' I moved back home in January of 1955. My mom passed away, and then my dad needed help running things. I was only coming home for a visit..." her voice trailed. Katy cleared her throat and began again, "but I guess I needed help as much as he did. Then Dad passed away in 1960. I thought about selling then, but I didn't have anywhere else to go so I ran the place. It was just me and a handful of hired cowboys until Jarvis showed up one day. He'd remember the year, but I don't. Must have been 1981 or 82, I'd guess. My sister and I were never close so I wasn't expecting her only son to show up here asking for work. He married and moved down to Cheyenne but commuted back here every day to work. Then when his wife passed a few years back, Jarvis sold that place and moved in with me. He said I needed the help." She smiled wanly. "He's been the only thing I've ever liked that my sister had a hand in, though I guess that since she's dead now, I shouldn't say things against her."

January 1955. The newspaper article had come out September 1954 and only four months later the course of her life was completely altered. Or maybe everything had changed the moment that article was printed. I considered asking about the article but changed my mind. I was beginning to think that Katy wanted to tell her story in her own way. She didn't need to be pushed with questions, but it'd be hard waiting for the parts I wanted to hear to come out. "It's beautiful country, but I think I'd get lonely."

"The days are too busy. But some nights...Of course, I haven't always been alone." Katy glanced over at Michele and asked, "How long have you two been together?"

"We're not together," Michele said quickly.

Katy turned her gaze on me, as if searching for a reaction to Michele's statement. "I'm not sure I'll open the box," Katy said finally. "Maybe it's enough knowing that she wrote me back."

She got up out of the recliner slowly, straightening up with focused effort. "No sense sitting here while the sun's shining. The hens are waiting for me. You two might as well follow along for a bit. Stretch your legs. You've got a long drive back to the Springs."

We followed Katy out to the henhouse. The hens lived in a blue shed, identical to the one near the apple tree, except for an attached wire pen. The squawking increased as we got closer to the henhouse and silenced as soon as Katy opened the shed door. She scattered a handful of corn and a dozen hens fought over the kernels while Katy filled an egg carton with the morning's cache. Once the hens were occupied with a second handful of corn, Katy slipped out of the pen and latched the gate. "We'll go check on Jarvis and Cody next."

A cloud of dust rose up from the arena, and as we got closer, it was quickly evident that Romeo seemed to have the upper hand in his training program. The horse was furiously tearing around the arena. Cody's shoulders were slumped. Jarvis did little more than nod in our direction when we neared the fence.

"He's looking at you anyway," Katy said.

Cody looked over at the gate, quickly realizing he now had an audience. "That's about all he's done. Well, that and run."

"That's a good start. You want him to pay attention to you. If they ignore you entirely, you're in for a hell of a ride."

"We left him out in pasture too long," Jarvis said.

"He's three years old. That's not too long." Katy shot back. "We gave him time to be a colt. They need to learn to love it here."

"Oh, he loves it all right," Jarvis countered. "He loves to run and he's used to getting away with it."

Katy nodded. "Good. We want him to love running. He's used to outrunning everyone. You came along and he met someone he can't outrun. But give him a break. He's still trying to figure out if you're gonna kill him." The horse interrupted her words with a loud nicker. Katy continued, "He's calling for help, boys. You need to wait for him to realize that killing him isn't part of your plan." Katy watched the horse closely, the faint lines of a smile pulling at her lips. She pointed over to the mare tied up on the opposite side of the arena. "Mom's worried about her boy."

"She looks so calm compared to him," I said.

"You should have seen her when I first brought her in from pasture. I've never had a horse that I thought was going to kill me, until her." She turned to me and smiled. Her face was suddenly the same one in the photograph. "I always fall in love with the wrong girls. Horses and women." Katy laughed. "By now, you'd think I would have learned better. But I can't help it. We never can, can we?"

I noticed Katy's subtle nod at Michele. Michele was staring at the mountains in the distance.

Katy continued, "I decided to do things different with Miss July. With her, I knew I couldn't rush things like you can with some of the horses. Took me a good long while to get her to trust me and I didn't want to spoil that." She pointed to the barn and then headed that way.

I tapped Michele on the shoulder and followed behind Katy. She opened the door of the barn and waited for Michele, who lagged a few feet behind. The barn was dimly lit, and it took a moment to adjust from the glaring sunshine outside.

Katy saw me standing still and said, "You'll get used to the smell after a minute or two."

The smell wasn't awful. Manure and urine were notable but so was the sweet smell of grain, and the hay overwhelmed the other smells as we passed stacks that towered up to the rafters.

Katy paused in front of the first stall. "We had a new arrival yesterday." She waited for us to peek over the top rails of the stall. A foal stood on wobbly legs, pressing his muzzle against his mother's side. "This one is Jarvis's favorite, but I named her, way back. Allie. You can guess who she's named after." Katy smiled wryly and turned to continue the tour. She paused at a few of the other stalls, remarking about the horses in each, and then came to stop at the last stall. She sighed and leaned against the stall door. Michele was a few stalls back, after lagging behind to watch the newborn foal. The stall where Katy paused was empty and the rubber mats inside were scrubbed clean. She pointed to the corner of the stall, under the feed rack. "One of the barn cats. Can you see her babies?"

I peeked through the rails, finally spotting a gray cat with two orange balls of fur and two gray balls of fur nestled against her belly. Michele came to stand next to me. She stepped up on the rails and smiled as soon as she spied the kittens.

"How old?"

"Two weeks, give or take."

Michele pressed her face against the rails again. I glanced over at Katy and something unspoken passed between us. Maybe I'd spent too long getting acquainted through the black and white portrait I'd kept in the bathroom or maybe we would have had a connection anyway. Katy felt like an old friend.

"Sometimes I think Alice knew all along," Katy said. Her gaze had turned to the mama cat and her kittens. She clicked her tongue and the mama cat meowed in response. "She's my best mouser."

"Knew what?" I asked.

"That I waited." Katy stared at me. Her gray eyes were moist. She cleared her throat. "One of her kids mailed me her obituary. Apparently it was in her will to let me know that she'd passed. No word from her for sixty years and then only a clipping from their local paper…The same day I got her obituary I stopped playing the piano. I'm old enough to claim it's the arthritis. Now the piano is out of tune anyway."

CHAPTER SIXTEEN

The drive home had been quiet. On my end, it wasn't because there was nothing left to talk about but because there was too much. Maybe Michele felt the same, but I didn't ask. She seemed occupied with her own thoughts and I didn't try to interrupt.

By the time we pulled on to Granite Avenue, I was certain that she was going to drop me off with little more than a goodbye wave. Instead, she parked and got out of the car, heading toward my front door without even checking to make sure I was following. She paused at the porch swing and waited for me to unlock the door, then walked inside, glancing around until her eyes settled on the guitar case. My heart sank when I realized that was all she was after.

"Well…" I couldn't think of anything to keep her from leaving.

She met my eyes and then looked down at the guitar case. "Well," she said, as if this was enough of an answer. She seemed to change her mind about leaving and took a seat on the bottom step of the staircase. She popped open the case and stared at the guitar. Finally she took it out and ducked her head and one arm through the strap. She shifted back against the stairs and looked up at me.

"You know that song about the cowboy who gambles away his money?"

"And the farm girl marries someone else because he doesn't come back for her," I said, nodding.

"It wasn't that Sarah wanted to sing lead on that song. She tried to convince me to sing lead, like we'd planned, but I chickened out at the last minute." Michele sighed. She strummed her red guitar pick across the strings. "There are so many things I want to tell you."

"That sounds like the first line of a song."

"I can't write songs." Michele shook her head. She played another chord and then began a song, not the one about the cowboy, but another country piece about a lost love. She followed this one with a Dylan song I knew well but had never heard her sing. When she finished, she set the guitar back in the case and started to close the latches.

"Can I make a request?"

She tilted her head, considering. "Maybe."

I was nervous about asking. After years of watching her play, I'd never once asked for a song. Most of the time I'd been happy to sit transfixed by the music, transfixed by the image of her fingers pressing the strings, transfixed by the movements of her body as the music carried her along, eyes closed and head tilted up when she reached for a high note, chin dropping with the low notes.

"First time I heard you sing 'Have You Ever Seen the Rain,' I thought, 'Damn, I'll never be able to listen to Creedence Clearwater again.' Your version was better, but it wasn't only that." I paused. Michele had picked up her guitar again, but she gazed out the window, eyes unfocused. "I'd never really listened to the words before, I guess. Somehow you changed what I thought that song always meant."

"What'd you think it meant?"

I shrugged. "Getting what you want—rain on a hot day?"

Michele slung the guitar strap on again and shifted her knee to balance the guitar. She looked right at me when she started to play. I could hardly hear the words this time. I watched her lips and knew the sound of her voice was filling the room, but a warmth swept over me and the only thing I could think of was how I wanted to stay in that moment. I'd picked a short song and the room fell suddenly silent. When it was over, she sang a Dixie Chicks song that I recognized but didn't know well, and then "Wagon Wheel"—which had been one of Roxanne's favorites to sing along with whenever Michele brought out her guitar. She ended "Wagon Wheel" and placed the guitar in the case without looking up at me. She latched the case and stood up.

We stared at each other for a long minute, and I wondered what I could say to make her stay. No words came to mind. I'd been leaning against the wall in the living room and the music or the long drive or a combination of both had paralyzed me in place. When she finally headed for the door, I reached out and caught her arm like a fish going for a hook with no thought involved. She glanced down at my hand, and I involuntarily released her.

"I'm tired and hungry."

"So am I. There's a restaurant we can walk to." I paused. "It's not far and they have half-priced tapas until five. We can talk."

She sighed. "I have to work tomorrow."

I watched her head for the door and didn't try to stop her a second time. The door closed behind her, and I leaned back against the wall, staring at the spot on the stairs where she'd been only minutes before. I knew there was no point in trying to hold her.

CHAPTER SEVENTEEN

If Molly had given me her phone number, I'd have called and canceled our date. A thousand excuses came to mind—and of course, there was always the truth. I was into someone else. Did it matter that that someone wasn't into me? Anyway, I didn't have Molly's phone number. I had her address on a crumpled napkin that I found Saturday morning in the front pocket of my cargo pants. Laundry day.

Molly lived on the west side of town one block up from Colorado Avenue. I'd rented a basement apartment on the west side years ago and the streets were all familiar. It didn't take long to find her place. She was sitting on her front porch wearing a cowboy hat and a red scoop neck top that showed off her curves. Since I'd only always seen her with the café apron on, I hadn't appreciated her figure before.

Molly greeted me with a big smile. She was beautiful—no wonder I'd flirted with her for so long. Why had I wanted to call this off? I'd clearly been distracted the past week. I was lucky to be going on a date with her.

When I'd climbed the last step up to her porch, she asked, "How attached are you to wine tasting?"

"Not at all."

"Good."

She stood up and caught my hand. I wasn't expecting it and felt a rush with her touch. *Relax*, I chided myself. *She's only holding your hand*. But she didn't let go. And the rush didn't let up. She led me back down the porch steps and across the street toward Colorado Avenue. The evening was warm and the sidewalk on the main thoroughfare was filled with people meandering in and out of shops and restaurants.

We crossed Colorado Avenue and then Molly led me down an alleyway. We passed along the side of an antique shop with crates piled up in the alley. Molly knocked on a back door.

I didn't have time to wonder what she was getting us into. The door popped open and an older man stepped forward, his arms piled high with broken-down boxes. We stepped out of his way, and he went to the Dumpster with his load, then turned around and considered us.

He glanced at his watch. "You've got an hour," he said brusquely. "I'm closing the shop at eight."

Molly didn't waste time with introductions. The man had already headed back inside, disappearing down a dark hallway lined with boxes. Molly followed and I had no choice but to do the same. The hallway opened up to a storage room with furniture and boxes stacked in a matrix of layers that touched the ceiling at points. A narrow path zigzagged from one end of the room to the other. All of the items were tagged with either orange or blue stickers but no prices.

"Roberto lets me scope out his estate sales before anything makes it to the front room. Tomorrow he'll have an agent come through and price everything. After that, Roberto decides what items he can get more money for online...and after a few weeks, all of this will slowly filter to the front where ordinary customers will see it for the first time. But tonight," she said, glancing around the room, "we have first dibs."

Molly opened a box and scanned through the contents, then quickly moved to the next box in the line. I walked around the room, checking out the furniture, most of it high quality and solid wood, the framed pictures leaning against the back wall and then the odd assortment of statues, vases and dishware. As much as I liked old houses and old furniture, I'd never had a budget for antiques. Without prices, I had no idea how much some of the items would go for.

I walked back over to where Molly stood hunched over a box. She saw me and grinned, then held up an old camera. She spun a dial on the top edge of the Kodak, aimed the lens at me and then snapped a shot.

"Often I'll find old film in these cameras. I always develop it but mostly it's a waste of time. The images faded long ago… but sometimes I get lucky." Molly rummaged through the box more and found an old video camera. She popped the side open, checking for a cassette. It was empty. She set the video camera back in the box and closed it. The Kodak she'd kept out. "I used to go to garage sales, but I start my shift at five a.m., so I was always missing the good stuff. Roberto makes my treasure hunting a lot easier."

When she opened the next box, I couldn't help but reach past her for the item on top. It was a jewelry box—almost identical to Alice's—but in bad shape. The carved flowers on the lid were chipped and a fine split ran along the length of the backside. The hinges were brass, like Alice's box, but one had been broken and then hammered back in place. Clearly someone had cracked this box open. It was unlocked now and empty, save for a few pennies that rattled at the bottom.

Molly was watching me. She smiled when I met her gaze. "Everyone always finds something they want."

"I wasn't looking for anything."

"But then it finds you," Molly said. She smiled.

I'd appreciated her smile many times at the café. And this time I knew she wasn't flirting to get a better tip. Somehow, though, the smile and the look that accompanied it brought on a stab of guilt. What was I doing on a date with her? Who was I trying to fool?

Roberto suddenly appeared. "My wife wants me home. I forgot we're having her folks over tonight. I'm going to lock up the front." He paused, eyeing the jewelry box in my hands. "That one isn't for sale yet."

"Why not?" Molly asked.

"I have someone who wants to look at all the jewelry boxes I find before I put them up front, a collector."

"And you have someone who always wants first dibs on the cameras." Molly sighed resignedly and held up the Kodak camera. "How much for this one?"

"Ten. Pay me next time you come by." Roberto stepped out of the room as quickly as he'd appeared.

"Sorry about the jewelry box," Molly said.

I shrugged. "Wasn't meant to be mine." *Like so many things*, I thought.

After the antique shop, Molly suggested a drink. She was still in the mood for wine, but she didn't want to try out the new place. When she pointed out that West Side Winery was only one block away, I didn't argue. West Side Winery was where Sarah worked, but I doubted I'd see her.

I'd forgotten that there was only a half-wall partition between the seating area and the grill. Naturally, Sarah was standing there, wearing her chef's hat and a crisp white jacket, and happened to glance at the door right as we walked in. I didn't know her well enough for her to come out of the kitchen to chat with us, fortunately. I wasn't sure she'd even remember who I was, and if she did, I doubted she'd mention anything to Michele. But if she did, would it matter anyway?

After our wine and cheese platter arrived, I didn't think of Sarah or Michele for the rest of the evening. Molly kept my attention. We polished off the crackers and cheese along with a bottle of wine and I hardly realized the time that passed.

We people-watched on our slow walk back to Molly's apartment, then paused to window shop at the same antique shop we'd been in earlier. There were music boxes and other jewelry boxes on display in the front window, but none of them reminded me of Alice's box.

Molly decided I wasn't sober enough to drive for a while and invited me up to her tiny apartment. The place was crammed with an odd assortment of antique furniture. She had more than her fair share of lamps, though she only turned one on. I counted five end tables that shared space in the small family room with two coffee tables and one sofa.

She set the Kodak from tonight's quest on a desk crowded with other vintage cameras. When I wondered aloud about the pictures the old cameras had taken, she pulled out a thick photo album and we spent the next hour going through strangers' snapshots. I thought of Katy Warren's picture at Uptown and then again of Alice's jewelry box and the duplicate from the estate sale, but I didn't say anything to Molly. Maybe later. Maybe it would never be a story I could share. Maybe it wasn't my story at all.

I took the long way home, driving past the street where my old apartment had been and idling on the quiet street for several minutes only to stare at my old front door. I'd been single the entire year I'd lived on 27th Street, but for some reason being alone hadn't bothered me as much then as it did now.

By the time I finally had showered and climbed into bed, it was two in the morning. Molly had given me her phone number. She'd programmed it in my phone so, she'd said, I'd have no excuse for not calling her. I fell asleep thinking of Molly, not Michele.

CHAPTER EIGHTEEN

"I'm calling for an appraisal," Carol said.

I set my microwaved dinner on the new granite countertop and went to the sink to wash a fork. I hadn't expected Carol to drop in, but unexpected visits were something I'd learned to accept as part of being friends with her. In many ways, Carol reminded me of my mom, though I'd never admit as much to her.

"There's no reason to wait," Carol continued. "The place looks great. Everything else that you need to do is touch-up stuff."

"I still have the hall bathroom to get to—that's more than just touch-up." I had managed to get the kitchen mostly finished. The cabinets were in place by the time the granite was delivered, and I had the new sink and faucet installed shortly after. Unfortunately, the stove was held up in the warehouse and I still had to paint, but aside from that, the kitchen was done. "Give me until after the holidays. I'll have everything finished by then. There's no rush to list the place now. I don't want to move before the first of the year anyway."

"Well, if it takes a few months to move, you're going to regret waiting."

"And you'll be there to tell me 'I told you so.'" I smiled.

She smirked back at me. "I could save you the wait and tell you now. The appraisal is only going to give us a ballpark number so we can get clients interested. In a week you'll have the kitchen finished. The appraiser can imagine what that half bath will look like with a face-lift." Carol waved her hand when I tried to argue. "One week. I don't want you pouring any more money into this place. I know what your budget looked like when you started and I have a good feeling you're over it."

"Don't remind me." I sighed. The last thing I wanted to think about was how far off I was from my initial estimate for the remodel. It wasn't even close to the amount I'd put into the place so far. Still, I was certain I'd get it all out in the end and then some. "What's your other reason for the rush? I doubt you're really worried about my checkbook balancing. Has Michele been asking about it?"

Four weeks had passed since the trip to Wyoming. I'd gotten one text from Michele since. It had been a request for "some time to figure things out." I didn't ask what she needed to figure out. Now that the college semester had begun, I knew work was going to be enough of a distraction that she wouldn't need to think of much else, but I'd hoped for a call or a text at least.

After the first week, it had been hard not calling and I'd come up with many excuses to talk. But I'd stubbornly waited. Four weeks of waiting and I had faced up to the reality that Michele didn't need my company as much as I wanted hers. Fortunately I had a distraction. Molly. Still, I thought of Michele all too often. Working on a friendship with her was going to be tricky. But Michele had never been easy.

I also hadn't heard from Katy, but I wasn't expecting to hear anything unless she finally got around to opening the jewelry box. Even then, she might not call. Before we'd left the ranch, Katy had given us both an invitation to come back for Thanksgiving. Aside from the hens, there was a good-sized turkey in the henhouse that she had named Mister November.

Katy had pointed Mister November out to us as we were getting in Michele's car. He was pecking the weeds along with the chickens and seemed much too happy a creature to ever roast in an oven. I didn't have any grounds for comparison, but he looked huge. I wondered how much more weight the bird would put on and doubted I'd be able to eat a named turkey that I'd met. But I was still considering Katy's offer. Michele would be with Lynn and Roxanne in California, and the idea of escaping to the ranch to avoid thinking of California was appealing.

"I haven't shown any properties to Desi or Michele for a while now. In fact, I'm beginning to wonder if they've decided to stay in the condo after all. But I have someone else interested. He's only looking at houses in this neighborhood and there isn't a lot on the market. I drove him by the other day and he wants a look inside. If he likes it, we don't want to lose him. He's a cash buyer and is ready to pay top dollar."

"I wouldn't offer it to some stranger over Michele."

Maybe I had become too attached to the house. Carol's arched eyebrows confirmed that she suspected as much. Or maybe I was holding out for a different reason.

"I'm not going to tell you that a house flip is a business transaction, not a labor of love, because I know you already know that."

"I know. But there's something about this place. If Michele was interested, I'd lose money on the deal to make the sale happen."

"You'd be losing money for Desi's sake, not Michele's. Desi's the one who's putting down all the money. Michele's only her roommate." Carol paused and squinted at me. "Is there something going on with you and Michele?"

"No," I answered. My response was too quick. Carol shot me back a smug look. "There's nothing going on." For better or worse, it was mostly true.

"Okay, fine. But if there was nothing to talk about, why'd you blush when I asked?"

"I don't know." I stared at Carol. It would be a relief to tell her how much I wished something was going on between

Michele and me and for exactly how long I'd been wishing, but I managed to keep my mouth shut.

"I had lunch with Michele a few weeks ago. She acted funny when I brought up your name."

"What do you mean?"

"I joked that we needed to set you up on a blind date to get you out on the dating scene again. She told me you could take care of yourself and got pretty annoyed when I suggested otherwise."

"You don't think I can find a date?"

"When do you go out, Jodi?"

Pretty often, as of late, I thought. But I didn't want to tell Carol about Molly. Not yet. I knew Carol would tell Michele. Maybe Sarah had mentioned that she'd seen me at the winery. With a date. Maybe that was why Michele had been curt with Carol… Part of me wished that Michele knew I was dating Molly at least so she wouldn't think I was staying home pining for her.

I waved to the empty space where the new stove would stand when it finally arrived. "Maybe I have better things to spend my time and money on at the moment."

"Better things? I think you try very hard to make sure you don't have even a spare moment to consider the fact that you haven't been out on a date since Lynn left."

"Lynn has nothing to do with it. I've gone on dates since Lynn."

"But there's no one serious."

I couldn't argue with her. As much as I had enjoyed my last few dates with Molly, we still hadn't done anything more than kiss. Kissing was nice…but I couldn't sleep with her while I was still holding out for Michele. I wouldn't do that to her.

Carol tapped her painted fingernails against the granite counter. She stared at me. "How long have you been waiting?"

"For what?"

"For Michele. I'm not dense."

"Too long. I think I've given up." Not admitting the truth was exhausting, and I knew Carol would see through all of my excuses. She had her ways of weaseling information out of me.

"Then give your next date a real chance. I hate to say it, but I don't think Michele even wants a relationship." Carol's look bordered on pity. "And she doesn't know what a good thing she's passing up with you. I said as much to Lynn when I first heard about Sal's promotion. I know it's no comfort, but in my opinion, Lynn should have picked you, sweetie, a hundred times over." She reached for her cell phone. "I'm calling for an appraisal. I think you need to move on."

"Move on? Are you talking about the house or Michele?"

"Maybe both." She sighed. "I'll tell the appraiser to schedule you for next week."

"No. I need another two months at least. I'll be ready to list the first of the year."

"You're going to lose the client I have right now. And you're going to be in even more debt."

"I don't care. I'm not rushing this house. I want this place to be perfect when I turn the key that last time."

She threw up her hands. I didn't follow her to the front door. She had let herself in, calling my name as she opened the screen door, and she could let herself out. The microwaved pasta dinner was decidedly less appealing now that it had cooled to room temperature. I turned up the volume on the radio and then went to my usual spot on the sofa. I picked at the food, listening to the news and wishing for a big screen television and a movie rental. We had finally finished the basement remodel job, but it was several weeks too late for the bonus. Still, Travis had decided that we needed a day off to celebrate. I had to remind him that the next day was Saturday anyhow.

The screen door creaked, and I expected Carol's voice. She'd only been gone fifteen minutes. Enough time to go home and realize she'd forgotten something. I glanced at the entryway, ready to ask what it was she'd left behind, but Michele stood in the doorway. She was dressed in her librarian's attire, a blue silk blouse tucked into a gray patterned skirt, and she held her purse as if she wasn't certain if she should set it down or keep it in her hand in case she wouldn't be staying long.

"Hi," I said. "I guess it's visiting day in the neighborhood. Did you and Carol both get a memo?"

"She sent me a text. I was waiting for an excuse."

"She sent a text telling you to come see me?"

"Not exactly." Michele's expression was hard to read. "Can I close this?" she asked, reaching for the door handle. "The wind's picking up."

"Sure. Summer's gone, I guess." I set the dinner plate on the floor and started to stand up, but Michele came over to the sofa and took a seat a good foot away from me. I wanted to reach for her, but I wasn't certain she would welcome the touch. She kept her purse in her lap and stared at my dinner.

"Have you eaten? I can make you something. Not this," I said, motioning to the pasta. "It was barely edible warm. And now it's cold."

Michele shook her head. Finally she set her purse down and shifted back against the pillows. "I should have called to tell you I was coming."

"You know you don't need to call. It's always good to see you."

She attempted a smile. "So you aren't upset that I showed up unexpectedly after not talking to you for nearly four weeks?"

"I figured you had your reasons. You told me to give you some time."

"I wanted to call."

"What would you have said?"

"Sorry?" Michele didn't look at me. After a moment, she stood up. "I have to pee." She stared at me for a long minute, seemingly about to say something, but then turned and went to the hall bathroom. I listened for the door to creak as it closed and then waited for the sound of the fanlight. I needed to replace it. A minute later the toilet flushed. The fan switched off, but Michele stayed in the bathroom. The only sound came from the radio on the windowsill.

I hadn't yet remodeled even one part of the hall bathroom. It was the last place where the old wallpaper remained and I wasn't ready to rip it off the wall. After a minute passed, I went over to turn off the radio, annoyed by the sound of the DJ's familiar voice. I stared at the bathroom door, wondering at Michele's thoughts, and then went to lean against the doorframe. I wanted to open the door, wanted to pull Michele into a tight embrace, wanted to say that we could fix whatever had gone wrong.

"I'm going to replace that fan," I said. A moment later, I added, "I hate noisy fans. But I wish I could leave the wallpaper in there. Carol would probably kill me if I did." I chuckled. "But she doesn't know the story. Even if she did, I bet she'd tell me it's time to move on. I can't bring myself to rip it off yet. Did you notice the light switch cover?"

There was no window in the bathroom, and I knew Michele was now in near complete darkness. I also knew that for some reason Michele wanted the darkness.

"It's the same cover as the ones upstairs. And the wallpaper matched the old stuff in the kitchen. I keep wondering if there's yellow plaid wallpaper underneath."

Michele was still silent.

"I lied to you earlier. You asked if I was upset. I was." I waited, straining to hear a response from Michele. "If we are supposed to be friends, why wait four weeks? I figured you were making me wait in the hopes that I'd stop liking you. The more I thought about that, I did kind of like you less. So if that was your plan, it almost worked."

I sat down on the floor with my back against the door.

"I don't like pretending I'm happy when I'm not. I wanted to call someone and complain, but I don't have anyone to call. Pathetic, right? Carol was here earlier, you know, and I guess I could have called her. But I didn't. I kind of mentioned that I have this thing for you, *had* this thing, I guess I should say... She basically told me to move on—that you weren't interested in relationships. I wanted to tell her she had you all wrong but I couldn't." I sighed. "These past few months have been such a fucking roller coaster."

I closed my eyes. I didn't mind that she kept the door closed. It was easier talking to her without her looking right at me. I could imagine I was only thinking out loud and that she wasn't even listening.

"These weeks that go by when we don't see each other...I feel like I'm sick, but there's nothing wrong with me, and then when you come back again I'm so happy that I almost forget you don't actually want to be with me." I paused. I pressed my ear against the door, listening. Michele's side was still quiet. "Sometimes I don't know if you're only playing a game or if you are more messed up in the head than I ever realized. Where'd we leave off?"

"I don't even know where to start," Michele finally said. After a pause, she continued, "Mostly I think about you at night...I can't sleep. I don't like falling asleep alone. Some nights are harder than others, and I'll pick up the phone to call you and say that I want to come over—I want to hold you while I fall asleep—but then I don't call. Because Carol's right."

"Right about what?"

"We shouldn't date."

"Carol said that? Carol needs to mind her own business," I argued.

"She didn't say that in so many words. But the truth is, we make good friends. Why screw it up?"

"Because it's fun and we both want it?" I hoped this much was true and was willing to gamble it.

"You just finished explaining how I make you feel like shit when I check out. I don't want to take advantage of you."

"Take advantage of me?" I laughed. "You know I'd be fine with that."

"Take advantage of your *friendship*, Jodi. And maybe you'd be fine with it tonight, but how would you feel tomorrow?"

There was no joking tone in her voice. The truth was, I'd feel like shit in the morning. She knew it. I knew it.

"So why did you say that you needed time? Time for what? If you only wanted an occasional fuck buddy or someone to fall asleep with, why did you need a month away?"

"I knew you weren't ready for that."

Of course she knew that. I cursed silently. "Maybe I'm ready now."

"Maybe. That's why I waited."

"In my head, your answer was better," I admitted. "In my head, you needed time to decide if we could be more than friends. But don't worry. I didn't actually think that you'd ever say that." I rapped my knuckles against the door. "Why are you still in there?"

"Come in, it's not locked."

I pushed open the door. Michele was sitting on the counter by the sink, her feet dangling above the linoleum.

"We haven't even hugged. Weren't you the one who said friends hug?"

Michele shrugged. "Maybe we're not ready for being the type of friends who hug."

"Screw that. If I have to settle for being friends, I want a damn hug."

"Settle?" She shook her head. "I wouldn't let you settle with me."

"Now you're going to tell me what to do?" I wanted to swear, but I held back the words. Swearing would be a cop-out. Suddenly I wanted to close the bathroom door. It was easier admitting how I felt without seeing her response.

"Sarah told me she saw you at the winery. I'm glad you're dating again. I was starting to worry about you. It's been a long time since your breakup with Lynn…"

My jaw clenched. Well, at least everything was out in the open now. "Molly's nice. She works at the coffee shop I go to…I like her," I paused. "But I feel guilty dating her when I'd rather be dating someone else."

"You don't want to date me, Jodi."

I opened my mouth to tell her exactly how wrong she was, but she held up her hand before I could say anything.

"You want someone who is ready for a serious relationship. You want a commitment." She sighed. "Hell, Jodi, you want a minivan and kids."

"I don't want a minivan. Or kids. And I don't need a commitment," I countered.

I thought of Molly. It was impossible not to. On our last date she told me she wanted a minivan. We'd laughed about it, but I could tell she was serious. She wanted a minivan and kids. She even wanted to coach her future kids' soccer practices. But it was more than funny. It was sweet. And maybe I could want that too, though at the moment I didn't. I wanted Michele. Period. In whatever package she came in, including no commitment, no minivan, no kids, no soccer practices.

"Maybe you should stop thinking you know what I want. Maybe you don't know me that well." I paused. "Maybe I only want to date you. I never said I wanted to get married to anyone. Maybe I'd only date you for two months and then leave you for some other cute girl that shows up onstage at the Metro. I could be the one who finally breaks up with you. Maybe you could use that first."

"You wouldn't be my first." Michele hopped off the bathroom counter. "Not even my second or third." She turned on the faucet and washed her hands, then splashed water on her face. She toweled off quickly and headed through the doorway. I reached for her hand, stopping her. Michele stared down at me. Her eyes were moist.

I stood up and waited for her, half expecting that she'd hug me. She shook her head and looked at the ground. I touched her hand and then stepped closer. Her fingers entwined in mine, and she looked up at me waiting. I couldn't resist kissing her. She moved into me and returned the kiss. I had to pull away when her lips parted. I wasn't certain I was ready for what my body wanted. I was certain, however, that Michele's body wanted the same thing. I brushed my hand across her cheek, then caressed from her neck down to her shoulder, feeling her relax with the touch. "Screw being friends. Let's go upstairs."

Michele closed her eyes. "I came here tonight because I wanted to talk to you, not because I wanted to sleep with you."

"Okay. No sleeping." I waited for Michele to counter my sarcasm. It didn't happen. "But I don't entirely believe you. I think maybe you're saying you want to be friends because it's a nice cover. I think you want more and you're scared of what happens next if things go well. Tell me if I'm wrong."

"It's not a cover." She sighed. "I don't think it's a good idea."

"I think you overthink things." I waited for a response, but Michele was silent. "I'm going to toss the dinner I didn't eat and go upstairs and shower. If you need to leave, fine. If you want to stay, you're welcome to stay. But I want to lie down. I'm beat."

I went over to the sofa and picked up the unfinished dinner tray, then headed to the kitchen without looking back at Michele. I dumped the cold pasta in the trash and then got out a box of cookies. After two cookies I finished the meal with a sip of milk straight from the jug and then headed back to the living room. Michele wasn't there, but her purse was still on the sofa. I headed upstairs and found her lying on my bed on top of the comforter. Her clothes were still on. She was lying on her side, facing the sliding glass door, and I couldn't see if her eyes were opened or closed. I started to say her name but stopped before the sound left my lips. What could I say that would change her mind? I took off my clothes and headed for the shower.

When I returned to the bedroom to fish out a pair of boxer shorts and a T-shirt from the closet, Michele hadn't moved from her spot on the bed. Her even breathing made me think she'd already fallen asleep. I slipped into bed alongside her, careful that I didn't brush against her. It was only nine, but I'd had a long day. If she wasn't ready to talk or do anything else for that matter, I didn't want to be awake anymore. I wondered what Michele had to say, but by her somber tone when she'd mentioned it, I doubted it was anything I'd really want to hear. For the moment, I was content to lie in bed next to her.

I awoke to the feeling of Michele slipping under the sheets. The room was dark, and I didn't have my phone to check the time, but I guessed it was after midnight. Michele's arm wrapped around me and I felt her lips press against my shoulder. She was either stealing a kiss while she thought I was asleep or she was trying to wake me. I lay still for a moment, listening to her. Even through my T-shirt I could feel her chilled skin. I rolled over and pulled her close to me.

"I should have covered you. You're freezing."

"You fell asleep so fast," Michele said. "I didn't want to wake you. I tried to keep still." She shifted closer to me. "But you were so warm. I couldn't resist. Don't worry, I'm still dressed."

"I'm not the one who was worried about us being in bed together." I kissed her and felt the hesitation in her response. "Tell me if I shouldn't kiss you again."

She placed one finger against my lips and then rolled onto her back, away from me. I waited several minutes, knowing she wasn't asleep but clueless as to what she wanted. Finally, I climbed on top of her. She wrapped her arms around me, holding me tight against her but didn't make any move suggesting she wanted more. Sometime later, she relaxed and I rolled off her. I didn't remember falling back to sleep, but I awoke to the feel of her body slipping away from me. I watched her climb out of bed, still dressed in the same clothes she'd been in last night. Sunlight was pouring through the sliding glass door.

I reached for her, but she only glanced back at me and then turned to go out to the balcony. The ends of her hair, lightened by the past summer's sun, caught the morning light. She reached her hands skyward, then let them fall to her sides in a slow arc. She repeated the movements a few times and then gripped the railing and leaned over the edge. When she straightened again, she glanced back at me.

"You're a sound sleeper."

"Did I snore?" I asked.

"No." She had moved away from the railing and now leaned against the doorframe, half inside and half on the balcony. "You lie so still—like nothing's troubling your mind."

"I have plenty of things to worry about, but by the end of a workday I'm too tired not to sleep. You have trouble sleeping?"

She nodded. "I don't know if I blame my conscience or too much caffeine. Probably it's both." She came inside and sat down on the bed. "Some days I feel so alone. It didn't hit me until after you and Lynn broke up. I have this whole busy life with work and friends, plenty of distractions, but then when you guys broke up, I realized most people I'm friends with hardly know me at all…"

"So let me in." I reached for her again, but she crossed her arms and looked out the sliding glass door.

"I came here last night to talk to you. There's things I want to say, things I need to tell you…but somehow I can't."

I waited for her to continue but she didn't. Finally, I said, "I'm breaking things off with Molly."

She shook her head. "I don't think you should. You need someone, Jodi. You haven't been happy since you broke up with Lynn…"

I wasn't happy before I broke up with Lynn either, I thought.

Michele continued, "You like her and she's nice—that's what you said last night. Why break it off?"

"Because she's nice and…" *And I'm stuck on someone else*, I finished. "Maybe someday I'll be able to date someone like her, but right now I'm too complicated."

Michele sighed. "I shouldn't have stayed last night. I promise I won't crash in your bed again." She glanced at her watch and then stood up. "And I'm going to be late for work."

Once Michele had left, I crawled back in bed and pulled the covers over my head. I lay there for several minutes until I knew that what needed to be done couldn't wait another day. I had to go to the coffee shop. I couldn't break up with Molly over the phone. It had to be in person. Regardless of what my head told me I ought to do, sleeping next to Michele had felt too right.

CHAPTER NINETEEN

Molly let me go almost too nicely. I stood on the other side of her counter admitting I wasn't there to buy coffee and that we needed to talk. She let me talk and no one came up to the counter to buy anything. When I'd said what I'd planned out, she'd brushed her hand over mine and said that she'd guessed it all along. She even asked if the one I was still stuck on was the same person that had been in the coffee shop months earlier—the one she'd dared me to go meet. I nodded and she only sighed and said, "*C'est la vie.*"

When she smiled sadly and told me goodbye, I longed to take back everything I'd said. I knew heartache was only a figure of speech, but the weight of my words had settled on that side of my chest. I reminded myself that I wouldn't make her happy in the long run. It wasn't only about Michele. Still it was hard to walk out of the coffee shop knowing I'd probably never go back.

Michele showed up at my house every night that next week. Each night when she knocked on the door it was like the sound of raindrops after a long drought, so unexpected that you rush to the window to make certain it isn't only the wind playing tricks. I worried that if she found out how happy I was having her company she might disappear altogether. She asked once about Molly and then never brought it up again.

She brought groceries and cooked while I worked or texted me to pick up takeout at one of the restaurants we used to order from with Lynn. The first few nights I'd hoped that she'd stay, but I soon realized she'd only wanted company for dinner and she always drove home afterward. She seemed to be trying to prove her point of how much we both needed company. After a few evenings together, she kissed me on the cheek when she said good night. It felt like a friend's kiss and nothing more. The next evening I kissed her cheek when she first walked in. A few times we'd ended up sitting close on the sofa, and when neither of us moved away, I'd reached for her hand. She let me hold her hand—almost pretending as if she didn't notice what I was doing. I didn't ask if we were the sort of friends who held hands.

Limiting our touch to hand holding and cheek kisses brought back memories of my high school girlfriend. I was more keyed up by the extended foreplay with Michele than I ever was in high school, but my high school girlfriend was a close second. My high school girlfriend, on the other hand, actually had wanted to be my girlfriend.

Almost touching was an easy thing to obsess about, and I went to bed every night imagining that Michele had stayed. I didn't dare ask what it meant by her coming over so often. She skipped the weekend but then showed up at my house the following Monday and I began to suspect that it was going to be our new routine.

On Tuesday, I cooked for her. Travis had complained about his back and we'd quit at three. I picked up a baguette from the bakery and her favorite raviolis, then cooked up a tomato and basil sauce, one of the few dishes I could do well. I texted her with the menu, and she showed up at half past five with a bottle of wine. She also had a shoulder bag I recognized from when she used to spend the night at Lynn's.

She saw me eye the bag but didn't mention anything when she tossed it on the first step of the staircase. Dinner passed as had become habit with each of us rehashing the best or worst moments of the day. She was dealing with a new professor who'd asked for help tracking down documents written during the time of the Spanish conquistadores. Her portrayal of the young professor with the nose-in-the-air attitude was hilarious and each day there was a new bit added to the story. After dinner, she said she wanted to change and I started on the dishes, wondering what to expect. She reappeared in a paint-stained white T-shirt and a pair of jeans with holes at the knees.

"I want to help," she said.

"With what?"

"I've been thinking about the hall bathroom all week. It's the same wallpaper and the same outlet covers. What if there's something hidden there as well?"

I'd considered this as well, many times. "You want to help strip the wallpaper?"

She nodded.

I finished scrubbing the saucepan and then dried my hands on the dishtowel. "All right, let's get to work."

Michele had brought a few CDs and popped one into the stereo while I started clearing out the bathroom. She sang along, somehow knowing every word on the album despite Creedence Clearwater Revivals' song lyrics being seemingly entirely random. Her voice, as she crowded into the bathroom alongside me, was as much a distraction as the low V-neck of her T-shirt.

I had an extra scraper and gave Michele a quick lesson in loosening the edge of the paper with the tool and then peeling it off. The bathroom was small and we bumped elbows frequently. She cussed frequently as well, but the first layer was off soon enough. The glue backing of the wallpaper took more patience. I sprayed it first with hot water and let it soak while Michele changed out the CDs. Soon Melissa Etheridge's voice was filling the living room. I knew the songs well and usually sang along, but Michele's voice was well suited to the music and I wanted to hear her voice more than my own. She continued when we went back to work, me sneaking glances at her every so often out of the corner of my eye. When she sang, every bit of emotion from the music was present on her face. I could hardly concentrate on what we were doing.

Peeling the glue backing was slow going. When we reached the last strips on either side of the mirror above the sink, Michele eyed me in the mirror.

"I'm not even sure what I was hoping to find," she said.

I picked up the light switch cover and turned it over in my hand. "I thought there might be something in here as well." I screwed the light switch cover back in place and washed my hands in the sink, then leaned against the cabinet while Michele finished peeling off the last narrow strip.

When she'd finished, she set her scraper next to mine and rinsed her hands. "I guess there's nothing left to the story. Alice left us just enough of a trail to piece together their story...We found KW. I think that's what she wanted us to do. It's probably only wishful thinking, but I wish there was something more."

"Like what?"

Michele shrugged. The song ended, and Michele brushed her hand down my arm. I turned to her and she pressed her hand against my chest as if she were trying to keep some distance between us.

"I need a shower after this," she said.

"You can shower here. It's late. You could spend the night." I hesitated. Her hand was still on my chest, and I wanted to push it away and find her lips. "Can you stay?"

"No one's given me a curfew." She pulled her hand away and stepped out of the bathroom. "But I don't think we should go down that road. I think we're doing pretty well as friends, don't you?"

I didn't bother lying to make her feel more comfortable with her own lie. I stood in the hallway watching Michele fish through her shoulder bag for something. She pulled out her Sutherland College sweatshirt.

"I wish we had a picture of Alice," I said. "I keep wondering what she looked like. I have this image in my head of this perfect fifties housewife up on a stepstool hanging wallpaper…"

"There was a picture of her in that newspaper obituary I found, but she looked like anyone's grandma in that shot. Who knows what she looked like when KW fell in love with her. Chances are she was beautiful. KW was good looking back then. And you don't spend the rest of your life longing for someone unless you're convinced they're sexy as hell."

"Is that how you know you're in love?"

Michele stared at me but didn't answer. Finally she swung the shoulder bag over her arm and motioned to the stairs. "I'm going to take you up on that offer to shower before I head out. Mind if I borrow a towel?"

CHAPTER TWENTY

"Hello?" The number was unlisted. I'd pulled my phone out of my pocket at the first ring hoping it was Michele. Travis didn't mind me taking phone calls, and it happened so rarely that he only looked concerned when I pointed to the phone and stepped outside. The cell phone reception was terrible in the cinder block garage where we were working.

"Hello, and how are you, and all of that. I went ahead and opened Alice's jewelry box," Katy said. She paused and cleared her throat. "It took me three weeks to make it through all of her letters, because I had to stop and wipe my eyes every damn minute. I don't think I've ever had tears like this. But I guess that's what happens when you get old." She laughed. "I never thought I'd become an old sap. Anyway, that isn't the reason I called. I know you're busy, so I'll get to my point. There's something I want you to have. It's more a favor than anything else."

I waited for Katy to continue, but the line was quiet. "You sure everything's okay?"

"Oh, I'm fine." The line went silent again and a long moment passed before she continued, "I don't trust the mail. Never have. Can you make the drive up here again?"

"How's this weekend?" I hoped that I could get Katy to tell me more of the story this time. Understandably she hadn't been ready to talk last time. I guessed from her tone that things might be different now.

"This weekend's fine. There's plenty of room here so don't waste your money on a motel."

Katy hung up before I had time to argue. Travis had gone out to his truck to grab the cooler. He stopped in front of me. "Lunch break?"

"Sure."

"Everything okay?"

I nodded. I'd made a habit out of not telling Travis anything too personal and didn't see a reason to change. But I wanted to talk to someone about KW and Alice's story. It was hard to resist not sharing.

"You've been distracted by something, but if you don't want to talk, fine by me."

"Okay, good."

Travis shrugged. Clearly he wanted to know what was going on, but I wasn't sure what was distracting me—Katy and Alice's story or the fact that my attraction to Michele hadn't changed despite our pretending to be friends. She wanted us to be friends and I knew that I ought to want that as well, but I was tired of reining everything back.

Travis had set the cooler on the workbench we'd set up. The day's project was to build a storage unit in a garage. The homeowner wanted the whole thing stained and finished like a piece of furniture and since he was willing to pay top dollar, Travis didn't argue. "I brought leftovers. Barbecue."

I reached for my water and downed the last of the bottle. "You barbecued?"

Travis shook his head. "Korean barbecue."

Travis handed me a Tupperware container and a fork. I poked at it with my finger. "Cold?"

"It probably would be better microwaved, but he didn't give us a key for the house."

"Guess he doesn't trust us."

Travis smiled. "If I didn't know you, I'm not sure I'd trust you either. You are way too quiet."

"Wait, you're blaming me? You're the one with all the tattoos."

"But everyone trusts a guy with dimples." Travis pointed to his dimples and smiled wide to show them off. His arms were covered with tattoos, as were his chest and back. The dimples did little to soften the image.

I shook my head. My cell phone rang again, and Michele's number popped up on the screen.

Travis reached for the phone before I could. He read the screen and then handed the phone over, grinning as he did. "Michele, huh? Is she the new girlfriend? I knew there was something up with you. You've brought leftovers for our lunches lately—and the food's been good. I had a feeling you weren't the one doing the cooking."

I waved him off and answered the call.

"I hate calling when you're at work. Am I catching you at a bad time?" Michele's voice seemed strained.

"Not at all. I'm on lunch," I answered. I pointed to the container with the chicken in it and signaled for Travis to save me some, then headed back outside. "What's up?"

"I need to ask a favor. Any chance I could borrow your truck?"

"Sure. When?" As far as favors went, I had a list of things I'd rather she ask besides using my truck. "Wait, are you moving?"

"How'd you guess?"

"No one's ever asked to borrow my truck unless they were moving. I've moved a lot of people."

"My landlord gave me notice. He gave me a month—but he'd like me out by the end of the month."

"As in this Sunday?"

"Or I can pay double the rent if I need to stay longer. He's letting his cousin move in and that guy needs a place as of next week. He wants me out on the first. It's ridiculous."

"I don't even think that's legal."

"I signed a one-year contract when I first moved in and it's been month-to-month since. I think I could probably argue with him that it's illegal to raise my last month's rent with only a week's notice, but I don't have the energy to do that alone. Desi has already decided to move in with her girlfriend. She started packing as soon as we got the notice. I think she was happy for the excuse to move in with her."

"Where are you moving?" Was it crazy to hope she'd ask to move in with me?

"I'm going to check out a place after work. And I'm going to need a truck. I wasn't planning on moving expenses this month...How would you feel about driving my Prius for the weekend?"

"Well..." I considered the drive back up to Katy's ranch alone in Michele's car. I'd save on gas money at least.

"Let me guess. You'd be thrilled. Right?"

"Thrilled to drive your Prius? Oh yeah," I agreed sarcastically. "I'd rather drive my truck and help you move actually. Unfortunately I already promised Katy I'd drive up to the ranch this weekend. She wants me to pick something up. Okay if I take your car there?"

"You're going to Wyoming this weekend? What does she want you to pick up?"

"She didn't say."

"Damn, I wish I could go with you." Michele was quiet for a moment. "She didn't drop any hints?"

"I'm not the detective here. She asked me to come pick something up, and I told her I would. But now I think I should call her back and reschedule. I'd rather stay and help you this weekend."

"No, I'll be fine. So long as I have your truck, that is."

I glanced at my watch. Travis would be getting antsy to get back to work. We rarely took more than a fifteen-minute break. "I have to get back to work. Can I call you later?"

"Yeah, sure."

I hung up the phone and turned around to see Travis staring at me. He was holding the side door open and waiting. "Break over?"

Travis shook his head. "You got another five minutes to eat. I'm going to start sanding down the pieces we cut, though, so you might want to eat out here." He handed me the container and my water bottle that he'd refilled. "You don't seem all that happy. I'd expect even you to be smiling if you were talking to your girlfriend."

"She's not my girlfriend." I didn't want to explain to Travis or anyone else why it was so difficult to say that sentence aloud. The past few weeks of dinners and spending every evening together had made things more complicated. Being friends with Michele was better than any relationship I'd had, excepting the sex. But I couldn't let go of wondering why she didn't want more. And too often I let my thoughts wander to what would happen if, or when, she met her next girlfriend.

"Fooled me," Travis said. "You sure looked like you were answering a call from a sweetheart when you said hello." He shrugged and headed back into the garage.

I watched the door swing shut behind him. Travis was right. Every time Michele called, I'd feel a rush of excitement. As soon as she'd hung up the line, I dropped like a rock falling in a half-filled bucket, the impact barely making any sound. It was too pathetic to voice out loud even to myself, much less to Travis, who was quick to trivialize and then push his solution to the problem. I knew what he'd say. He'd tell me to forget about her and go looking for the next girl. Or maybe he'd understand why I was ready to settle on a friendship so long as sex was part of the equation. Travis had been married three times already and didn't seem capable of long-term anything.

I parked in the empty spot next to Michele's Prius. It was ten to five and I guessed Michele would be leaving work right at five if she had plans to check out an apartment that evening. I hadn't texted her to say that I was coming. I wasn't even certain that I wanted to see Michele until the moment I got into my truck to drive home. As soon as I imagined Michele packing up her condo and loading up the truck alone, I knew I wanted to help. Michele wouldn't ask for help and clearly didn't have the extra money to hire anyone.

Michele came out of the library with her sunglasses on and a purse slung over one shoulder. She was awkwardly carrying several folded boxes and I hopped out and met her as she was stepping off the path. I followed her over to the Prius and she smiled her thanks. She unlocked the hatchback, waiting for me to set down the boxes, then dropped her purse in the passenger seat and turned to look over at me. She opened her mouth as if to say something but clamped it shut nearly as quickly. She seemed to be waiting for me to say something first.

I had spent the afternoon coming up with a plan but wasn't sure Michele would go for it. It was ridiculous to be this nervous around her. I glanced down at Michele's black leather flats, wondering if it would be possible to start from the beginning and simply ask her out on a date. I already knew the answer.

I met Michele's gaze and said, "I've been thinking...You have pretty decent furniture and I need some things to stage the house." In my head, the plan had sounded more convincing. Maybe I'd rehearsed the line too many times.

Michele cocked her head to one side and said, "If you are trying to say what I think, that has got to be the least romantic way I've ever been asked to move in with someone."

"Good. I'm not trying to be romantic." In fact, her criticism was the encouragement I needed. At least she had been expecting the question. "Aside from needing to stage the place, nights are getting colder and it doesn't make sense to heat the place for one person. If you move in, we can split the gas bill." I paused. Michele had crossed her arms and was leaning against the side of her car, watching me. The sunglasses made her expression hard to read. I continued, "You could save on rent money...I'm not going to list the place until after the first of the year. Carol's crazy if she thinks anyone is going to jump on a remodel that isn't finished, especially this time of year. You'd have time to look for a nice place and if you wanted to move out sooner than the first, that'd be okay too."

"Can we take a step back?"

I waited, guessing what was coming next.

Michele continued, "You know, we've been hanging out almost every night for the past few weeks. It's been nice—like old times…But I'm still not sure that you're okay with only being friends."

"Relax, I'm fine with it."

She hesitated. Finally, she nodded and said, "Okay, good."

"In fact, we could be even better friends if we were living together."

Michele smiled but looked down at her shoes. I knew what her answer was without her saying.

"You know what, forget about it." It was too late to take back what I'd said, but now I wished I hadn't asked at all. "I'm sorry."

"Don't apologize." Michele shook her head. "Truth is, I'm not sure I'm ready for us to be roommates. I think things could get complicated if I moved in."

"Complicated? Isn't that how things are now?" I continued, knowing I probably shouldn't, "I don't know if you're ever going to be ready for being more than friends or more than casual girlfriends. With anyone, not just me."

Michele's jaw muscles tensed, and I knew I'd hit a tender spot. She didn't say anything in response, making me all the more certain I'd said too much. Two students passed through the parking lot, one glancing in our direction, the other loudly discussing his chemistry test.

"I think we need to take things slow so nothing happens that we regret," Michele said finally. She was clearly choosing her words carefully. "I know you aren't asking me to move in only because you think my furniture would spruce up the place."

"No, but you need a place to live and I've got an extra room. I'm asking you to move in to my house as a roommate, not as a girlfriend, obviously."

"Obviously," Michele repeated. "I don't think it's a good idea to move in together. We're not ready." Michele climbed into the driver's seat of her car. "I need to go check out this apartment. I'll call you later."

I watched Michele drive out of the parking lot. When she had disappeared from view, I climbed back into the truck and stared at the rearview mirror, half expecting to see the Prius roll back into the lot. No Prius appeared.

I turned the key in the ignition and sat a moment longer. I'd grown too accustomed to eating dinner with her and wasn't interested in eating alone again. The cramp of loneliness was most like being hungry. It was something you could ignore until you saw what you wanted right in front of you.

I drove the five miles south of the university without considering why I wanted to go to Uptown. There were fewer parking places than I'd remembered from the last visit, but I found a spot near the guy I'd pegged last time as a drug dealer. He was staked out in front of the bar in nearly the same position as the last time and his grimace as I passed his corner was not entirely endearing though it was familiar.

I pushed open the door and stood a moment in the entryway. The bartender looked up at me, paused for a moment as if trying to place my face and then said, "Find a place to hang Grandma's picture?"

"Yep," I answered, pulling up a stool at the bar. There were a handful of men clustered at one end of the bar and a gray-haired couple at a table. The woman was playing a game of solitaire on an iPad and the man was staring at the television screen, his feet kicked up on a nearby chair. I decided Val was more attractive than I'd remembered. Her hair was dyed a dark red and the cut was shorter. Maybe it was the new style that I liked or maybe it was her smile. Either way, she was a welcome sight.

"Want to try the boss's new favorite beer?"

I nodded and waited for Val to fill a glass with a frothy dark beer. She pushed the glass in front of me and then wiped up a drop that had spilled. When I took a sip, she stepped back to the spot where she'd stood earlier, half leaning against the counter by the sink and distractedly glancing from the television screen to her customers and then to the door. I felt the afternoon's tension slowly relax as I sipped the drink. No one stared at me or seemed to care that I was alone at the bar, quietly sipping one of the best-tasting beers I'd ever had. I might give up Cherry Cokes, I thought, if all beer tasted this good.

Val glanced over at me a few times, as if she was expecting that I'd come with something to say. This time I had no agenda. I didn't feel out of place in the least bit, despite the fact that I was a good thirty years younger than everyone else, excepting Val, and had never spent any time in a straight bar, excepting the last time I'd been to Uptown.

"I wasn't expecting to see you in here again," Val finally said. "Nice surprise. What brings you back? I'm guessing it isn't the ball game."

"This time I only wanted a beer. And I didn't feel like drinking alone. Some days I want a girlfriend more than others."

Val laughed. "Well, you don't have to explain that one to me. I've been single for too long to admit. I get it."

"But some days I'm fine being single, you know? Months will pass and I don't even think about it. Then all of a sudden you realize how lonely you are and you start to wonder if maybe there's a reason you're alone…At the moment I'm stuck wondering if maybe I'm still single because there's something wrong with me. Maybe I'm not that interesting."

"I could give you a hundred reasons I've thought of for why I'm single. Mostly it's probably I get tired of the guys I date by the time we've had our second or third date." She laughed. "Anyway, you're interesting enough. I can tell."

"How's that?"

She shrugged. "You get to know a thing or two about people in this job. Trust me, you don't want to be too interesting anyway. You wouldn't believe some of the stories people tell me…I hear things these old guys have done in their lives. The older ladies as well. I wonder what I'm going to say in twenty or thirty years when some punk asks whether I have any regrets working all my life in a run-down place like Uptown, never getting out of my hometown, never traveling…"

I took another sip. "This is really good."

Val nodded. "My boss travels. He got this up in Vancouver and brought some back for me. I told him we needed to get some on tap. We don't have much left. The old guys hardly taste it so I don't give them the good stuff…I'm thinking of taking the trip. Never even been out of this state—that's how boring my life is."

"Would a trip to Canada make it any more interesting?"

"I don't know. I'd have a good drink at the end of the drive so maybe it wouldn't matter."

One of the guys in the far corner motioned to Val. He wanted another drink and a refill on the bowl of peanuts. Val filled his drink and then went off to the storeroom for a new jar of peanuts. A text message beeped on my phone and I glanced at the screen. Michele had texted two words, "Total dive."

I wrote back, "My offer still stands."

It was possible that I was making a bad decision even suggesting that Michele temporarily stay with me. I wasn't certain I could handle having her in the house, sleeping in the room across the hall, using the same shower, sharing the same sofa, all while keeping the relationship platonic. Alternatively, maybe it would give us the time together that we needed to sort our feelings out. It was easy to imagine things going fairly well…at least until Michele brought home a girlfriend.

Regardless of whether Michele moved to an apartment or bunked in my spare room, I had to admit that she did have a point about wanting to take things slow. We needed to be only friends, not friends with benefits or girlfriends, for at least a few months. She was too much of a cliff for me—one step forward and the fall would be immediate. The question was—were we taking things slow or were we not going anywhere at all?

Val came back to her spot at the bar and said, "So when are we going to Canada?"

I laughed.

"Is that a no?"

"Even if I thought that would make me more interesting, I'm too broke to take off the time."

"Yeah, me too," Val agreed. "And this is the reason we aren't more exciting. We pay the bills. Exciting people have unpaid credit cards and photo albums full of their tan butts leaping off Costa Rican waterfalls."

"Maybe."

"I bet your grandma had some good stories."

Val's comment threw me momentarily. Of course she was referring to Katy. "You know, she didn't tell me all that much. I wish she'd told me more." I wondered if Val had noticed my hesitation.

"Since she ended up on our back hall, I'm guessing you missed out on some damn good stories."

I glanced down at the phone, hoping Michele would text back a reply. As much as I wanted to drive up to Wyoming to see Katy, I'd find a way to reschedule if Michele asked for help moving.

Val motioned to the phone. "Waiting for a call?"

"Yeah."

"Someone important, by the look on your face."

"I've been in love with this woman for two years…"

I stopped when I heard the words. Somehow I'd ignored this reality by not voicing it. Calling my attraction to Michele a crush had been easier to deal with, but I knew the feelings were much more serious than a crush. And much more complicated now.

"And you think she's gonna call tonight?"

"She lost her lease on her condo and I told her she could stay with me. I've got a spare room." I tossed the phone on the counter. "So now I'm waiting for her to text me to say that of course she wants to move in—and that she's hopelessly in love with me. But the thing is, her life is so much more interesting than mine that I've started to wonder if I'm boring." I paused. It sounded like a ridiculous concern, but the doubt nudged at the back of my mind and I had no reason not to say it out loud.

"Maybe she only seems interesting because you're in love with her."

"No, it's not just that. She's a singer in a band. She's got a cool job. She goes on dates all of the time…She has more of a social life than I'd ever want. I'm stuck trying to figure out if she doesn't want to date me because I'm boring or if it's just that I'm more into her than she's into me."

"You want my opinion?"

"Why not?" I shrugged. "I'm hopelessly in love with someone who thinks we should only be friends."

Val sighed. "You might not seem that interesting to yourself but," she spread her hand out to motion to the rest of the customers and added, "no one else here is waiting for a call like that tonight." She crossed her arms and leaned back against the counter. "Is it unrequited love?"

"Meaning, is there a chance she loves me? As a friend, yes, but as something more?" I'd considered this question too many times. My immediate answer was yes, but I hesitated. Maybe I'd been leading myself on all this time. Maybe Michele only wanted to be friends with me but some nights she got lonely and thought of doing more. I shook my head. "I don't know."

"*You* know. Stop second-guessing that feeling and move on. Let's say for the moment that she loves you as much as you love her. Now, the next question: What's holding her back?"

"Do you moonlight as a therapist?"

"I got my bachelor's in psychology from this place." She jabbed her finger on the counter. "And I've read enough that I think I know what I'm talking about." She pointed to my chest. "Trust yourself."

"My head says one thing…"

"And your body says something else," Val finished.

The phone screen lit up and Michele's name flashed on the screen: "Home?"

I knew I wasn't ready to see Michele again tonight. I started to type a response and then deleted the words and tossed the phone back on the counter.

Val grinned, watching me type. "You're hopeless, but you aren't boring."

After I finished the drink, I went to use the bathroom. I studied the new face in the frame that KW had filled. Linda Blenheim had long blond hair with feathered bangs. Her frozen smile didn't capture my imagination any more than the other strangers crowding the space on the walls. I took out the phone and texted Michele: "Heading home now."

I left the front door unlocked. It was against my better judgment, mostly because I'd grown up in cities. The houses on Granite Avenue were only occasional targets of burglars, and they mostly came for easy-to-pack electronics. It was a safe neighborhood otherwise, so I decided to take my chances. Michele had texted back several hours after I'd left the bar to say that she might come over. This was enough to make me unlatch the deadbolt. By nine o'clock, I'd given up waiting for her, however, and was settled under the covers.

My phone beeped with a text before I fell asleep. Michele was parked out front. I climbed out of bed and pulled on jeans and a sweatshirt. I didn't bother with shoes and the cold pavement stung my feet as I picked my way over to Michele's car. I slipped into the passenger seat and warm air blasted at my toes.

"You were already in bed, weren't you?"

I nodded, stifling a yawn.

"I shouldn't have come so late."

"We could fill a book with shouldn't haves."

"And should haves," Michele agreed. "Are you sure you want to rent out your room?"

I didn't want to admit all of the doubt that welled up with Michele's question. "I'll need to check your references, of course," I joked. Somehow joking with her was harder than ever.

"I need to know if you are okay with us living in the same house."

"Don't worry, I already thought about this. I'm going to stop thinking you're cute. Living together will probably make me realize that you're a big pain in the ass. Before long I might be convinced that you'd make a crappy girlfriend. You do have a lot of issues. After a few months I may decide I don't even want to kiss you."

"With all of my issues, that should be an easy decision."

"Easy to say, less easy in practice." Michele's eyes were locked on mine, and I wondered if she could tell how it was all a front on my end. Could she tell I'd been in love all along and nothing had changed? I had to look away from her eyes. "Anyway, I don't like being in a relationship with roommates. It always makes the issues of whose turn it is to clean the bathroom or vacuum more complicated. And you're already going to be a complicated enough roommate. So I'm just going to stop liking you."

"Convenient that we can control how much we like someone, isn't it?" Michele's sarcasm fell flat. She sighed. "I'm not sure this is a good idea."

"What's the worst that can happen?" I had considered many possible worse-case scenarios. I picked one of the more mild ones that had crossed my mind. "We decide we don't like each other after all?" Usually, it was easier to joke with Michele than have a serious conversation. But our jokes now were only thinly veiled covers for the truth.

"I wish things weren't so complicated," Michele said. She glanced up at the house, avoiding my gaze. "Truth is, I want to live here." She added, "With you."

I wanted to kiss her. I wanted to grab her and hold her body against mine and tell her everything I'd held back for two years. Instead, I said, "Okay."

"Can I start moving a few of my things in tomorrow evening?"

"Sure. I'll help." I had every intent of making her realize exactly how helpful I could be with my sleeves rolled up and my muscles flexed.

"You know, it might be hard to only be friends if we're living together."

"It's been hard for years. Look at the bright side—we've had plenty of practice. I don't think it will be that big of a deal."

"Until one of us gets a girlfriend."

"That thought has crossed my mind. I won't if you won't." I hadn't been back to the coffee shop and was certain Molly had moved on. Still part of me wondered what might have happened between us if Michele hadn't shown back up on the scene. *C'est la vie*, I thought.

Michele sighed. "I'm going home. I'll get tomorrow's dinner. Can you meet me at my condo after work?"

"I'll be there." I kissed her on the cheek and climbed out of the car. I waited until her car had disappeared from view before heading back to the warmth of my bed.

CHAPTER TWENTY-ONE

The drive seemed longer the second time round. We'd already had the first snow of the season and in the time since I'd last made the drive, the fields had all turned from green to brown. Some stubborn leaves clung to the trees that spotted the rolling hills, but the only bits of green were the scraggly ponderosa pines.

Other than the color change, the scenery was predictable and I had only the radio to distract my thoughts. This distraction didn't last long. At the second wave of static I switched the radio off rather than search for a CD.

All of Michele's furniture was out of her condo, but many more things remained to be moved, namely everything in Michele's closet and the overfilled kitchen. Desi had promised to help clean the place once everything was out, but the deadline to hand off the keys was fast approaching. It took Michele until Saturday morning, after we'd finished moving her bedroom furniture into the room adjacent to mine, to admit that a drive to Wyoming simply wasn't in the cards. I knew how much she wanted to go, but I was relieved, partly, to have the time alone. The past few days had been jammed full and I needed time to download.

Alice's house, as I had started to think of it in my mind, had been transformed by Michele's furniture. A certain character suddenly filled the space. It had gone from being a workspace to a home with the addition of only a few things—a coffee table, Michele's favorite overstuffed chair that didn't match the sofa but didn't fight it either, a portrait of a sleeping dog that I'd hung over the fireplace and a dining room table and chairs. She didn't have many items, so the house still felt sparsely decorated, though now things were more elegantly allocated compared to the spartan design I'd managed with for months. She'd also clearly saved up for each piece, going for Crate and Barrel quality over Walmart quantity.

I stopped for gas and a late lunch when I neared the Wyoming border and then stopped again only to pee. The sun was setting as I pulled up to Katy's ranch. I angled the Prius for the apple tree where Michele had parked at the first visit. The branches were stripped clean of the apples, and the leaves had all turned yellow. I got out of the car and was quickly accosted by a small pack of yipping collies. None of the dogs seemed to have any desire to do more than slow my way from the tree to the house, their barks serving as more of a greeting than warning. Katy soon appeared to call them off. The dogs responded to her voice immediately and their yipping ceased. She waved her hello, and then when I followed her up to the house, she turned around and hugged me.

"You came alone," Katy said.

I nodded. "Michele is moving out of her condo this weekend."

"Fine by me. I'm not one for crowds. Besides this way I can be nosy and ask questions I couldn't ask if we had company. Starting with why aren't you two together?"

"I've asked myself that same question too many times."

"Good. I'm glad you're at least asking the right questions." Katy patted my shoulder. "Let's go inside. I've been out working all afternoon. I need a long sit and a cool drink."

She led us in through the garage this time, passing first into the family room and then into the kitchen. She filled two water glasses and handed one to me. She drank half of hers and then went back out to the garage after something she'd forgotten, leaving me the chance to have a second look at the place. The old picture we'd brought her wasn't up on the wall anywhere that I could see, but I'd guessed she wouldn't be the type to hang an old headshot. I hadn't noticed the piano in the corner of the living room last time. It was an old upright with the keys covered and a sofa positioned in front of it as partial concealment. A guitar case rested against its side.

I spotted Alice's jewelry box atop the piano and suddenly felt an odd sense of camaraderie with it. The little box had been hidden for so many years and was now prominently on display in an entirely foreign room. I thought of the damaged jewelry box at the antique store. I was glad I'd resisted breaking Alice's open.

I walked over to the piano and brushed my finger along the red lacquered oak. There was no layer of dust. It was a beautiful instrument and I wished I could hear the sound of it filling the room when Katy played. I found myself staring at Alice's box with a bit of sympathy. I guessed that Katy had removed the letters. After treasuring love letters for years, it would seem somehow inappropriate to serve only as an empty case on display. Then again, maybe it wasn't empty. Maybe the letters were inside, safely hidden from view in plain sight.

Katy came back into the kitchen carrying a manila folder. She set it on the kitchen counter and then nodded in the direction of the piano. "I got it tuned."

"You started playing again?"

Katy nodded. "But I won't sing anymore. At least not aloud. There's always a song or two in my head…I never was the singer that my mother was. She had a song for every minute of the day and pulled out a new one the moment someone asked. She had the voice."

She came into the living room and sat down on the recliner, then motioned to the sofa for me to sit as well. "I've always played the piano well enough to distract people from listening to my singing." She winked.

"But the joy was in writing the music. Nothing sounded as good when I sang it as when I'd heard it in my head. And I knew no one, aside from maybe the crowd at Uptown, was going to pay money to hear me sing. But it wasn't the money. I wanted my songs to have a chance. They were my babies...I realized the only way they were going to get anywhere in life was if I sold them to better singers. That's when I finally started seeing some money come in. Not a lot, mind you, but money was never the point. I wanted my music to have an audience. I didn't need to be famous, but I guess I needed to be heard."

"Any famous songs?"

"Famous enough for me, but I doubt you'd have heard of any of them. Several songs played on the radio, and a few even made it to the top forty—when that happened...well, I'll tell you, there's nothing like hearing your song announced in the top forty. Didn't matter that I wasn't the one singing—the words were mine. But all of that was years ago. Years and years...seems like someone else's lifetime."

"I want to hear one of your songs. Before I leave, can I write down some of the titles and look them up?"

"Sure. I might even remember the singers' names." Katy laughed and added, "Maybe. No promises. I don't remember names the way I used to...That picture you found at Uptown brought back so many memories. Good and bad. I remember the name of the photographer who took that shot of me. She was a real piece of work." She grinned. "We dated for a bit, but I dropped her quick when I met Alice."

I shifted back on the sofa. This was the conversation I'd been waiting for. "Did you and Alice meet at Uptown?"

"No, no. I think I may have ruined her when I took her there that first time!" Katy laughed again. "I still remember how the color drained out of her face when she saw two women kissing at the bar. She wouldn't even look at me—kept staring at her feet after that. She panicked a bit when she realized I was leaving her alone at the bar to get up onstage. But after a few more trips to Uptown she settled in all right." Katy grinned.

"No, we met at the university. Her husband was a professor. I was a grad student—not his grad student, fortunately. He and I were in different departments, but everyone knew everyone else back then. I saw her, that first time, at a picnic on campus. She dropped potato salad in her lap, and I showed her where the women's room was so she could wash up."

Katy hesitated for a moment, glancing at the window and then back at me. When she began again, her voice was more somber. "Back then, you could say I fancied married woman."

"Really? Were there many others?"

She nodded. "And I thought I'd fallen in love each time. But Alice was different. No one else hurt that much. The truth was, though, Alice came after me. She was from Kansas and didn't know anyone in town. She said I was the only one who'd talked to her that day. I knew she was lonely and when she asked me over for lunch, to thank me for the help with the potato salad, I said yes only thinking I was being nice to a lonely girl from Kansas…But we kept having lunches together after that and maybe my intentions weren't quite as pure then as they were at first. Her husband was ten years older and a notorious ladies' man. He'd swooned Alice and she'd dropped out of college for him. They married a few months later. Then he went on to swoon many more women, most of them also undergrads, but she stayed married to him through it all. Alice was loyal."

I didn't argue that Alice wasn't exactly loyal since she'd clearly been in love with Katy. Her husband was only a cover. "Why do you think she stayed through all of that?"

Katy shrugged. "What'd you say earlier when I asked you about your gal—'I've asked myself that same question too many times'? We were in love, but it wasn't in the cards." She paused and stared out the window for a long moment. "Turns out all of the love songs I wrote before Alice were dead wrong. The only way you know how hard you've fallen is when you get up to walk away and realize your chest is hollow." She paused. The room had darkened as the sun dropped below the mountain range, but Katy didn't get up to turn on the lights. A moment later she said, "There's no flesh wound. You wish there was so you could fix your mind on that, but there's no wound—nothing to clean and so nothing that heals. It isn't a showy sort of pain. The lights go out and the room gets quiet…No one's in the room with you so no one asks, 'What are you thinking?'"

"Was it that McCarthy list? Is that why you two ended things?"

"That list didn't help, and neither did my arrest. But in the end, that only cost me my position in grad school. I stayed in town, wrote music and played to a packed room at Uptown nearly every night. I was never the main attraction, but I liked it that way. Different singers would travel through…Back then, Uptown kept a little band so the singers wouldn't have to bring their crew. I had a regular job playing piano and sometimes if the main act was late, I'd sing a couple of my pieces and the crowd didn't mind. I didn't make much, but the drinks were free and I had a bed in a little room on the third floor. I wrote songs like a fiend back then and would give them away for a kiss. And I had plenty of takers back then."

She smiled sadly. "It'd be easy to blame McCarthy, but I finally realized Alice wasn't going to leave her husband. I couldn't stay around making her feel miserable for cheating on him, though everyone knew he was doing the same to her and, more than that, making myself miserable. One day I came to the realization that Alice might only be playing a game with me, saying she'd leave him someday but knowing in her heart it was an empty promise…So, I told her I wanted all or nothing. I was hoping she'd prove me wrong, hoping she'd say that she wanted me more than him, but I never believed she'd have the courage to leave. After I read her letters, something occurred to me that I'd never thought of then…I think maybe me not believing in her was part of our downfall. She needed me to trust her—to trust that she could leave him when the time was right. But I didn't trust her with my heart. I was too young and foolish to realize I'd already given it to her anyway."

"I figured it would have been Alice who broke it off. Knowing it was your choice to leave somehow changes the story in my head."

"Choice is funny, isn't it? Leaving wasn't my choice, but I did it, so then it became my choice. She chose staying so I had to choose leaving. Those first few months were hard." Katy sighed. "I moved in winter, which is a terrible thing to do to a body that's already grieving a lover. Nothing worse than remembering the feel of a warm body next to yours when you've got nothing but ice-cold sheets. But spring came soon enough and calving time keeps ranchers busy. Then I met someone new that summer. If you'd asked me then, I would have said I'd moved on. Her name was Ruth Ann and she sang like a bird...We sat on the piano bench together and she'd sing while I played and in those moments, I'd nearly forget about Alice. But then when the song was over and Ruth Ann kissed me, I knew that there was no forgetting Alice.

"Truth was, there's no moving on when part of you stays behind. Alice kept a part of me and I was a different person, missing that piece. I loved other women after her, but it was never the same. Ruth Ann realized it eventually, as did the ones who followed. I was too damn stubborn to ever give up on Alice. I'd broken it off, but I thought for sure she'd chase me down. Ego or pride or both...She didn't come find me. Not 'til the end."

I followed Katy's gaze up to the jewelry box. Part of me envied Michele for having read all of the letters and yet in some ways I'd read enough to understand exactly how much Katy had lost. "Must have been tough for every woman who came after Alice."

"They never stood much of a chance," Katy agreed. "There was one who was with me for the long-term or so I thought. We were seeing each other, off and on, for nearly twenty years. She even talked about moving in with me here. But then time drifted us apart..."

"Did you write to Alice after she moved to Atlanta?"

"No. There's only so long you can write to someone without getting any reply. But I kept writing songs for her. I always imagined she'd hear one playing on the radio and maybe, even if it was someone else's voice she was hearing, maybe the song would make her think of me...'Course I hoped she'd pick up the phone and call. I'd given her the ranch number that last time we said goodbye. I think I knew then that I'd end up back here if I didn't end up with her. For a long time, I truly expected a call. She never was one to send a letter so I didn't expect that."

Katy braced her weight on the arms of the recliner and stood up. She'd aged in the telling of the story or the day's work was catching up with her joints. She went to get the manila folder she'd left in the kitchen as well as her glass of water. "Parched," she said, taking a sip. "Jarvis isn't one for conversations. I think I'm out of practice talking." She handed the folder to me and retook her seat.

I opened the folder. Several pages of sheet music were inside, paper clipped together with a sealed envelope that had Michele's name written across the front. I couldn't read the music notes, so I only scanned the words penciled underneath the lines.

"I wrote that music years ago, but I struggled with the words. Then I read Alice's letters and reread mine." She leaned back in her seat and closed her eyes.

I looked again at the words and realized that Katy had pieced together the bits from their letters to create the lyrics. I only recognized a few of the lines, but I was certain most of it had come straight from the letters. "This is beautiful."

Katy's eyes were still closed. She had been humming a tune that I didn't recognize, but she paused now. "Not yet it isn't. Right now there's only notes on a page. This is why I asked you to drive up here. I need a favor."

I spent the night at the ranch, at Katy's insistence. There was no point in arguing. I was learning that once Katy had decided on something that was the way it was going to be. A hotel room wouldn't be any more interesting than a night in Katy's house anyway. She brought out a cot and advised I dust it off and look for spiders while she defrosted our dinner. I found webs but no spiders. Jarvis and his son were out of town for the night, doing business in Cheyenne. The hired ranch hands apparently took care of most things on the ranch in their absence, but Katy fretted that the men couldn't be trusted to remember the hens, and once she had the thawed stew in the pot, she handed me a wooden spoon to stir it and hustled out to check that the henhouse was locked for the night. Through the kitchen window I followed her flashlight's path out to the henhouse and then over to the milking barn. Even in her eighties and with arthritis stiffening her joints, she could hustle. The flashlight darted from the milking barn over to the horse barn. Clearly she didn't trust the hired hands to do much of anything and was double-checking their work. I had the stew in bowls and the rolls browned and buttered by the time she returned.

We sat down to eat, and Katy didn't stop to look up from her bowl until she'd swiped the last of the stew up with a remnant of her roll. She wiped her lips with a handkerchief, took a sip of water and then leaned back in her chair. I finished up the last bite of stew, save for the peas which were too freezer-burned to swallow. I carried our bowls over to the sink, hoping Katy wouldn't notice the peas.

"Does Michele cook?"

I glanced over my shoulder at Katy. I rinsed the bowls and then set to work on cleaning the soup pot. "She gets by in the kitchen, but I don't think it's anything she loves doing. We eat a lot of takeout."

"Alice loved to eat good food. She could cook anything you asked for. And she always made big dinners, so she could save enough for us to have the leftovers the next day when we lunched in the park. I used to wonder if her husband ever thought of the leftovers, went looking for them at midnight or whatnot. I would have…Do you cook?"

"Sometimes. I've cooked for Michele a few times if that's what you're asking. When I was still with my ex we used to have dinner parties all the time and Michele and I would cook together. I never liked cooking until I had her directing me around the kitchen."

"You should cook together more. The way to the heart is through the belly, you know. Find out what she likes to eat and go buy a cookbook."

"I doubt I'd woo her by us making dinner together. I don't think either of us is that good in the kitchen."

"Would it hurt your chances to get better at it then?"

I laughed. "You're giving me dating advice? Well, truth is, I probably need it, so go ahead."

"I'm not the one to give advice, I suppose. What I've learned has only come through studying regret. For one, I know I never tried hard enough. That took me a long time to learn…At the time, I thought that love should be left up to fate. Turns out fate doesn't give a rat's ass about love."

"A rat's ass?"

Katy nodded. "I need chocolate." She stood up and went to the pantry, returning with a jar of candies. Silver-wrapped Hershey's Kisses fought for space with gold-wrapped Rolos and black and orange-wrapped butter toffees. "I have a sweet tooth," Katy admitted. She took out a Rolo and a Kiss and pushed the jar toward me. "Tell me about your gal."

"I don't know where to start." I picked out a butter toffee and unwrapped it. I sucked the toffee. The syrupy sweetness filled my mouth. "We're only supposed to be friends, but I know we both want more. Part of the problem is she only does short-term relationships and I'm looking for more. I don't know if she can commit to more. For a long time I thought there must be some reason why she never wanted a long-term relationship with anyone, but I'm starting to wonder…"

"What do you mean?"

"Sometimes I think maybe it's that she's never had practice. She's used to leaving before things get hard. But why? Maybe she's scared of how you start to depend on someone in a long-term relationship. I know she doesn't like to depend on anyone. Or maybe she doesn't want anyone depending on her, doesn't want anyone holding her down…"

"Or maybe she's never let herself fall in love," Katy guessed. "Why stick around if you aren't in love?"

"Maybe. She's dated some nice women, but she seems to do everything she can to make sure no one gets close."

"Maybe she's scared. Too bad she's beautiful and you're already in love, huh?" Katy whistled.

"Beautiful, talented, funny…If I were smarter, I'd walk away. Instead I asked her to move in with me."

"I think you two are perfect for each other, but I'm not the best judge. My track record is terrible, in fact," Katy smiled. "But you'll sink yourself with regret if you never go for it."

Katy slept in the master bedroom. She said Jarvis usually had the second bedroom while his son had the room off the garage, but since both Jarvis and his son were gone to Cheyenne for the weekend, those rooms were empty. Katy had offered either of them or the cot. I didn't mind the cot. It fit between the piano and the sofa with a narrow walkway along one side. Katy went to bed early, saying that she'd grown used to waking in time for milking the few cows they kept, though she grumbled that Jarvis had retired her from that job since she'd fallen on the slick floors of the milking parlor.

I laid out the bedding Katy had left, a crisp cotton sheet and two thick wool blankets, dark gray in color and smelling faintly of moth balls. She had forgotten a pillow so I folded my hands under my head and lay still on the cot. The springs complained loudly when I shifted my weight. Finally I folded up my jeans, placed them under my head as a pillow and settled into what I'd decided was the only comfortable position. The ring of my cell phone was deafening. I hurried to answer it, worrying that the noise would wake Katy.

"Hey," Michele said. "How's Wyoming?"

"It's good." I added, "Too bad you couldn't make the trip. Katy and I spent the evening talking." I crawled back into the cot and pulled the blankets up to my chest. The family room was drafty, and I'd gotten cold running out to my car for the overnight bag. "I wasn't missing you much earlier, but now I wish you were here."

Michele laughed. "Why's that?"

"I'm cold and want a girlfriend to cuddle with. Anyone would do," I joked, "but you'd be a nice option."

Michele didn't answer. I didn't wish to take back the words however. The conversation with Katy had left me more determined to not apologize for how I felt. If Michele needed to push me away, I'd deal with the rejection. What I couldn't handle anymore was biting my tongue every time I wanted to say "I love you."

"So is it weird being in my house without me there?" I asked.

"A little. I'm still trying to get used to Alice's ghost."

"Ghost?"

"Well, I'm not hearing anyone dragging chains across the floor or seeing flickering lights...but I imagine her in every room. She always seems so sad."

"Maybe she's not sad. Maybe she's only waiting."

"For Katy? Well, I guess I could try imagining that."

Katy's manila folder with the music sheets was sitting on the piano bench by my head. I reached for this and said, "Katy wrote a song. It's called 'Waiting for a Love Song.' She wants you to sing it with your band and send her the recording. But it's a country piece, and I remember you saying that Sarah doesn't like to do country songs."

"I think she'd let the band do one country song. I might have to remind her that she owes me more than one favor. Did she play it for you?"

"No." I read over the first few lines. "She wrote it based on the letters. I can't decide if I like it because I know the background story or if it's just really good. You can feel how much they longed for each other."

"I wish I could be there," Michele said.

"I feel like I'm hanging out with my grandma. But my grandma was never this cool." I paused. "Katy is different this time. She's more at ease compared to last time. I think Alice's letters changed her."

"It'd be nice to see Katy again, but she isn't the one I'm missing tonight."

"Tonight," I echoed.

"Don't get on my case, Jodi. It's been a long day. Yeah, I'm missing your company tonight. And yeah, I get what you're implying by that comment." Michele's tone was sharp.

"I wish I knew if I should give up waiting for you," I said softly. "Sometimes I think I must be crazy thinking someday you'll change your mind. Crazy or stupid. Maybe both."

Michele was silent.

"Anyway, I'm beat and I know you are too," I said. "Maybe we need to say goodbye."

"You mean, 'good night.'"

"Yeah, that's what I meant." I *had* meant to say good night. I wasn't pulling a passive aggressive move at all, but I could tell by her tone that she'd taken it as such. She was being overly sensitive, but I wasn't about to say that out loud.

"Damn it, Jodi."

"All I meant was good night." I was too tired to argue.

"Yeah…you're right. We're both tired." She sighed. "And I'd never ask you to wait. You can do whatever the hell you want to do. Anyway, good night."

I stared at the phone and then at Katy's music sheets. I set them both on the piano bench and shifted back under the blankets. The grandfather clock ticked off the passing time and I struggled not to fixate on the sound, knowing sleep wasn't going to come quickly.

After a half hour of trying to stop my mind from rethinking the conversation with Michele, I got up to get a glass of water. The floorboards creaked as I crossed the room and I heard one of the dogs give a low growl. Five of Katy's dogs slept in a heap in the garage, but one kept post on a floor mat at the front door. Katy didn't explain why she let the one dog inside after shooing the others out to the garage, but now I realized he was the night watch.

I went back to my cot with the water but didn't lie back down. I knew the jewelry box was rightfully Katy's now, but I reached for it anyhow. The key was easy to find, taped to the underside of the box. I sat on top of the blankets with it in my lap, one hand on the wood and the other on the key, debating whether I had any right to peek inside. Finally I loosened the masking tape and slipped the key into the lock. The letters were gone. One sheet of paper remained. I took it out and held it up to the weak light. It was a page cut from the front pages of a book and there was a handwritten inscription. I squinted to read the faded cursive. The page had gotten wet at one point or another and the ink was smeared. Only the last bit of it was legible: "May you hold love." It was signed: "Fearless" but this part wasn't in cursive but in blocky print as if the signer had pressed down hard on the pen to get each letter stamped into the page. The page was blank save for this inscription and a printed dedication above it: "For Isabelle." There was no way of knowing what book the page had been cut from or who had written the inscription. Fearless was no one I knew.

I replaced the sheet in the box and locked the lid. The masking tape held the key securely enough to avoid anyone's noticing that I'd used the key. I leaned back on the cot, the jewelry box balanced on my chest, wondering whether Katy had kept this page to remind herself of what she'd lost or what she'd had. I decided on the latter, but I wasn't entirely convinced.

CHAPTER TWENTY-TWO

The gray ball of fur wedged itself between my thigh and my elbow for the first three hours of the drive. I kept glancing down at him, making certain he was still a round ball curled up with the head tucked between the forepaws and not being squished flat by the seat belt. When I stopped for gas, his nails dug into my jeans so I scooped him up and slipped his bony frame under my coat. He stayed there for the rest of the drive, making only an occasional noise and then falling asleep once more.

I'd woken early to help with the milking mostly because I wanted to see how it was done and then stayed on because I wasn't quite ready to leave Katy. She mentioned the letters only briefly as we had our coffee with the morning's fresh milk. She served me biscuits and scrambled eggs. I ate my fill and then had seconds. She'd said that reading Alice's letters had given her everything she needed to know. Finally. I almost asked her what Alice looked like, but I had such a clear image in my head now that I didn't. I wanted to keep the picture of her just as I'd imagined her. We didn't talk about what Katy wished had happened, and there was no longing in her voice when she mentioned the last time she'd seen Alice. Now that she knew Alice had loved her, as much or maybe more than she'd ever hoped, she could finally let her go. In the end, it was enough to know that Alice had wanted to be with her even if she never was.

She'd given me the kitten as I rolled down my window to wave goodbye. The kitten was sunning himself in the middle of the driveway and she'd caught him by the nape of the neck and, in one fluid movement, tossed him through the window and onto my lap. "This one isn't going to make it on the ranch. He doesn't have the sense to get out of anyone's way. I found him in the chicken pen yesterday. The rooster was about to do away with him," she said.

I'd been caught off guard and didn't think to argue until I was two hours away and realized I had no litter box or food for him, not to mention that I had no real desire to have a cat. I hadn't owned a cat since high school and if I'd had a choice in the matter then would have picked a dog instead. When I reached Colorado Springs, I found a pet store and with the gray ball still tucked under my coat, picked out food, litter and a toy mouse dangling from the end of a stick.

Michele was sitting on the sofa with her feet up on the coffee table. She had a magazine on her lap and the television on, but the volume was muted. She eyed the box of litter as I set it down in the entryway. I dropped the bag of kitten food on top of this and then kicked off my boots.

"How was your trip?" she asked.

"It was good. Katy says hello." The kitten had awoken since the trip into the pet store and wriggled under my coat. I fished him out and in one hand held him out to Michele. "She sent you this."

"Are you kidding? A kitten?" She grinned and reached for him. "All gray—she's beautiful!"

"And this." I set the folder with Katy's song sheets on Michele's coffee table and watched Michele with the kitten.

"I love gray kittens," she admitted.

"Good. He's all gray and all yours. I'll set up the litter box and food if you watch him for a minute." I went out to the truck for the rest of my things and then set up the kitten's litter and food in the hall bathroom.

Michele walked over with the kitten in her arms. "She's purring. I'm naming her Alice."

"I think it's a boy."

Michele shook her head and then lifted the tail. "There's too much hair back here to tell." She set the kitten in front of the food bowl and folded her arms. "I'm still calling her Alice."

"Even if it's a boy?"

She nodded. "But I'll bet you money it's a girl."

I stuck out my hand. "This time you're paying for dinner. I'm going to win this bet."

"Deal. You don't mind that we have a kitten here?"

I shrugged. "I didn't have a lot of time to argue about this one. He'll have to be a good boy and stay out of trouble."

"She'll be perfect," Michele promised.

Michele had ordered pizza and a two-liter of Cherry Coke. We watched a movie and ate pizza while the kitten rolled on the floor between us, intermittently attacking the toy mouse and our toes.

I glanced over at her. "This feels like old times."

She smiled. "Pizza and movie night…we had some good times. Now instead of a seven-year-old kid trying to get our attention, it's a kitten."

"This kitten might be cuter," I admitted. "I like seeing all of your furniture here. Definitely spruces up the place."

Michele tilted her head and eyed me for a long moment but didn't say anything. I scooped up the kitten, whose nails were digging into everything in his reach, including my wool socks, and planted him on the sofa between us. He attacked the sofa and then spun around and lunged at Michele's hand. She caught him midjump and laughed as he swatted the air.

"I think I agree with you. Kittens are cuter than seven-year-olds." She played with the kitten for a while, both of us ignoring the movie now that the kitten was better entertainment. She carried the pizza box and our plates to the kitchen, and the kitten followed her, pouncing after her slippers. I liked seeing Michele in slippers. She'd never worn them when she was over for the evening. But now she lived here, and the slippers were somehow tangible proof.

Michele had left the magazine she'd been reading earlier on the coffee table. It was open to an article about Santa Fe; a young couple was pictured standing next to a line of brilliant red peppers with an adobe house in the backdrop. I closed the magazine and kicked up my feet. My heels rested on another picture of Santa Fe on the magazine's cover with the promising title: *Romantic Getaways*. I'd been to Santa Fe years ago, but I'd gone alone—and now suddenly wanted to ask Michele if she wanted to go there for a long weekend. But that was something girlfriends would do. "Damn 'romantic getaways,'" I said grimly.

Her cell phone beeped with a text. She'd left it on the coffee table by the magazine and I glanced at the screen without thinking. I stared at the words and felt the room shift, though I was still sitting on the sofa and hadn't moved an inch. Michele walked back into the room and the kitten followed a half step behind. I stared at the television as if I could still focus on the movie. She sat down on the sofa, picked up her cell phone, glanced briefly at the screen and then set it facedown on the arm of the sofa. Maybe my response would have been different if she hadn't set it facedown. I felt sick and wished I hadn't eaten a third piece of pizza.

The text had read: "Hey Mom." I hadn't read anything past the first line. The words repeated in my head in an endless thread. I swallowed down the surge of questions. After several minutes debating all the possible ways I could ask if the text was sent to the wrong number, I gave up any pretense of watching the movie and stood up. My legs felt shaky. I blamed the drive, though I'd been fine earlier. "I'm going to take a shower."

Michele looked up at me. "Want me to stop the movie?"

"No, you can tell me how it ends. It's been a long day. Katy had me up at five to help with the milking. I'm beat. Can you get the kitten settled for the night?"

She nodded and I headed upstairs without meeting her gaze. I didn't want to look at her now. I couldn't risk seeing her expression. And I didn't want her to read the mix of emotions on my own face.

CHAPTER TWENTY-THREE

Sometimes I wonder how long we would have gone on pretending—or if she would have told me at all if not for that text.

Knowing someone's keeping a secret can tear you up inside. I've never liked secrets. They are too close to lies. I found out the tooth fairy was a hoax long before I ever lost a tooth, but I slipped those teeth under my pillow anyway. As much as I didn't like it, I knew I needed to keep up my end when my parents gushed about the fairy trading coins for baby teeth. What did I have to gain by not spoiling everything with the truth this time? I wondered. There was no silver dollar waiting for me.

I was exhausted but couldn't sleep. I'd heard Michele shower not long after I'd gone to bed, and hours had passed since then. I padded downstairs in search of a glass of water or some other distraction. Michele's bedroom door was ajar, and the kitten shot out of the room as I passed by. Alice followed me downstairs to the kitchen, slipping between my ankles as I tried to walk and meowing as I filled a glass from the tap. I stared out the kitchen window at a dark soup with no moon or stars to keep me company. I scooped up the kitten when he tried to taste my toes. Underneath the gray fluff he was so scrawny I could feel every bone in his back and the ribs too. He started a loud purr when I rubbed my thumb on his head. I heard footsteps behind me and turned to see Michele.

"I left my phone in plain view." She leaned against the far counter, not looking at me. She continued, "I don't blame you for reading the message."

"I only read part of it." Suddenly I wanted to lie, to pretend as if I hadn't read the important part at all. But it was too late to go back to the moment before I'd seen the text and there was no way I could keep up the pretense. "I only saw the words 'Hey Mom.' I couldn't have read anything after that even if I'd been trying."

Michele nodded. Her distant look made me wonder if she'd heard what I'd said or simply already knew what I was going to say when she'd followed me downstairs. What did she want me to say? I waited for her to speak, but she only stared out at the dark sky. Alice twisted in my hands when he grew tired of my petting. I set him on the ground and he bolted out of the room. When I finished my water, I headed out of the kitchen.

Michele caught my arm before I could slip past her. She let go as quickly as she'd grabbed me, but we were shoulder to shoulder when she whispered, "We need to talk." In a louder voice she added, "We need to talk tonight. Neither of us is going to sleep if we don't."

"I don't get it," I said. "You have a kid and didn't tell me?"
She nodded.

"What the hell? Why would you lie to me?" When she only stared at me, I turned and walked out of the room. I hoped she wouldn't follow me upstairs. I didn't want to "talk" tonight. I closed my bedroom door and sank facedown on the bed. Several minutes passed before I heard the door open and then felt the mattress give as Michele sat down next to me.

"My son's name is Peter. And I'm married, on paper anyway, to a guy named Nicolas Grady." She paused. "I was young and stupid when I fell for Nic. He left six months after we got married. He never even met his son."

I turned her words up and down in my mind like a puzzle piece, as if I turned it one more time it might fit the image I had. Maybe I could imagine she'd been married, long ago. But I couldn't imagine she had a kid.

I considered that what I knew of her maybe didn't fit because I'd invented most of it, hoping it was true. Someday she'd settle down with a woman and have a couple kids, not with me but maybe with someone, I'd told myself. She was old to get pregnant herself, but it was possible... Or if she met someone who wanted to be pregnant, I'd thought that she'd jump at the chance to have a family... Because why? Because she'd always struck me as someone who would be a great mom. Funny that this was still true when everything else was suddenly wrong. The puzzle piece she'd handed me didn't fit my puzzle at all. I shifted onto my side. "How old is your kid?"

"He's not a kid anymore. Pete turned twenty-one in June."

"Twenty-one?" I did the math. She'd had him at twenty. "Where is he now?" I sat up and pulled my pillow onto my lap.

"College. UCLA. He's got this dream of being a movie producer." Several minutes passed before she said, "It feels like I've lived two different lives. Part of me still thinks like a single mom in Tucson trying to make sure my kid eats his vegetables and the rent gets paid. But that isn't me anymore. I'm a librarian with a side gig as a backup singer in a band." She paused. "Instead of trying to scrimp together tips to pay for my kid's school clothes, I'm looking for a fun no-strings-attached hookup and splurging on a new outfit. I send Peter money every month, but I still have a little extra most of the time. Some days I wake up, get dressed in a skirt and blouse, and as I'm brushing my teeth, I catch my reflection in the mirror and wonder— who the hell is that? Who is this person with bleached blond hair in an outfit that I never could have afforded five years ago staring back at me? I used to have shoulder-length hair—kind of medium brown—I'd always pull it back in a ponytail. And when I'd be getting ready for work, I never used to stare long at my reflection in the mirror. I worked six days a week and always in the same restaurant uniform. It wasn't much to look at in the mirror. Anyway, I was too busy trying to get Pete out the door in time for school and then trying to get to work on time to think about much other than—had I remembered to brush my teeth? Somehow, I had to make sure Pete had dinner and had finished his homework before I dropped him off at the babysitter in time to make it to my night classes…It doesn't feel like one life followed the other. I was living a different life then."

"I think I'm still stuck on the fact that you have a son." I wasn't sure where steady ground was. Questions flooded my mind. The questions I wanted to ask most were the ones I knew I probably shouldn't ask. Why hadn't she said anything before? Why lie? "Why didn't you mention him before?" I had to ask.

Michele shrugged. She stared at the dark sliding glass door. "If I told you about Peter, I knew I'd have to tell you everything. I spent so many years in Tucson explaining that, yes, I was a single mom, and, yes, I was technically married to a man, but I wasn't straight. When I moved here, I didn't want to be the single mom with the husband who'd left her anymore. I wanted to be a free forty-something singing backup vocals in a band. I didn't think of it as a secret at first.

"After Nic, I only dated women. So from twenty on…But that didn't seem to matter to a lot of the women I dated. They'd meet Pete, hear the story about Nic and then…most of them never called me back for another date after that. The ones who stuck around were always worried that I'd decide to go back to men if the right guy came along—as if I didn't hear that line enough from my mom and my sister.

"My goal when I moved here was to let go of my past. I guess I figured if I ever got close to someone, then I'd tell them about Peter or maybe they'd even meet him and the story would come out naturally…But with you I waited too long. How do you tell a close friend that you've been lying to them for years? Or if not lying, omitting something that important?"

"When I asked you about Arizona in the car ride up to see KW—you lied then. I asked you about your family."

"Did I lie or did I simply not tell you everything that I could have told you?"

"Would you have told me if I hadn't seen his text?" I strained to keep the anger out of my voice.

"I wanted to—so many times… I wanted you to really know me if we were going to be friends. How could you know me at all if you didn't know this really important part?"

Do I know you at all? I shot back silently. How could she keep all of this from me? "Were you scared to tell me?"

"At first I wasn't scared—I just wanted to be free of all that baggage. Not free of Peter, but I wanted to let go of Nic and everything that I'd hated about my past." Michele shook her head. "Getting married was only one of many bad decisions. I wanted to move on. But over time, I began to worry about you finding out somehow and then I was scared that you'd be pissed that I'd been lying all this time. I know I would be."

"Did you tell Lynn?"

"I've known Lynn for years, you know that."

"And?"

She sighed. "Yeah, Lynn knows. Lynn was one of the reasons I moved here. I told you it was the job and it was…but I applied for the job at Sutherland because of Lynn. She'd emailed me the job posting and encouraged me to go for it. We'd met through a friend in Tucson. Turns out we had an ex-girlfriend in common." Michele smiled weakly. "The only other people who know all live in Tucson."

"So you aren't staying out of Tucson because of the heat or your Bible-thumping sister."

"I didn't lie about that. My sister is a total piece of work. But she isn't the reason I left—and only part of the reason why I don't like going back. I'd planned on leaving for a long time. I had to wait for Peter to graduate high school. The weekend he left for college, I moved up here. When I passed the Tucson city limits I remember thinking—maybe I'll never be back. But I can't convince my mom to fly, and she doesn't like long car rides, so of course sometimes I have to go back. When I do, it feels like I haven't been away at all—like there's no life up here for me and Tucson is all there is…Time's stood still and Tucson's been waiting for me."

"But then you come back here."

"And then I come back here and I have a completely different life. I've never regretted having Peter. But being a single mom meant I had to put so many things on hold. There were times when I went to bed, completely exhausted, and thought—I'm twenty-five, or twenty-six, or twenty-seven, and I should be out at a dance club with friends, but I'm home with my son. I know how that sounds—but it's true. My twenties slipped away before I knew it. When I turned thirty, I decided I needed a plan. Don't get me wrong—I loved being a mom even when Peter was challenging. But no one loves the stress of being broke all the time, and it's hard putting your role as a mom above everything else you dream about doing."

I thought of the times I'd watched Michele with Roxanne and how part of me had been jealous of how easy their relationship seemed. Roxanne loved spending time with Michele, and Michele always seemed to know how to brighten Roxanne's mood. She'd taken the role of Aunty seriously. Now it was clear that at least part of the reason interacting with kids had seemed so natural for Michele was because she'd had plenty of parenting practice.

All this aside, I still couldn't imagine Michele with a grown son in college. It was too much of a stretch for the image I had of her. And then there was the issue she'd only briefly mentioned. Why was she still married? Was this the reason why she always ended relationships before they became serious? "You said your husband left before Peter was born. That was twenty years ago…" I hesitated finishing the thought.

"Why didn't I divorce him years ago? Trust me, I've tried. He needs to sign the papers. I can't find him. I hired a lawyer when I had the money for the fees. Turns out I'm not the only one who can't find him."

I thought of how quickly Michele had pieced together the identity and whereabouts of Alice and KW. Apparently she'd had practice sleuthing. And apparently I'd never make it as Sherlock. "What'd you think I was going to do when I found out? Did you honestly think I was going to be upset that you were married twenty years ago and have a son?"

"I don't know…Mostly I thought you were going to be pissed that I'd been keeping all of this from you."

"Well, you're right about that part."

I wanted to say that it didn't matter. That now that everything was out in the open we could move on. But it wasn't true. How could I let go of the fact that she'd kept all of this from me for so long? And it was worse knowing that all along Lynn had known.

"For better or worse, I'm glad you finally know. I've hated myself for not telling you. And now you probably hate me." Michele pulled her knees up to her chest. She rested her forehead against her knees.

"Mostly I'm mad at myself for not being able to see when someone I think I know pretty well is hiding something."

"I'm sorry." Michele waited for me to respond and then brushed her hand across my arm. "I really am."

I pulled away at the touch. Michele stood up as if she were going to leave, but she only stood in the middle of the room watching me. Michele had said that she'd come out when she was in her twenties and hadn't dated men since. Omitting the fact that she was still married wasn't a huge issue, but I couldn't understand why she'd omitted her son.

She opened the sliding glass door and stared out into the darkness, then stepped onto the balcony and glanced back at me. I sat on the bed for several minutes watching her, then finally got up and joined her on the balcony. I kept to the side near the door to give us both space. The mountains were shrouded with fog and the breeze smelled of rain. It was warmer than I expected, but I shivered anyway.

"I've wanted to tell you for so long," she said. "I'd rehearsed in my head how it would go and never once did I expect you'd read a text from Peter and find out that way."

"Does it matter how I found out?"

"Yes, of course it matters. I should have told you myself."

Michele wiped tears off her face, but I didn't offer anything to comfort her. Several minutes passed with neither of us speaking. I thought she'd turn and walk back inside, but both of us stayed on the balcony shivering when the wind gusted. I didn't want to look at her.

"After Lynn, I decided I needed someone who wasn't going to keep things from me. Someone I trusted as much as I trusted you. Funny, huh?"

Michele didn't smile at my sarcasm. "Lynn and I got in an argument once—she thought that I should tell you about Peter. I should have listened. He came into town unexpectedly and I had to cancel on one of our weekly dinners…But there were things she was keeping from you as well, and when I brought that up, she didn't raise the subject again."

"You and Lynn have that in common."

"We have a lot in common," she agreed. "I thought you would be pissed that I was married. I remember you teasing Lynn about her being only 'half gay' because of that."

"Not because she was married to a man years ago, before Sal, but because she's bi, and you missed her giving me an earful later about how I had no business judging someone's gayness."

Lynn had left the dude because of Sal—and that, she said, was the important part. Since she'd left me for Sal as well, I'd decided that her leaving a man for a woman wasn't exactly the important part. Sal was her one true love—plain and simple. It wasn't about her being bi at all. Anyway, I'd learned my lesson and never joked about her being bi again. It was stupid at the time. "Sometimes when someone isn't that interested in you, you want to believe there's a reason that has nothing to do with you."

"Well, you were right—only her reason had nothing to do with being bi. She never got over Sal breaking up with her. She always held on to the idea that they would get back together again."

"You could have told me that a long time ago."

Michele gave me a tight-lipped smile. "Add it to the list."

"Lynn had a habit of omitting important things, and I didn't ask enough questions. But I thought I learned something from that relationship. I guess 'gullible' is written across my forehead."

Michele brushed her fingertip across my forehead. Her touch nearly brought tears to my eyes. I blinked and looked away.

"There's nothing written there," she said. She slipped her hand into her pocket as if she'd realized that I'd need time before she could touch me again. "One of the reasons I hated not being honest with you was that you are so trusting. After Lynn left, as much as it would kill me I kind of hoped you'd fall for someone else. I knew you didn't need someone with more baggage."

"Maybe you shouldn't have tried to guess what was best for me."

"For some reason, I thought I could keep my past separate from my future. I convinced myself that my past didn't need to be part of anything here. Peter was in LA and I wanted to leave everything else behind in Arizona." She laughed softly, then added, "I'm not going to pretend like this is no big deal. But I don't want you to pull away because of it. I don't want to lose you…I'll answer any questions you need to ask. I promise I won't keep anything from you again."

Michele waited for a response, but I clenched my teeth and looked away. After a while, she said, "This is why I couldn't agree to anything more than being friends. Hell, legally I'm still married to Nic."

"I don't care if you were married to some guy twenty years ago."

"Still married."

"Only on paper," I argued. "Damn it, Michele, you should have told me. A long time ago."

She nodded. "I wanted that part of my life to be over. Now I want that even more." She started to reach for me, but then paused, as if second-guessing if her move would be welcomed. I didn't want to be touched and was relieved when she let her hand fall to her side. She continued, "At least now all of my cards are on the table."

"So what now?" It wasn't so much a question for her as it was for me.

"Somehow I find a way to convince you to trust me. Any ideas?"

"Not at the moment."

She shook her head. "I've always been the one who had issues trusting people. I never wanted to tell the women I dated about being married or about Peter because I didn't trust them enough to think that they would stay. I was so worried about their reaction that I became the one who wasn't telling the truth."

"Funny how things work out," I said. I wouldn't smooth over the sarcasm now.

"When we started to get close, I knew I had to tell you. After you asked about my past and I lied…I felt terrible for weeks. I didn't even want to face you. Then I decided I was going to tell you. I did try. Do you remember the night when I sat in your bathroom with the lights off? I came over because I had something to tell you."

I knew exactly which night she was talking about. It was the night I'd finally admitted everything. I'd been honest. Too honest. And I hadn't asked enough questions. I never did.

Michele continued, "I chickened out. After everything you told me that night, I couldn't bring it up… I figured that if I said something then you'd never trust me again and I wouldn't blame you. When do you decide to tell the truth after keeping up a lie for so long?"

"Before now."

"I'm so sorry." She stepped toward me and kissed my cheek.

I may have winced at the touch. I don't remember. But the expression on her face when she turned away was so full of hurt that I wondered what I'd done. Hurt and something more. It took me a moment to register it. Longing.

CHAPTER TWENTY-FOUR

I tried to call it an omission because in my mind that sounded better than a lie, but it wasn't easy to pretend that nothing had changed between us after everything she'd disclosed. Neither of us mentioned it the next morning, and I tried to convince myself that I didn't really care. The new details did change the picture of her in my mind, but when I looked right at her, none of those new details mattered. Especially after a few days had passed. This confused me more than anything else. How could I still be in love with someone who'd lied to my face?

We settled into the habit of living together. Four weeks slipped by, and Alice went to the vet twice, once for his shots and again when he'd chewed the power cord on my sander. He singed his lip but was otherwise fine. I hadn't realized that it'd been a month since Michele moved in, but she did. She brought it up in the middle of dinner.

"I should be paying part of the rent," she'd said. "It's been a month and I haven't paid anything. You even paid for Alice's vet bill."

"But I won the bet because of that vet visit." I smiled. The vet had agreed. Alice was unequivocally a boy. We'd decided not to change the name. "Anyway, it's not rent when you're paying the bank. It's mortgage. I wasn't expecting you to pay my mortgage when I asked you to move in. You buy most of the groceries. We're fine." I set down my fork and reached for my water glass.

"I want to pay my share," she argued quietly. "I can afford more than the grocery bill. You buy us takeout half the time anyway."

In fact, I only bought takeout twice a week, but I knew that wasn't the point. Her point was that she wanted the situation to be more like roommates and less like lovers. If we were only roommates, we'd split the house payment. I closed my eyes, wanting to go back to the moment before she'd brought up the rent, the moment we were only having dinner—as if we were a real couple. Only we weren't.

"Are you working with Travis tomorrow?" she asked.

I nodded.

She reached for the salt and sprinkled it on the vegetables. "We never talk about this sort of stuff."

"We don't talk about a lot of stuff," I argued. I watched Alice in the kitchen. He was spinning around in a circle chasing his tail. At the moment, I couldn't look at Michele. I heard her sigh and then felt her hand touch mine.

"So let's change that. We need to start talking about things."

I glanced up at her. "Okay. You first."

"If I paid half the mortgage, could you afford to stay here? I know you've put most of your savings into remodeling this place."

"All of it, actually." My job with Travis was paying the mortgage each month and slowly working down my credit card debt. I hadn't bought the hall bathroom toilet and sink yet. I had a cabinet on hold at the warehouse. I was tapped out.

"But could we stay if I paid half the bills?"

"I never planned on staying here, Michele. This was always just a job."

"Maybe it *was* just a job, but is it now?" She paused. "And this is more than a conversation about being housemates, isn't it?"

I waited for her to continue, but she didn't. Finally she pulled her hand away and went back to eating her vegetables.

Michele was already out of bed when I woke the next morning. Usually I was the first one up, but we kept similar schedules. I heard the shower and went downstairs to pee, turning on the coffee before coming back up to dress. Alice attacked my ankles as I passed him on the stairs and I had to turn back around to go fill his bowl. When I headed back up again, Michele met me at the top of the stairs. She was wrapped in a towel and had a toothbrush in her mouth. She pulled the toothbrush out to say, "We need to talk," and then went back to the sink to finish brushing.

I pulled on long johns, then thick work pants, wool socks, a long sleeve T-shirt and a flannel shirt. With all that, along with my heavy work coat, I might manage to stay warm. Travis had scheduled a two-week outside job for us right before a cold front had settled in. With an expected high of nine, I was already dreading the day's work. I finished dressing and went to find Michele. Her room was right across the hall from mine. She usually made a point of dressing in her room with the door closed; today she'd left it open. I leaned in the doorway. "Should I be worried?"

"No. I want to talk about some things—that's all. We agreed we would talk more last night, didn't we?"

"Okay." I didn't move away from the doorway and she didn't seem to mind that I was still standing there. The bed was fully made. She already had her underwear on or I would have averted my gaze. I'd seen her naked once and only in passing since she'd moved in. She didn't try to hide her body, but she always had a towel on after her shower and I never really let myself look at her. She had flowers on her underwear today. Not little demure daisies but great big Hawaiian sort of flowers. It was hard not to stare. She had a fuchsia-colored bra with thin straps that would be easy to slip off her shoulders. The bra quickly disappeared under a silk camisole. Navy slacks and a navy blazer were laid out on the bed. She pulled a cream-colored knit blouse on over the camisole.

"Can you give me a hint?"

She glanced over at me and then sat down on the bed to put on her socks. She pulled them up past her shins. "I don't think you need a hint. I think we both know what we need to discuss."

Every evening we spent together made me think that I could say "I love you." And yet I hesitated. "Tonight then?" I knew her schedule well. She was home a little after five every night and only went out on Thursday and Sunday nights for either band practice or a performance. But she could have something else to do.

"Yeah. Tonight works." She buttoned the slacks and reached for the blazer. No one except me would know that she was wearing Hawaiian-flowered underwear and a fuchsia bra.

"I'll probably be home early. Last night's weather report said we'd get a few inches of snow this afternoon. I'm guessing Travis will probably call it quits as soon as the snow starts. I'll make dinner."

She went over to her dresser and opened the top drawer. She pulled out an envelope, glanced at it briefly and then handed it to me. "This was from Katy. It was in the folder with the music sheets."

I recognized the envelope. Michele's name was on the front in swirling cursive. "Yeah, she asked me to give this to you."

"Will you read it and tell me why you think she gave it to me?"

"But it's your letter."

She shook her head. "It was for Alice."

By noon the snow was coming in sideways. Travis had settled with the homeowner that the hot tub cabana was going to have to be delayed until the weather improved. I huddled up to the heating vents in my truck when he went to let the owner know we were leaving for the day. Even in two pairs of gloves, my fingers were numb at the tips. Travis knocked on the passenger window and then climbed in the truck. He leaned back and sighed. "So, the new weather prediction is that we're stuck with this storm for the next three days. And it's going to get worse before it gets better." Travis gestured back to the house. "He's fine if we put this on hold until the storm passes. But at the moment, I don't have anything else lined up. I'll go home and see what else I can drum up. Sorry. This is bad timing for both of us."

He knew I was hoping for more hours in the next paycheck. I had broken my rule of not telling Travis anything personal when Michele moved in with me, and since then, it was as if the floodgates had broken and I'd told him nearly everything. I hadn't told him about Katy or Alice, only because that still didn't feel like my story to share, but I'd admitted my feelings for Michele and then told him about her secret past. It was Travis's response, or lack thereof, that made me think I could get over her lying.

That morning I'd also mentioned Michele's comment about splitting rent and how I'd wished she hadn't brought it up, yet the truth was I could use help with the bills. Travis had told me he was currently running the business on managed credit card debt and was month to month on all his bills. We were in the same boat, but it wasn't much comfort.

He got out of my truck, promising to text if any new job came up and hurried over to his. The snow was thick, and even with the wipers and the defrost both going, I only had a narrow arc of the windshield cleared well enough to drive. I had settled on making soup and bread for dinner mainly because I had one of Lynn's old recipes for a thick barley vegetable stew memorized. I stopped at the nearly deserted grocery store to get what I needed and was soon home peeling potatoes. All the ingredients went into a pot to boil, then simmered for the rest of the afternoon.

Michele was home by five. Her coat was dusted in snow and she kicked off her boots in the entryway, complaining about wet toes. She went upstairs to change and came down a few minutes later wearing her University of Arizona sweats and puffy down slippers.

She handed me a blue-and-white-striped gift bag with yellow tissue poking out of the top.

"It's not my birthday."

"I know. Open it," she said. She lifted the lid on the stew and stirred the contents. "This smells amazing."

"The bread is warming in the oven. We can eat as soon as you like."

"I love coming home to dinner." She set the spoon down and glanced over at me.

"Well?"

I pushed the tissue paper out of the way and reached into the bag. I knew what it was immediately. The feel of the wood and the carvings were unmistakable. I pulled out the jewelry box and ran my hand over the lid. "Where'd you find it?"

"At an antique shop on the west side. I stopped in a few weeks ago to pass the time before a gig at the winery. When I spotted this in their window display, I couldn't look at anything else."

"I love it."

"It needs to be polished and there's a split in the wood. One of the hinges is broken too...but I thought you could probably fix it up."

"Thank you."

"Too bad this one's empty," she apologized.

"It's perfect." I'd never even considered that the jewelry box collector wouldn't be interested in it.

She smiled. "So, did you guys freeze today? I kept looking out the window and thinking you must be miserable."

"We had to quit at noon." I loved the fact that she thought of me while she was at work. "And I have the next few days off unless the storm lets up."

I sliced the bread while Michele dished out the soup. We ate our meals on her dining room table now, and I had to admit that it was much more comfortable than eating on the couch.

Michele was halfway through her soup when she tore off a piece of bread and looked over at me. "Travis pays you an hourly rate, right? So you won't get paid if you have days off because of the snow."

I nodded.

"We should talk about money."

"I have credit cards. I'm not worried. This month's going to be tight, but I'll be fine." I dipped my bread in the stew. "Is that what we're supposed to talk about tonight? Money stuff?"

She shook her head. "But I think we should split the bills."

"Okay."

"That's it? Okay?"

I nodded. "We are roommates, right? I thought about it and I think you're right. Roommates split the bills. But if that's what we are doing here, I want to split the grocery bill too." I finished up the last of my stew with the heel of the bread and shifted back in my chair waiting for Michele to answer. Finally I said, "I didn't get a chance to read the letter from Katy."

"There's no rush." She ate slowly, pushing the peas and carrots away from the potatoes with the edge of her spoon and then scooping them all up in one bite. "This is delicious," she said. "I think there's enough to save for tomorrow's dinner as well. We could add some green beans or even cauliflower."

"Yeah, sure." I didn't care about the stew. Whatever was on Michele's mind, she was clearly reluctant to start the real conversation if she was procrastinating thinking of leftovers. "I don't like cauliflower though."

"I forgot about that. Okay, no cauliflower."

"How was your practice session last night?" This wasn't the question I wanted to ask. Now I was the one procrastinating. Her band and Katy's song was a safe topic for both of us.

"We've been working on Katy's song nonstop. Mostly because of me. I've fallen in love with that song. I want it to sound as good as we can make it. Well, I want it to sound even better than that…Sarah wants me to sing lead. It's not written for a soprano." She finished up her soup and then took my bowl as well as hers over to the sink. She rinsed the bowls and stared out at the dark window.

"Katy's going to love that you're singing lead."

"I hope so. We're not ready to perform it yet, but I think maybe in another month or so, we'll be close."

"I'd love to convince Katy to come down to see it live. She told me she has no intention of leaving Wyoming until she's dead."

"And then she'll go find Alice." Michele filled the dishwasher and rinsed her hands. She dried her hands on a dishtowel and then tossed it at me. "You're making me nervous."

"Me? Why?"

"You keep staring at me."

"I'm waiting for you to tell me what's going on. You're the one who said we needed to talk." I threw the dishtowel back at her. "Maybe I'm nervous too. What is it you wanted to talk about?"

Michele hung the towel and then headed for the living room. I'd already a started a fire and the living room was several degrees warmer because of it. She sat down on the sofa, crossing her legs under her and then grabbed one of the throw pillows and hugged it to her chest. I poked at the fire until sparks flew up and added another log. When I looked over at her, Michele patted the cushion next to her.

I reluctantly sat down. "This morning I thought maybe this was going to be a good conversation, but tonight I'm not so sure."

"I want to stay in Alice's house. I want us to figure out a way to make that happen."

"Do you play the lottery? I like it here too. A lot. But neither of us can afford Granite Avenue." I sighed. "You don't want to see my credit card statement. I need to sell this place. Soon."

"But we could afford it together," she argued.

"It's not that I haven't considered it. This past month has made me consider a lot of things…" I kept my eyes trained on the fire. The new log I'd pushed onto the flames was smoking some, but an edge of it had already begun to flicker.

"So how are you feeling about what we aren't talking about?"

"The text?"

"Yeah." She stared at the fire. "You haven't asked me any questions about Peter. I'm not sure if you're waiting for me to bring it up or if you don't want to talk about it."

"I didn't bring it up because I didn't want you to think it was a big deal for me."

"I lied to you, Jodi. Lies of omission but still…I know it's a big deal."

"Okay, so what do you want me to say? Want me to be pissed that you lied? Pissed that you still aren't talking about it—that we are pretending it isn't a problem?"

"Maybe. Maybe I want you to be pissed." She had raised her voice and quickly checked the volume when she added, "Look, I want to know how you feel about it. I want to talk about it."

The trouble was, I wasn't pissed. "I've tried to forget about that text, but then as soon as I'm starting to feel comfortable, like I know your routine, know that you have a bagel for breakfast every day through the week and then eggs on the weekend, I remember that you have this whole other life that I know nothing about…And maybe I'm crazy, but I haven't wanted to talk about it, or even think about it for too long, because I've had this feeling that if I brought it up, I'd ruin everything else."

"'Everything else'?"

I contemplated my answer. It was hard to justify not being honest. I'd fallen hard for her long ago and the text hadn't changed my feelings. Now I was only pretending I wasn't in love with her to make her feel more comfortable. "It's been nice having you as a roommate. Maybe even too nice. But the truth is, you're not the easiest roommate for me."

"Why?"

I knew she could guess the answer, but I wanted to say it aloud anyway. Maybe she finally wanted to hear. "The fact that I like you might have something to do with it. Your room is only across the hall. Your bed is so close to mine."

"And mine's more comfortable."

"I'm glad you can joke." As soon as I said it, her expression turned tight-lipped and I realized her light tone was only a cover. We were both standing on the edge of a cliff. "The thing is, I'm not pissed that you lied. I am pissed that it didn't change how much I want you. 'Cause it'd be easier for me if the fact that you lied made me not want to kiss you. But it doesn't."

She crossed her arms, and I knew it was too late to take back the words. I didn't want to anyway. "Since you moved in, I've tried really hard to pretend that I'm not interested. I'd almost convinced myself that we could make it as friends, but then I catch you coming out of the shower in nothing but a towel, and I know that as soon as you find a girlfriend, I'm going to be miserable."

"You know, you're not the easiest roommate either."

I looked over at her. "Good. I hope I'm really difficult."

"Some days you're impossible. Impossible not to fall for." After a long moment, she said, "You're really okay with everything? With Peter and with me being married and all of that?"

"You can't lie to me again. Not about something that important. We won't make it as roommates—or anything more—if you do. I like living with you, but..."

"I like living with you too," she interrupted. "A lot."

"That might change when one of us has a girlfriend over."

"I haven't had anyone else over because I don't want anyone else," she said.

"At the moment. But what happens when you meet the next girl? I can't afford this place on my own, and I don't want to live here if you're sleeping with someone else in the room next door."

Michele was quiet for several minutes, and I wondered if our conversation was over. I wanted to ask her if she really meant it when she said I was a difficult roommate. Was being across the hall from my room as hard for her as it was for me? One of the logs was smoking, so I got up to poke the fire again. Alice was dangerously close to the flames, the tip of his gray tail twitching as he stared down the sparks. I put up the screen and tried to push him away, but he reared up to attack my hand. In some ways, he was still every bit a ferocious barn cat.

"What's he like?"

"Pete?"

I nodded.

"He's sweet, always has been. A bit of a daydreamer, but somehow he always remembers to call me on Sundays. And he's always been sensitive—the kind of kid who cried when another kid doused a snail with salt. I used to worry that the world would harden him, but I think that's something all mothers worry about." She sighed. "He's tall, like his father, but otherwise he looks a lot like me, poor kid."

"Yeah, poor kid. I bet he's got it tough finding dates." If he had half his mother's looks, I doubted that Pete was having any trouble filling his social calendar.

"Sometimes I even appreciate your sarcasm." Michele smiled. "I know I said I wanted us to be friends. I do...but... something's changed, hasn't it?"

Michele's question hung in the space between us. I glanced over at her.

She continued, "When I can't sleep at night, the only thing I think about is how easy it would be to slip into your bed and curl up against you. I feel like for the first time I'm in the right house, but I'm in the wrong bed."

"What are you saying?"

Alice pounced on Michele's lap and then a moment later shot up the staircase. Michele followed him with her eyes and then looked back at me. "I'm saying this is different from every other relationship I've had. And I like it. A lot. Maybe I like it too much."

I wanted her to come out and say what I thought was right on the tip of her tongue, but of course she only stared at me. "But we aren't in a relationship. We're only roommates, remember?"

She shifted back on the sofa pillows, keeping her eyes trained on me. "Are we?"

"And this is only a house that I remodeled to make money. I know you like living here, but I need this place flipped. Soon." I let my eyes wander about the room. This was Alice's house. Of course it wasn't only a flip. Not anymore anyway. The possibility of making it my home was all too appealing. But the money simply wasn't there. "I don't know, Michele. Maybe we should both ignore what we feel. We're fine being friends. Why rock the boat?"

"Because we want more. Don't try arguing with me on this. The truth is, I've wanted more all along. I was holding back before. I hated that I was too scared to tell you about Peter and being married and all of that. I hated that I kept up a lie. I made everything so much worse by waiting too long. And then you found out…But it's done. You know and for some reason you don't hate me. So, now I don't want to hold back anymore."

I reached for her and she held my hand. The touch was enough to make everything else in the room fade into the background. Her skin was soft against mine, and the feel of holding her was intoxicating.

"You have no idea how many times I'd gone through everything in my head," Michele continued. "How could I let go of someone I'd been falling for for over two years now all because I couldn't tell them the truth?"

"You've been falling for me for over two years and you wait until now to tell me?"

"Did I say that?" Michele blushed. "I want to date you. And I want an official first date—like going out for dinner at a place with real flowers on the table…Or maybe a movie with theater popcorn and you holding my hand the whole time. Hell, I want to go to Santa Fe for the weekend."

"Santa Fe?" I smiled. "Why?"

"I want to travel—I've never had a chance to before. And now I have someone that I want to take with me."

"Maybe we should start with holding hands."

"I want the real flowers and the popcorn too. I want all of it."

"And after two months of that, if you still don't want to break up with me or if I don't want to break up with you—"

"Don't," Michele interrupted. "Maybe I deserve that, but… I'll be different with you. And I need you to give me a chance to prove that."

I wanted to say "I love you" in response, but I only nodded.

"I know I've been a pain in the ass and confusing and all of that but…You don't know how many times I've wanted to kiss you. At Lynn's house when we used to cook together. At the Metro. Every day I've been in this damn house—every time we pass each other in the hall—I want you to reach for me. I've wanted to kiss you so much that I couldn't even look at you some days." She paused. "If we're going to do this right, we need to forget about what happens if we break up. I want more than hand holding."

"Me too." It was strangely hard to admit this. It was hard to say anything at all. I only wanted to kiss her.

"Then what are you afraid of?"

"You."

Michele shook her head. "You're not afraid of me. You're afraid of getting your heart broken."

"Like Katy?" I asked the question and answered it in my own head a moment later. That was it exactly. "I think we both are."

She shifted to close the space between us. "I want to sleep in your room tonight."

"I might need to be convinced that's a good idea." I was only half teasing. I felt shaky, scared and turned on like I'd never held a woman's hand before. Michele's gaze was full of desire. I'd seen the look so many times before, on other faces, other women, but they were all fuzzy memories now. I knew exactly what would come next and yet I didn't. It'd never been just like this.

Michele let go of my hand and headed for the stairs. I followed her to my bedroom. Our only light came from the night sky shining in through the sliding door. It cast shards of bright and dim light across my bed.

I didn't resist when she slipped off my shirt and brushed her hand across my chest. I watched her take off her shirt, staring unabashedly at her breasts cupped in the fuchsia bra. I looked up when I realized she was watching me. The look of desire in her eyes was enough to make me take off my pants, feeling her wanting eyes on my body all the while. When I was naked, I stepped closer to her, but she pushed me back and looked at me for a moment longer, a half smile playing on her lips.

"It's hard to resist touching you," I said, after a long moment of waiting.

"I thought you were going to need some convincing," she teased.

"You convinced me."

"We've had two years to practice resisting. Maybe I want to savor it this time." She paused, then reached toward me, her fingertips tracing the line of my jaw. She continued the light caress down my neck, over my shoulder and down my arm, stopping when our fingertips touched. A shiver raced down me, and I stepped toward her. She shook her head. "Are you going to complain that I'm taking my time?"

"Maybe. Maybe I'm done resisting."

She pulled me toward her. I lost myself in the kiss, lost hold of everything that I'd warned about, lost hold of every hesitation. How could I have thought that being friends was enough?

Michele undid her bra clasp and slipped it off, then shifted forward to feel my hands against her breasts. I encircled each nipple with a fingertip, then bent low and let my tongue follow the same pattern. Michele's responding murmurs were more a command not to stop than any sign of contentment. I undid her pants and pulled them off, then pushed her back onto the bed. I gazed down at her and felt a rush of emotion that choked me. Michele's face and chest were illuminated in the weak moonlight, pale skin and tousled blond hair sharply contrasting the dark blue sheets, almond eyes searching mine and lips that I'd long watched forming oohs and ahhs in every song, parted now, waiting for mine.

I slid closer and she pushed up into me, her kiss demanding as she opened and waited for my tongue. When I shifted away, she pulled me back, moaning softly and pressing her teeth into my neck. I felt the pressure but not the bite. She had held back but barely, and her intentions were obvious. When I pulled away again, she said, "Don't get second thoughts." Her voice was a husky whisper in my ear.

It's too late for that, I answered silently. I wanted her more than I could admit and the response of my body, already wet and wanting her fingers, unsteadied me. I followed her movements, pressing into her each time her hips rocked up. I kissed her neck, her breasts and down her belly, my hands moving between her legs. I shifted lower and slipped my tongue across her swollen clit and then slid fingers inside, watching her face as I did, her low moan all the encouragement I needed. I licked faster as she pulled me into her.

When she climaxed, her eyes squeezed closed and her mouth opened with a moan, her body clenching around my hands. A minute passed and I hoped that she'd never ask me to move, that I could lie with my lips between her legs, my fingers deep inside her warm folds, watching her chest rise and fall with each breath, her body beginning to relax. She shifted away from my hand finally and pulled me up to a kiss, then wrapped her arms around me. I shifted so my full weight wasn't on her, but she murmured an argument and pulled me back on top of her, holding me tighter this time.

I kept my position for several minutes, loving the feel of her skin under every inch of mine. Underneath me, Michele's frame felt petite, but when she stood, she was only a few inches shorter than I was. I shifted so my weight wasn't pinning her down and then tentatively surveyed her body. Even in the dim light, my tanned skin was a stark contrast to her pale color. My calloused hands felt much too rough against her smooth belly. I didn't dare speak or look at Michele's face for fear of breaking the spell that had led to this moment. What had led to this? What had changed? Her breathing set the rhythm of my own and I tried to relax.

When Michele finally moved to her side, I rolled off her. I pulled the sheet up to cover our bodies and curled up against her. I was too keyed up to sleep, but I tried to quiet the urge to reach for her hand. Several minutes passed and I wondered if she was already asleep.

She touched my cheek. "Don't think I'm going to let you sleep tonight. You might change your mind tomorrow."

"I won't change my mind." *Ever*, I added silently.

She pushed me onto my back and then climbed on top, wet brushing against my thighs. She pushed the sheet to the end of the bed and stared down at me. "I want to see all of you." She pinned my hands against the bed and kissed me hard.

CHAPTER TWENTY-FIVE

I felt Michele get out of bed and rubbed my eyes. I didn't want to move and didn't want to admit it was morning. Michele returned after a few minutes and crawled back under the covers. We had slept, after all. Briefly. Then woke again sometime in the still dark morning and made love again. We were both too greedy to let sleep have much say. Michele wrapped her arm around me and closed her eyes. I lay still, waiting for her to drift back to sleep. She slept on as sunlight brightened the room. I finally eased free from her arms and went to pee.

When I came back to the room, Michele stretched and looked over at me. "What are you smiling about?"

"I like seeing you naked in my bed." That wasn't all. Parts of me were buzzing that I hadn't felt buzz in years. I didn't want the buzz to stop. I wanted to touch the spots that had made her cry out my name last night. Had it all been last night? I wanted to lie on top of her and kiss her breasts down to her wet center all over again. "Want to call in sick?"

"Yes, but I'm not going to." She sighed. "The downside of a desk job is you have to work even when it's snowing." She reached for my phone and glanced at the time. "Shit, I'm going to be late."

I waited until Michele had left for work to find Katy's letter. It was still in the cargo pocket of my work pants and the corners of the envelope were bent. The envelope was addressed to Michele, but the letter inside was addressed to Alice. Although I hadn't read all of the letters in Alice's jewelry box, I knew this note had never been in the box. Instead of a page ripped out of a journal, this was written on proper stationery. I sat on the bed with the comforter pulled up over my legs. The smell of Michele was still on the sheets and I had no desire to rush the morning.

Dear Alice,

I know it's been too long. Too long to expect you to remember how it felt the first time we held each other, or the first time we kissed, or the first time you said, "I love you." But I remember it all. Some days I wish I could forget. Today I'm stuck remembering. It's this blue sky. You used to say that the blue sky was only wide enough for lovers. I wondered what you meant but you wouldn't explain. Now I feel lost in all this blue sky. Days pass and all I do is long for the company of clouds.

Years change some things. The latch on the milking barn is rusted and needs replacing. You'd never guess that my Ford was once blue. My hair's streaked with gray as well but I don't mind. I don't look in the mirror often. My dad's favorite Jersey passed away of old age last month. Animals rarely go of old age around here but she was Dad's favorite. She was born the same spring I moved back home. I wouldn't expect you to remember that spring but I do. I remember my dad holding that calf up to her mama's teats to get her to nurse. She was born early and we'd had a frost the night she arrived. She was too weak to stand so he brought her inside the house and nursed her by hand. That's why he got attached. Before he passed, I promised him she'd live out her life without ever knowing the butcher. Some things are too precious to be practical, even here.

But some things don't change with time. I still think of you every day. You wander into my thoughts and catch me off guard. Sometimes I'll be out on a ride, other times I'll be having my morning coffee… And suddenly I'm thinking of you. I can't remember if you drink your coffee with milk and sugar or if you like it black. I poured you a mug the other day and let it get cold before I tossed it out. I wonder if you are happy. I wonder if you think of me sometimes, maybe.

Remember the first afternoon you came to my room at Uptown? I heard a knock and thought it was the manager wanting my rent. I saw your face in the hallway and nearly cried. You had an excuse for why you'd come but I didn't let you finish talking. I pulled you inside and the rest of the afternoon was ours. I wish I could remember everything we did that afternoon, everything you whispered, but I don't. I only remember how you felt in my arms. No matter how many others I've held, I haven't been able to shrug the feel of you.

I won't send this letter. I know it's too much risk for you to receive it now and there's no way of knowing how time has changed your mind. I suppose I've always been too much risk for you, haven't I? You were too much risk for me too, but not in the way you think of it. When I said 'Goodbye' it was only because it was far easier for both of us than 'I love you.' We were never fearless but we did hold love. And maybe once is all you get in this life. I don't regret anything that happened between us. We each had our reasons. I only regret that I wasn't fearless.

Yours always,
KW

"Damn it, Katy," I said aloud. No one except maybe Alice was listening. The cat was stretched out at the foot of the bed, and his ears twitched at my voice. I got up to shower and Alice didn't move.

The water pelted my skin and I leaned against the cold tile, enjoying the contrast with the steaming water. If she had sent the letter, would anything have changed? The more I thought about it, the more I found myself agreeing with her decision not to post this last letter despite my knee-jerk reaction of exasperation that pushed on tears. Maybe this wasn't even the last letter she'd written. Maybe she had a box full of letters that had never been sent. Of course, Alice might have had unsent letters that we never found as well. Maybe her kids would unearth them someday and realize the truth about their mom. Or maybe they'd never go looking for the truth.

I'd bought a cookbook on Katy's advice and spent the better half of the morning flipping through the recipes and distractedly surfing the Internet. I had plenty of work to do around the house, of course, but I couldn't bring myself to do anything, not after last night. It was hard to believe that Michele had slept in my bed despite the fuchsia bra I found tangled up in the sheets at the foot of the bed. There was no way I was going to have second thoughts. But would she? I finally settled on a promising-looking coconut curry and headed for the grocery store.

* * *

"Something smells good."

As she came into the kitchen I kissed Michele on the cheek, as had become our custom, and realized only when she smiled back at me that I could have kissed her on the lips. "I read Katy's last letter," I said. "The one she didn't send to Alice."

"And?" Michele went over to the stove and lifted the lid on the curry. She dipped the spoon in and stirred, nodding approvingly.

I wanted to grab her and kiss her again. But she was so restrained—such the librarian, I thought with a grin. But not last night. The memory of her naked body next to mine distracted my thoughts. She lifted the spoon to her lips and blew to cool it. Those lips, I thought...

"And what'd you think?" she asked.

"About what?"

She laughed when I stared back at her. "The letter? What are you thinking about, Burkitt?"

"The letter," I lied. I loved her innuendo. I'd heard it so many times before, but this time was different. It wasn't only a tease.

"Yeah right." She laughed again and tasted the curry. "This is delicious."

"So, why do you think she gave the letter to you?"

"I think she wanted me to read it before I sang the song. There was a note that she wrote to me inside the envelope as well. But I didn't want to give that to you."

"Why not?"

"Because she mentioned something about you. I'm allowed to keep some secrets. But don't worry. This one's innocent."

"I thought Katy was on my side."

"She's on both of our sides."

I pushed away a twinge of jealousy at the secret I wasn't privy to. I knew Katy was only trying to help my cause. "You hungry?" I asked, checking the rice.

"I've been hungry all day."

Her tone was almost too distracting. "So, back to Katy's letter…" I dished out two bowls of rice and then ladled on the steaming vegetable curry. "Why'd you want me to read it?"

"I wanted to know what you thought about it."

"It's depressing. Like all of the letters. What else?"

She took the bowls to the table. "I love that you cook."

I smiled. "Maybe I'm trying to hook you."

"That was last night, wasn't it?"

Hearing her admit it out loud made my head spin. What had happened between us last night was real—here with all the lights on as well as in the dark of the bedroom. I wasn't going to ask her to define our relationship now. I wasn't going to worry about what might happen when we broke up and if we could keep our friendship after. Today I didn't care. "Ever feel fearless?"

She shook her head. "Do you?"

"Today I do."

"Maybe you can be brave enough for the both of us."

"Okay. I'm up for it."

Michele laughed. "Who are you?"

"Someone you should have dated years ago."

"Tell me about it," she said, grinning.

I sat down at my usual spot, feeling that this meal was anything but usual. We'd had dinner together too many times to count, but this was the first time she slipped her leg between mine. Then she leaned across the table and kissed me. I wanted to skip dinner and find a bed.

"'Fearless,' huh? Wonder what KW would say…" She took a bite of the curry and murmured her approval again. "At first I thought maybe she gave me the letter because of the meaning in the song. You know the line in the first verse, 'you were only trying out I love yous when I found the one thing I couldn't lose'?"

"'This blue sky day's only wide enough for lovers, Alone and I'm looking for the gray,'" I said, continuing the song. I paused.

Michele sang, "'And I'll be waiting for that love song, when all this sunshine turns to rain.'"

"Doesn't get less depressing, does it?"

"I don't know." Michele paused. "When you take it line by line, it's sad. But Katy manages to make me believe that it all turns out okay."

"But it didn't."

"Maybe not with her and Alice…I don't know. In the end, the song has a resolution that's hopeful. Everyone gets a love song. What's more positive than that?" She took another bite of the curry. "Then I think maybe she gave me that last letter for an entirely different reason. Maybe it wasn't because of the song at all. Maybe she only wanted someone to read that last letter. I wish Alice could have been the one to read it."

"Sometimes I hate Alice for never sending Katy any letters."

"She's dead."

"I can hate a dead person."

Michele shook her head. "I fell in love with Alice a long time ago, and I'm going to stand by her always. You never read the letters she wrote to Katy."

"She never sent them," I countered. "How can you stand by her? She broke Katy's heart."

"Katy made her choices. Like she said in that last letter—she wasn't fearless. And she was the one who left Alice."

"I'm not going to win this argument, am I?"

Michele smiled. "No. You might as well give up now. By the way, I'm telling Lynn."

"About Katy and Alice?"

She shook her head.

"Telling her what?"

"That you're a better cook than you ever let on." She smiled again. "And I want her to hear it from me first. Before you and Lynn got serious, there's a chance I told her that...well, I may have admitted that I'd ask you out if she didn't." She reached across the table and touched my cheek. "You're blushing."

"No, I'm not."

Michele laughed. "It's true. Lynn beat me to you. Anyway, I know she's going to be upset, at first, but I want to tell her so she doesn't find out through someone else. And there's another reason. I want you to come with me to California for Thanksgiving. Roxy already asked if I could bring you as my carry-on."

"I'm not sure Lynn is going to be happy about any of that, but I'd love to come. I'd like to see Roxy. And going on a trip with you wouldn't be all that bad either."

"Not 'all that bad'?" Michele nudged me under the table. "Don't try and play coy, Jodi. I can see right through your act."

"You always could," I admitted.

"There's something else I've been waiting to tell you."

"Uh-oh," I teased.

"Relax, this is good news. Remember how Lynn always has that annual ski trip with her sister in Breckenridge? Sal wants to go too this year."

"I thought you said this was good news." Lynn had never asked me to go on the annual trip to Breckenridge. I'd stayed home with Roxy each year. But chances were good that Lynn hadn't asked Sal to come with her this year either. Knowing Sal, she'd invited herself.

"Roxy can't stay home alone, and Lynn says this is her annual vacation from parenting. She asked me if I'd take Roxy for the week," Michele paused. "All three of them are flying into Denver, and I'll be picking Roxy up and driving her down here."

"Roxy will be staying with us for the week? And Lynn's okay with that?"

"She will be when I tell her all the reasons it's a good idea. They're flying out the first week of January."

I started thinking of a list of things the three of us could do... Last year, Roxy and I had gone to Travis's cabin in the mountains for a few days while Lynn was at Breck. We'd made hot cocoa and a fire every night and spent the days hunting for the best sledding hill. I knew Travis would let me have the cabin for the whole week if I asked.

"Don't worry about Lynn. You know Roxy will be thrilled." She added, "Lynn has said several times that Roxy needs a second auntie in her life. Now I'll make my case for why you would be perfect."

I *was* worried about Lynn regardless of what Michele said. How could I not be? It was her decision that had cut me out of Roxy's life before. But with Michele on my side and everything different between us, I hoped there was a chance... If Lynn agreed, I'd take the role of aunt in a heartbeat. In fact, now that Michele had suggested it, I realized that'd been my part all along.

CHAPTER TWENTY-SIX

I couldn't do much about the split in the wood, but I'd sanded down the spots where the flowers had been chipped and replaced the broken brass hinge. With a fresh coat of stain, the jewelry box shone like new.

When the second coat of stain had dried, I set the jewelry box on the mantel above the fireplace. Michele came home as I was starting a fire. She carried a bag of groceries into the kitchen and then came back to the front room. When she spotted the box, she picked it up to admire my days' work. In fact, I'd had a few other projects, but the jewelry box had taken up more time than I was willing to admit. I'd gotten attached to the little box at first sight and wanted to make it perfect.

"Now it looks even more like Alice's. Almost an exact replica," Michele said, setting the box back on the mantel.

"When I'm as old as Katy, I'll open that box and remember their story…and this house."

She smiled down at me. I had a tender flame going and had to concentrate to get the next bit of kindling to catch fire.

When I had a good bit burning, I stood up and kissed Michele. I doubted I was going to grow tired of the simple pleasure of doing that.

"I haven't started dinner."

"It's my turn tonight," Michele said. "I'm making your favorite."

"What's my favorite?"

She grinned. "You're about to find out."

"It's a good thing you moved in when you did. I was getting tired of frozen dinners."

"I like living with you too," she said, punching my arm playfully. "You know, we never finished our conversation about the house the other night."

"Which part?"

"About us staying here."

"I think we hit the main points. I don't have the money to stay." I needed to list the house the first of the year. Moneywise, I didn't have a choice. "Even if we split the mortgage, I have too many bills I'm going to need to pay come January." I paused. But maybe it could wait until after Roxy's visit. "I can probably stretch things until February, March at the latest…Anyway, why do you want to stay in this house? We could find another place with a mortgage we could afford…"

"Because I love *this* house. And because it's Alice's house. I've looked at plenty of other places. Nothing compares." She glanced around the room. "I love that I know some of the secrets that the walls have heard, and I love living with you, but I also think it's a great house. Why leave?"

Saying she loved living with me was not what I wanted to hear. I wanted to test out an "I love you" simply to hear if there was a deafening lack of response from her or if she'd repeat the words back to me.

"When are we going to finish the bathroom? I still think there's more here, hidden…Maybe there's something in the basement. We haven't even begun to explore past that rickety staircase. I took a peek down there the other day. You know, if you finished it off and added a couple rooms down there, this place would be worth a hell of a lot more. There's even more potential here."

"I know. But I'm out of money."

"You keep saying that, but you know I'm willing to help—not with only splitting the rent. I could help with the remodel costs too. Why not say yes?"

"I'm not going to let you put your money into the remodel. It will get too complicated if we have to sell and I don't want to risk losing anyone else's money."

"Unless we don't sell. What if we agree to a year?" She paused. "I was going to sign a year's lease somewhere—why not let me sign it with you? Let's live in Alice's house for a year and keep working on it."

"One year would only make me miss you more when you've gone."

Michele crossed her arms. "You promised you'd give me a real chance."

"I would give you a hundred chances," I admitted. She might as well know the truth. "But you don't do long term."

"*Didn't*. Past tense. What if it's a year lease on the house and a relationship? I know I have a bad track record, but that doesn't mean I don't want long term. It's never felt like a possibility for me. I'm still technically married, you know. For the time being, anyway."

She went over to the entryway where she'd left her boots and coat. "There's something I wanted to show you." Next to the puddle left by the snow melting off the boots was her briefcase. She brought the briefcase over to the coffee table and popped it open, then pulled out a printout filled with names and addresses. She pointed to a Nicolas McMullen midway down the page. "He changed his name. McMullen is his mother's maiden name."

"How'd you find him?"

"After I told you about everything, I realized how much I wanted that part of my life to have some conclusion. I hired a private investigator. I went in to talk with her a week ago. She called me today to say that she thought she'd found Nic and wanted to send me a picture. I didn't believe her until I saw everything. It's all online. As soon as I saw the picture, I was sure that it was him. Twenty years have done him no favors. He's bald and overweight, but it's Nic all right. Apparently Pete was only one of the kids he fathered. There are multiple people looking for Nicolas Grady and most of them want child support. I only want his signature. He still lives in Tucson. Some of the past addresses that he's had were in my old neighborhood. I could have driven right by his house and never known."

"Are you going to try and contact him?"

"I have no reason to ever talk to Nic again. All I want are signed divorce papers. I've already called my lawyer in Tucson. He's going to have a courier hand deliver everything on Monday."

"Almost too easy."

"I know. All these years and I only needed to call the right person. This investigator knew what she was doing…I don't think I'll be able to believe it until I'm actually holding signed papers." Michele sighed. "You have no idea how this has been hanging over me for all of these years. For the first time, I think that I can finally end this chapter."

"Are you going to tell Peter?"

"Peter doesn't know I ever was married to his dad. He's never met Nic, never even asked…I'll probably let him know where Nic's living and let him know the new name, but I doubt he'd be interested in meeting him now. You never really know what someone's thinking, though, do you? I used to think that maybe he never asked about his dad because he didn't want to make me feel bad. He's always been a sensitive kid."

"I want to meet Peter. Someday."

"Someday you will. Maybe sooner rather than later." Michele looked over at me. "He mentioned wanting to come to Colorado for Christmas."

"We could have a spare room."

She tilted her head. "If I slept in your room on a regular basis?" She smiled. "You wouldn't mind if he stayed here?"

"I like the idea of having family around. Your family."

"Maybe someday we'll feel like we're part of the same family. You, me, Roxy, Pete, even Lynn and Sal."

"Sal? I guess every family has to have someone who's overbearing and obsessed with the weather."

"That's Sal." Michele laughed. "But she makes a damn good cake."

Michele couldn't possibly know how much I wanted to be part of a family just like she'd described. "You already feel like part of my family."

"Good. You've felt like part of my family for years." Michele smiled and reached for my hand. "You don't have plans after dinner tonight, do you?"

CHAPTER TWENTY-SEVEN

It didn't matter that I'd offered to drive her both ways, Katy put her foot down about leaving the ranch, and I realized after two phone calls about it that I wasn't going to win an argument with her. She was more stubborn than anyone I'd ever met, either by her nature or by eighty years of cattle ranching. All she needed, she insisted, was a recording of the song. She didn't need to see Olive and Slim perform or hear the song live, and she added that she didn't need a video either. "I only need to hear it once, Jodi, that's all," she'd said. But I had a feeling she'd listen to the song more than once.

Michele had practiced her part on the guitar and sung enough around the house that by the time the band had decided they were ready to perform Katy's song, I had all the words memorized too. The tune was catchy and I'd found myself humming it at work as well. I knew I wanted a recording for myself almost as much as for Katy.

I was at a table near the middle of the lounge and close enough to the stage so that I had a perfect view. For the first time, I didn't care who noticed that I was staring right at Michele as the band set up. Carol and Desi were sitting with me. They were drinking wine and discussing real estate. I had ordered a Cherry Coke, but I was too nervous to drink. I set up the iPad I'd borrowed from Carol's daughter and waited. Desi was again looking for a place to buy and had mentioned that she was still interested in Granite Avenue. Carol helpfully piped up with a comment about other properties in the neighborhood; I was relieved to be left out of their conversation.

Sarah came up to the microphone, and the audience quieted down when she tapped her hand against her thigh, counting, "One, two, three." The first songs were two of their usual crowd-pleasers and the round of applause that followed was enthusiastic. Sarah stepped back from the mic and as Michele stepped forward, I hit the record button on the iPad screen. My hands were shaky. I balled them into fists and kept my eyes on Michele.

"Our next song was written by Katy Warren. It's called 'Waiting for a Love Song.' You all are lucky enough to be the first audience to hear it." She paused and glanced back at Sarah and then at the bass player. She strummed a chord and then said, "I hope you enjoy it."

The familiar guitar chords filled the room and I relaxed back in my chair. The look on Michele's face was serene. There was no nervous tension. When her lips parted and her voice first rang out, the notes were spot-on. Michele was singing this song for Katy and maybe for Alice as well. The audience was only dressing on the side tonight.

I didn't wait for Michele to join our table after their set. I went out to the back alley and met her there. She threw her arms around me and I lifted her off the ground, kissing her as she landed.

"That was amazing!"

Michele beamed back at me. "You think Katy is going to like it?"

"You're going to make her cry. It was that fucking good."

"It was, wasn't it? Damn that felt good."

We went inside to meet up with Carol and Desi, but Michele was still buzzing from the performance and could hardly sit down. Finally she grabbed my arm and said, "Let's get out of here before the next band starts."

I didn't ask where she wanted to go until we were headed for the highway. Her hand was on my leg, making it hard for me to concentrate on the road. When I looked over at her, she answered with one word: "Home."

I unlocked the door and waited for her to walk in first. She set her guitar down in the entryway and then spun around and grabbed me. Her kiss was hard and made my blood rush. She pulled me toward the sofa, kicking her shoes off along the way. I dropped my keys and wallet on the coffee table and watched as she sank down on the sofa and started unbuttoning her coat.

"Right here, huh?" I teased.

She pushed off her coat and nodded, reaching for my belt. I let her unbuckle the belt and then move on to my jeans as I slipped out of my coat and shirt. I wanted her now more than ever. I pushed her back on the pillows and climbed on top. She stretched across the length of the sofa and pulled me into another kiss.

"We could go upstairs," I suggested.

She shook her head. "I want you right now."

"Right now...and what about tomorrow?"

She kissed me again. "Oh, you're mine then too. And the day after, and the day after that..."

"A little greedy?"

"No," she said, wrapping her arms around me. "A little in love."

"Me too."

"That's all I get? A 'me too'?"

"That's not all." I kissed her and then whispered in her ear, "You also get an 'I love you.' Because I do...so much." I'd said the words in my head for years, but it hadn't felt right to say them aloud. And "I love you" was something that had to be said out loud. "I love you." I could say it over and over again now.

"Me too," Michele said. "I love you too."

Bella Books, Inc.

Women. Books. Even Better Together.

P.O. Box 10543
Tallahassee, FL 32302

Phone: 800-729-4992
www.bellabooks.com